Dafidi and Abdul
Beyond Friends

Order this book online at www.trafford.com
or email orders@trafford.com

Most Trafford titles are also available at major online book retailers.

This book is a work of fiction. All the primary characters are fictional. Any semblance to actual persons
is coincidental.

Note for Librarians: A cataloguing record for this book is available from Library
and Archives Canada at www.collectionscanada.ca/amicus/index-e.html

Printed in Victoria, BC, Canada.

ISBN: 978-1-4269-2102-5 (sc)
ISBN: 978-1-4269-2101-8 (dj)

Library of Congress Control Number: 2009940183

*Our mission is to efficiently provide the world's finest, most comprehensive book publishing
service, enabling every author to experience success. To find out how to publish your book, your
way, and have it available worldwide, visit us online at www.trafford.com*

Trafford rev. 11/18/2009

 www.trafford.com

North America & international
toll-free: 1 888 232 4444 (USA & Canada)
phone: 250 383 6864 ♦ fax: 812 355 4082

Dafidi and Abdul
Beyond Friends

Dr. Joe Ordia

To all who enrich the lives of others and the world through unconditional friendship and selfless giving.

To peacemakers everywhere. To individuals who sow love where there is hatred. To those who protect our environment.

To healers of the body, and healers of the soul.

And to all who sacrifice and work through groups such as the Red Cross, Médecins Sans Frontières, Bill and Melinda Gates Foundation, and other humanitarian organizations.

Contents

Acknowledgements

I am profoundly grateful to all who have directly or indirectly played a role to make the writing this book a reality.

I appreciate the support of my family and friends. I thank those who made constructive and editorial comments.

I also thank everyone who joined me in·conducting research for portions of the book.

It is a privilege for my son to write the Foreword, and my good friend Dr. Richard Lapchick, to honor the book with the Introduction. Many thanks.

Dr. Lapchick, and my father Dr. Abraham A. Ordia, played keys roles to hold the then South Africa, accountable for its apartheid policies. My father led the international boycott of sporting contacts with apartheid South Africa (SA) and its friends. In the mid and late 1970s, he fought a battle of wills with the then Prime Minister of New Zealand (NZ) Mr. Robert Muldoon who refused to end sporting contacts with SA. The Prime Minister refused to meet with my father who was visiting Australia and NZ, and Muldoon told him that he could "stew in his own juice." Muldoon further infuriated the civilized world when he remarked that he would have permitted a NZ sporting tour of Germany even in 1933 when the Nazis were slaughtering Jews. My father did not relent until apartheid was shattered, and the new South Africa was born.

I say a special thank you to my patients, who inspire me by their courage and perseverance.

I thank God for everything.

Foreword

The story of Dafidi and Abdul is an inspiring tale about meeting and overcoming life's many challenges and the incredible strength of friendship. As the two friends come of age and begin to encounter personal hardships amid the backdrop of an increasingly volatile world, they encourage us to remain faithful to the ideals of friendship, perseverance, and sacrifice. The experiences of Dafidi and Abdul hold profound lessons for children and adults alike. As the larger global community continues to experience unprecedented levels of social and cultural intolerance, this heartwarming story reminds us of the existence of those inalienable positive human qualities that bind us all together and enable us to accomplish great things by working together.

The world we live in today is smaller and more connected than it has been at any other point in history. Students in America can connect in real-time via video conference to counterparts in Asia and the Middle East. Researchers from Europe can collaborate with peers in Australia to meet and overcome complex challenges in medicine and the physical sciences. Entrepreneurs in emerging markets in Africa can raise investment capital from other businesspeople across the developed world. The new reality of global connectedness, made possible by the Internet and specifically social networking technologies, has allowed the instant and free flow of culture and information across the planet between previously disconnected societies. As you read this book, several more young people from various geographies, cultures, and languages will connect and form life-long friendships like that of Dafidi and Abdul. It is my belief that in this century we will experience an unprecedented increase in global cultural awareness that moves us decidedly towards a world without the painful and unproductive conflict that we've experienced in the recent past.

My father Dr. Ordia's own life experience has brought him from West Africa to institutions of higher learning in the U.S, and ultimately to the forefront of global medical research at Harvard University,

Boston University, and beyond. Along his journey, he has collaborated with leading medical professionals and treated patients from every continent on the planet. His travels have also taken him to some of the most conflict-torn regions of the world including Africa and the Middle East. These experiences have instilled in him a profound appreciation of the world's many different cultures and the qualities that bind us all together as citizens of Earth and children of God. The story of the friends Abdul and Dafidi should serve as a reminder to us all about the incredible ability for tolerance to overcome fear, and of friendship to overcome hardship.

Joe E. Ordia
President and Chief Executive Officer,
Ordia Solutions

Introduction

Dr. Joe Ordia has given the world an enormous blessing with his book, *Dafidi and Abdul: Beyond Friends*. I have been saying and writing for many years that there is "something about sport." It can bring us together when we are apart. It can unite communities that are divided. In the huddle, it does not matter what we look like, what faith we believe in, if we are rich or poor. If we are going to win, we have to get beyond any differences. That is precisely what happens in *Dafidi and Abdul*.

Dafidi and Abdul come to realize that it is a blessing to live in the United States of America. While we surely have to fight discrimination, we can only imagine living in a place where everyone looked, spoke, and acted the same. Our world would not carry the same notion one shares in a global village. We are all human. Even with blessings counted, the color of one's skin, an ethnic background, or even the slight variation of which god you pray to can cause the world to shift from beneath you. Instead of seeing the many similarities we share as human beings we focus on the small nuances that make one different from another. Our society is obsessed with small differences instead of BIG similarities. We know that the world is comprised of people of all shapes and sizes, but yet still we criticize based on physical features.

Before meeting someone named Abdul Rashid many would perceive a male from the Middle East practicing the religion of Islam. When you see his mother wearing a head scarf it only reassures you of their faith. In reality, his name is of Arab origin, but Abdul is a Catholic. This is a simple example of what goes on in our daily lives. Another example of prejudging someone based on their name would be Dafidi Abraham, who is the main character in the book. He was born in Africa but of the Jewish faith. In today's society you would think that since Palestine and Israel are consistently at war people from such communities or religious backgrounds would not get along. The media reinforces that each day with news reports from the Middle East. Many Jews and Muslims want to end the war and bring peace back into their lives. By categorizing people from a turbulent part of the world as natural combatants and born enemies, the inherited assumption is that peacefully coexisting with one another is impossible. Ignorance has led us to believe that two distinct individuals (Abdul and Dafidi) could not see eye to eye, let alone build a friendship due to their divergent backgrounds.

In today's society children are slowly starting to see past color and more into a person's soul. There are a lot more biracial children being born because communities are beginning to see past stereotypical physical qualities of an individual, and are focusing more on the inner qualities of a human being. Everyone needs unconditional love whether it is from a parent, guardian, sibling, or child. Even from a community.

Today's fast pace and busy lifestyle have created immense levels of stress in people's lives and households. Being a parent in today's society has brought busy work schedules, overtime, grocery shopping, driving to and from basketball practice, homework help, and a slew of other responsibilities and priorities. The pressure to over provide for their children becomes suffocating as some parents consistently take extra shifts doing all they can to meet their children's needs. This selfless intention proves to work counter intuitively as not enough time is focused into actually raising their child. This flaw in thinking that you are providing a better life for your child by filling a void of love with money has only lead families into unhappiness. Parents do not realize by doing so they are putting their child on the bottom of the priority list.

Once arriving home the parent is flustered, unhappy, throws in a microwavable dish and often does not have the patience to answer all of their children's questions. Children, who may not show their discontent with the perceived lack of love and attention, may eventually falter in other areas, becoming disconnected, misbehaving in school, and even rebelling.

Parents need to pay attention to their children and show them that they love and care for them. Children need to be praised for their hard work, and stay motivated to continue moving in the right direction. Eventually everyone needs to be LOVED unconditionally. It is as simple as breathing, but because of the busy times we constrict ourselves in, it is sometimes forgotten to even have existed.

In this wonderful book the life experiences of Dafidi and Abdul, who come together because they play on the same high school basketball team in a Boston suburb, shatter the stereotypes for the families and then their friends. It was all summed up in an interview that Dafidi gave as a star player at Boston College where both boys went to College.

"I am the child of Jewish parents, yet I am attending a Catholic university. My best friend is Christian, but of Arab descent, and has many relatives that are Muslim. In today's violent and prejudiced world, this may seem odd to many people. However, to me and my friend, we are just alike – two young men seeking to find our place in the world and trying to come to grips with it. We both feel strongly that our friendship has transcended our ethnic and religious differences and has enriched our lives for the better. We wish to share our experience with other young people and to enable them to know others of different cultures so that they, too, can become true friends. It all goes back to the saying, "friends are the family we choose for ourselves." Maybe the contribution Abdul and I make will allow children all over the world to think of their friends as 'family' and through this, religious prejudice and violence will end. That is our goal."

So I say thank you, Joe, for this gift of understanding and love.

Richard Lapchick
Director, The Institute for Diversity and Ethics in Sport
The University of Central Florida

Preface

This is a story about two devoted friends, about brotherhood, and about sharing and giving. Though one of the principal characters is of Jewish heritage and the other Arab, this book is not about Jews and Arabs. However, nothing would bring me greater joy than to see peace between Jews and Palestinians. During my visits to Israel and to the West Bank, I found both people to have the same fervent aspirations for peace and security. They are one people, brought together by destiny. All children of Abraham. This book is not about ethnicity or religion. Diversity is a source of strength, not weakness. For selfish and egotistic reasons, cultural, ethnic, racial, religious, and other perceived differences, are exploited to sow the seeds of discord and antagonism. This is a story about an unbreakable bond of friendship. It is about devotion, and unconditional giving. This book is also a call to service and sacrifice.

All people are created in the image of God, not physically but spiritually. Because God is loving, giving, and forgiving, we are all inherently good, and innately full of love and compassion. Why then is there so much hatred and violence in the world today? Everywhere, brutality overshadows compassion.

A resounding majority of people are peace loving. There is more love than hatred. More generosity than selfishness.

Acts of kindness don't make headlines, and the voices of good are hardly heard. This book recognizes and honors those acts, and makes those voices heard.

History shows us that individual acts of kindness and generosity can spread like wild fire and make the world a better place for all.

Mother Teresa, through her kindheartedness and abundant compassion, became the greatest advocate and crusader for, to borrow her own words, "the hungry, the naked, the homeless, the crippled, the blind, the lepers, all those people who feel unwanted, unloved, uncared for throughout society, people that have become a burden to the society and are shunned by everyone." She fought her cause with the courage of a lion. Today, she is considered by many to be a saint.

Oskar Schindler was relentless in his determination to defeat a system that condemned innocent people to death. He spent all his wealth and risked his own life to keep hundreds of helpless people from the gas chambers. He was a life jacket in rough seas.

The compassion of Mother Teresa and Oskar Schindler supplanted poverty, hopelessness, and tyranny, with kindness and hope. They were their brother's keepers and their sister's keepers.

Our challenge today is to go and do likewise.

Chapter 1
Goodbye to Kansas

By Spring of 2008, Dafidi Abraham and his mother, Peggy, had been living in Olathe, Kansas for eight years. They moved there upon their return from Africa where Peggy had conducted research on mountain gorillas. Her husband, Jack Abraham, left her and her small son precipitously when they were in Africa, but she remained behind to protect the gorillas from poachers. However, a short time later, when her mother died, Peggy felt it prudent to return to the United States to help her father manage his hardware store.

Returning to Kansas, where she grew up, was tough on his mother, but Dafidi loved living there, especially since they shared his beloved grandfather's home. Peggy felt constrained living with her widowed father. However, she knew that her father provided a strong role model for Dafidi, and she was grateful for his care. Dafidi enjoyed fishing with his grandpa, and when they were not doing stuff together, Dafidi loved dancing around the house, creating new intricate steps. When his grandfather died, Dafidi missed him greatly. Andrzej Bach provided his daughter and her son with a stable and loving home life, and Dafidi blossomed into a healthy, confident child.

Peggy enrolled Dafidi in a special school where he gradually made new friends. Unfortunately he was in constant pain due to deformities in his leg and back. His mother took him to Boston where he could receive the sophisticated medical care which he desperately needed. Once Dafidi's condition was successfully treated at Boston's Children's Hospital, Peggy moved back to Olathe with her son.

While in high school, Dafidi developed a love for basketball because it allowed him to express his athletic skills, especially his jumping ability. He was further inspired by watching videos of Michael Jordan. Dafidi thought that it was really cool that "Air Jordan" could jump so high and seem to almost fly. The young athlete soon became the star player on his high school's basketball team. He felt his life was on track and loved going to school each day. Near the end of the school year, as the warmer May weather brought forth multitudes of richly colored wildflowers on the Kansas plains, Dafidi looked around him and thought he was in paradise.

Things were soon to change. The downturn in the economy left many people tethering on brink of bankruptcy. Early one rainy spring morning, Peggy Abraham sat quietly at her father's old roll-top desk, holding her coffee cup in both hands, scanning the Excel spreadsheet on her laptop. The figures were worse than she had expected.

Her father, Andrzej Bach, left his only daughter, Pelagia, a thriving long-established business. Although the store was small, it was stocked with everything do-it-yourselfers needed to complete their household renovations. As the spring of 2008 continued, however, sales began to severely decline. Many homes in suburban Kansas City were going into foreclosure, and their owners had no interest in fixing them up. Those who still owned their homes were struggling to pay their mortgages. The business just wasn't there to sustain the legacy her hard-working father had left her.

Peggy was soon forced to shut the store. Dafidi was devastated. It seemed as if his whole world had come crashing down on him. Lying awake at night, he thought up ideas to help his mother, but none seemed really viable.

Dafidi even began to feel that he had let his mother down by not accepting previous offers to become a professional dancer after winning the TV Dance Contest. Dafidi's secret pleasure was to dance. Like many boys his age, he emulated hip-hop stars. Unlike those boys, however, he also revered Alvin Ailey and Bob Fosse, who to him were almost magical figures in the way they conjured movement from their dancers.

Dafidi worried incessantly about his mother. He didn't know how to comfort her as she sat by the kitchen table crunching numbers and trying to figure out the best thing to do to keep herself and her son safe. His heart broke to see her so tired and stressed.

After searching for better employment for what seemed like ages, Peggy finally accepted a post at Johnson County's *Ernie Miller Park and Nature Center* in Olathe, working as a research associate studying birds of prey. Although she preferred studying primate behavior, her Master's degree in Biology and Wildlife Management, and her certification by the Association of Zoos and Aquariums enabled her to do research on various types of animals. Though she enjoyed her work immensely, her position was unfortunately soon eliminated due to lack of funding.

Luckily, Peggy had made friends in the Boston area when she took Dafidi for treatment at Children's Hospital. One friend had even offered her an entry-level management position at Franklin Park Zoo, if she was willing to relocate. She mulled it over and thought it would be the best option, but was concerned about taking Dafidi away from the school and friends he loved so much. For his part, although saddened that he had to leave his friends in Kansas and possibly might not have the opportunity to play basketball, Dafidi realized the plight his mother faced and knew she had to take the position that had been so generously offered. He also knew that she would love working at the zoo and that his mother's love of animals was second only to her love for him.

Soon after making the decision to move to Boston, his mother flew there to find housing for them.

The phone rang early one evening as Dafidi was cooking a hamburger for dinner. Holding a spatula in one hand, Dafidi raced to the living room to answer it. Hearing his mother's upbeat tone through the receiver, he knew the decision to move had been the right one.

His mother's voice was calm and upbeat. "Hi, honey. Just to let you know I found us a really nice apartment in a suburb named Brookline. It's a bit more congested than Kansas City, but I think you'll like it. I've sorted out all the necessary paperwork for you to apply to the high school, so we should be hearing in a few weeks if there is room for you there. I'll be home tomorrow night about 6, as my flight arrives around 4."

"Great, Mom. I've got to rush because my burger is burning. I love you!"

Dafidi replaced the receiver and ran back to the kitchen just in time to flip his somewhat blackened burger. As he removed the pan from the stove and began putting ketchup on the bun, he thought about the new school. Anxiety crept into his thoughts, but he tried to stifle those feelings, knowing his mother would worry about him if she knew he was at all afraid of the move.

Six days passed before the letter arrived from Brookline High. Opening the envelope with shaking hands, Dafidi was glad his mother wasn't home at that moment. As he read the somewhat long and formal letter, his shaking abated and a smile crept across his face. He was ecstatic. Not only had he been allowed to transfer, but he had been awarded a basketball scholarship!

Dafidi felt an urgent need to share his good news with the one person who had made his dream of playing sports possible. Picking up the phone, he dialed long-distance to his neurosurgeon's office in Boston. After identifying himself to the receptionist, she told him to wait just a moment and then put him through to Dr. Joe.

As soon as her heard the doctor's voice say "hello," Dafidi began speaking.

"Hey, Dr. Joe, guess what? I'm moving to Boston! Not only that, but I'm going to play basketball at Brookline High. Can you believe it?"

Dr. Joe chuckled and said, "That's great news, Dafidi. Brookline High is a great school. You are going to obtain a first class education. And you must invite me to a game. When are you moving?"

Dafidi outlined his mother's timetable, and after speaking to the doctor for some time, put down the receiver and sat down in the nearest armchair. He felt in shock. His world was changing so quickly, it put him off balance. He sat there for a long while, just mulling over what the school and his future might look like. When his mother arrived home in the late afternoon, she found him napping on the sofa, completely worn out from the stressful burden he had carried for so many weeks.

Chapter 2
Brookline Beckons

On an overcast morning in June, Dafidi and his mother packed up their Subaru Outback and hugged their next-door neighbors good-bye. As they drove slowly away from their small ranch house, Peggy's eyes began to fill with tears. Her mother and father had moved to this tract of tidy homes in the early 1960's, when she was still small and the world had seemed so big and welcoming. Now that she was a parent, moving with her son to a new city out of necessity, the world seemed smaller and somewhat threatening. She grieved the loss of her parents and her old life in Kansas, and felt as if she was climbing out on a limb that could crack at any time, flinging her into the unknown.

Dafidi looked out disconsolately at the flat fertile fields as they drove east on I-70. He knew these plains and rolling hills of Kansas for as long as he could remember, and he loved their simplicity and the feeling of freedom they engendered in him. He couldn't imagine leaving them or his friends and school, and he had no concept of what life would be like in Boston. *Brookline* was just a name to him, and he was unable to visualize what the city would look like. The only urban area he had really experienced, Kansas City, was no longer the burgeoning brick mid-western cow-town it had been in the twentieth century; it was now a city of new office towers and urban renewal, sushi bars and Starbucks. Would Boston be the same?

Peggy turned on the radio and they listened quietly to the news. Neither mother nor son felt like talking at first, each wrapped up in their own thoughts. However, as the hours and miles passed, distancing them from their old life, they began to open up to each other about their hopes and fears, gingerly at first, each afraid of hurting the other's feelings. Peggy was afraid Dafidi would find it hard to make friends, and Dafidi feared the same for his mother. He knew she would always put work first, seeing it as their protection. She had worked long hours managing the hardware store, and he knew that she often put her own emotional and physical needs aside to make certain they were financially secure. He had heard her come home late, sighing from exhaustion as she took off her coat and hung it and her purse on the oak hall tree. Many nights, he would awake to find her at the kitchen table going over bills, leaning her forehead on her hand and looking depressed. Dafidi wanted more for his mother. He wanted to hear her laugh and to see her smile more.

Driving on the highway all day, they reached the Chicago suburbs at rush hour. Stuck in traffic for what seemed forever, they both felt the need to bypass the city and head further east to spend the night. Once the famous Chicago gridlock eased, they drove towards Indiana and merged onto I-90, headed for South Bend. Dafidi suddenly felt a bit excited and asked his mom if they could stay there for the night, as he wanted to see the University of Notre Dame, whose football team he followed closely. There was also a connection between the university and one of Boston's famous teams. The head coach of the University of Notre Dame Fighting Irish football team, Charlie Weis, served as offensive coordinator for the New England Patriots from 2000 to 2004.

Peggy was tired and easily acquiesced. As she exited the highway, steering the car towards the toll booth, they could both see Notre Dame's famous golden dome ahead, looming like a beacon of hope.

Finding a motel proved easy and they slept soundly that night. Early the next morning, they treated themselves to a big mid-western farmer's breakfast at a coffee shop on Dixie Way South, and then drove to the university. Both mother and son were impressed by the beauty of the school. The golden dome shone in the late spring sunlight and the verdant shrubbery was in full bloom. They walked leisurely around the campus, visiting the famous grotto with its statue of the Virgin Mary, and the school's elegant and venerable Morris Inn, where many famous people had stayed.

There was something about the university that made Dafidi feel secure spiritually as well as physically. Unknown to his mother, he had been researching Boston College, a similar school near to their new home in Brookline. Although it was a Catholic university, he felt she would approve of it, as it had a solid reputation for both academics and sports.

After realizing that they spent the entire morning and part of the afternoon exploring Notre Dame, they reluctantly walked back to the car. Starting the car's engine, Peggy turned to her son and looked at him quizzically.

"Dafidi, you seemed entranced by Notre Dame. Would you like to apply there when the time comes?"

Her son smiled. "Mom, I really liked it, but it would be too far from Boston and probably too expensive, unless I could get a scholarship or something. Also, doesn't it bother you that it's a Catholic school?"

His mother looked him at him directly. "Dafidi, God is God and those who worship him differently are still His children. I respect others' views and want you to be open-minded and to do the same. In the end, we all want peace, love, health and happiness. If going to a Catholic university would make you happy and give you a good education, it's fine with me."

As they drove north to I-90, Dafidi looked at the car's clock. It was already mid-afternoon. He felt relaxed and suddenly very tired. Closing his eyes, he gave in to the temptation to nap. His mother smiled fondly, seeing her son's head loll against the passenger window. She began to relax herself, feeling that maybe, just maybe, everything would be all right for them in their new life.

Having had such a late start, Peggy pulled off the highway around 6 pm, just as they encountered horribly heavy traffic just west of Cleveland. As they drove off the highway onto a suburban street in Lakewood, Ohio, they saw a Hampton Inn to their left. Peggy made a snap decision and pulled into the driveway. She was tired of driving and knew her son was hungry. She told Dafidi to wait in the car while she went in to try to book a room. A few minutes later, Peggy returned with a room card and moved the car to the guest parking area.

After sprucing up a bit, mother and son walked across the street to a shopping mall, and found a nice restaurant. Relaxing over dinner, they both realized they were enjoying their trip to Boston.

Dafidi voiced this to his mother. "Mom, even though I miss Kansas, I'm kind of excited about moving to Brookline. Maybe it will be really good for us there. I just feel that the zoo job will be a lot more fun for you than granddad's hardware store, and who knows – maybe Brookline High will be ok."

Peggy set down her wine glass and smiled at her son, laughter bubbling at the edge of her lips. "Daf, you never cease to amaze me. How did you become so wise at such a young age?"

"Oh, mom. It must be genetic!" Dafidi laughed also and reached for more bread and butter. His appetite was always a good sign of his emotional state, and if his desire for tonight's dinner was any indicator, he was really happy.

Peggy couldn't believe the drivers on the Massachusetts Turnpike. Between Stockbridge and Springfield she'd seen two major accidents and had been tailgated, cut off, and witnessed people driving 70 mph in the emergency lane. She was beginning to feel she was driving on the Autobahn in Germany rather than a major expressway in the United States. It took all her concentration to avoid hazardous drivers. For his part, Dafidi was speechless, mainly from fear.

As they finally approached the western suburbs of greater Boston, Peggy told Dafidi to look closely at the map and tell her what exit to take. She knew they had to pass I-95 before the turn-off, but all the signs said I-95 and Rte. 128 and Peggy had no idea how these two roads related to one another. Dafidi solved the mystery by examining the map.

"Mom, this is really weird. 128 and 95 are the same road in places! I think you should get off the turnpike at Exit 17 in Newton. Once we get off the road, let's stop, and I'll show you the red line I've drawn on the map to show you the route to the apartment in Brookline." Dafidi thought to himself that he would buy his mother a GPS if he ever had enough money.

Exiting the highway as Dafidi had directed, Peggy pulled over into a parking space on a suburban street and perused the map. Dafidi did a remarkable job of finding the most direct route to their new home. Taking a swig from her water bottle and inhaling a deep cleansing breath to release the stress of navigating Massachusetts traffic, Peggy turned off the car's engine and looked towards her son, smiling.

"Dafidi, we are going to be all right, you know. You do know that, don't you?"

"Yeah, mom, I know. I feel that too now. Let's go home."

***

On Monday morning, many students entered the glass-windowed door to the English class with only moments to spare before the bell rang. One nervous youngster, flinging his backpack on a desk, hurriedly unzipped it and took out his Shakespeare notes. He wasn't looking forward to the test on Friday as he couldn't comprehend half of what was being said in the language of the Bard. Sliding onto the hard wooden seat, Abdul composed himself and put the notes in order. At least he had studied over the weekend, albeit reluctantly.

Just then he saw a tall dark-haired young man come through the classroom door, looking hesitantly at the teacher and asking if this was Room 306. Mrs. Thiebault smiled and affirmed he was in the right place. She then looked at the note he was carrying and turned to the class, saying, "Let's all welcome a new student, Dafidi Abraham, to our class. Have a seat and make yourself comfortable, Dafidi." Smiling, she added, "I just hope I'm pronouncing your name properly."

Looking at his class schedule, Dafidi thought her comment ironic, as he had no idea how to pronounce *her* name. Finding an empty desk at the back of the room near the window, he sat down quietly. He felt awkward and embarrassed to be introduced to all of these kids he didn't know. He had only been in Boston two days, and already felt like a fish out of water. The young people he saw when he and his mother went grocery shopping in Brookline all looked stylish, affluent and confident. In Kansas, the kids he hung around with wore more modest clothing and seemed less sophisticated.

He couldn't even get over the grocery store they visited; *Trader Joe's* was totally different than the grocery section of the local Wal Mart in Olathe, Kansas. Foods he had never seen before lined the aisles, tempting him to try things from all over the world. On top of that, the cashiers all wore Hawaiian print shirts. It seemed as if his entire frame of reference had been pulled out from under his feet, leaving him in limbo.

Mercifully, Mrs. Thiebault launched immediately into that day's lesson, leaving Dafidi to settle in. As the teacher spoke, Dafidi discreetly looked around him at his classmates. They were listening attentively to the teacher and seemed enthralled by Shakespeare's words. It seemed as though teenagers in Brookline knew the value of education and were anxious to avail themselves of it. In Kansas, he remembered some kids tuning out and passing notes in class. None of that was evident here however. Everyone seemed engaged.

The teacher asked a few students to read out loud. One young man in particular did an excellent job of putting emotion into Shakespeare's words and actually made them decipherable to his classmates. Another stumbled over the prose, struggling to complete his assigned section. Dafidi felt empathy for the student, knowing that he, too, would have trouble acting out the part of Julius Caesar. He smiled at the young man as he completed the segment, raising his eyebrows to let him know he empathized with his plight. The smile he received in return was warm, welcoming and unpretentious. Dafidi immediately felt more comfortable.

The bell rang, signaling the end of the class. Dafidi gathered up his notes, plunged them into his backpack, and shouldering it, stood up. As he did so, the young man with whom he had empathized walked over to him and offered his hand to shake.

"Hi, I'm Abdul Rashid." Laughing ruefully, he continued, "I'm not exactly a Shakespeare scholar, as you could see."

Dafidi shook his hand and laughed too. "Don't worry. I can't understand any of it either."

Abdul then asked Dafidi what other classrooms he had to find and offered to help him navigate the huge old building. Dafidi gratefully accepted, feeling as if he had been rescued. At least he would be walking with someone the other kids knew and wouldn't look as much like the stranger that he was.

As they walked down the long noisy hallway, the two boys asked each other questions. Dafidi was the first to bring up basketball, asking Abdul if the Brookline team was any good. Abdul laughed at this, saying since he was on the team it must be good. As he left Dafidi at his Calculus class, Abdul asked Daf if he was wanted to join in a pick-up game scheduled for that afternoon after school. Daf readily accepted. He might not know Brookline but he knew basketball.

Walking down the steps of the large brick building that afternoon, Dafidi reflected on his first day at Brookline High. The thought that took precedence was that the school was challenging, both academically and physically. Unlike his school in Kansas, that had been built as a rambling campus of one-story buildings set around small quadrangles, Brookline High was a massive brick building harkening to an early 20th century design, with three floors, the stale scent of over-stuffed lockers, and congested stairwells. Just managing to make it from one class to another in time was a challenge. In addition, and most importantly, the curriculum was demanding. Dafidi knew he would receive the best education here, but it would be tough and he would have to study a lot. He had always been a good student, but he instinctively felt that more was now required of him. He needed to excel, and to do so would require hard work.

Stopping at the bottom of the stairs, he took his cell phone from his backpack and rang his mother at the zoo number he had written on a small piece of paper that morning. Peggy answered in a chipper voice after the second ring, and Dafidi could hear the happiness in her voice when she described her first day on the job. Dafidi then asked his mother if he could stay after school to play basketball. Knowing that the sport was her son's passion, Peggy readily agreed, although she grilled him as to where and with whom he would be playing. Once she was confident that the game would be on school property and that he at least knew one of the players, she felt confident that he would be all right and enjoy himself.

"Daf, call me when the game is over, and I'll pick you up in front of the school. I think we could both benefit from going out for pizza tonight, and I've heard from people here at the zoo that if we go into Boston to the North End, we'll feel as if we are really in Italy. What do you say?"

"Great, mom. Italy it is. I'll see you around 5:30, OK?"

"Sounds fine. I'll plan on being there even if you forget to call."

"Oh. Mom, I won't forget!"

"Right, Daf. See you then."

After his mother rang off, Dafidi walked towards the basketball courts where he could see others practicing. As he approached the benches, he heard his name being called and turned around to find Abdul standing behind him with another student. The other young man was extremely tall and thin, with sandy blond hair and glasses. *Wiry* was the word that sprung to Dafidi's mind. Abdul introduced him as Jason Kelly, the team's star shooter.

Jason smiled at Dafidi and then asked him about his previous school's team. Dafidi didn't really want to brag, but he knew he was the best player there, and he had to somehow relay to Jason that he knew the game and could play well.

After hesitating a second, Dafidi said, "We were state champions, and I actually won an award, if you can believe it."

Jason laughed and said, "Yeah, but that was Kansas. This is Boston, home of the Celtics. We live for basketball here."

Dafidi felt the rebuke but was determined not to accept the bait the other boy offered. Deciding to take the high road, he said, "OK, let's see what you've got."

It turned out that what Jason had was speed, flexibility and especially, height. He could slam dunk like a pro. At 6' 5", he stood almost even with the basket and a head above most of the other players. He moved rapidly and with precision, not wasting any motion. He was the player that Dafidi's coach in Kansas, Papa Jackson, had dreamed of.

After playing for almost two hours, the game broke up. Dafidi conducted himself respectably, blocking numerous shots and keeping up a strong defense. Abdul complimented him on his prowess, suggesting he try out for the school's team. Dafidi couldn't bring himself to tell his new friend that he had already been sent a letter asking him to join the team and had received a small scholarship based on his basketball skills. He felt it would be rude to tout his talent to Abdul, who seemed to be a good player but not a star.

After parting from Jason and the other players, the two young men walked like buddies towards the front of the school. Seeing his mom's Subaru parked across the street from the school's patrician entrance, Dafidi told Abdul he'd see him the next morning. Abdul smiled and waved to him as he and Peggy drove off.

As the car inched through the increasingly thick traffic on Commonwealth Ave., Peggy told Dafidi about her first day at the zoo. In her new position as a Department Coordinator, she would be responsible for scheduling the staff, appointments and medical care for the animals in the primate wing. The job would be stressful but rewarding, and most of all, she would be working for the benefit of her beloved gorillas, apes and monkeys. Peggy spoke animatedly as she snaked through the traffic, keeping ever alert to the cars that came at her from all directions at once. By the time they approached Boston, Dafidi knew his mother had made the right decision. Her new job was perfect for her and offered an incredible chance to help the animals she loved so much.

"Mom, I'm so happy for you. The job sounds perfect. I can't wait to come see you at the zoo."

"Oh, Daf, you're wonderful. How did I ever deserve a son like you?"

Seen through the window from the pavement, the tiny trattoria on Hanover Street looked as if it couldn't hold another person. Peggy opened the heavy wooden door and she and her son stepped into another world. Tiny white fairy lights shone from the ceiling, and travel posters of Sicily lined the walls. The smell of garlic wafted from the kitchen as steaming plates of lasagna and fried calamari were hoisted above the waiters' heads. Diners sat at square oak tables laden with crusty peasant bread and bottles of Chianti. The atmosphere felt as if one had entered a family home in Italy. In one corner, two tables were pushed together to accommodate a large party of college students. They were laughing and pounding the table good-naturedly, obviously enjoying their meal and their friends. The ambiance of the entire restaurant spoke of welcome.

Peggy and Dafidi were led to a corner table where they squeezed into their seats, narrowly avoiding tripping a waiter. A large woman dressed all in black came to their table with menus, and told them the day's special dishes. Dafidi had no idea what half of them were, but Peggy seemed comfortable ordering for both of them, so he relaxed and let his mother choose. Once the woman left for the kitchen, a waiter came over with a glass of Chianti for Peggy and water for Dafidi, a basket of bread, and bowls of dipping oil and olives. Gingerly dipping his crust into the oil, Dafidi tasted it. A smile spread across his face.

"Mom, this is delicious! Try it."

Peggy did as he asked, savoring the new tastes and textures. She was exhausted from the day's challenges, and was content to let the food and wine work their magic on her.

When their food arrived, Dafidi attacked it with gusto. As he and his mother ate in silence, they both relaxed. After a quarter hour or so, Peggy finally asked Dafidi a question. Holding her wine glass with both hands and peering down into it, she quietly asked, "So, Daf, what was your first day at school like?"

Dafidi took a moment to gather his thoughts before replying. There was so much to say and yet, he felt he needed to digest some of it before sharing his thoughts with his mother. He looked up from his plate of lasagna and looked Peggy in the eye.

"It's difficult, mom. I can't quite put my finger on how I feel. For most of the day, I was nervous, but I was also happy. Most of the kids sort of ignored me, and that was OK. At least I didn't stand out like a freak. One kid was really nice – the one you saw waving to us. His name is Abdul Rashid. Funny, but his name sounds Arab, even though most of the kids had Irish, Italian or Jewish last names. He's the one who asked me to play basketball this afternoon."

Looking up at her son with a serious look on her face, Peggy replied cryptically, "Don't stray too far from the path, Dafidi."

Daf wasn't quite sure what his mother meant but knew the comment had something to do with Abdul's religion. Although Peggy was usually very open-minded, he knew she felt antipathy to the aberrant variety of religion practiced by extremists. Raised in a reformed Jewish household, Peggy had grown up supporting Israeli causes. The recent rise in violence from some Palestinian groups against Israel had only reinforced her beliefs.

Dafidi calmly replied, "Let me find my own path in life. We must stop the knee-jerk reaction to any issue that has to do with the other side." Peggy was dumbfounded and speechless.

Peggy felt that she needed to draw out her son to talk about his first day at school. Sensing his hesitation to resume the conversation, she asked, "So, how did the game go? Did you meet anyone else who plays on the varsity team?"

"Yeah, I did. This one guy, Jason Kelly, was so good, I couldn't believe it! He practically flew through the air and landed every basket he shot. Coach Jackson at my old school would have given his right arm to have him on his team."

Peggy chuckled. Her son always saw the *big picture,* seeing and feeling what others saw and felt. He had adored Coach Jackson and must be missing him terribly. Hopefully, she thought, he'll find a new mentor in Brookline towards whom he can feel that loyalty.

Just at that moment the waiter returned, bearing another basket of bread. He asked Peggy if she and Dafidi were tourists, and when she answered that they had just moved to Brookline, he smiled and said to Dafidi, "Wow, you're one lucky kid. Brookline High has just about the best basketball team in the state. Do you play?"

Welcoming a kindred spirit, Dafidi smiled and looking up at the thin young man, responded, "I'm actually going to be on the team there and I can't wait! I got a scholarship when we moved. Hey, have you ever heard of one of their players, Jason Kelly?"

The waiter nodded. "Yeah, he's pretty famous around here. The Globe did a piece on local high school players and he was listed as one of the best. Watch out, though. He's got a reputation for being really aggressive on the court. A few players have been injured because of his antics. He's reputed to have a really bad temper. One of the guys in my dorm at BU had a run-in with him a few years ago and ended up with a broken nose."

Dafidi couldn't answer immediately, even though he wanted to. He had sensed something about Jason Kelly he hadn't liked, but he hadn't been able to put his finger on what it was. Now he realized he sensed an undercurrent of hostility in the young man. He felt grateful to the waiter for putting what he felt into words.

Peggy answered for her son. "Thanks for the warning. I'm sure Daf appreciates knowing what he'll be up against."

The waiter smiled. "Sorry if what I said sounded scary. Kelly's probably just a typical conceited jerk who can't stand to lose." Reaching towards the table, he scooped up their empty plates and headed back to the kitchen.

Peggy looked at her son, saying, "Daf, be careful. Just play your best and stay out of the fray. We're new here, so that kid might try to test you. I don't want you getting hurt."

"No sweat, Mom. I can handle him."

Dafidi's words were brave, but in his heart he was fearful. He'd soon be tested on the court and hoped he could match his bravado with action.

Soon, the young waiter returned, bringing each of them a cappuccino and a plate of tiramisu. Mother and son were silent as they enjoyed these new flavors, once more relaxing in each other's company. Just as they pushed their empty plates to the side, the large older woman in black brought the check and put it gently on the table.

Peggy reached for her purse and took out her American Express card, and then signaled to the waiter to come over. He soon came, and taking the check and the card, retreated back to the kitchen's alcove to process the transaction.

Returning a few minutes later, he handed Peggy the credit card and receipt and told her, "I've written my name and cell number on your copy of the receipt. If your son has any problems with Jason Kelly, call me and I'll ask my roommate to talk to him about how to handle the situation. Good luck!"

Thanking him and smiling, Peggy reached out and handed him a $10 bill. "I know how hard it is to be a student, so take this. We really appreciate the excellent service and the information."

The young man thanked her profusely and shook hands with Dafidi, wishing him well, as Dafidi turned beet red with embarrassment.

Getting up from the table, mother and son walked out of the small eatery and into the late spring evening. Peggy was the first to speak. "Daf, let's take a stroll and explore a bit. I want to get to know Boston."

They walked leisurely down the narrow streets, marveling at the old brick buildings and taking in the new sights and sounds. Voices speaking Italian could be heard from all sides, and they saw Italian magazines in the news agent's window. It really did feel as if they were in Italy. When they saw and smelled the luscious scents emanating from a bakery on their left, Peggy couldn't resist the temptations it offered.

"Daf, come on; let's get some pastry for tomorrow morning."

The two entered the small shop, ooh-ing and ah-ing over the beautiful pastries. Choosing some chocolate dipped macaroons and two huge cannolis, they exited the shop just as the proprietress said "Ciao." For two people who had just moved from Kansas, they felt as if they had entered an exotic new world.

Driving back to Brookline, Daf mulled over what the waiter had said. He felt apprehensive but then told himself to buck up. After all, he, Dafidi Abraham, had been through so much in his life that this was just one small possible problem. He had faced back surgery that had enabled him to overcome a deformity, and he had faced up to the typical taunts of grade-schoolers who couldn't resist tormenting a student in a cast. He was strong and could handle the Jason Kellys of the high school world.

Only two weeks after arriving at Brookline High, Dafidi was to be tested with his first basketball game there. He had been practicing with the team every day, and his new coach had repetitively complimented him on his skills. However, despite this assurance, he still felt a lingering fear that Jason Kelly would pull something during the game.

The day before his first game, Dafidi, Abdul and another boy named Yosha were practicing hook shots after school. Shooting from the pivot was something Dafidi felt he needed to practice. In Kansas, he had perfected landing outside hooks off the backboard, but he always had problems with laying them over the rim when moving down the center of the court. Yosha was demonstrating his exceptional skill at this, and both Daf and Abdul were trying to emulate his movements. Both boys appreciated the help of the stocky red-haired athlete. Yosha was friendly and upbeat and seemed to like to teach them. Unlike Jason Kelly, he had no taint of conceit.

As the boys played, they talked and laughed. It was clear that all three would become friends and would hang out during the soon to be enjoyed summer. Dafidi and Abdul were catching on quickly as Yosha instructed them, and Daf only wished he had more time to practice the new moves before the next day's game.

As dusk began to settle and the light dimmed too much to play, the boys reluctantly stopped their practice. Dafidi and Abdul walked towards the bus stop where each could board a bus home. As they approached the stop, they heard Dafidi's name being called. Turning in unison, they saw Jason Kelly standing on the pavement about 10 feet away.

He looked directly at them and said in a sarcastic tone, "Hey, Abraham. I can't wait to see you strut your stuff tomorrow. We'll see if you walk the walk the way you talk the talk."

Daf and Abdul turned around slowly and continued walking the remaining distance to the bus stop. Neither said anything. They knew Jason's words were a veiled threat. He alone wanted to be the school's star player and couldn't stand any competition. He had warned Dafidi of as much, and now the ball was really in Daf's court.

The first bus soon arrived, and as Abdul boarded it he turned and gave Dafidi the thumbs-up sign, saying "Daf, it'll be OK. See you later."

Dafidi smiled and nodded. His friend was so positive and cheerful, but he himself was anything but that. The lumbering bus pulled away, and Dafidi ruminated over the coming game as he waited a few more minutes for his own transport home. When it arrived he was grateful. Dafidi just wanted to go home and seek the solace of his room.

An overcast sky heralded the day of the game. Looking out of his bedroom window, Dafidi saw dark clouds scuppering across the horizon and could feel rain in the air. The somber sky matched his mood. He was nervous and unsure of himself, knowing this game would be the big test for him – his entrée into the high school's hall of fame or its dreaded wall of shame. He was determined it would be the former.

When he arrived at school, he immediately noticed the big banners hanging from the second story windows, advertising that afternoon's varsity basketball game against Walpole. The pressure was on.

Dafidi had trouble concentrating as his classes and the day slipped by. Luckily, there were no tests or quizzes scheduled, so he was able to keep a low profile and maintain a calm exterior despite his roiling stomach.

After his last class of the day, American History, he walked slowly to the gym to suit up for the game. As he entered the gym's locker room, a voice could be heard expostulating on the game ahead.

"I can stop Walpole. If you guys give me the right support against their defense, I'll be able to set up shots from the sides, the corners and even back of the foul line. You all know I'm a great one-handed shooter from far back, but I can also dribble and cut with the best. Just set me up in position and I'll do the rest."

The voice was that of Jason Kelly, the team's star shooter and Daf's nemesis. Jason constantly criticized Dafidi's performance, taking pleasure in putting him down in front of the other players. Daf could handle these verbal attacks because he saw Jason as what he truly was – an insecure bully. What Dafidi couldn't stand was the way Jason made fun of Abdul. Although he was not a star, Abdul was a solid player. Daf also knew that Abdul frequently played while in pain from a previous sports injury, popping aspirin and other pain killers before a game and sometimes even in class. He hated that Jason sensed Abdul's vulnerability and exploited it. It reminded Dafidi of a lion he had once seen in Africa chasing a wounded wildebeest calf, waiting for it to expose its injury so the huge beast could go in for the kill. Unlike the prowling lion, however, whose violence was directed by its survival instinct, Jason hunted the weak as a selfish ploy to build up his own ego.

Dafidi wasn't the only player who knew how Jason operated. Dafidi had seen Yosha Stern stand up for Abdul on previous occasions, inserting his stocky athlete's body between Jason's extreme height and Abdul's slender form.

Jason frequently tried to pull rank on the other players. Today was no exception.

As he reached his locker, Daf heard Jason call his name. "Hey, Abraham - got what it takes to beat Walpole?"

Dafidi opened his locker slowly before turning to answer. "Jason, the whole team thinks we have a chance to win. Why are you asking me?"

The taller boy snorted, curling his lip in a gesture of disgust. "Because if we lose, it'll be because of your pathetic playing."

Dafidi turned back to face his locker, ignoring the troublemaker, and began pulling his green jersey over his head. As he reached inside the locker, a hand slammed the door closed. Only because of his quick reflexes were Daf's fingers not caught in the banging metal door.

Dafidi looked to his right to see Jason grinning maliciously. "Damn, Abraham. You're quicker than I thought."

Dafidi returned to the locker, holding its door firmly with his right hand while extracting his team shirt with his left. After pulling the shirt over this head, he reached inside for his uniform shorts and carried them to a stall in the bathroom. Once inside with the door locked, he changed into them quickly. There was no way he was going to give Jason a chance to torment him when he was wearing only his underwear.

As he went back to the locker room in his playing gear, he saw Yosha and Abdul donning theirs. Walking over to the pair, Dafidi told them about Jason's taunts. Yosha was the first to respond.

"Daf, you're a totally awesome player. Don't let that idiot get to you. When we're playing we have to help him set up shots, but we don't have to like him. Just play the game and ignore him otherwise."

Abdul nodded his assent. "He's right, Daf. You're the best and Jason knows it. He only torments you because he's afraid you'll steal his thunder."

Just at that moment, Coach Tom Rebor called out to the players that there'd be a pre-game meeting in two minutes. After scrambling into their sneakers, the boys ran out to their assigned meeting spot in the hallway. There they saw the coach holding a clipboard and perusing it.

Looking up from the clipboard, the coach glanced first at Jason and then at Dafidi. It was obvious to the two boys that he was mulling over something important. After making a tick mark on the clipboard with his pen, Coach Rebor looked up at the assembled team and finally spoke.

"Walpole's going to be tough. They've got Nick Sabatino and LeShawn Johnson as shooters, and we all know how crafty those two can be." A nervous chuckle emanated from the team.

The coach continued. "What Sabatino and Johnson don't know is that we have a surprise of our own. I want you all to work hard to support Dafidi Abraham as he plays his first varsity game with us. With Abraham and Kelly both going up against Sabatino and Johnson, Brookline will win hands down. Now let's hear an energetic roar and let's get out on that court."

In unison, the team gave their signature pre-game roar and ran out to the court.

The game began slowly, with neither team scoring a shot for what seemed like ages. The crowd watched as Yosha Stern drove the ball down the court, dribbling with textbook precision as he eluded the opponent's wily defense. Keeping his fingertips lightly on the ball, he changed pace and direction frequently to fake out the opposition. When he stopped just short of the basket and effected a front pivot, the crowd held its breath. Swiveling, Yosha threw the ball and landed a one-handed shot. The ball hit the backboard and dropped cleanly into the basket. The Brookline crowd went wild, shouting "Yosh, Yosh, Yosh."

Yosha waved to the crowd before walking to the bench, grabbing a towel and wiping his face with it.

A scowl crossed Jason Kelly's face. Attention was being directed at his teammate's success rather than his own. He vowed to take the glory away from Stern.

Early in the first period, it was obvious to Jason that Walpole had chosen to execute a zone defense strategy. He laughed, knowing that a strong shooter such as himself could easily land a clear shot. He also saw that Brookline's strong offense was tiring the Walpole team. Even the crowd was becoming bored. Walpole's weak defense made it just too easy for Brookline to score.

The thought that went through Coach Rebor's mind was that the Walpole team lacked consistency and other than a few shorter, faster front men in their zone, the team lacked speed. By the end of the second period, Brookline had a 21 point lead. Here they were, halfway through the game, and Brookline was decimating Walpole.

Halfway through the third period, however, Brookline's strong lead began to unexpectedly dwindle as Walpole gained speed and strength. It was clear that Walpole had stepped up their game, and by the end of the period, Walpole was leading by 6 points. Seeing his team begin to falter, Coach Rebor made it clear to the players that they needed to tighten up both their defense and offense or they would hand the game to Walpole.

Midway through the 4th period, the lead flip-flopped between the two teams. The crowd watched with concentration as the two teams battled doggedly. Brookline was struggling as Jason Kelly seemed to have a cold hand when making shots. Something was wrong and it was evident he was off his game.

As the 4th period wound down, Coach Rebor saw the writing on the wall and pulled Kelly from the game. Calling Dafidi from the bench, he slapped him on the back and whispered, "You can do it, Daf. Go get'em."

With one minute to go, Dafidi realized that the game was on the line and that it was up to him to bring his team to victory. Playing his heart out, he managed to break through the Walpole defense and make a jump shot, to reduce the Brookline deficit to 2 points.

As Walpole sought to inbound the ball, Daf stole it from LeShawn Johnson and pivoted. Stepping behind the 3 point line and brusquely raising the ball in the air, he threw with all his skill and strength and landed a clean basket. The cheering crowd went wild. Brookline had won the game.

The Brookline players jubilantly huddled around Dafidi, laughing, slapping each other on the back and giving one another the high-five.

Smiling from ear to ear, Coach Rebor came up to Dafidi and grabbed him in a bear hug. Dafidi felt overwhelmed and joyous, feeling secure for the first time since he had arrived in Brookline.

Jason Kelly stood on the sidelines, with a stony look on his face. Seeing this, Coach Rebor walked over to the tall young man and looking up at him directly, said, "Kelly, you have what it takes, but you just didn't give it your all today. Regroup and take stock of what you did wrong and next time will be different. Let the new kid have his glory."

Jason nodded mutely, knowing he couldn't contain his anger if he spoke. Coach Rebor was one of the few people he respected, and he didn't want to antagonize him.

As the jubilant roar of the crowd wound down, the team retrieved their towels and water bottles from the benches and headed towards the locker room. Dafidi and Abdul walked next to each other but didn't speak. Their happiness was obvious and the two friends had no need for words.

As they entered the locker room, Jason Kelly stepped over to Abdul and asked him, "Trying to bask in your new friend's limelight, Rashid? Guess you are, 'cause you'll never have any of your own."

Dafidi didn't speak at first. He knew that Jason's taunt of Abdul was really directed at him but he couldn't figure out how to retaliate effectively without making matters worse. Finally coming to a decision, he turned to Jason and looking up at the taller boy, said, "Kelly, we're all supposed to be on the same team. Let's just do our best for Coach Rebor. We all have our own talents and let's use them to win."

Having expected an angry jibe, Jason didn't know what to say. He turned around and walked away, much to the relief of the other two boys.

Arriving home that evening, Dafidi found Peggy at the stove making dinner. Looking up as she saw him come through the kitchen door, she smiled and asked, "Hey, how did the game go?"

Throwing his backpack on the floor, Dafidi sat down at the kitchen table and grinning, began eagerly telling her about his triumph.

Peggy was ecstatic. When moving to Brookline, this was the outcome she had dreamed of for her son: acceptance by his peers, nurturing of his innate talent, and pure happiness.

Seeing his joy, she grinned back. "Daf, I was making chicken stew for dinner, but I think this calls for a celebration. Let's go get Chinese and grab a DVD from the video store. You get to choose!"

"But, Mom, you've already started cooking. Why don't we just have this tonight, and maybe Friday night, when I don't have any homework, we can celebrate."

"All right. Hey, why don't you invite your new friend over then? I'll pick up tons of goodies at the market tomorrow, and you guys can celebrate to your heart's content."

"Great idea. I'll ask Abdul tomorrow if he can come over on Friday."

When Dafidi approached his friend the next day, Abdul happily accepted.

That Friday, Mrs. Rashid dropped Abdul off at the Abrahams' apartment, but declined to go upstairs with him to meet Dafidi's mother. Abdul knew his mother was shy and didn't press her, but he thought that Mrs. Abraham might take offense that the other woman made no attempt to meet her. He mentioned this to Dafidi later in the evening, as the two boys were rifling through various DVD's, trying to decide what sci-fi film to watch next.

Dafidi listened to his friend's concerns and smiling, answered, "Don't worry. Next time, we'll just think of some excuse for your mom to have to come up here. She'll love my mother. Mom is really friendly and open to meeting other people."

Abdul agreed with Dafidi's assessment and assented to the plan. Mrs. Abraham made him feel totally welcome in her home and left the two boys to their own devices. She seemed to trust Dafidi and didn't hover around them the way many parents of their classmates did.

While stuffing themselves with Chinese food and popcorn, the two settled in to watch two really awful films, laughing all the time about the corny plots and bad special effects. When Abdul's mother telephoned to say she was leaving just then to come pick him up, her son found himself wishing he could stay longer at Dafidi's. After politely thanking Peggy for her hospitality, he walked to the elevator with Dafidi.

"Thanks for having me over, Daf. It was fun."

Dafidi smiled at his new friend as Abdul pushed the elevator button labeled Lobby. "We'll do it again soon. Let's just hope we can celebrate another winning game next week!"

The elevator doors closed and Daf walked the short distance down the carpeted hallway to his apartment. When he came through the door, he saw his mother cleaning up the cartons and bowls on the coffee table.

"Mom, I'll do that. We made the mess, after all. Just go relax and veg, and I'll make certain everything is cleaned up."

As he saw his mother smile and thank him, Dafidi noticed how tired Peggy looked. He knew she worked long hours at the zoo, and he felt awful that he couldn't help more around the house. His school schedule was grueling and basketball practice took up almost all the rest of his free time. He knew his mother put academics first, so he could justify the long hours he spent studying, but he wasn't as certain about the time he spent with the team. He knew that some kids at school had part-time jobs, and wondered if maybe he should try to find one. Seeing his mother's drained look and drooping shoulders, he posed the question to her.

"Mom, would it be better if I tried to find a part-time job to help out and got off the basketball team? I love playing, but maybe I should be helping you out financially. After all, I eat a lot."

Looking quizzically at him, Peggy smiled and answered her son

"Daf, I just want you to be happy, and my biggest dream is for you to fulfill your potential. You are a bright and ambitious young man and will go far academically. You are also a very talented basketball player. Both sides of your nature are valuable to me, and I want you to nurture them both. We might not be as rich as many people in Brookline, but we'll survive just fi ne. My job at the zoo is tiring, and I know I look exhausted tonight, but I really love my work there. Let's just be grateful for all the good things we've found here in Boston and keep going along as we have been. It'll be all right, honey."

Walking over to Peggy and hugging her affectionately, Daf said, "You're the best, Mom."

Chapter 3
Summer of 2008

A few weeks later, the school year ended. As Yosha, Abdul and Dafidi exited the building together after their last class, the three agreed to meet up the following Monday to practice. They knew that the pressure would be on them to succeed in their senior year, and all three were hoping to obtain college basketball scholarships.

Meeting back at the school's basketball courts on Monday, they practiced for over three hours, trying new shots and new moves. Yosha Stern was a great teacher and Abdul told him so.

"Yosha, you should really look into coaching as a career. You're a born teacher."

Yosha laughed, answering, "Must be genetic. All my uncles are rabbis and as we all know, that word means teacher!"

Dafidi laughed too, saying, "I don't think that Abdul knows too much about rabbis, but he is definitely right. You definitely know basketball and you really know how to teach it."

Yosha smiled. "I would love to coach, but my dad wants me to become a lawyer and join his practice. Who knows, maybe I can specialize in sports contracts."

Abdul commented. "I'm in the same boat. My dad wants me to become an IT whiz and work for a big corporation like he does. He's always telling me how great the benefits are and how lucky he is to work there. He never says anything, though, about how much he has to travel for business. It seems as if he's always calling Mom from airports."

Dafidi sensed the unspoken thoughts behind Abdul's words. He knew his friend missed his father a lot when he traveled. Dafidi, however, couldn't put himself exactly in his friend's shoes, as his father had left so many years before when Daf was just a toddler; he had never really known him at all.

Yosha dribbled the ball over to Abdul and gave it to him, saying, "I've got to rush home. My parents are taking me and my sister to a concert at Brandeis tonight. Call me on my cell tomorrow and maybe we can get together again late in the week."

As he walked away, Dafidi turned to Abdul and asked, "Hey, why don't you have dinner at my house tonight? I'll call my mom and she can pick us up."

"I can't tonight. Dad's taking me to *Best Buy* tonight to upgrade my old laptop. Maybe tomorrow?"

"Sure, no sweat. I'll call you in the morning."

Waving to his friend and smiling, Abdul walked off towards the bus stop with the basketball in his arms.

Strolling slowly towards home, Daf took out his cell phone and rang his mother at work. When she answered, he asked, "Hey, mom, can I have Abdul over to dinner tomorrow night?"

"Sure, Daf. No problem. I'll catch up with you at home tonight about it. I'm really busy right now and can't stay on the line."

"OK, Mom. Talk to you tonight. Bye." As he closed his phone and put it back in his jacket pocket, Dafidi felt deflated. It seemed as if his two new friends always spent time doing things with their parents, and especially their dads. He wished his mother didn't have to work so hard and could spend more time with him. He couldn't visualize having a father but, from what he'd heard from his friends, it was fun to have one most of the time.

When Peggy arrived home that evening, she found her son making spaghetti in the kitchen. Looking at the disorder on the kitchen table and counters, she knew he was trying to put together a complete meal for both of them. As tired as she was, she was grateful to him for the attempt, even though she knew she'd have to go cleaning up after him. Daf always tried to clean up after himself, but he just didn't view cleanliness in the same exacting way that Peggy did.

Peggy slumped gratefully onto a kitchen chair and said, "Thanks for making dinner. I am so tired tonight. We had budget meetings all day today and then the health inspector came by. I'm totally shattered."

"It's just spaghetti, but I added onions and mushrooms to the bottle of sauce."

Peggy smiled. Pushing herself slowly out of the chair, she walked to the fridge and extracted the bottle of cold water she always kept in its door. She then walked over to an overhead cupboard, reached for a small wine glass and filled it with water.

Taking a glass from the cupboard, she filled it also and carried both glasses over to the table. Sitting down again, she sipped from the glass, sighing with contentment as the cold water soothed her dehydrated throat. It had been a long, grueling day at the zoo.

Dafidi turned off the cooker's right front burner and removed the pan of spaghetti sauce. Setting it on a cool rear burner, he began ladling the sauce on to two plates of pasta. He then brought both to the table and set Peggy's in front of her.

Peggy smiled mischievously at her son, saying, "I think it would be easier to eat the spaghetti with forks instead of with our fingers."

Daf laughed and opened a drawer, pulling out cutlery. He reached into another drawer and pulled out two white paper napkins. After handing his mother a fork and setting his on the table, he folded a napkin carefully and handed it to his mother.

Peggy couldn't resist teasing him. "Maybe you should become a waiter at *Bettina's*. Then we could get all the free spaghetti we wanted!"

Daf laughed but a serious thought entered his mind as his mother said this. A moment later, he voiced it.

"Mom, maybe I could call that waiter we met and he could help get me a summer job at *Bettina's*. We could really use the money, and maybe I could meet that roommate he said had graduated from Brookline. That way, I could get the scoop on Jason Kelly from him."

Peggy mulled this over for a moment, and taking a last swallow from the glass of cold water before answering, said, "You know, Daf, even though I was joking about you becoming a waiter, that might not be a bad idea. It wouldn't hurt to gain a little work experience and *Bettina's* seems like a nice place. I think I still have the receipt with the waiter's number on it. I'll look for it after we eat."

Daf smiled at his mother and nodded. Reaching for the jar of parmesan cheese, he shook a tremendous amount on top of the huge mound of pasta. As he began eating heartily, his mind was racing with thoughts about *Bettina's* and what it would be like for Dafidi to work as a waiter.

After they finished eating, Peggy got up and poured a small amount of red wine into her glass. Taking a sip and savoring it, she walked out to the living room and picked up her pocketbook from where she'd left it on the coffee table. Reaching inside, she removed her wallet and rifled through one of its zippered compartments. After removing and examining various receipts and coupons, she found what she wanted and returned to the kitchen with it.

"Here, Daf. You can call the waiter tomorrow morning. I hope he remembers us."

Taking the receipt, Dafidi looked at it and responded, "Great, Mom. Will do. Just think - maybe I'll make a fortune and be able to take us on a trip to Italy!"

Peggy laughed and took another sip of her wine. The son she loved so much was beginning to grow up, but his dreams were still those of a child.

Late the following morning, Dafidi got up the courage to call the young waiter's number. The phone rang three times before being answered.

A soft young man's voice said, "Hello."

Daf nervously cleared his throat. "Hi, I don't know if you'll remember me, but my mom and I had dinner at *Bettina's* and you wrote your number on our receipt."

The voice on the other end answered in a friendly tone, "Sure, I remember you. You're the kid from Brookline that plays basketball with Jason Kelly, right?"

Dafidi relaxed. "Yeah, that's me. The reason I'm calling is that I'm sort of looking for a summer job and wondered if *Bettina's* was hiring waiters. Your job seemed kind of cool."

The waiter laughed. "It is cool, at least when I make good tips and the customers are nice. Every now and then it's a hassle, but all jobs are sometimes, right?"

Dafidi answered, "I don't know. I haven't really had a job before. This would be my first."

The waiter's voice had a hint of laughter in it when he responded. "Well, you have to start somewhere. Can you come to *Bettina's* this afternoon around three when I start my shift? I'll introduce you to Bettina herself and she can decide. She's a really neat lady, and she usually hires a few extra kids for the summer to handle the tourist rush."

Dafidi couldn't believe it – he had a job interview! Trying to remain cool, he said, "Great, I'll be there at three. Oh, my name's Daf Abraham."

"Great, Daf. My name is Tom Gill. I'll meet you there this afternoon. Bye now."

"Bye, Tom." Dafidi hung up and beamed from ear to ear. His mother would be so happy.

That afternoon Dafidi took the Green Line train from Brookline and managed to navigate successfully through the subway system to the Haymarket stop. He walked from there to the North End and Hanover Street, reaching the block where *Bettina's* was located about 2:45 pm. Just as he approached the restaurant, he heard his name called. "You must be Daf. I'm Tom."

Turning around, Dafidi saw the young waiter walking towards him. Tom was dressed in a navy hooded sweatshirt over his uniform of white shirt and black pants. He smiled as he came up to Daf.

"Let's go inside and track down Bettina. I rang her this morning and said I was bringing by a friend who was looking for a summer job."

Tom opened the heavy wooden door and both boys stepped inside the fragrant eatery. At this time of day only one table was occupied. The older couple seated there were obviously tourists, as they had a digital camera placed on the extra chair along with a canvas tote bag with "Boston – A Revolutionary City" printed on its side.

Tom told Dafidi to sit at a small table near the kitchen, and he went through a door in search of Bettina. A few moments later, the heavy-set woman in black who had seated Dafidi and his mother on their previous visit appeared. She smiled in a sincere way at Dafidi and said in a heavily accented voice, "Welcome. I'm Bettina Guarini. Tom said you're looking for a job. Have you ever worked as a server before?"

Dafidi answered politely, "I'm trying to find a waiter job for the summer but no, I've never been a server before. I need to save money for college, so I thought it would be a good way to earn some."

"Can you work late afternoons on weekdays? We get lots of tourists coming for early dinner after they walk the Freedom Trail. Also, how did you get here? Parking is a big problem in the North End, especially in the summer."

"I can *definitely* work late afternoons, and I took the T to get here from Brookline. It was pretty easy, actually."

Bettina was an excellent judge of character, and she also remembered the young man and his mother from their earlier visit. What stuck in her mind was the laughter that emanated from their table. It was rare to see a parent and their teenage child enjoying talking together so much. It reminded her of her relationship with her mother in Sicily. The eldest of seven children, Bettina was very close to her beloved mother.

"OK, you've got the job. Tom knows the place inside out, so I'll have him train you. Can you stay for two hours this afternoon and follow him around? That way, you can start officially tomorrow afternoon."

Dafidi was beside himself with joy. "Sure. I can call my mom on my cell and let her know when I'll be home. Thank you so much, Mrs. Guarini."

"Just call me Bettina like everyone else does. Tom said your name was Daf. I've never heard that name before. Is it a nickname?"

"Yeah, it is. My full name is Dafidi Abraham. Dafidi is just another spelling of David."

"Ok, Dafidi Abraham. You and Tom get going and I'm sure he will get you up to speed. I'll be in the kitchen cooking. Ciao." With that, Bettina turned and pushed open the door to the kitchen, her stout frame in its black apron disappearing as the door closed.

Dafidi turned to Tom and said, "Thanks, Tom. I really appreciate this. My mom works really hard and truthfully, we need the money. I'll try to learn as fast as I can."

***

The summer seemed to fly by as Dafidi developed a routine that would allow him to maximize the number of hours he could work at *Bettina's* but would also allow enough time to practice basketball with his friends. At first, he only worked shifts when Tom Gill was scheduled so that he could learn from his friend. Now he was a seasoned waiter with one full month behind him, he was able to take on shifts when Tom wasn't there. Dafidi felt pride when he counted the dollar bills in his apron at night. Some nights he brought home only $20 or so, but on nights when hordes of tourists descended on the small restaurant, he counted hundreds of dollars. On those nights, he stuck the precious money in his sock before leaving for home. By the end of July he had opened a savings account and was putting money in it almost daily.

As August arrived, Abdul began talking to Yosha and Dafidi about college applications. Abdul's father wanted him to go to a university out west, either to Stanford or UCLA. Abdul's mother, however, wanted him to stay in Boston.

Yosha and Daf tried to pry out of Abdul what he wanted. It was during these discussions that Yosha and Dafidi realized that there was a different cultural imperative working in the Rashid home. From what they could glean from their conversations with Abdul, Mr. Rashid's decisions were final and to be obeyed, whereas in their own homes, a more collaborative process occurred. Yosha's father truly desired his son to become a lawyer, but if Yosha felt that his true vocation lay somewhere different, Mr. Stern wouldn't try to force law studies on his son. Dafidi's mother hoped her son would attain success, but she left it to him to define what that success was.

Talking to his mother one morning over breakfast about the situation at Abdul's house, Dafidi expressed his concern about his friend's future happiness.

"Mom, how can he be happy if he just does what his dad wants and doesn't question it? I don't think Abdul wants to go out west, and I think he really wants to become a history professor, not a computer wizard. He reads about history all the time and he talks about ancient cultures constantly."

"Daf, you might be right, but you have to respect his father's wishes. Each family has its own dynamic, and it also might be a cultural difference because they are Moslem. Help Abdul find his own way and support him, but don't try to change his mind, whatever he and his family decide."

Dafidi listened to his mother's logic and understood her point of view, but it was really tough to follow her advice. A few weeks later, he decided to be pro-active and take an action he thought would help Abdul. As the two boys were walking home from practice, Dafidi invited Abdul and his mother over for brunch the following Sunday. He had already asked Peggy if he could do so and she had agreed, thinking it would be nice to finally meet Abdul's mother. She also wanted to get a sense of the other mother's attitude towards religion. If Peggy found the Rashids to be fundamentalists, she would find it necessary to talk to Dafidi at length about his growing friendship with Abdul and would attempt to convince him to cool it off.

When Dafidi heard the buzzer and went downstairs to greet Abdul and his mother on Sunday, the first thought that crossed his mind was how humble Mrs. Rashid looked. Asiya Rashid was 43 years old and petite, dressed in a conservative grey dress. Her head was covered with a grey silk scarf that encircled her oval face. Mrs. Rashid's beautiful bright blue eyes and gentle smile enlivened the severity of her outfit, and she emanated a calm beauty. Dafidi led Abdul and his mother to the elevator and took them upstairs.

Peggy heard voices as the three entered the apartment. Abdul politely introduced his beautiful mother as Peggy extended her right hand in welcome. The smaller woman gracefully took it and smiled, thanking Peggy for her hospitality.

Once they were all seated at the table, Peggy brought out a pot of herb tea and served everyone. She was very careful not to offer any liquor in deference to the Rashids' religious strictures, whereas she usually offered Mimosa or Bloody Mary to her female guests.

As they began eating, they talked about many things. Peggy found it easy to talk to Asiya Rashid. Abdul's mother seemed bright and knowledgeable about many subjects. Although her demeanor was subdued, there was a spark of humor in her eyes. Asiya was totally different than Peggy had expected.

Conversation flowed easily, soon leading to a discussion of the boys' college plans. Dafidi was the first to raise the subject.

"Mrs. Rashid, Abdul and I have been looking into applying to Boston College and Notre Dame, but I wondered about something. Would it be against your religion to have your son attend a Catholic school?"

Asiya Rashid laughed and looked at Dafidi with a twinkle in her eye. "And what religion of ours would that be?"

Dafidi felt awkward answering. He had been put off base by her response and wondered if he had offended her by asking the question. However, he had to say something in response, so he decided to voice his true thoughts.

"Well, I ...excuse me for asking, but I thought that since your family is Moslem, maybe it would be a problem. I'm really sorry if I've offended you with my question." Dafidi bit his lip and looked down at his lap, embarrassed and not certain what else to say.

Expecting a stony silence, Dafidi and his mother were surprised when both Asiya and Abdul smiled and laughed. The Rashids seemed to see some joke in Dafidi's words that had eluded Peggy and her son.

Choking on his laughter, Abdul answered. "Oh, Daf, that question is so typical of Americans. You look at Mom and think because she is wearing a head scarf that she is Moslem. Did you ever think she might just be having a bad hair day?"

Asiya doubled over laughing at her son's comment, hugging her stomach as she endured a fit of giggles.

Dafidi and Peggy were more confused than ever. This was the last thing they had expected.

Finally composing herself, Asiya smiled at Peggy and said, "It is just that we endure these assumptions so often. The truth is that my family brought me up as a Coptic Christian, which is a fairly common religion in my mother's country, Egypt, and my husband was raised as a Roman Catholic in the West Bank city of Bethlehem. We are now members of Most Precious Blood Parish and about as Catholic as one could get!"

Peggy turned beet red with embarrassment. She finally stammered, "Oh, I am so, so sorry. I feel as if I am one of those "Ugly Americans" all the Europeans talk about. I am totally embarrassed right now. Please forgive my ignorance."

Asiya smiled gently at Peggy and patted the other woman's hand, saying, "There is no reason to feel embarrassment. All people stereotype others to some degree, and the media in the United States has fanned the flames of prejudice recently towards those of Middle Eastern descent." Asiya laughed before continuing, "And anyway, you're from Kansas, so I don't think you've met many Arabs."

Peggy relaxed and smiled back at the other woman. "Thank you for being so gracious. I just learned a really good lesson."

Abdul looked at Dafidi and said, "So, I guess we can go ahead with those applications. The only problem now is how to explain to my dad that I don't want to go out west to college."

Asiya Rashid looked at her son, saying, "Abdul, just because your father would prefer you to study in California doesn't mean you have to do so. He just suggested that because he was so successful in his graduate studies at UCLA and wanted you to have the same advantages. He loved living in Los Angeles when he was studying for his PhD, but he'll be happy as long as you get good grades and can find a good job after graduation. He just wants you to succeed, feel fulfilled and to be secure."

Abdul looked directly at his mother and answered, "Thanks for saying that, Mom. I was kind of worried he'd insist on Stanford or UCLA. I really want to stay in Boston, if possible."

Peggy got up from the table and clearing her guests' plates, said, "Let's go into the living room and I'll bring out dessert. Anyone for coffee?"

After dinner at the Rashid home that night, once Abdul had left the table to play computer games in his room, Asiya told her husband about the luncheon at the Abrahams. Maroun Rashid laughed but then became somber. He took his wife's hands in his own and looking her straight in the eye, said, "Maybe it would be best if Abdul does stay in Boston. I never intended to have Abdul feel he had to attend school out west. I just thought he would enjoy it as much as I did."

Asiya smiled fondly at her husband. She touched his cheek with her right hand and said in a soft voice, "You are such a wonderful father. Abdul is so blessed to have you. I am, too."

Maroun reached over and pulled his wife to him, hugging her. They sat there in silence for a few moments.

Finally, Maroun asked his wife, "So, how is the new school year going for our son? I've been so busy at work that I haven't had time to really talk to him about it."

Asiya began telling him about Abdul's classes and his comments about his teachers and basketball teammates. She also mentioned in passing that Abdul's sports injuries had seemed to be bothering him recently.

Her husband asked, "When is his next appointment with Dr. Simmons?"

Asiya looked down at the dining table and sighed. "He seems all right most of the time, but I saw him taking an aspirin after breakfast yesterday, and I think he might be in pain but isn't telling us. I'm actually a bit worried about him."

Her husband reached over and put his arm around his wife's

shoulders. Asiya relaxed into his embrace and the two sat mutely at the table for a time.

Finally, Maroun spoke. "It will all be all right. Our son is in God's hands, and for some reason, I just feel everything will work out OK."

Chapter 4

Senior Year Begins

The month of August flew by for Dafidi. He was working as much as possible at *Bettina's* and between playing basketball with his friends and researching colleges online, he was constantly busy. Peggy could see the pride in her son when he told her how much he earned that week. Dafidi was happily engaged in his new life and Peggy was relieved that the move had turned out so well for both of them.

Classes resumed at Brookline High in the second week of September. After scurrying around to find their new classrooms on the first day, Abdul and Dafidi met up at the basketball court to practice and decompress. Dafidi was tired from the day's stress, but he saw that Abdul was totally exhausted. His friend was off his game and kept rubbing his left side with his hand as if he had pulled a muscle.

Dafidi asked him if that was the case, and Abdul just shook his head, saying, "I don't know what it is. My back has been aching for a few months. No worries, though. I've got my aspirin with me, and Mom has me scheduled to see a doctor next week."

Dafidi accepted his friend's answer and teenage boy that he was, brushed off any worry. Both boys were athletes and were used to playing with injuries and sore muscles.

Dafidi had arranged to work only on weekends at *Bettina's* during the school year, so it felt great to relax on the court for an hour or so before heading home to tackle his homework and chores.

Abdul finally said, "Let's call it a day. My sore back is getting in the way of my game. Anyway, I need to sit down tonight with my dad to go over the essays I need to start writing for early admission to BC. Have you started yours yet?"

Dafidi shook his head. "No. Mom has been really busy at work the past two weeks, and this is the first week I haven't had to work afternoons. I need to talk to her tonight about it. Anyway, I already got the online application info from Mrs. Herrero, my Guidance Counselor."

The two boys picked up their gear and started walking home. Both were trying to save money for college and decided to save on bus fare when the weather was good. Walking the short distance home on a warm September afternoon was pleasurable as the soft sea air blew inland from the Atlantic and the numerous trees along their route had just begun turning colors. Neither boy spoke much as they passed brick homes with manicured lawns and high-rise apartment blocks. At the corner where their paths diverged, Abdul gave Dafidi a high-five and waved as he turned and walked off.

Dafidi continued walking and five minutes later, he punched his entry code into his building's security system. He was glad to be home.

That night, Dafidi felt restless. Something was nagging him, but he couldn't put his finger on what it was. He tossed and turned in bed and finally got up and walked to the kitchen to get a glass of water. As he reached in the cupboard, he saw a half-empty bottle of aspirin on the shelf. Looking at it, something snapped in his brain. That was it…Abdul was in pain. The more Dafidi thought about it, the more he realized that Abdul was in constant pain and that there might be something really wrong with him. Dafidi had seen him taking a handful of aspirin in class, leaning down under his desk to take a secret swig from his water bottle. Students weren't allowed to bring drinks or food to class, so Abdul was breaking the rules. His friend was such a good student and usually so strict about following school regulations that this behavior was totally out of character. Something had to be really wrong.

The next day Dafidi approached his friend to ask about his aspirin use. Answering, Abdul made light of it and changed the subject. However, Dafidi was not easily fooled. He knew Abdul well for almost a year and could tell when his friend was being evasive.

At home that evening, Dafidi voiced his concerns to his mother over dinner. Peggy listened intently to her son's comments and began to feel concerned herself. Coming to a decision but not telling Dafidi about it, she vowed to telephone Asiya Rashid later that evening and tell her what Dafidi had said. Maybe Abdul's mother was unaware that her son was in pain.

Around 8 O'clock, Dafidi headed to his room to finish his homework on the computer. After he did so, Peggy walked into her bedroom and retrieved her address book from the bedside table. Picking up the phone, she dialed the Rashids' number. Peggy was nervous and felt a bit as if she were betraying Dafidi's confidence, but she was truly worried about her son's friend and put his welfare above her scruples.

Asiya Rashid answered the call after the second ring.

After prefacing her comments, Peggy told Asiya about what Dafidi had said. Listening to Peggy, Asiya sighed and remained silent for a time. Finally, she said, "Peggy, I'm very worried about Abdul too. Our doctor has scheduled tests for him on September 20th and I'm afraid of what they will find. Abdul has seemed to be in more pain recently and has been practically gobbling aspirin and ibuprofen. He's been injured a few times while playing basketball, and I know his back aches a lot. I'll let you know what the doctor says as soon as I know. I really appreciate your concern. You and your son have become true friends to our family."

When Peggy hung up the phone she was more worried than previously. However, she decided to keep her worries to herself until she heard back from Asiya. Maybe it was just a minor sports injury. After all, Dafidi had experienced many of those and none had been serious. They just have to wait and see.

The morning of Friday, September 19th ushered in a balmy Indian summer day. Dafidi enjoyed his walk to school, savoring the warm sunshine and soft air. As he approached Brookline High, he saw Yosha Stern walking towards him with a smile on his face. Once the two boys were within hearing distance, Yosha said, "Hi, Daf. I can't wait for the game tonight. We're going to steamroller Newton South. Hey, did you remember to bring your health clearance form for Coach Rebor?"

Dafidi nodded. "Yeah, I have it. I've heard he's pretty strict about not allowing guys to play until they give him their clearance paperwork."

Yosha nodded. "Yeah, I've heard that too."

The two boys continued talking until Yosha waved and walked leisurely off to the stairway to head for his AP Spanish class. Dafidi opened the door to Mrs. Thiebault's room and walked over to his regular seat. The sun was streaming through the tall windows and a bright ray illuminated Dafidi's desk. As the class progressed, he found it increasingly difficult to concentrate on Samuel Johnson and Boswell. With a beautiful morning outside, it was just too tempting to daydream about being outside on the basketball court.

Dafidi glanced over at Abdul and found that his friend was looking out the window, seemingly feeling the same restlessness. Feeling instinctively that someone was looking at him, Abdul turned around and smiled when he found it was Daf. He then moved his head in a subtle gesture towards the front of the room where Mrs. Thiebault was expounding on Samuel Johnson's love of London society. Daf nodded to his friend, understanding that they were supposed to be listening and that Abdul didn't want to get into trouble with the teacher. Both boys tried their best to concentrate on the teacher's description of Johnson and Boswell's era, taking copious notes to study later. After what seemed like an eternity, the class ended and the two young men headed out into the hallway.

Abdul was the first to speak. "Daf, I'm really worried that I won't get to play in tonight's game. Mom scheduled my check-up for tomorrow morning, so I don't have the health clearance to give to Coach Rebor. Do you think he'll let me play anyway?"

Daf replied honestly, shaking his head in a quizzical manner. "I don't know. Yosha and I were talking about it this morning, and he seems to think Coach is really strict about it. You'll just have to ask him directly, I guess."

Abdul's body language showed him to feel deflated. Hunching over a bit and shifting his backpack, he replied, "Yeah, I've heard that too. Oh well, at least it's just Newton South tonight. We're going to beat them no matter who plays, so if I have to miss a game, this is probably the one to miss. See you later this afternoon. I've got to rush, or I'll be late to Calculus." With that, Abdul turned to his left and almost sprinted down the long hallway that intersected the main one down which Dafidi walked.

That afternoon at practice, Coach Rebor asked the entire basketball team to present their health clearance forms. As he went along the line taking paperwork from each boy, he briefly looked at each form and nodded. When he reached Abdul and saw the boy wasn't holding anything, he queried him. "Rashid, where is your form? You know I won't let anyone play without a clearance, and you're scheduled for tonight's game. What's going on?"

Frowning at the coach, Abdul shrugged. "My mom has my doctor appointment scheduled for tomorrow, so I can't get it signed until then. Could I just play the one game without it? I'm sure I'm OK."

Coach Rebor shook his head and answered, "No, Rashid, you can't play. A rule is a rule, and this one is there to protect both the players and the school. The liability is just too great. If you were injured, we'd all be in trouble. I'll put in Mike Ramsay instead of you tonight. Just make certain you bring the form on Monday so you don't miss next week's game."

Abdul looked disconsolately down at the parquet, stinging from the coach's comments. He finally looked up as Coach Rebor gave the team directions for that day's practice.

Seeing and hearing the entire situation, Dafidi kept quiet until their coach was out of earshot. Standing next to Abdul, he leaned towards his friend and whispered, "No sweat. This game isn't a big one, and it wasn't your fault the doctor couldn't see you until tomorrow. Coach understands. He wasn't mad or anything. Just focus on next week, OK?"

Abdul nodded discreetly. Both boys then ran to their assigned positions and concentrated intently on the practice session.

The following morning, Asiya Rashid and her son drove the short distance to Dr. Simmons' office in the big medical building on Route 9. After dropping Abdul off in front of the building, his mother scoured the busy lot for a parking spot while her son took the elevator to the 4th floor. Abdul didn't feel any unease going to Dr. Simmons; he just wanted to get the appointment over with, grab the signed clearance form and head to the basketball court to practice all afternoon. However, when he entered the office and saw how busy the waiting room was, he realized it was going to take a lot longer than he had hoped. Sitting down in the nearest available chair, he grabbed a *Sports Illustrated* from a side table and began leafing through it. Forty-five minutes later, Abdul was ushered into an examining room by a nurse and sat there waiting an additional five minutes until Dr. Simmons finally opened the door and smiling, said, "Hi, Abdul. How's my star basketball player?"

Abdul returned the doctor's smile. "Not too bad, Dr. S. I'm doing great except for that backache that seems to come and go, but we both know that was from that fall at the Natick game last year, so nothing has changed. It's probably a waste of time for me to even be here today. I just need that form signed, and then you can go help someone who really needs it."

Dr. Simmons smiled at the chatty young man. He told Abdul to lie down and began examining him. When the doctor felt the boy's lower back, Abdul winced. Dr. Simmons palpated the spine and the flank and observed that there was muscle spasm. However, Abdul's strength and reflexes were normal. He concluded that Abdul had muscle strain. Going back to the waiting room, he invited Mrs. Rashid to join them in his office. He prescribed ibuprofen and instructed Abdul to take it with food to protect his stomach from developing an ulcer. He also sent him to have physical therapy. Unfortunately, we would not be cleared to play basketball for 10 days. Though disappointed, Abdul and his mother were relieved that he did not have a more serious problem.

That night's game with Newton South High ended just as Abdul and Dafidi had predicted. Brookline won handily. Abdul laughed about how boring it was to just watch the action from the bench, and he told Daf that he had given Coach Rebor the signed clearance form after the game so that he would definitely be allowed to play the following week. Both boys were in good spirits as they waved to each other before climbing into their respective mothers' cars. As they drove home, Peggy queried her son about the night's game, and he regaled her with all the mistakes the Newton South team had made. The pride in Daf's voice was evident as he explained how Brookline won the game.

As autumn progressed, the entire nation watched the Presidential election contest closely. In their Government class, the teacher meted out joint assignments about voter participation to the pupils. Dafidi and Abdul were assigned the task of interviewing ten voters each and then writing up their findings and presenting them jointly to the class. They worked diligently on the project each night throughout October, canvassing their neighborhoods door-to-door, asking people about their political views. Some neighbors were friendly and helpful; others slammed doors in their faces. It was a learning experience in human nature for both boys.

They finally gave their presentation on Halloween. As each boy in turn began reciting his findings, they felt that the class was distracted by imagining that night's holiday activities. They could see some of their classmates looking out the window distractedly or writing discreetly in their notebooks. The few who really paid attention were those that Dafidi and Abdul knew to be activists in the community and were already politically savvy.

At the end of their presentation, a hand flew up in the back of the class. The teacher, Akiro Miyakawa, called on the student to ask her question.

Sara Mendelssohn asked Abdul, "So, as a Muslim do you feel that your people will now get a fair shake in this country if Barack Obama wins the election?"

Abdul couldn't answer for a moment. He was taken aback by the question and wasn't certain how to respond. Finally, he said, "Well, first and foremost, Barack Obama is a Methodist. Secondly, I'm Catholic, so if you mean 'will Catholics get a fair shake?' ...well, yes, I think they will. However, I think you assumed that because I have an Arab name that I must be a Moslem. How about that other famous Abdul, Paula? Her father was born in Syria, but is Jewish. So, in answer to your implied question, yes, I think they will get fair treatment also."

Sara looked abashed. "Sorry, Abdul. I just thought..." As embarrassed as she was, she couldn't finish the sentence. Sensing both students' unease, Mr. Miyakawa wisely called on the next two students to give their presentation.

When the two boys met at the basketball court for practice that afternoon, Abdul told Dafidi how embarrassed he had been by Sara's question.

"Why does everyone assume I'm Moslem or something? I'm so sick of it! Mr. Miyakawa is of Japanese descent, but nobody accuses him of starting World War II. For that matter, Sara has a German last name, but I don't see anyone asking her if she has any Nazis in her family."

Dafidi heard the hurt in his friend's voice and answered softly, "Sara's question was well-meant but it showed her ignorance. It was just like when I had my back problem and kids would ask if I was a hunchback. I had to educate them. Maybe that's what we need to do now."

Abdul sighed, "How can we get people to understand when every night on TV Arabs are wrongly portrayed as violent? Most Arabs are regular people who want peace. What can we do? After all, we're just high-school kids in Brookline."

Dafidi thought for a moment before responding, "Well, maybe we could write a joint letter to the *Boston Globe* editorial page. It might get people's attention to hear from a Jewish kid and an Arab Christian who are friends. I know my mom reads that part of the paper every morning. Maybe a lot of other people do too."

Looking down, Abdul shook his head. "No one would listen to us. We're nobodies."

Dafidi laughed. "Speak for yourself. We did a really good job on our presentation today, and I think we could make people change their minds if we worked hard at it. Maybe Mr. Miyakawa could tell us if it a good idea to write the letter. He might also give us extra credit for it, and that wouldn't hurt if we want to ace that class."

Abdul looked up at his friend and saw the sincerity in his face. He said, "Well, even if we don't convince too many people, it would sure feel good to get our point across. But before we agree to do it, let's ask Mr. Miyakawa tomorrow what he thinks, OK?"

"No worries. We'll ask him." With that, Dafidi began dribbling the ball and the two practiced blocking and shooting. Two hours passed before the two finally went home for dinner.

In between bites of his chicken, Dafidi told his mother about the proposed letter to the *Boston Globe*. Peggy listened and thought about it carefully before answering.

"Daf, I think that's a great idea. What matters is that you and Abdul are voicing your true thoughts. Even if nobody reads the column, you would still feel good about expressing what you feel. I think, though, that readers will respond. I know that I would, even if I weren't your mother."

"Thanks, Mom. That makes me feel at least a little more confident. I wasn't sure if it was a dumb idea or not."

Three weeks later, a letter from Dafidi Abraham and Abdul Rashid appeared in the Editorial Page of the *Boston Globe*.

We wish to bring to readers' attention a pervasive problem occurring in the Boston area, and for that matter, probably throughout the entire United States, and possibly the world. The problem is stereotyping by presumed ethnicity. In our case, it is stereotyping related specifically to Arabs and Jews, but it could also be directed towards anyone else.

Both of us attend high school in an affluent suburb of Boston. The area in which we live is predominantly populated by white, upper middle-class families who represent the typical ethnic mix of greater Boston's suburbs – Jewish, Irish, Italian, and African-American. However, there are also students of many other ethnic and racial backgrounds at our school, although they are definitely in the minority. We have experienced first-hand what stereotyping feels like and please, believe us when we say it is not a pleasant sensation.

We are two 17 year-olds who think alike and look similar. However, one of us is Jewish and one is an Arab Christian. When we encounter people who don't know us well, they seem to always assume that one of us practices Islam and that the other one should not be his friend because of this. Nothing could be further from the truth.

Although we are of different backgrounds, we share one outlook: we want peace in the world and have faith that it will eventually come to pass. Our paths to this faith are different, but they converge at the intersection of hope and trust. We both believe that all children are descended from the same essence of good and mercy. We are both children of Abraham!

Why, then, do people stereotype us when they meet us? It is because of our surnames and their own ignorance. They just don't understand that ANYONE can be of any ethnicity, despite his or her name. What about someone who has a Japanese mother and an Irish father and is named John Reilly? If someone saw that name in a phonebook or on the internet, they would assume the person was of Irish descent. But if they saw the individual in person, they would see he was part Asian. Why should that make any difference in how they view him? He would still be John Reilly, despite his appearance.

It is now almost fifty years since the great scandal of prejudice erupted in Boston's public schools. Thank God, we have come a long way in America, yet we, as high school students, still have to endure racial and ethnic stereotyping. It is time for this great nation of ours to end this practice. We ask you, the readers, to begin speaking honestly to your neighbors about this subject and to start a dialogue of peace in your community.

Please help us bring stereotyping to an end and promote acceptance of all people.

Peace,
Dafidi Abraham and Abdul Rashid
Seniors, Brookline High School
Brookline, MA

The response by readers was huge. Letters began pouring into the *Boston Globe* not only from people who lived locally, but also from others around the world who had read the boys' letter. Most of the response was positive and supported the boys' viewpoint. However, a few respondents were openly hostile, slinging racial epithets and slanderous accusations. The editor witnessed in these letters the kind of stereotyping mentioned by the boys.

Suddenly, the *Boston Globe* itself was front page news. Both local and national television newscasts covered the debate about the letter's intent and its ramifications. Reporters swarmed Brookline High trying to get interviews with Dafidi and Abdul. The principal put his foot down and forbade any cameras on school property. This didn't prevent camera trucks from parking down the street and reporters hounding any students they could lure into speaking on air.

One of these interviews was that conducted with Jason Kelly, the school's star basketball player. The cub reporter who was assigned to the school story for the 4 pm local newscast thrust the microphone in Jason's face. The tall young student beamed, enjoying his five minutes of fame. When the young female reporter asked him his opinion of the letter, Jason felt no hesitation in answering, his answer showing both his immaturity and his obvious prejudice.

"Abraham and Rashid are just trying to get attention from the letter because they aren't very good on the basketball team. I'm the star player, not them. Also, Rashid is an Arab, so I don't understand why Abraham, who is Jewish, would even have anything to do with him."

The reporter was astounded by the stupidity of the student's answer. She quickly pulled back the microphone and turned slightly, saying, "And now back to the studio." The cameraman took her cue and quickly swiveled the camera towards the school building and away from Jason's face.

Late the following Friday afternoon, Dafidi was astounded when a customer at *Bettina's* recognized him as the writer of the letter to the *Boston Globe*. As Dafidi brought bread to the customer's table, the older man looked at the waiter's name badge and smiling, asked, "So, I assume you are the Dafidi who wrote the inspired letter to the Globe?"

Surprised by the man's question, Dafidi almost dropped the bread basket. Recovering, he leaned over and slid it onto the table before answering "Yes" in a shy whisper.

As Daf straightened up, the customer looked at him and commented, "Son, you and your friend are on the right track. I just wish more people would see the world the way you do. My parents were Armenian immigrants, and when they moved to East Boston, people would avoid talking to them. When I was your age, kids used to make fun of my parents' accents and clothes. It just wasn't right."

Dafidi relaxed and extended his hand to shake. The stocky grey-haired man rose from his seat and took the young waiter's hand in both of his, saying, "Nice to meet you, Dafidi. I am John Petrossian."

Dafidi talked to Mr. Petrossian a few moments longer and then excused himself. Tables were filling up, and he knew Bettina liked to get orders in as soon as possible so that customers would be served their made-to-order food promptly. As he moved from table to table, his mind was spinning with the idea that the letter he and Abdul wrote had actually been taken seriously by readers.

He couldn't wait to get home and call his friend to tell him.

The next morning, Dafidi telephoned Abdul and told him about the conversation with Mr. Petrossian. Both boys voiced their surprise that their letter had been so well received, thinking that as high school students, their opinions might be ignored by adult readers. They agreed to tell Mr. Miyakawa about the encounter and to thank him again for his help in writing the letter. Before hanging up, Abdul said, "Daf, I really wanted to practice this afternoon with you and Mike Ramsay, but my back is really aching. Can I take a rain check until next week?"

"No problem. Actually, I volunteered to work one of Tom's shifts at *Bettina's* this afternoon anyway. I need to start saving more money before summer."

Abdul answered, "I can relate. Go do your thing, and I'll see you Monday in class."

"OK, bye. Feel better." With that, Dafidi hung up the phone and plopped down on the sofa to vegetate in front of the television to watch an old black and white *Three Stooges* film. He was roaring with laughter when Peggy came through the front door laden with grocery bags.

Seeing what was on the TV screen, she smiled and said, "If you can pull yourself away from that erudite fare, could you help me with these bags. I don't think I can hold onto them much longer."

Daf jumped up and grabbed a heavy bag from his mother's arms, ejecting an onion from it onto the floor as he did so. He bent down and retrieved it before walking into the kitchen and setting the bag on the counter. He then threw the onion towards the vegetable basket on the top of the fridge, trying to make a jump shot as he would with a ball. The onion missed and rolled behind the fridge. Peggy laughed at her son's antics as he fought to slide out the heavy refrigerator and retrieve the rogue vegetable behind it. He finally succeeded and gently placed the onion in the basket. When he felt his mother looking at him, he turned and saw she was chuckling. He smiled sheepishly in return and said, "Well, can't blame me for trying, right?"

After dinner, mother and son sat and watched a news special about the election and inauguration. Peggy was amused that so much time was spent theorizing on what Michelle Obama would wear to the swearing-in ceremony if Obama won the election. With the world in such dire political and economic straits, it was inconceivable to her that a world-renowned newscaster would spend precious time interviewing two famous dress designers about what they thought the new First Lady should wear. As the show continued, however, more substantive questions were asked of members of the House and Senate, and Peggy came away from the program with a better view of Obama's plans for the country.

Peggy's feeling of optimism was short-lived. As the week progressed, the ramping up of the Gaza conflict became the primary focus of the nightly news. Scenes of immense devastation flooded the airwaves as foreign correspondents in flak jackets breathlessly described missile attacks while racing to seek cover themselves. The conflict escalated daily, with Israel and Hamas exchanging missile strikes.

The world watched in horror at footage of toddlers with arms encased in bandages wailed for their mothers, many of whom had died. Mothers on both sides of the conflict were interviewed and responded remarkably alike that they just wanted peace and a secure world for their children. World leaders bemoaned the conflict but offered no substantive solutions.

Although of Jewish heritage, Peggy prayed each night for children on both sides of the skirmish. She lay awake at night imagining how terrifying it would be to hear artillery bombarding one's home, to find no rest for days at a time. She envisioned mothers shielding their children with their bodies as they heard walls collapsing around them. Her heart broke for all the mothers and children trapped in a conflict not of their making.

Dafidi watched the news and couldn't understand how land could be so important that people's lives were expendable to obtain it. Both sides had claim to the same land. Why couldn't they negotiate a just settlement that would benefit everyone?

Asiya Rashid watched the news each night in horror. She was raised in Nazareth as an Israeli citizen, a Christian, yet Arab. Her lineage was interwoven with both sides of the conflict; her family's blood ran in the veins of both Israelis and Palestinians alike. Yes, her immediate family was Christian, but who knew what religion was practiced in previous millennia by her forebears? She wept as she watched the coverage, feeling the pain of the mothers on both sides, just as Peggy did.

Election Day

On election day, Dafidi and Abdul felt restless and, like most people in the United States, were anxious to start seeing the election returns come in. As soon as school ended, the two boys set off for the Abrahams' apartment to watch local news coverage of the exit polls. By the time the polls closed, both boys were fairly confident that Obama would win, but they still hovered in front of the television, eating snacks and listening to the various news commentaries.

Abdul laughed as he dipped a corn chip into a dish of salsa and said, "Can you believe this? Both of us are actually interested in politics. That's the last thing my mom or dad would have thought!"

Dafidi chuckled too. "Yeah, I usually get bored watching the news. But you know, this really is an awesome election. We're watching history being made. Just think, someday when we have kids, we can tell them all about it the same way your mom always brings up stuff about President Kennedy."

Abdul smiled. "Yeah, Mom quotes him a lot. I think she was really into politics in high school and college. When she met my dad at the University of Haifa, they used to go to political lectures a lot. Not very exciting dates, huh?"

"Yeah, like we're always taking girls to exciting places. Oh, the thrill of Coolidge Corner Theatre!" Dafidi laughed at his own joke. He knew that his infrequent movie dates weren't in the same league as experiencing the conflict in the Middle East first-hand the way his friend's parents did.

A big smile on his face, Abdul responded, "Speak for yourself, Abraham. Personally, I think any girl would be excited just to go out with me at all!"

"Oh, give me a break!" Dafidi mischievously grabbed a brown throw pillow and threw it at his friend.

Holding up both hands and giggling as he ducked to avoid the pillow, Abdul said, "Enough, enough...I almost dropped salsa on your sofa. Your mom will kill me if I do."

"Ok, truce. Hey, why can't it just be this easy in Israel? Why couldn't the Israelis and Palestinians just throw pillows at each other instead of gunfire. Just picture what the news would be like..."And now a green down sofa cushion is flying over Gaza. Wait – did we see two brown plaid pillows being launched by Hamas?"

Just then Abdul threw a cushion back at Dafidi and shouted, "Incoming missile!"

Both boys laughed hysterically, visualizing such a battle. Just at that moment Peggy arrived home to find both boys doubled over with laughter in front of the 6 pm news, sofa pillows scattered on the floor. As she put down her briefcase and took off her jacket, she smiled and asked, "So, you two, what is so funny?"

Dafidi almost choked with laughter as he answered, "Pillow imbroglio, Mom."

Looking puzzled, Peggy said to her son. "Ok, explain that to me over dinner because I have no idea what you are talking about. Abdul, would you like to stay and eat with us?"

"Thanks, Mrs. A. but I told Mom I'd be home by seven, and I should get going." Rising from the sofa, Abdul picked up his jacket and backpack and walked towards the front door. As he turned its handle to open it, he looked back at Peggy and Dafidi and said, "Well. We'll see who wins. My guess is that it will be a landslide for Obama. See you tomorrow."

Peggy seemed as anxious as her son to watch the election results, so after a hastily eaten meal, the two settled themselves on the sofa and listened intently to the coverage of the election. They sat there entranced for two hours, until Peggy finally got up and told her son she was just too tired to watch any more.

"I'm going to bed, Daf. If you want to, you can stay up. After all, this is history."

"Thanks, Mom. I'll head off in a few minutes. I just want to watch the 11 O'clock news before I do. Sleep tight."

After his mother left the room, Dafidi turned off all of the lights and sat listening to the news in darkness. The enormity of the election slowly dawned on him. He really was watching history being made. As he listened to the newscaster's voice in the darkness, he leaned back into the cushions and relaxed. So it was that at 6:15 the next morning, Peggy found her son sleeping soundly, sprawled across the sofa still in his clothes. She tapped him gently on his shoulder and he responded with a sleepy "huh"? Once awake, Dafidi rushed off to shower and change. Skipping breakfast so he wouldn't be late to school, he ran out the door twenty minutes later.

***

December 2008 saw the US economy falter even further than it had in the previous months. Dafidi lost some of his basketball teammates when their families were forced to move away to find employment elsewhere. One of those who moved away was Yosha Stern, a great defensive player and a good friend to both Dafidi and Abdul. Yosha's father was working for a large investment firm in Boston, but it went under. Mr. Stern accepted a lesser position with a bank in Framingham, and the Sterns were forced to move into a two-family house in Natick, owned by Yosha's grandfather. Although the actual distance from Brookline to Natick wasn't that far, it seemed like a million miles away to high-schoolers dependent on public transportation.

The three boys still kept in touch by text messaging. Dafidi found out that Yosha was offered a basketball scholarship by Boston College. Daf was ecstatic for his friend, but he now felt even more pressured to get into the school himself. He and Abdul had finished their entrance essays, and during the previous week had emailed their paperwork to the various universities to which they were applying. Now they had to endure the hardest part – waiting to hear if they were accepted. Dafidi and Abdul's emotions ran the gamut, swinging from confidence that they would be accepted at every school, to despondency that they would never be accepted anywhere. As January arrived, both boys began fearing the worst, although their counselor told them they might have to wait until April or May to receive their acceptance letters.

Dafidi knew that Yosha was granted early acceptance in December, not just because of the basketball scholarship, but because he was also an outstanding student and a true scholar. Yosha was fluent in three languages and had garnered numerous awards for his science projects. He was a National Merit Scholar and was offered full scholarships to Brandeis and Carnegie Mellon. Choosing to accept the offer from Boston College was because of his love of basketball and the opportunity to live in Brookline again. Yosha's uncle was a rabbi at a nearby reformed temple, and he could live rent-free with his uncle's family, thus helping out his struggling parents. The Sterns were grateful to their son for making such a considerate choice, and they put up no resistance to his going to a Catholic university. They knew it was a good school and just wanted him to be happy. They also knew he missed his friends from Brookline.

On Martin Luther King Day, Monday, January 19, Peggy had the day off. Early that morning, she and Dafidi drove the short distance to the Rashid home and picked up Abdul. The three then drove to Natick to collect Yosha, and the party went out for a huge breakfast before returning to the Abraham's Brookline apartment. As both Brookline and Natick had cancelled school for Inauguration Day, the plan was for Yosha to spend the night and to watch the Inauguration on television with his friends the following day, and Peggy would take him home early in the evening on Tuesday.

Once they arrived back at the apartment, the three boys sat and talked for a while before heading out to the basketball court, just as Peggy expected. Arriving there in the late morning cold, they immediately began practicing. Abdul was amazed at Yosha's skill. If anything, Yosha had become an even better player since leaving Brookline. Try as he may, Dafidi couldn't get a ball around his friend, and Yosha managed to block every shot he attempted. Laughing, the boys kept trying to outdo one another.

A familiar voice interrupted the friendly play. "Hey, Stern, what the H--- are you doing here? I thought your dad went bankrupt and you had to slither away in shame."

The voice was that of Jason Kelly, who stood to the left of the players near the benches, his orange parka glaring in the bright winter sun. Jason himself was also glaring.

Abdul was the first to speak. "Hey, lay off, Jason. We're just practicing. It's no skin off your back."

Jason laughed malevolently and responded, "Looks like you need another player to even the score. Why don't you and I go against Daf and Yosha? That way, each pair will have one great player and one loser."

Although none of the three boys wanted Jason to play, they accepted to save face. Dafidi voiced this to the interloper. "Right, you're on, but don't be so certain there are any losers here."

Jason smirked and answered. "OK, Abraham. Let's see what you've got."

The boys played for almost two hours. Abdul and Dafidi fought to keep up with the other two players, whose superior expertise was immediately evident. Dafidi kept silently telling himself that it was good to be pushed to work harder. After all, Coach Rebor always told them to model themselves after better players.

At one point, Abdul was inadvertently knocked down by Jason. As the smaller boy slid on the ground, he could feel a sharp pain in his side. Finally getting up, he gasped as he stretched to his full height. It felt as if a hot poker were being thrust into his back.

Not wanting to let Jason see his pain, Abdul half-turned away. Taking in two deep breaths, he then planted a firm smile on his face and turned back around to face the other boys. Jason began dribbling without so much as a glance at Abdul, as Yosha tried to steal the ball. Only Dafidi could sense Abdul's pain.

Seeing his friend was suffering, Dafidi said the first thing that came to mind. "Hey, I'm hungry. Let's head back to my place and get some lunch. See you later, Kelly."

"Yeah, right, Abraham. I need to leave anyway." Jason resented the fact that he hadn't been invited to have lunch with the others, but he would never let them know that. In his mind, power resides with those who never needed others.

Yosha dribbled the ball carelessly as the three walked along the busy street. He turned to Daf and Abdul and asked, "So, have you heard anything back from Notre Dame or UCLA yet?"

Abdul shook his head. "No, not yet. It might be too soon though. They get tons of applications."

Dafidi then asked Yosha a question that had been bothering him for ages but he had been afraid to ask. "So, since you're going to move in with your uncle, does that mean that BC didn't offer you room and board as part of your scholarship?"

Yosha answered immediately. "Actually, they offered a partial subsidy, but my dad isn't doing very well right now, so it just seemed best to stay at Uncle Bernie's for the first year. I might move into a dorm or an apartment later on if I can find a part-time job. Anyway, this way I get to enjoy Aunt Rachel's cooking!"

The other two boys laughed at this comment, as they had enjoyed his aunt's incredible fare the previous Thanksgiving. Rachel Stern's turkey and stuffing was the best they had ever tasted, and her apple raisin pie could have won an award.

Dafidi joked with his friend, "Just don't enjoy the food too much. You don't want to get so fat you can't play on the BC team. We don't want you nicknamed *Yosh the Nosh*!!!"

Laughing, Yosha answered, "No worries, my friend. I'll be working out every day and playing basketball every night. Between that and my studies, I'll probably have hardly any time to eat at all. It's just that when I do, the food will be very, very good!"

The three strode on in friendly silence until Peggy buzzed them into the building. Once in the elevator, Yosha turned to the other two and made an unexpected comment. "I think Kelly wanted to come back with us. He was just too proud to ask."

Not knowing how to respond to this perceptive remark, both Abdul and Dafidi remained silent.

Inauguration Day

Inauguration Day dawned bright, bracingly cold and blindingly sunny. Peggy got up early and left the boys a pot of hot coffee on the counter and some homemade cinnamon rolls in the oven. Despite having the day off, she had decided to go into work for an hour or two to tie up some loose ends, arriving back home in plenty of time to see the actual Inauguration ceremony.

Around 8, Abdul woke up and strode out to the living room in his navy fleece pajamas to turn on the television. The Inauguration festivities were already being broadcast, so he went back to the bedroom to wake up the other two boys. As he opened the door, he almost tripped over the sleeping bag occupied by Yosha, who exclaimed in a fuzzy voice, "Hey, what…" and then yawned.

"Get up, guys. The fun is about to begin. Daf, your mom left us coffee and rolls. Come on, you two. This is a once in a lifetime opportunity."

With that, Abdul walked out of the room and back to the kitchen. Grabbing a clean mug from the dish drainer, he poured coffee into it and sipped it slowly and thoughtfully. Just as he was opening the oven door to extract the cinnamon rolls, Dafidi and Yosha came through the doorway. Yosha looked as if he were still asleep; his eyes were half closed and his hair stood up in a cowlick from the static electricity in the overheated apartment. Abdul laughed affably upon seeing his friend.

"Yosh, you look like a zombie. Get some coffee!"

Yosha yawned again and reached for one mug and then another. He handed one to Dafidi, who walked over to the coffeemaker and poured the steaming liquid into his cup. Yosha followed suit and for a few moments, none of the three spoke as they savored the hot, flavorful coffee.

Finally, Dafidi got some plates down from the cupboard and said, "Let's take the rolls into the living room. We'll miss everything if we eat in here."

The three settled into the sofa, drinking coffee and munching on rolls as the newscaster described the scene in Washington. What made a huge impression on all three boys was the mammoth number of people who converged on the Capitol. Spectators were everywhere; people of all colors, sizes and ages were spread across every conceivable corner of Washington to witness history being made.

As the morning progressed, Obama and his wife were whisked from place to place by the Secret Service in discreetly armored black Cadillac limousines. From meeting with the outgoing President and his wife for the traditional farewell coffee, to attending St. John's Church, known as "The Presidents' Church" for its traditional role in offering a prayer service before each new President took the oath of office, the pair were now at the mercy of government-appointed handlers who choreographed their every movement with clockwork precision.

Dafidi, Yosha and Abdul sat watching intently as Barack Hussein Obama took the oath of office, stumbling as Chief Justice John Roberts misplaced the word "faithfully" as he administered the oath. It was a minor misstep, probably caused by both men's nervousness at being the focal point of the ceremony, and the crowd accepted it as such. Thus, there was no diminishing of the loud roar of applause that followed this momentous occasion. As television cameras panned the enormous sea of people witnessing this unique historical event, viewers saw smiles and tears of joy on the faces of those in attendance. As one, the diverse crowd cheered, sending the world a vision of unity. Like so many people worldwide, the three boys watching in the living room in Brookline felt chills go down their spines. They were witnessing history in the making and what they perceived to be the beginning of a new era of brotherhood.

As they became engrossed in the pageantry, each boy realized how momentous the occasion they were watching really was.

Dafidi voiced his feelings. "Obama did it. He became President. If he can, anyone who is smart can. My mom used to talk about the *American Dream* and I never quite knew what that was. I guess this is it."

Yosha nodded. "Just think, maybe one day there'll be a Jewish President."

Abdul commented, "Isn't it really the point that it doesn't matter what ethnicity or religion the President is, as long as he or she is a good person and will do their best to help the country?"

***

The day after the inauguration was hectic at Brookline High. In keeping with the historic nature of the event, teachers were directed by the Principal to devise ongoing assignments that were relevant to the new President's stated goals for the country. Therefore, that morning, Abdul and Dafidi's US Government teacher assigned each student an essay about how they, as individuals, could personally help to heal the country's economic and social problems. If approved by their parents, each student was directed to pair up with another class member to jointly complete 10 hours of volunteer work before the end of the semester and to document this in a journal. The pair would then give a presentation on their project at the end of June. The teacher handed out parental authorization forms, telling the class to think carefully about their assignments before committing themselves. Students discussed this as they left the classroom, and many were heard to say they felt powerless to do anything really constructive.

That evening, as Dafidi and Abdul studied together at the Rashid's kitchen table, they bounced ideas off of one another, striving to find viable projects to execute and what to write about. Abdul was the first to voice his thoughts. "Maybe we could find a charity and volunteer for it; maybe something to do with kids?"

Dafidi nodded assent, "Yeah, that would work and actually, it might be fun. Maybe we could help them with basketball."

Abdul laughed and asked, "So, how will basketball solve the country's economic problems, other than making the NBA players really, really rich?"

Dafidi smiled and answered, "Yeah, you're right. But look at it this way: maybe we could work with some group that helps kids learn good sportsmanship. Wouldn't that qualify because it would make them more responsible citizens?"

Abdul thought for a moment and then slapped his forehead with the palm of his head. "How could I forget? BC has a group called *Baldwin's Bunch* that lets little kids attend games for free. Maybe we could contact them and if we worked there, maybe it would help our chances of getting into BC."

Dafidi said, "Maybe, but I'm not sure it's a charity. Google it and let's see what they've got."

Abdul reached across the table and pulled his laptop towards him. Doing as Dafidi asked, he brought up the BC website. There he found information about *Baldwin's Bunch*. Moving his chair a few inches closer to Dafidi's so they could both view the screen, he scrolled down and both boys read about the group. As they read, they realized it was a membership based children's group, so it wasn't strictly a charity. However, they both felt that if they got accepted to BC, it might be a group for which they would like to volunteer.

Dafidi looked at Abdul and said, "Not exactly what we thought, so let's go to Plan B."

Abdul answered, "Yosha used to belong to the Boys Club in Allston. Maybe they could use us to coach or something. That's a charity, right?"

"Yeah, good call. Let's check out their site."

It took a few minutes for the boys to find the website because the actual name of the charity was the West End Boys and Girls Club of Allston. As the boys read about the club, they became increasingly certain that it met the criteria for their project. Picking up the phone, Abdul called the club's number and asked to speak to someone about volunteering. A few moments later, a friendly, soft-spoken woman listened to his explanation about the school assignment, answered his questions and invited both boys to meet with her the following day after school. After hanging up, Abdul smiled and said, "This is great. Not only will it give us a good grade on the assignment, but it will give us coaching experience too. Maybe they'd hire us to work there during the summer."

Dafidi laughed at his friend's exuberance. "Whoa, my friend. Let's just get this project sewn up first."

At 4:30 the following day, Dafidi and Abdul stepped down from the bus on the corner of Allston Street and headed towards the club building. After stating the reason for their visit to the receptionist, she led them to a small cluttered office where a heavy-set woman with curly salt and pepper hair was working on her computer. Upon hearing a knock at her half-opened office door, the woman turned and stood up, smiling at the pair and introducing herself as Miriam Hernandez, the club's volunteer coordinator. Both boys could feel warmth and sincerity in her greeting.

After hastily removing papers and notebooks from two straight backed wooden chairs, she asked Dafidi and Abdul to sit and tell her about their school project. As they spoke, she nodded and smiled. Finally she spoke.

"Well, boys, it just so happens that we need assistance with our after-school sports program and could use your skills. We run a basketball clinic for middle-schoolers on Tuesday and Thursday afternoons from 5-7pm. Would it be possible for one of you to work on Tuesdays and one on Thursdays?"

Grinning, Daf spoke for both boys, "That would be perfect! When can we start?"

Miriam responded, "We'll have you begin next week. You'll both need to fill out some paperwork today, and I'll have to run a CORI on each of you, which should take a few days. Come here on Tuesday around 4 pm and I'll show .you around and introduce you to the kids. Even though this is a school project for you, I think you'll really enjoy them and have some fun."

Dafidi smiled and asked Abdul, "What is a CORI?"

With a sullen look on his face, Abdul replied, "That's what they do to us all the time. When your name is Abdul or Ahmad, they have to check to see if you have any criminal record. CORI stands for Criminal Offender Record Information." Dafidi could see that Abdul's feelings were hurt.

"Come on Abdul, don't take it personally. I think it's something they do for all their employees and volunteers. They are just trying to protect the kids from possible abuse."

Dafidi and Abdul explained their project the next day to their teacher, who was very positive about their submission.

He smiled and said, "West End House has a long-established program. I think they've been around for about a hundred years. They have a great reputation for mentoring inner city kids. I think you've made a good choice, and I'll look forward to your presentation."

Both boys felt relieved. They knew their senior year grades were crucial and felt that they had to excel. The teacher's comments reinforced their feeling that coaching at West End House was exactly the right choice for their project.

The following Tuesday, Abdul and Dafidi arrived at Miriam's office exactly on time at 4 pm. She led them through the building to a gym where they saw numerous boys and girls practicing basketball. Children of all sizes and ethnic groups were laughing and dribbling, running and blocking. As they heard the players' good-natured bantering, it seemed as if the kids were really enjoying themselves. Miriam and the boys watched as a tall girl scored a jump shot and the children erupted into a rap style cheer.

Miriam introduced Abdul and Dafidi as new part-time Coaching Coordinators. Neither boy had thought he would be given such a lofty title, and they were amazed at the respect the children showed them.

Daf had the presence of mind to bring a notebook with him, and he asked each child to write his or her name in it and alongside it, what part of the game they wanted to improve. The children politely passed the notebook around, and Dafidi could see wheels turning in the youngsters' brains as they carefully noted their weak points and dreams of glory. Once all the children had completed this task, Dafidi and Abdul broke the group into two lines and had them practice shooting free throws from the foul line. The new coaches wanted to size up the children's abilities before devising a coaching strategy. Abdul and Dafidi had allocated that night after dinner at the Abrahams to sit down and write up a detailed plan for their new charges. Both boys took their new responsibilities seriously.

Just before 7 pm, Miriam Hernandez came back to the gym and began closing down the session, telling them that Abdul would be back on Thursday evening for their next practice. The kids walked by smiling, giving Abdul and Dafidi high-fives, with many saying, "Next time, man" or "See ya."

As they walked out towards the bus stop, both boys felt gratified with that day's experience. Abdul was the first to speak of it once they were seated on the bus for the short journey home.

"Wow, those kids were great. They made me feel… I don't know, like an adult or something."

Dafidi turned sideways to look at Abdul and said, "Yeah, I felt the same way. It was like they really wanted us there to help them play better."

Abdul nodded before saying a bit somberly, "Now the hard work begins."

Passover

Thursday, April 9th marked the first night of Passover. Rachel Stern had been cooking since early that morning, and by 4 pm she felt she deserved a break. As her chicken soup was simmering on the stove, she sat down at the breakfast bar and shook off her shoes. Dangling her legs from the high stool, she relaxed and rested her head on her hands, closing her eyes as the comforting scents of her kitchen lulled her into a semi-somnolent state. Just as she was falling asleep, the doorbell rang. Lifting her head groggily and rubbing her eyes, she slipped off the contemporary metal stool and padded towards the front door in her bare feet. She opened the door a crack, leaving the security chain engaged. Once she saw who her visitor was, however, she burst into a big smile and unhinged the chain to fully open the door.

An elderly man carrying two enormous baskets of fresh flowers entered the house. He smiled at Rachel and walked over to the coffee table and deposited the baskets on it. Rachel walked over and touched the flowers, bending down to take in their heady scent. As she lifted her head, she said, "Mr. Petrossian! The flowers are beautiful. Come in and have some coffee."

"Thanks, Rachel. I could use a break."

John Petrossian, 68 years old and suffering from osteoarthritis, pushed himself at work, delivering flowers himself rather than hiring a courier to do it for him. He had been on the road all day, delivering flowers to all areas of greater Boston, heaving great baskets of blooms into hotels and homes. The familiar pain in his lower back was acting up and he was grateful to be asked by Rachel to sit down.

Rachel leaned down again and took in the scent of the exquisite bouquet. As usual, the flowers were beautifully perfect. *Petals* in the nearby suburb of Watertown was considered a top-flight establishment and consistently won awards. The owner prided himself on always delivering the freshest, most fragrant flowers to his clients and his dedication to quality and hard work had paid off handsomely.

Rachel's mother, Ruth Glass, had attended high school in East Boston with John Petrossian and she watched him grow from an impoverished but ambitious youth into a confident and successful businessman. For as long as Rachel could remember, flowers from *Petals by Petrossian* had graced her mother's holiday tables. When she and Bernie Stern married and established a home of their own, she carried on the tradition.

Beginning with their wedding reception 22 years earlier, Rachel relied on John Petrossian to provide flowers for all family gatherings and holidays. The Sterns' wedding took place on a frigid February afternoon, but Rachel insisted on fresh lily-of-the-valley for her bouquet. Unbeknown to her or her parents, Rachel's bouquet cost Mr. Petrossian more than he charged. He felt it was a gesture of goodwill to his longtime friends. Having been invited to the wedding, it gratified him to see Rachel beam with joy as she carried the delicately fragranced blooms down the aisle to the flower-draped *hoopah* where her husband-to-be waited. Witnessing the gentle couple take their vows reminded him of his own wedding to his beloved Anna many years before.

Raven-haired Anna Hagopian was petite and feisty, loving and generous. She was known to all in their close-knit Watertown neighborhood as 'Auntie Anna' because she volunteered for so many years to help with children's outings at the Armenian Orthodox Church the couple attended. As her two daughters, Sofia and Alia grew, Anna babysat most of her neighbors' children at some time or another, and her exceptional warmth and generosity was well-known. She also was a regular contributor to charitable events at the church her family attended, making her delicious baklava for the get-togethers. When Anna died at 62 of invasive breast cancer, the entire community mourned her.

Anna was also a savvy businesswoman, and when the yuppie craze resulted in the gentrification of many old Boston neighborhoods, she counseled her husband to modernize his business's name to fit in with the trend. The florist took down his outdated 1970's style yellow, pink and orange *Petals by Petrossian* sign and replaced it with an elegant forest green and white sign that stated simply *Petals*. The result was an exponential increase in business from companies wanting exotic flowers for corporate events and young professional women wanting to have beautiful bouquets at their weddings. John watched in amazement as his balance sheet became flush with capital.

Seven years had passed since Anna's death, and during those years, John Petrossian threw himself into his work, seeking solace in frenetic activity. The result of this was a thriving florist's establishment known to caterers and wedding planners as the *crème de la crème*. To say that one's wedding bouquet came from *Petals* was the desire of most society brides. Such was the sea change in Boston society in the 21st century that the former society outcast now provided a highly desired service. John had no idea how he was regarded; he just truly loved flowers and knew he was good at this craft.

Rachel brought two cups of coffee out to the living room and handed one to John, saying, "Excuse me for saying this, but you look really tired. Maybe you should look for someone to help you at work. After all, you're not getting any younger."

John laughed, "You sound just like your mother. Actually, I have begun thinking about getting someone to help out. With the new store in Wellesley, I have to travel back and forth all day. Any chance your nephew Yosha might be interested? He's a strapping young man."

Rachel looked down into her coffee cup considering this before answering, "Maybe. Did you know his family had to move when his father was laid off? They're living in Natick now, in a two-family house they share with his grandparents. His dad got another job, but it doesn't pay anything like what he made before when they lived in Brookline."

John frowned, responding, "Typical of what's happening everywhere, isn't it? So many people losing their jobs. Maybe a bit of extra cash would help Yosha. Have him call me over the weekend, if you can reach him by then."

"I will. You know, you are a very good man, Mr. Petrossian, or should I call you 'Uncle Flower' the way I did when I was really little?"

John laughed. "I always loved it when you called me that. You were so cute. Well, as much as I would love to sit and chat, I have two more deliveries before the day's end. Have a lovely Passover dinner and give my best to your family."

As the man struggled out of the low leather chair, Rachel could see he was in pain, and she felt she owed something to this wonderful man for all he had done for her and her family over the years.

"Why don't you join us for dinner tonight? After all, on Passover we are supposed to invite strangers to share our *seder*. Although you are anything but a stranger, you aren't Jewish, so you qualify. I know Mom and Dad would love to see you. Please come."

John heard the sincerity in Rachel's voice and it touched his heart. It had been many years since he attended a family gathering, and he would enjoy seeing Rachel's mother, Ruth, and her husband again.

"All right, missy, you're on. I'd like to come. What time should I be here?"

Rachel smiled. "Everyone's invited for 7:30. Don't dress up or anything. We're pretty informal around here."

"OK, I'll be here. See you then." With that, John opened the door and waved goodbye as he walked towards the curb where his white delivery van with its distinctive green logo was parked.

Ruth and Arthur Glass were the first to arrive for dinner. As Rachel opened the door, her mother hugged her and pressed a small wrapped gift into her hand.

Rachel kissed her father and took his coat to hang in the hall closet.

Returning to the living room, she found her father helping himself to a glass of wine from the bar. She walked over and sat next to her mother on the arm of the sofa. Opening the small box that her mother gave her, she gasped, "Oh, they're beautiful. Where did you find them? Oh, Mom, thank you so much."

Rachel held up a pair of tiny gold earrings in the shape of lily-of-the-valley. Taking off her pearl earrings, she substituted the ones her mother had given her. Rachel walked over to the mirror above the high black walnut table that served as a bar, and looked at her reflection, smiling.

"Mom, these are the earrings I wanted for my wedding that we were never able to find. I can't believe your remembered! I'll cherish them forever." Rachel walked over to her mother and reached down to hug her.

Ruth smiled, and answered, "Actually, I was at a Hadassah luncheon and one of the women there was wearing the same pair. They reminded me of you, and I asked her where she got them. And please cherish them – they cost a small fortune!"

Arthur Glass laughed at his wife's comment and said, "And a hug for your old dad would be welcome, since I'm the one who ultimately paid for them!"

Rachel walked over to her father's chair and kissed him tenderly on the cheek. Just then the doorbell sounded again. Upon opening the door, Rachel welcomed Yosha and his parents, Edie and Benjamin Stern. Just as she was going to close the door, she saw Peggy Abraham, her son Dafidi and his friend Abdul coming down the front walk, with Dafidi carrying a box of chocolates.

"Welcome, you're right on time. Have a seat, and I'll have Bernie get you all something to drink."

Everyone began talking and there was an air of relaxed calm in the room. After a few moments, the doorbell rang again. Bernie answered it, a drink in his hand, and smiled when he saw who it was. "Mr. Petrossian, welcome. We are so happy you could join us tonight."

John Petrossian came into the room and nodded at everyone. He suddenly felt very shy. Seeing his hesitation, his old friend Ruth rose and walking over to him, took his hand and said, "Come, John, let me show you Rachel's back garden. I want your opinion about how we should plant the flower bed I helped her to dig last weekend."

With that, Ruth and John headed towards the kitchen and the group could hear them exit the back door and close it. The room was silent for a moment before Rachel spoke.

"Ben, my mother's old friend, John, needs someone to help him deliver flowers. He asked about Yosha possibly helping. Any chance you and Edie would let him?"

Ben shrugged and answered, "It's fine by me as long as Yosha wants to do it. What do you think, son?"

Yosha could not believe his good luck. He had been trying for weeks to find a part-time job, but with the economy being so bad, he hadn't had any luck so far. Delivering flowers sounded easy and the old man seemed nice.

"Sounds good to me. Where is the shop located?"

Rachel answered. "Actually, he owns three shops. The main one is in Watertown, right on Mt. Auburn Street. The second shop is on Newbury Street in the Back Bay, and he just opened a new shop in Wellesley Center. Since you now live in Natick, I thought the Wellesley location would be a good fit. I think there is a bus you could take. And, who knows, maybe after a while you could save enough money to buy a car."

At that moment, the kitchen door opened and Ruth and John returned to the living room, seating themselves on the sofa next to Ruth's husband, Arthur.

Seeing that the entire group was now assembled, Rachel called for them to join her at the dining room table. She had put a small place card at each seat, and at her two male non-Jewish guests' places, *yamulkas*, the traditional caps. John and Abdul donned these out of respect for their hosts, and were especially thankful for this small token of thoughtfulness, as they noticed all the other men wearing them.

Both men felt themselves to be outsiders at this most traditional of Jewish festivities, even though they felt warmly welcomed by the group around them.

After putting the traditional white prayer shawl on over his sports jacket, Bernie said the required *Kiddush* prayer over the wine and then handed the carafe to Ben who filled each of the glasses in turn. Bernie then reached for the Seder plate and broke the large matzo on it into two pieces, the smaller of which he returned to the plate. Abdul was astounded by Bernie's next action, as the rabbi took the larger piece of matzo and slid it under the tablecloth. It seemed like such an odd thing to do, and Abdul couldn't think of any reason why one would do that.

Bernie then recited a summary of the Passover story. After this was completed, he handed Yosha a paper on which Abdul could see was written *The Four Questions*. Yosha stood up and began speaking "Why is this night different from all other nights?"

Yosha continued until he had asked the prescribed four questions. When he finished, Bernie, sensing the confusion of his non-Jewish guests, explained the various traditions, including that of the larger piece of matzo, the *afikoman*, which had to be hidden until the end of the meal. He also explained the tradition behind asking four questions and drinking four glasses of wine, and then went on to tell them about 'four sons' spoken of in the Haggadah: the wise son, the evil son, the simple son, and the son who does not know how to ask questions.

As Dafidi listened to Rabbi Stern, he felt confused. He knew that his mother was raised in the Jewish faith, yet he could not remember ever having attended a Passover *seder* before. He wasn't certain he felt comfortable enough to ask his mother about this, even though he really wanted to do so. Daf also wondered how Abdul was reacting to the traditions. Knowing Abdul as well as he did, however, he knew that his friend would offer his opinion without being asked.

Peggy, for her part, was almost moved to tears as she heard the prayers recited by Bernie and his nephew. She remembered Passover at her childhood home. Her mother cooking the traditional foods and her more conservative father donning a silken white wraparound robe, called a *kittel*, instead of a prayer shawl, before blessing the wine. When she moved to Africa, the religious holidays she had traditionally celebrated with her family got lost in the shuffle. There just never seemed to be enough time or energy to go through the motions required of this ancient tradition. Now that her father and mother were both deceased, Peggy felt the loss of her family heritage even more. As she sat at the Stern's dinner table, she vowed to reinstate the celebration of Passover in her own home.

John Petrossian was equally moved by the meal's traditions. He could sense the kindness in Rabbi Stern and could see how his son strove to correctly perform his role. John also recognized Dafidi from the day he met him while eating at *Bettina's*, and he wondered how the young man came to be at the Stern's Passover dinner. As he looked around the table, John thought how blessed this family was to have such a close group of friends.

At the prescribed time, Rachel brought out her apple-walnut *charose*t and each diner put a tiny amount on a matzo and ate it. Abdul was amazed by how sweet and delicious it tasted. Bernie had explained that *charoset* represented mortar, so Abdul thought it would be bitter or bland.

The fourth glass of wine was finally drunk, and the *afikoman* was broken into pieces the size of olives and distributed to everyone. This was the signal that the dinner had ended. All rose from the table and wandered back into the living room to talk. Although stricter Jewish homes forbade eating or drinking for the remainder of the night after the Passover meal, Rachel and Bernie allowed their guests to enjoy coffee or tea.

The diverse group sat and chatted warmly, replete with delicious food and relaxed by the calming atmosphere and the hot drinks. John Petrossian sat next to Dafidi on the sofa, and they began talking, and laughing about their coincidental meeting at *Bettina's*. John finally stated, "You know, young man, I don't really believe in coincidences. I think we met for a reason. I just don't know what it is yet."

Dafidi reflected on the old man's words. He too felt that sometimes things happen for a purpose. So it was with Yosha accepting Mr. Petrossian's job offer. Yosha needed as much money as possible to be able to attend college, and the offer was made just in time. Dafidi remembered the old expression his grandfather was fond of saying, "God works in mysterious ways, His wonders to perform."

Throughout April and into May, Dafidi and Abdul acted as coaches at West End House, documenting their Tuesday and Thursday sessions in a jointly held journal. Every Saturday morning before basketball practice, they met at Dunkin' Donuts to go over their journal notes and plan their coaching sessions for the following week. As the weeks progressed, so did the proficiency of their charges. Kids who had been weak players became stronger and the strong ones became stars. Their mentor, Miriam Hernandez, noticed the success the two boys were having and telephoned their teacher to apprise him of it. When he received 'letters of reference' forms from Notre Dame, Boston College, Brandeis and Stanford to fill out for Dafidi and Abdul, he was more than happy to give the two boys glowing references.

At one of their breakfast meetings in late April, Yosha met up with Dafidi and Abdul. He was spending the weekend at his aunt and uncle's house, and the three boys were going to practice later that morning with Mike Ramsay. As Yosha entered the coffee shop, he had a big grin on his face. Abdul was the first to speak, "Ok, what is it, Yosh? You look like the cat that ate the canary!"

Still grinning, Yosha answered, "Look outside, you two."

Neither boy could see anything special outside – just a line of parked cars. Shaking their heads and looking at Yosha in bewilderment, they signaled their confusion at his remark.

"OK, I guess it's not that obvious. Look at the 1998 silver Honda Civic to your right. What do you see in the window?"

The boys looked and saw a Boston College sticker on the car's rear window.

Then it dawned on them and they both smiled.

"You got a car!" Dafidi said.

"Yep. Can you believe it? I managed to save $800 from my job, so Uncle Bernie told me he would pay for the rest and the insurance as a graduation gift. We went on Wednesday night to buy it, and I went to the RMV yesterday after school and got the registration. It's all mine!"

Dafidi said, "Yosh, that's fantastic. Just think how much easier it will be now to get around. Not to mention dating!"

The other two boys chuckled at Dafidi's comment and Yosha

replied, "Yeah, but I had to promise Uncle Bernie that I would use it primarily for work and school. Anyway, with my schedule, there won't be too much time for dating. I hope there will be, but I'm not counting on it, at least not for the first year."

The three sat there for a half hour, drinking coffee and hot chocolate, wolfing down sugary donuts and discussing strategies for the upcoming game with Needham. Afterwards, they piled into Yosha's tiny car, and he drove them to practice, parking the car carefully in the school lot located off of Greenough Street. As they were climbing out of the car, Dafidi hailed Mike Ramsay, who was walking across the parking lot towards them. Mike waved back, and after all four had discussed and examined Yosha's new car in detail, the group walked to the court and began playing. Three hours passed as the boys ran around the court, trying out new moves and pleasantly teasing as they strove to block one another's shots.

Looking at his watch as he bent over to grab some breath after a particularly energetic session, Dafidi said, "Sorry guys, I've got to go. I volunteered to work Tom's shift at *Bettina's* tonight, and if I don't leave now, I'll be late."

Yosha responded, "No worries. I'll drive you home."

With that, the two left the court as Abdul and Mike waved at them and then returned to playing.

Thanks to Yosha's new car, Dafidi arrived home in plenty of time to shower and change and even arrived at *Bettina's* ten minutes early. He stood in the cluttered restaurant kitchen drinking a Coke, waiting the few moments before he could clock in for his shift. As he did so, he thought how wonderful it would be to have a car of his own.

Bettina's was crowded that night. As the weather began to warm, tourists descended on Boston's popular restaurants in the North End to lap up the local flavor. Saturday nights were always busy at the restaurant, and Dafidi loved working when it was full of customers and the tips were good. As he swiftly walked the short distance back and forth to the kitchen, he thought about his good fortune and said a silent prayer that it would continue.

While Dafidi was at work, Peggy was out shopping with Asiya. The two women stopped for dinner, and they began talking about their sons. Peggy sensed that Asiya was worried about something and tried to draw her out. Finally, Asiya got to the point.

"I'm worried about Abdul. We haven't heard yet from any university. What if none of them accepts him?"

Peggy hesitated before answering. "Asiya, you really shouldn't worry. I know there aren't any guarantees, but Abdul has good grades. He shouldn't have any problem getting in. Anyway, there are always other schools if his first choice doesn't pan out. Have faith. I just know it will be OK."

Asiya frowned. "I worry about my husband's reaction if Abdul doesn't get in. Maroun is so set on Abdul being accepted at UCLA and Stanford, and I know Stanford is especially difficult to get into. It would hurt him greatly if those schools rejected his only son. He would take it as a personal failure."

"Oh, my. Then we must just pray. What else can we do? The ball is in the schools' courts now so to speak."

Asiya nodded in assent. "I know that. I'm just very concerned, and I had to vent my frustration. You are such a good friend, Peggy, to let me babble."

"You do the same for me. Let's order something delicious and decadent, and forget calories tonight."

With that, the two friends perused their menus, ordered food and wine and sat chatting and enjoying their meal when it arrived.

When Dafidi got home that night, he found his mother curled up peacefully asleep on the sofa, the TV remote still in her hand. He turned off the television and lifted the beige woolen throw from the back of the sofa and gently covered his mother with it. As he turned off the lights and headed towards his bedroom, he thought how peaceful she looked.

The next morning over breakfast, Peggy told Dafidi about the conversation with Asiya and how worried her friend had seemed.

"Mom, there's nothing you can do. We're all nervous right now. We should be getting letters from the schools any day now, so all we can do is to hope and pray."

"I know you're right, Daf, but let's pray that Abdul gets accepted. I just feel sorry that Asiya is so worried."

Without saying anything further, Peggy rose from the table and poured another cup of coffee. Cup in hand, she turned to her son and asked, "So, what would you like for a graduation present? Within reason of course."

Dafidi laughed, saying, "So I guess that rules out the Celtics season tickets, the beach house in Aruba, or a trip to Africa!"

Peggy laughed at his comment before saying, "No, seriously. What would you like?"

Wrinkling his forehead in thought, Dafidi considered the question. Finally, he hesitantly replied, "Well, I've saved up a pretty fair amount of money from my job for school next year, but I really could use a car so I can work part-time at *Bettina's* when I am not playing basketball. I know money is tight right now, but if I could buy the car out of my own money, could you maybe help me with the insurance?"

Peggy looked at her son and realized how lucky she was that he was so mature for his years. Looking at him fondly, she answered, "A fair request. I think I could swing it. The only thing is that you have to make certain you still have enough money for school expenses before you buy the car. Could you wait until the end of summer to buy it? By then, we'll have a better idea of where you'll be going and how much it will cost."

"No probs. Oh, Mom, you're the best!"

Dafidi rose from the table and walked over to hug his mother, spilling her hot coffee in the process. Peggy shrieked when the hot liquid hit her hands, but then began laughing. "Are you trying to do your old mother in? You're killing me with kindness!"

As his mother rinsed her sore hands in cold tap water, Daf reached for paper towels and began wiping up the floor. When he rose, Peggy saw tears in his eyes.

"What's wrong, honey?" she asked.

His voice cracking, Dafidi answered, "It's just that it's been s-so hard for so long, and now things are getting better. I just hope I don't fail or anything. Maybe I won't get in anywhere either!"

Peggy reached out and hugged her son. "Don't even think about that. You will get in, and you won't fail. You are smart and ambitious, and I am immensely proud of you just as you are."

Embarrassed by his childish tears, Dafidi pulled away from his mother and wiped his eyes on his shirtsleeve. "Thanks, Mom. I just hope you're right."

Chapter 5
Decision Time

A soft rain ushered in the next day. Mondays were always hectic at school and the day flew by for Dafidi. He went to the Brookline library by himself after school to study for a math test and remained there until after 6pm. Feeling he couldn't concentrate on numbers for another moment, he pushed in the desk chair and lifted his heavy backpack onto his shoulder. Leaving the library in the early spring dusk feeling agitated and restless, he chose to walk home in the misty drizzle, forgoing the bus. He couldn't put his finger on what was bothering him; he just felt confused.

He arrived home to an empty apartment and set his backpack on the hardwood floor by the front door to dry out. Taking off his sneakers, he placed them beside the backpack and walked in his socks to the kitchen. There, he opened the door of the fridge, took out a carton of orange juice and reached into a cupboard to take down a glass. As he poured juice into it, he mulled over his day. "Maybe I'm just nervous about the test tomorrow," he thought.

Just then, the front door opened and Peggy came in smiling from ear to ear.

After shaking out her sodden black umbrella, she put her overstuffed briefcase down next to Dafidi's shoes and walked straight into the kitchen. In her hand was a pile of mail. Still smiling she said, "OK, Mister, time to face the music. It looks as if you have letters from two schools here."

Dafidi swallowed nervously and almost choked on his orange juice. Sputtering and coughing, he held up a hand as if he were warding off evil. As he finally recovered, Peggy poured a glass of water and thrust it into his hands.

"Sorry about shocking you. I wouldn't want to have to do the Heimlich maneuver or CPR on you. Here, drink this and then we'll open these. I don't know about you, but I can't wait to see what they say."

Peggy and her son sat down at the kitchen table. As she handed him the two envelopes, he took them with shaking hands, saying, "Mom, I can't open them. I just can't. Can you do it?" Placing the envelopes back on the table, he stood up from his chair and began pacing nervously, covering his face with both hands.

Peggy smiled apprehensively. "OK, if that's what you want. I can't stand the suspense anymore, so here we go."

Tearing open the first envelope, which was from Brandeis University, Peggy read out loud, "It is with pleasure that we hereby confirm your acceptance as a new undergraduate student at Brandeis University. We hope your academic career will be everything you anticipate. Please go to the website listed below and fill out the required forms. We look forward to welcoming you to as a Freshman in September."

Peggy couldn't continue reading. Tears of happiness were streaming down her cheeks. Finally, she said softly, "Your grandfather would be so proud. I wish he could be here to read this. I know he would be saying 'Mazel Tov, Dafidi'."

Dafidi was speechless. He was accepted at a top-flight school. He just couldn't believe it.

Peggy reached for the other envelope but hesitated before opening it. The logo on the envelope said Boston College. Although she knew her son wanted desperately to play basketball for BC, she preferred for him to go to Brandeis. After all, the university was named after the famous Jewish U.S. Supreme Court Justice, Louis D. Brandeis. The university was noted for its excellent academic record and history of matriculating many famous Jewish scholars. Although she truly felt no prejudice towards people of other faiths, Peggy felt that Dafidi might feel like a fish out of water at a predominantly Catholic university, whereas at Brandeis he would be just one of many students of Jewish descent.

Peggy opened the envelope slowly. She read the letter silently through before saying anything. Dafidi sat there in a paroxysm of anxiety because he saw the envelope's logo. His hands were shaking and his knees were knocking. Chills were running down his spine.

Finally, Peggy put the letter down on the table and looked Dafidi in the eye, saying, "You have a big choice to make. Read the letter carefully and then think about it before you say anything."

With shaking hands, Dafidi took the piece of paper and turned it over to read it. As he began reading, he was awestruck. He shook his head in wonder and re-read the letter again. He felt like jumping up and dancing with joy. Following his mother's instructions, however, he sat there for a few minutes internalizing the letter's contents before speaking, and when he finally spoke, it was with the utmost care.

"Oh, Mom, I can't believe it. A full scholarship to BC with housing included. First, I can't believe I was accepted at both schools, but to receive a full scholarship just blows my mind."

Smiling, he added, "But Brandeis is where Grandpa wanted me to go, and I just wish that he were here today with us. I just can't believe I got into such a good school. How am I ever going to choose?"

Peggy looked at Dafidi and said, "You have time to decide. You still have other letters to come, so let's wait and see what they say."

Dafidi nodded. He felt conflicted, and he could not stand the thought of letting his grandfather down. His grandfather had told him over and over again about the virtues of Brandeis, and yet he knew he really wanted to play basketball for BC. There was also the financial consideration: BC offered a full scholarship and Brandeis offered none. Could his mother even afford to send him to Brandeis? He would have to apply for financial aid and loans if he decided to go there.

Rising from the table, Peggy walked over to the sink and poured a glass of water, drinking it to steady her nerves. She then said, "Daf, let's put away the letters for now. I want you to sleep over it and think about things. Remember, you've got that test tomorrow too. I'm going to start dinner. Why don't you go watch TV for awhile, and I'll call you when it's ready."

Dafidi took the two letters and carried them to the living room. He opened the left-hand drawer of his mother's old roll-top desk and put the letters carefully inside it. Peggy kept all her important papers in that drawer, and he knew they would be safe there.

He then walked over and absentmindedly turned on the television. The nightly news was on, broadcasting the horror of political warfare around the world. Dafidi sat on the sofa half aware of what was being said. When Peggy finally called him to dinner, he walked into the kitchen like a zombie and sat down without saying anything. Peggy knew enough to remain quiet and just let her son digest the information he had received. The pair ate in silence.

Just as they were finishing, the phone rang. Peggy walked over to the wall phone and answered it and then said, "It's Abdul. He sounds happy and wants to speak with you."

Dafidi rose slowly from the table, placing his white paper napkin down next to his plate. He walked over to the phone and lifted it to his ear saying, "Hi. What's up?"

Abdul's voice was bubbling with happiness. "You won't believe it, Daf. I got my letter from UCLA today and they accepted me! Dad isn't home from work yet but he'll be so happy. I just can't believe it."

Dafidi owed his friend an enthusiastic response. This was Abdul's father's dream. Shaking off his shock induced stupor, Dafidi smiled and said, "That's fantastic. You are one lucky dude. Your mom must be smiling right now."

Abdul laughed and Dafidi could hear him say to his mother, "Hey, Mom, Daf can see you smiling through the phone!"

Just then, Dafidi could hear the voice of Mr. Rashid in the background, and Abdul said, "Dad's home. Have to go. Talk to you tomorrow" and hung up.

Dafidi hadn't even had a chance to tell Abdul his own good news.

Maroun Rashid sat at the breakfast bar beaming from ear to ear. He grabbed his son in a bear hug and said, "I knew you could do it. I am so proud of you."

Abdul could feel the emotion in his father's words and he was overcome with happiness. He knew his father had struggled financially to finish his PhD and that he worked long hours so that his wife and son could live what he thought of as 'The American Dream' in Brookline. Maroun Rashid had sacrificed dreams of opening his own IT consulting firm, choosing instead to work for a large corporation that offered exceptional pay for long hours, grueling travel, and unreserved loyalty to the company.

Asiya touched her husband gently on the shoulder and said, "Let's have some dinner and toast our son's good fortune." With that, she drew down a bottle of champagne from an overhead kitchen cabinet and handed it to Maroun to open. After he expertly uncorked it, he poured two small glasses and he and his wife brought them to their lips. Maroun looked directly at Abdul, and said, "Here is to the success of my wonderful son, the light of my life. May you be as happy and successful at UCLA as I was."

As his father said the words, Abdul was gripped by guilt. He really didn't want to go out west to attend university. His father, however, already considered it agreed upon. Abdul knew he might not get into any other school and might have to attend UCLA, but he wanted to wait and see what the remaining letters would say. He just had no idea how to tell this to his father.

The next morning Abdul met Dafidi at the door to their math class and said, "Let's talk after this is over. Good luck. I think we'll need it."

The two boys sat at their desks engrossed in trying to answer the difficult questions. Dafidi was happy he had studied for so long at the library. Even though he had to concentrate hard to answer some of the questions, he felt he was doing all right on the test.

Abdul was having a difficult time concentrating. He kept hearing his father's toast over and over again in his mind. Finally, he became harsh with himself and gave himself a mental pep talk. After finishing the test and handing it in, he looked at Dafidi and raised his shoulders in a shrug, as if to say he had done his best but who knew if it was good enough. Dafidi understood and nodded. The bell finally rang, and the two boys got up and exited the class. Once they were in the hallway, Dafidi said, "I have something to tell you and it's important. Walk with me as far as the stairs."

Once they were outside of hearing range of other students Dafidi turned to Abdul and said, "I wanted to tell you last night but you hung up too fast. I got my letter from BC yesterday and I got accepted. Not only that – they've offered me a full scholarship."

Abdul stopped walking. He looked at Dafidi and responded, "I-I can't believe it! That's awesome."

Before he could say any more, he realized they had reached the stairway. Dafidi grabbed his arm and said, "Meet me at the courts at 4. Let's talk about all of this then. I am totally confused."

Abdul nodded assent and ran up the stairs. As he did so, he thought, 'What does Daf have to be confused about? I'm the one who's confused.' With that thought in mind, he walked into his French class.

All that day both boys only half concentrated on their schoolwork. Finally, they made their way to the basketball courts and at five minutes past four, Dafidi waved to his friend as he saw Abdul walking towards him. Abdul came up to the bench where Daf was sitting and plopped down beside him, placing his backpack between his ankles and not making eye contact as he looked down at it. From his friend's subdued demeanor, Dafidi sensed something was wrong.

Turning sideways Daf asked, "What's going on? You should be ecstatic that you got into UCLA, but instead, you seem really down."

Abdul raised his head and looked at Dafidi. "I am happy for my father that I was accepted at UCLA, but I really don't want to go there. I want to stay in Boston. How can I tell him that when this has been his dream ever since I was born?"

Dafidi didn't respond. He had no idea what to say. He realized that no matter which choice Abdul made, someone would be unhappy. He finally said the only thing he could think of, "You have to do what *you* think is best. This is *your* life and *your* choice, not your father's. He enjoyed his choice and you deserve to enjoy yours."

Chapter 6
Gang of Five

LeShawn Johnson woke up late Sunday morning. He had stayed up until the wee hours the previous night, not wanting to miss a moment of the Boston College vs. North Carolina game. His hero, BC senior Tyrese Rice, had again given the Tar Heels a run for their money. Since his 25-point showing in the Eagles' 85-78 upset against previously undefeated North Carolina in January, Rice had become a household name in Boston. LeShawn longed to emulate his hero.

The Johnson family lived in a comfortable but unassuming cape style house in Walpole. LeShawn's father, Lester, was a pharmacist and his mother, Tonya, was a nurse at the neonatal intensive care unit at the Beth Israel Deaconess Medical Center. Both parents had instilled a respect for education in their three children. LeShawn's older sisters, twins Lena and Lenora were both graduate students; Lena was studying at the prestigious Harvard Business School, and Lenora was pursuing veterinary medicine at Tufts.

As far back as he could remember, his sister Lenora had rescued stray animals, frequently bringing them home secretly and bribing her younger brother to hide them in his room.

LeShawn got up and walked to the kitchen in his plaid pajamas. His mother was at work and his father had gone to church, so he had the entire house to himself.

He poured a cup of coffee from the pot his father had made previously and took it over to the kitchen table. As he tasted the leftover coffee, he grimaced at its bitterness. His father had left the Sports section of the *Boston Globe* on the table, and LeShawn picked it up and began reading. Just as he was finishing a long article about football, the phone rang. He got up and walked to the hallway to answer it. Picking up the receiver, he said, "Hello."

A voice he recognized said, "Hey, Johnson. Guess what? I got accepted at BC. Just thought you'd like to know. Your ass is grass."

LeShawn answered, "Kelly, is that you? You're a sorry piece of work." With that, LeShawn abruptly hung up.

Jason Kelly and LeShawn Johnson had a running rivalry since the beginning of high school. As the stars of their respective schools' basketball teams, they had fought it out repetitively on the court, each trying to outdo the other. It wasn't just about basketball. Kelly was overt in his bigotry, and Johnson was vocal about his disgust with Kelly's prejudiced attitude. Both boys had been reprimanded by coaches for trying to duke it out on the court. Both had fouls called against them for shoving the other.

Like Jason, LeShawn dreamed of playing basketball on the BC team. He applied to the school in December but hadn't yet received any response. Now that he knew Jason was going there, he felt it would be a debt of honor to also be accepted. There was no way he was going to let Jason Kelly show him up.

As he hung up the phone, LeShawn heard his father's car come up the driveway. He walked over to the front door and opened it, leaving it ajar before returning to the kitchen. As he opened the fridge and pulled out a carton of eggs, his father came through the kitchen door.

"Hi, son. Hey, if you're making eggs, make me some too. I was late to church, so I just had toast before I went and I'm starving."

"Sure, Dad. Can you make some fresh coffee? That stuff you left in the pot is pretty gross."

Lester laughed. "Well, it was good when I drank it at 7 this morning. Guess it cooked a bit on the burner between then and when you got up."

"Yeah, I did get up late. I stayed up watching Rice score in the BC game last night. Some old man sitting next to me on the sofa slept through it all and snored a lot. I guess that's why he woke up so early."

"OK, son. Enough. I have to put up with your mother's flak about my snoring, so I don't need it from you too!" Lester chuckled as he said this, taking any animosity out of the statement. His loud snoring was legendary in the family and a frequent cause of humor.

The lanky young man pulled a frying pan out of the cupboard and cracked eggs into it. As he stood there cooking them, he fantasized over what it would be like to win a game for BC the way Rice had done. Returning to reality, he slid the eggs onto two plates and carried them over to the table. Handing one to his father, he said, "Dad, I sure hope I get my acceptance letters this week. I can't stand not knowing where I'll end up."

Lester smiled fondly at his son. "Don't worry. Your grades are excellent, and your counselor said you'll probably qualify for a basketball scholarship after your exemplary record on the Walpole team. Just go with the flow."

LeShawn chewed in silence as he buttered a piece of toast. He had applied to Penn, Tufts, Rutgers, Boston College and his 'safety' school, Colby. Surely, at least one of them would accept him. His dad was right - he just needed to relax.

Lester got up, made more toast and brought it over to the table. Father and son ate and read the paper in silence. When he was so full he couldn't eat another morsel, LeShawn got up and took his plate to the sink and rinsed it off before putting it in the dishwasher. He then turned to his father and asked, "Can you drive me to Brookline this afternoon? Mike Ramsay called and there's a pick-up game at 3. Luis Ayala-Marquez from Natick is going to be there too. Mike thought it would be a good idea to practice playing against real opponents more, instead of just against our own teammates."

Mike Ramsay lived in Walpole from the time he began kindergarten until he started high school. When his father got a promotion to the company's main office in Boston, the family moved to Brookline for a better commute. When they moved, Mike was heartbroken at leaving behind his best friend, LeShawn. The two had been inseparable since first grade; they had bonded immediately - two extremely tall, skinny children who were constantly teased by their classmates.

Teasing turned to envy, however, when the two boys excelled on their respective schools' basketball team. Each had become an exceptional player, and they were regaled as stars by their classmates. Both were also exceptionally nice young men, excellent students and hard workers. With no taint of conceit, they earned respect from both their teachers and peers alike.

Mike missed LeShawn and invited him to play with the Brookline group whenever possible. Dafidi and Abdul liked LeShawn and found that playing against him sharpened their skills. The boys talked constantly about attending BC and playing on the same team together.

Lester drove LeShawn to the Ramsay home in Brookline. As he pulled up to the curb in front of the large brick house, he said, "Call me on your cell when you want to come home. Let it ring a few times, though, because I'll probably be out in the yard mowing the lawn."

"Great. Thanks, Dad. See you later."

LeShawn uncoiled his long legs and got out of the car, rising to his full height of 6' 5". Glancing over at his son as he drove off, Lester thought how grown up LeShawn looked.

Mrs. Ramsay opened the front door at LeShawn's ring of the doorbell and smiled at her son's friend. "Hi, come on in. Mike is out taking the dog for a walk, but he'll be right back."

LeShawn smiled at Cathy Ramsay. He always felt extremely comfortable around the friendly blonde woman, with her soft voice and calm demeanor. He remembered her walking him and Mike home from school when his own mother was working days, and he stayed after school with Mike's family until Tonya picked him up there. Cathy always had cookies or sandwiches waiting for them at the Ramsay house when they arrived, and made LeShawn feel like one of the family. Mrs. Ramsay's famous cranberry chocolate chip cookies always brought back memories to both young men of afternoons after school full of play and fun.

Mike appeared at the front door, his faithful black lab, Dexter, standing beside him. Dexter scampered in his clumsy big dog fashion into the hallway and jumped up to put his paws on LeShawn's shoulders, licking his cheek. LeShawn, said, "Ugh, Dex, you have bad breath!" and gently shook himself free of the overly affectionate dog. He then bent down and lovingly rubbed the dog's ears, saying "You're such a little mutt, but Uncle LeShawn loves you anyway." The dog licked the young man's hands and wagged his tail in delight.

Mike said, "We'd better get going. The game starts at two. See you later, Mom."

Cathy smiled at the pair and said, "Call me if you want a ride home. Have fun."

With that, the two boys went out the front door, Dexter trying desperately to follow them but held back by Cathy's firm hand on his collar.

Fifteen minutes later, they arrived at the basketball court and found only Abdul and Dafidi there. Looking around, Mike asked, "Have you seen Luis yet? He was supposed to be here today, wasn't he?"

Abdul answered, "He called me about an hour ago. His mom got stuck at work, so he's going to be late. He said he should be here by three at the latest."

"Great. Let's get going then."

With that, the four boys split up into pairs, each pair taking a side of the court. They began playing one on one, Abdul vs. LeShawn and Mike vs. Dafidi. As they ran around the court waving their arms to block their opponent's shots, they each realized how good it felt to play against someone of equal ability. The group had been practicing periodically like this for a year, seeking to sharpen their skills. Even though they were opponents when playing on their respective school teams, they were friends when playing casually. Therefore, this Sunday game was all about fun, not competition.

A few people stopped to watch them play. Unheeding of their stares, the four boys concentrated on the game. Little did they know that Jason Kelly was with the group watching, and that he was seething with anger that he hadn't been invited to join the game. He finally couldn't take it any longer and stomped off in fury. He wouldn't give them the benefit of even knowing he was there.

With no skill at deflecting his anger, Jason wound himself into a rage as he walked down Greenough Street. He thought to himself how he would get back at the four boys. The Needham game was coming up, so he could sabotage three of them then. LeShawn was another matter; he would have to think of something different but equally evil for him.

While Jason was walking down the street thinking conniving thoughts, Luis Ayala-Marquez and his mother drove up. Luis rolled down the window and yelled, "Hey, Jason. Are you playing with us today?"

Jason looked up and made a rude gesture, much to Mrs. Ayala-Marquez's dismay. She told her son to roll up the car window and she accelerated towards the school parking lot. As she pulled into a parking place, she said, "Luis, stay clear of that one. He is no good. You should be glad he isn't playing today. Your other friends are good boys, like you."

Her son responded, "Jason's just conceited because he's such a good player. He'll get over it. He shouldn't have been rude in front of you, though."

Smiling, Mrs. Ayala patted her son's hand and said, "OK, get going. I'll pick you up at six. I'm going to treat myself to a movie at Coolidge Corner while you play. Call me on my cell if you need to leave earlier."

"OK, will do. Hasta luego." Luis got out of the car and waved to the four boys who were waiting for him. As he did so, LeShawn and Mike started singing, "Louie Louie," laughing as they forgot the real lyrics and made up their own. The song had become Luis's trademark since he scored a big win for Natick against Brookline the previous season. Now, at every game, the cheerleaders sung it when he came onto the court, as a fitting tribute to a boy whose name had the same sounds in it.

Luis walked over and high-fived the other boys. He then said something that gave them pause.

"What's up with Jason Kelly? I just saw him walking in front of the school and when I waved at him, he gave me the finger. What's up with that?"

Mike shook his head in exasperation and said, "He's such a jerk. He just can't get it through his thick head that just because he plays basketball really well, it doesn't make him perfect."

Luis nodded. "Yeah, he's a bully. He keeps goading all of us. I can't wait for him to go off to college somewhere far, far away. May be Alaska, or even Russia!"

LeShawn looked at Luis and said, "No luck. He called me this morning to gloat about being accepted to BC. If any of us go there, we'll have to put up with him."

Abdul and Dafi di looked at one another frowning. That was not good news.

Chapter 7
Worries

As the school week progressed, Abdul became more and more anxious. For one thing, he was really nervous about the Needham game because his back had been acting up, making his movements stiff and awkward. The most important reason for his anxiety, however, was that he still hadn't received any more acceptance letters. To make matters even worse, every night at dinner he had to listen to his father extol the virtues of California – the beautiful weather, the open-minded people, the sumptuous suburbs that surrounded the UCLA campus. Abdul felt he just couldn't take it anymore.

Arriving home from school on Wednesday, he found his mother sitting at the breakfast bar talking on the phone. She waved distractedly to him and continued her conversation, babbling away in Arabic. Abdul understood very little of his mother's native language, and he tuned out the conversation. Going to the fridge, he took out some bread and cheese and made a slapdash sandwich, not even bothering to put it on a plate. Munching happily, he walked out of the kitchen and up to his room, sitting down on the corner of his bed and opening his laptop computer.

Signing on, Abdul immediately went to the BC website. He deviated from his usual routine and didn't bother to even glance at the basketball stats, instead choosing to read about admittance procedures. As he found the information, he scanned it for any dates, thinking it would tell him how long he had to wait to hear about his application. As he read, a new thought came into his mind – maybe letters were sent out alphabetically. That would explain why Abraham and Kelly had been notified before Rashid. Feeling that must be the answer, he began to relax a little. Slapping his forehead, he thought, *I've been so stupid. Of course, that's it!*

Rising from his desk, he suddenly felt like going outside. Picking up his basketball, he went downstairs and out through the kitchen door to the backyard. There he shot baskets at the hoop attached to an adjustable portable stand. As he shot, he entered a state of complete relaxation; playing was a form of meditation to him. Everything else fell away from his consciousness as he dribbled and shot.

Suddenly, he was gripped by an intense pain in his left side. He doubled over and held himself by his mid-section with both hands. The pain then subsided as fast as it had occurred. Lifting his head and releasing his hands, he stood erect and took a deep breath. I must be really out of shape, he thought.

Deciding to take a break, he walked back into the kitchen and poured himself a glass of water and swallowed a couple of extra strength acetaminophen. His mother was still on the phone. He couldn't believe it; she never spent much time phoning people and rarely spoke in Arabic. Something weird was going on.

Looking disconsolate, Asiya finally hung up and put the receiver down. The news from her aunt was not good. Her cousin, Alia, was wounded while working as a volunteer nurse at a Gaza hospital. Alia was staying at the hospital when the wing in which she was sleeping was hit by a mortar attack. The young nurse was alive but critically wounded, her right leg crushed and almost severed from her body.

Alia was transported out of the war zone by the humanitarian group Médecins Sans Frontières, and taken to a hospital in Haifa that specialized in orthopedic surgery. Asiya's aunt had telephoned to apprise her of the situation and to let her know the name of the hospital.

Asiya sat there thinking that she should go to Haifa to be with her beloved cousin. The two girls grew up together and were as close as sisters.

However, she didn't feel comfortable taking money out of the bank when Abdul was so close to having to pay college expenses. Although Maroun earned an excellent salary, Asiya had seen her friends' husbands being laid off right and left in the faltering economy, and she just couldn't risk endangering her son's future.

No, she would just have to stay in touch by telephone for the present. Asiya said a silent prayer for her cousin.

Asiya then went into the living room and took her checkbook out of her purse. As they were retired and living on a small pension, she knew her aunt and uncle were not well off. She couldn't afford to go to Israel, but she could at least send them some money to help with Alia's expenses. She felt compelled to write out the check and mail it immediately. Just doing so was tangible proof of her love for her most beloved family members, and it was all she could do to help from so far away.

After writing the check, she picked up her purse and walked towards the front door. As she opened it, she turned and shouted to Abdul, "Be back in a little while. I need to go to the post office." With that, she closed the door and within minutes, Abdul could hear her car backing out of the garage.

That night during dinner, Abdul finally had some relief from his father's monologues about California. Asiya had kept her own counsel all afternoon, but now felt she needed to tell her husband and son about her cousin's injuries. As she told them in detail about the air strike and Alia's condition, Maroun and Abdul were astounded by the brutality of the situation. Here was an Israeli citizen, a nurse, volunteering with an eminently respected humanitarian group, injured while trying to help innocent victims of an ongoing war. Alia was a peacemaker, a healer, not an enemy combatant.

Maroun shook his head, saying, "The hatred on both sides must end. How can two groups of people who have both lived in the same region for thousands of years not see that they should share their historical lands in an equitable manner? The people are destined to live together. Their heritage is intertwined, their religions grew from the same rootstock, and their bloodlines are mixed. In truth, they are really one people, not two."

Abdul related in the only way he knew how, saying, "It's like an all-star basketball team made up of members of separate teams. They all love playing the same game."

Maroun nodded. "If it were only that easy, my son."

***

On Saturday night, Abdul and Dafidi arrived at the gym just as the team carrying the Needham team was driving into the Brookline High parking lot. The two boys realized they were running late and hurried into the building. Upon reaching their lockers, they changed quickly into their uniforms and ran out to the basketball court, finding most of the team already there. As soon as the three remaining missing teammates showed up, Coach Rebor began their pre-game meeting.

"Tonight is a big game, guys. Needham is tough. Just remember that we're tougher. Abraham and Kelly, you know what to do. I'm relying on you, Ramsay, to keep the opposition off our backs. The rest of you, follow their lead. Let's go win this."

The game began to heat up quickly. Needham's offense was exceptional. Dafidi and Jason were running the fastest game of their lives. Mike Ramsay and his crew was struggling to block the Needham offense. It seemed as if the Needham players were giants. In truth, six players were over 6' 6" and incredibly muscular.

The lighter weight Brookline team had to concentrate on skill, speed and agility instead of brute force.

At one point in the game, Dafidi could have sworn that he saw Jason move aside swiftly so that Needham's biggest offensive player, Tom Thornton, could mow Mike Ramsay down. As Mike slid across the parquet, Jason tried to hide his smile, but Dafidi saw it and recognized the treachery in it. Dafidi was appalled. Mike was the best blocker on their team; they were supposed to support his efforts not sabotage them. What was going on?

Despite his aching back, Abdul did his best, moving skillfully from side to side with arms extended, to block the behemoths. At one point, he managed to deflect a pass that could have resulted in Needham winning the game. A cheer erupted from the Brookline crowd, "Rashid, Rashid, Rashid!"

Finally, with 20 seconds to go, Brookline scored a free throw and won the game by two points. The Needham players were astounded; they had thought the game was a shoe-in. As the two teams walked off the court, one enormous player on the Needham team was heard to say, "I can't believe those skinny lightweights beat us." Their team had learned a good lesson in how clever strategy and quick movement could win over sheer size and force.

As they waited for Mrs. Rashid to pick them up after the game, Dafidi told Abdul about what he thought he had seen Jason do to Mike Ramsay. Abdul shook his head in disbelief and asked, "But why go after his own teammate? Why not go after Thornton or one of the other Needham stars?"

Dafidi answered, "I think he hates us – and by 'us' I mean you, me, Mike and LeShawn. He might even hate Yosha and Luis. I don't know. I don't get it either. What have we ever done to him?"

Abdul reflected a moment and said, "Well, we never include him when we practice. But that's his own fault because he's so mean, nobody wants to be around him."

"Yeah, and if we did include him, he'd probably just beat someone up." Dafidi said this and then reached for his gym bag, saying, "Hey, your mom is here, let's go."

Chapter 8
At the Kelly Home

Jason was rudely awakened on Sunday morning to the sound of the ancient bathroom pipes making their water hammer serenade. He got out of bed and ran to the bathroom and turned the shower on and off quickly. The loud banging subsided, and he walked back to the room he shared with his younger brother and climbed back into bed. Jude Kelly was sleeping soundly and snoring loudly, so Jason threw a pillow at him to shut him up. As Jason saw it, here it was only 8:30, and the day was already turning into hell.

Jude woke up upon feeling the pillow strike his face. Pushing it away from him, he struggled into a sitting position and groggily rubbed his small, elongated blue eyes. Looking across the room at his brother, he asked, "Did you throw the pillow at me?"

"Yeah ,stupid, I did," Jason replied, not moving from the position in which he was lying, staring up at the ceiling with his hands folded under his head.

Maybe if he didn't move or say anything else, his brother would go back to sleep and leave him alone.

The younger boy yelled, "I'll tell Mom, I'll tell Mom" and clumsily jumped out of bed and stumbled out the bedroom door. Jason could hear him pattering slowly down the old scuffed wooden staircase.

A few minutes later, Jason's mother, Mary, appeared at the doorway, anger distorting her tired face. "Jason, stop tormenting Jude. He doesn't understand half of what you say to him, and when you tease him he thinks it's mean. I can't take it anymore. It has to stop."

"Yeah, Mom, right." Jason tuned out most of what his mother said. All she ever did was criticize the way he treated his brother. Ever since Jude was born with Down Syndrome, Jason's life had changed. Before that, it was just him and his older sister, Jennifer to share their parents' love. When his father was alive, Mary and Michael Kelly had made it a point to pay equal attention to both siblings. Everything changed after his father's death from cancer three years previously. Jason now felt he was expendable – just another mouth to feed for the overworked and underpaid Mary.

Jason's older sister, Jennifer, had left home, choosing to move into an apartment with a girlfriend immediately after high school. Jennifer was smart and ambitious, and worked hard at her job at the cosmetics store in the mall, rising to assistant store manager at the age of 20. Once in management, she took advantage of the company's tuition reimbursement program and went on to acquire a business degree from Suffolk University. She was now a regional manager and oversaw twelve stores in the Northeast. Mary Kelly was proud of her daughter, and she let Jason know in no uncertain terms that he was expected to succeed also.

Jason hated the way his mother harped on him. He hated the way she constantly extolled his sister's virtues. To Jason, his sister was a loser who just sold make-up. When he succeeds, he would be a real success. Jason's dream was to become a famous trial lawyer. That was why he studied so much. He wanted to be in a powerful position where he could call the shots.

When Jason telephoned LeShawn to tell him of his acceptance at Boston College, he thought he only did it out of spite. What he didn't realize was that he felt compelled to tell someone, anyone, of his first real success in life. His mother was working a double shift at the supermarket, and he was home alone all day with his brother when the mail arrived. Opening the letter elated him, but not having anyone to brag to frustrated him. He hoped that his mother would be home by midnight, and he waited for her, but he fell asleep on the sofa by the time she came home.

The next morning he felt obsessed about telling someone, and the first person he could think of was LeShawn, whom he knew desperately wanted to play on the BC basketball team. Jason loved one-upping people, and this was as good a chance as any, or so he thought. What he didn't realize was that LeShawn didn't think in the same devious way, and so was completely unaffected by Jason's call.

As the sunny Sunday morning went on, Jason began to wish that he could move to BC immediately. The school offered him a full scholarship, complete with room and board. Jason didn't know that his counselor at Brookline High had apprised Boston College of the Kelly family's poverty when she wrote his reference letter. In her letter, the counselor told of the death of Jason's stonemason father three years before, and the disability of his younger brother. Although she knew

Jason didn't help out much at home, the counselor wove a tale about how committed the young man was to his family. In doing so, she hoped that the college would grant him the one shot he had to escape the misery he was experiencing. Luckily for Jason, the experienced counselor saw the hurt beneath the boy's brusque manner and hoped her efforts would enable the intelligent man within to grow out of his youthful defensive shell. Jason would owe her a lifelong debt of gratitude; he just didn't know it yet.

When Jason walked to the school basketball courts later that Sunday afternoon, intending to escape his brother's efforts to engage him in play, he had anticipated to shoot baskets on his own. However, as he approached the courts, he saw a group of people watching a pick-up game. Joining them, he saw Dafidi, Abdul, Mike and LeShawn playing one-on-one, and it infuriated him. Although Jason didn't have the emotional depth to question himself about why it bothered him so much, he felt the pain intensely.

When he walked away and then heard Luis hailing him from a car, he knew that Luis was joining the group. That was the last straw: that he, Jason Kelly, star basketball player of Brookline High, was the only one left out of the game. Although his dysfunctional defenses kicked in, telling him he didn't need the group or their approval, down deep he really needed it more than anything.

Jason walked home in fury. Arriving and opening the battered green wooden door leading into the downstairs flat of the shabby two family house, he could hear his 10 year-old brother singing along off key with a Disney CD. Walking quickly into the small bedroom they shared, Jason picked up the CD player and threw it against the wall, sending Jude into torrents of tears. Jason then walked out of the room and back out the front door. He sat on the stoop with his head in his hands and thoughts racing across his mind. He had to get out; he couldn't stand it any longer.

Mary Kelly heard the commotion and abandoned her bread making to check on her younger son. When she saw what had happened, she took Jude in her arms and comforted him, holding him until his tears abated. Leading him gently into the living room, she turned the television to a children's program on PBS and told him to sit down on the sofa and watch it. Jude was soon enthralled by the show, and once his mother brought him milk and cookies, he was set for the night. When she saw he had calmed down, she opened the front door and walked out in search of Jason.

Seeing her elder son sitting on the front stoop with his head in his hands, she sat down beside him and looking straight ahead, said, "You just don't get it, do you? Jude will always need help of some kind. I gave birth to him, and I am responsible for him. You can leave and go off to college and get a job. I can never leave."

Jason had never heard his mother speak that way before. He turned towards her and saw that she was gazing off into the distance, unseeing. He struggled to find something to say, but in his typical narcissistic manner, all he could come up with was, "So, I'm expected to help you with a half-wit?"

Mary turned and slapped Jason hard on his right shoulder. Her face distorted in pain and she began to cry. Dropping her head into her hands, she whispered to herself through her tears, "Oh, my God, what have I become that I would strike my own son?"

Jason finally felt some pity for his mother and reached to put an arm around her shoulders, but she pushed him away, screaming, "You are an insensitive lout. Do you hear me, Jason? Your brother has a genetic condition; he is NOT a half-wit. He does the best he can, whereas you, who are so blessed with much intelligence, don't try at all. I am sick and tired of your attitude and your anger. I work long hours at two jobs to keep us in Brookline so you can attend a good high school and play basketball. Think about that for awhile."

With that, Mary stormed off through the front door and headed back into the kitchen. She took out her aggression by kneading the dough she had left to rise earlier. As she did so, her anger abated, but the misery of her situation became even clearer to her. She was forty-six years old, a widow, tired and poor, saddled with debts and a disabled son. Now she had to contend with an older child who had anger management problems. It was just too much to comprehend. Always resilient, however, Mary vowed she would find time to discuss her problems with an elderly friend who was a nun. Maybe Sister Dorothy would have some suggestions.

Jason sat on the stoop until dark. He had nowhere else to go and nobody to talk to. He was tired and hungry and fed up. Finally, as the sun set and the early spring evening began to chill, he opened the front door and walked slowly into the kitchen. As he did so, he smelled the comforting aroma of freshly baked bread. He found his mother and brother sitting at the small oak table eating chicken casserole and green beans. Jason sat down in his usual seat where Mary had set a plate and silverware for him. He reached over silently and scooped some casserole onto his plate. Still not speaking, he did the same with the green beans and then began slowly eating. The entire meal passed in silence, with neither mother nor sons having the energy or inclination to speak.

After Mary cleared away the dishes to wash them, and Jude was once more settled in front of the television, Jason retreated to his room. He closed the door and sat propped up against pillows on his narrow twin bed. Turning on the lamp that rested on the bedside table, he reached for his Calculus textbook and his notes and tried to finish his homework. As he became engaged in the work, compartmentalizing his thinking to focus on integrals and derivatives, his mind calmed. When he finished, he felt extremely sleepy, and curling up on his side into the fetal position, he fell into a deep slumber, not even waking up when his mother put his brother to bed and turned off the light.

Jason's dreams that night were totally foreign to the reality to which he would wake up the following morning. He dreamt of being a Celtics player, driving around in limousines and playing at TD Garden. In his dreams, he could see himself being interviewed by sports announcers, and answering their questions brilliantly. He saw himself making jump shot after jump shot perfectly. Fans cheered and beautiful girls flirted with him. He was the star he had always wanted to be. Suddenly, he heard a bell ring. Still dreaming, he assumed it was signaling the end of a game. Unfortunately for Jason, it was actually the alarm clock his mother had set for 7 am to wake him up for school on Monday morning.

Chapter 9

Good News

The day at school on Monday passed quickly and happily. Abdul, Mike and Dafidi were complimented by their classmates for their defeat of the Needham team.

The three boys left school that afternoon feeling relaxed and confident. Since the weather was warm and sunny, they decided to walk the short distance to the Rashid home and study outside in the back yard. Mike and Dafidi sat at the white wooden outdoor table while Abdul went inside to get drinks and snacks for them all to share.

They expected him to be gone for some time, but he reappeared almost immediately, grinning from ear to ear and screaming, "I can't believe it! I got in! I got in!"

Wildly waving a piece of paper around, he ran to the table and gave it to Dafidi to read. Dafidi smiled and laughed, handing the letter to Mike as he jokingly remarked, "Now I'll never get rid of him. It'll be the 'Dafidi and Abdul Show' throughout all of eternity!"

Mike laughed too and then said, "Well done, my friend. The Eagles are going to fly high with you two on the team!"

Abdul sat there smiling and then said, "We need to make plans. We have to choose a dorm, go shopping for stuff, find out who else will be trying out for the team…" As his best friend babbled on, Dafidi couldn't bring himself to tell Abdul that he hadn't made his decision yet between Brandeis and BC. Dafidi then realized he had to choose soon. He vowed to talk to his mother that night.

LeShawn arrived home from Walpole High around 5 pm, just as his mother was getting out of her green Toyota Camry. Clad in blue scrubs and clogs, she crawled out of the driver's seat and closed the door. LeShawn waved to his mother, and she waved back halfheartedly. As he observed her, he realized how exhausted his mother looked. She had just finished a twelve hour shift at the hospital and seemed physically worn out. Her son walked over and hugging her said, "Hey, Mom. Let's just get pizza tonight. You look tired and Dad has to work late anyway, so why not?"

Tonya smiled serenely at her son and said, "You are a prize, Mr. Johnson." Fishing in her purse, she extracted a twenty dollar bill and giving it to LeShawn, said, "How about a large mushroom and pepperoni from *Luna Bianca*? You go get it, and I'll go take a shower and change while you're gone."

"No worries, Mom. I'm on it."

After kissing his mother on the cheek, LeShawn turned around and began walking back the way he had come. *Luna Bianca* was a small neighborhood restaurant only two blocks away and was the family's regular place to get good takeaway food. As the exceptionally tall young black man entered the little restaurant, he was greeted warmly by Giuseppe, its owner. Twenty minutes later, LeShawn was exiting the eatery with a hot, savory pizza in a huge square box. *Luna Bianca* was noted for the size of their pizzas, as well as for their delicious taste and moderate cost. That was how the restaurant had survived for 17 years in the same small location.

As he walked through the Johnson's front door with the pizza, LeShawn noticed a pile of mail had fallen through the letterbox onto the floor. Setting down the box of pizza on the hall table, he bent down and picked up the mail. As he did so, two envelopes drew his attention: the first was from Rutgers University in New Jersey, and the second was from Boston College. Standing up again, he gathered up the remainder of the mail and walked into the kitchen, where he found his mother making a salad. Looking over her shoulder, she said, "So, Honey, where's the pizza?"

Seeming as if he were in a daze, LeShawn nodded to his mother and walked back to the table to retrieve the pizza. He returned to the kitchen with it and set it down on the kitchen table. As he put down the box, his mother asked, "Anything interesting in the mail? I forgot to pick it up. I was that tired when I got home!"

LeShawn pulled out a kitchen chair and sitting down, stretched his long legs out as far as they could go. He placed the pile of mail on the table and then looked over at his mother and said, "Mom, two letters came today. Two! One from Rutgers and one from BC. I'm so nervous, I don't know if I can open them."

Tonya Johnson grinned. Always pro-active, she walked over to the table and riffled through the mail, extracting the letter from Rutgers. Still smiling, she sat down and opened it. LeShawn could see his mother's mischievous look as she hesitated in giving it to him and said,

"Are you sure you want to read this?"

He couldn't take it anymore and reached for the letter. As he began reading a slow smile stretched across his face. Not only was it an acceptance letter, but he was also granted a small partial scholarship. His mother was beaming at him and asked, "So, my intelligent son, how about opening the other letter yourself?"

LeShawn hesitated but then figured, 'What the heck?' I've gotten into one school at least so I'm safe. He removed the Boston College envelope and tore it open. As he unfurled the letter and began reading, he jumped up and started to scream with joy.

"Mom, I got in! I got into BC. Not only that - they're giving me a full scholarship! I can't believe it!"

Tonya stood up and hugged her son tightly, her head only reaching as far as his chest. As she held him, she could hear his heart beating fast with excitement. She was so proud and couldn't wait until her husband got home to tell him the good news. She released LeShawn and said, "Rules or no rules, call your father at work and tell him. This is an emergency!"

LeShawn's hands shook as he dialed the number of the pharmacy where his father worked. After a few moments, his father came on the line. As he heard his son's words, he felt like jumping up and down with joy. Unfortunately, Lester was constrained by the formality of his workplace and had to say guardedly, "Very important news, my son. We'll talk about it at length when I get home. Thank you for calling me immediately."

LeShawn knew that his father's boss, Mr. Patel, was an old-fashioned pharmacist trained in post-war England, who believed in strict decorum at work. Therefore, he wasn't at all offended by his father's lack of spontaneity or excited congratulations over the phone. He knew his father would be over the moon with joy at the news.

Tonya and LeShawn talked excitedly about BC during their improvised dinner. His mother knew that it was LeShawn's dream to play basketball there, so she had no doubt he would choose it over Rutgers. Besides, who would turn down a full scholarship to their favorite choice of school?

When Lester arrived home from work later that night, he grabbed his son in a bear hug and patted him furiously on the back with joy. He then opened a drawer in his desk and pulled out a manila folder. Opening it, he extracted six savings bonds, each in $1,000 denominations. Lester looked at LeShawn and said, "When I went to pharmacy school, I had to work two jobs to pay for it. I vowed that if I ever had kids, they wouldn't have to work that hard. When you and your sisters were born, I began stashing away savings bonds, until I had six for each of you. It isn't a lot, but it will mean you won't have to work, at least for the first couple of years. With the scholarship, you might even have enough to buy a car or take a trip to Europe. You're on your way, son; you're on your way!"

Father and son hugged again, and LeShawn told his parents how much he loved them. He then ran to the phone and called Mike Ramsay to tell him the good news. Mike was overjoyed at his best friend's good fortune. Laughing, he said, "OK, I'm the only one now who still has to get in. Cross your fingers and eyes, because I haven't received any letters yet. Hopefully, I'll be calling you with good news in a few days."

Mike had applied to Brown, BC, Notre Dame and Northwestern. His maternal grandparents lived in the Chicago suburb of Skokie, Illinois, and he had visited them many times and had always felt comfortable there. Brown appealed to him because of its more relaxed class structure, but his first choices were Notre Dame and Boston College. He felt both schools would offer him a fair chance of playing on their basketball teams, and basketball was Mike's passion, just as it was for the other boys. Unlike the others, however, Mike really liked Chicago and felt that he might enjoy leaving Boston to attend school near his grandparents' home. Notre Dame was only about 50 miles east and easily accessible by a commuter train that ran between South Bend and Chicago's Union Station. Mike decided that he would be happy with either of his choices and would just let the chips land where they might. Therefore, he felt much more relaxed about his ultimate acceptance than his friends had been.

After LeShawn hung up, Mike telephoned Dafidi and told him the good news. Dafidi was ecstatic for their friend and said he would telephone Abdul to let him know. After he did so, he realized that almost everyone had been accepted at BC. He became anxious and restless as he realized this.

Dafidi had been waiting for some sort of sign to direct him in his correct choice between Brandeis and BC. Earlier that day, he received two more acceptance letters, one from Tufts and one from George Washington University in St. Louis. Neither school had really appealed to him, and neither letter had offered a scholarship. This was the sign for which he'd been waiting. It was time to talk to his mother.

Peggy arrived home from work late that night. She had been stuck in heavy traffic on the Southeast Expressway for almost two hours and felt drained and exhausted. As she entered the apartment, Dafidi could see she was tired. He looked up and said, "Mom, you look wiped out. Let me make dinner tonight. It might not be great, but at least you won't have to cook."

"Thanks, Daf. You're on." Peggy flopped into the nearest armchair and shook off her shoes. She yawned and said, "You know, I think I could have gotten home faster on horseback than by car tonight. How can a medium sized city like Boston have so much heavy traffic?"

"Poor city planning. I learned about it in school. Most roads into Boston were originally for bringing livestock in to town. Just think of the Southeast Expressway as a cow path that went wrong!"

Peggy laughed and said, "I'm going to go take a shower. Start dinner, and I'll meet you in the kitchen in 15 minutes. And no tuna sandwich. That's what I had for lunch."

Dafidi walked into the kitchen and opened the freezer. Scanning its contents, he removed a box of fish fillets and then reached for a bag of frozen French fries and a packet of frozen peas. Turning on the oven, he read the directions on the box of fish and the bag of fries carefully. He set the temperature to 425°F, pulled a large cookie sheet out of a lower cabinet, and after placing four pieces of fish and a mound of fries on it, inserted it into the now warm oven. He was pouring water into a saucepan to boil the peas when his mother emerged in the doorway, wearing jeans and a sweatshirt, with her wet hair wrapped in a towel.

Peggy reached into the refrigerator and brought out a bottle of white wine. She poured a glass and sat at the kitchen table watching her son as he cooked. His movements were orderly and spare and very composed. No one looking at the young man would ever guess he had hardly before cooked a thing in his life. His mother smiled fondly and thought how he was growing up. Soon he'd be in college and she'd have the apartment to herself. The thought frightened Peggy a bit. It seemed just yesterday that Dafidi was a toddler struggling to walk and to overcome a back problem, rather than this tall, athletic young man who will soon be in college. Taking a small sip of wine, Peggy asked her son, "So, any decisions yet about which school you'd like to attend?"

Dafidi almost dropped the hot cookie sheet as he took the improvised fish and chips meal from the oven, his hands encased in Peggy's flowered yellow cotton pot holders. He put the sheet on top of the stove and closed the oven door before answering. Just as he was about to respond, he noticed the water on the peas was boiling down rapidly, the signal to take them off of the stove. Turning off the burner, he hesitated for another brief second before turning around and answering his mother's question.

When he turned to face her, Peggy already knew what the answer would be. Dafidi had a furtive, guilt-ridden look about him. Oh, how she longed to go over and hug her tall, gangly son and tell him that his grandfather would not want him to feel such guilt. Repressing her anxiety, she remained where she was, took another sip of wine and waited.

She didn't have to wait long. Dafidi walked over, pulled out a chair and sat down across the table from his mother. He looked down at his hands for a moment, composing himself, and then looked directly into her eyes. In a serious tone, he said, "Mom, I've been thinking about it every day for a month. I feel guilty because Grandpa wanted so much for me to go to Brandeis, but I just feel that I am meant to go to BC. They've offered me a remarkable opportunity with the scholarship. Just think, Mom. You won't have to struggle to pay for my tuition or pay back loans for years. Not only that, but I can play basketball where I've always dreamed of. Abdul, Yosha, and LeShawn are going there, so I'll have friends right from the beginning. I just feel it is meant to be. I'm sorry."

Peggy's eyes welled up with tears and she said softly, "Oh, Daf, you have nothing to feel sorry about. Your grandfather always just wanted you to be happy. He would never have insisted you choose Brandeis. He just wanted you to make good decisions and thought that suggesting for you go to his alma mater would be helpful. Also, Jews of his generation could never have imagined that their grandchildren could be accepted at a Catholic university. We've come a long way in America. No, you have no reason for guilt. You have reason to be proud of your choice. I can tell you analyzed the choices carefully. I can also tell that you agonized about telling me. You are truly an adult now, a man who can make his own choices. I am very proud of you, and I love you very much."

Daf looked at the tears falling down his mother's face and began sobbing himself. He dropped his head on his hands and wept.

Peggy stood up and walked over to him and put her arms around his shoulders, leaning her head against the back of his. Sighing, she lifted her head slowly and walked back over to the refrigerator. She took out the bottle of white wine, reached into an overhead cupboard and took down a tiny liqueur glass, into which she poured a small amount of the golden liquid. She then placed the miniscule glass next to Dafidi's head and then walked back over to her chair and sat down.

Raising her wine glass to her lips, she looked at her son and said, "Dafidi Abraham, beloved grandson of Andrzej Bach, please join me in a toast to the new member of the Boston College Freshman class of 2009. Mazel Tov!"

Despite himself, Dafidi laughed at his mother's words and reached for the glass. He raised it to his lips and took a hesitant sip of the unfamiliar drink. Thinking that it tasted like mouthwash, he forced himself to drink a little. Then he raised his glass and splitting his middle fingers into the Star Trek gesture of benediction, said his own toast "May the force be with us!"

Peggy doubled over laughing, almost choking on her wine. Her son might be an adult in some ways, but there was still a trace of childish mischief in him.

On Wednesday night Mike Ramsay telephoned Dafidi to tell him he had received two letters that day. First, he imparted the happy news that he was accepted at Notre Dame and was offered a partial scholarship. Unfortunately, the letter from Northwestern was not positive, so that choice was now off the table. It still remained to be seen if BC would accept him. Daf told him to keep a positive thought and hung up after congratulating Mike on being accepted at Notre Dame.

Although Dafidi truthfully preferred that his friends would all be able to go with him to BC, he secretly thought to himself, 'If Mike does go to Notre Dame, then I can visit him and go to their football games. Cool.'

Chapter 10
A Second Chance

Thursday morning found Miriam Hernandez sorting through a huge pile of paperwork on her already cluttered desk. West End House was always chaotic at the end of the school year, with parents and their children queuing to sign up for summer programs. Miriam sighed and took a sip of her Earl Grey tea as she reached for yet another application. She always performed a preliminary sorting by age and interest, an effective habit she developed over the many years that she worked there.

As she read the application in her hand, she realized that it was signed not by a parent but by Sr. Dorothy Brennan, a nun and trained psychologist who worked as a counselor at St. Elizabeth's Hospital. Sr. Dorothy had referred children to West End House many times in the past. They were usually inherently good kids who acted out, making trouble to attract the attention they missed at home. Miriam worked closely with these children over the years, seeking to instill in them a sense of self-esteem. Her guidance provided limits – secure but gentle bonds that told the children they were valued.

In her accompanying letter, Sr. Dorothy told the story of Jason Kelly, a 17 year-old boy with an exceptionally high IQ, very low self-esteem, and severe anger management issues stemming from the birth of a younger brother with Down Syndrome, and from the death of his father. She also told the story of his mother, Mary, a woman so overwhelmed with money worries, responsibility, and anxiety about her children's futures that she came to Sr. Dorothy for counseling.

Sr. Dorothy said that she thought that Jason needed a job. Her logic was that he needed structure, and to experience having responsibility himself so that he could learn to relate to his mother's situation. She went on to say that besides being an excellent student, Jason was an accomplished athlete at Brookline High, and that his mother let him focus on athletics because she thought it gave him an outlet for his anger. Sr. Dorothy agreed with this, but she felt that athletics alone had not provided him with a sense of self-worth. Jason felt that his only worth came from obtaining perfect grades and his prowess on the basketball court, and therefore he judged others solely by those qualifiers. Because of this, he wasn't well-liked by his peers.

Sr. Dorothy suggested that Jason be added to the summer coaching squad. That way he could also earn money for college, money that was sorely needed. She appealed to Miriam's spirit of compassion. Here was a troubled boy with tremendous potential who just needed a structured environment in which to blossom. Miriam took the bait and telephoned the Kelly house.

The phone rang just as Mary Kelly was putting a load of laundry in the washer. She hurried into the kitchen and picked up the receiver, transferring a light haze of soap powder to it as she did so. Dusting off the Tide dust, she said, "Hello."

Miriam introduced herself, careful to immediately say that she was a friend of Sr. Dorothy Brennan. She then told Mary about a part-time summer coaching position at West End House that she thought would be perfect for Jason. Mary listened as Miriam's soft melodic voice enumerated the benefits this would have for her elder son.

After Miriam finished and asked, "So, what do you think? Would Jason possibly be interested?"

Mary responded appreciatively, "I think it would be perfect for him. Oh, thank you so much, Mrs. Hernandez. I can't thank you or Sr. Dorothy enough."

Miriam's voice had a smile in it as she said, "Great. Have him come by Friday after school to see me. I'll be here until six. There is some paperwork he needs to fill out. And Mary, don't worry. I've worked with a lot of kids like Jason and he'll turn out fine. He just needs someone other than a family member to give him some guidance."

Gently hanging up the phone, Mary sat for a moment and then began to cry. Tears of relief streamed down her cheeks as she abandoned herself to a rare feeling - hope.

Mary immediately told Jason about the job when he arrived home from school. She felt that if she waited, she might lose her nerve. All afternoon she had thought about how to approach the subject, and she discreetly left Sr. Dorothy's name out of her explanation. When Mary finished speaking, her son's reaction was totally different than she had expected.

"Oh, that place on Allston Street? Abdul and Daf coach there part-time for a school project so the work can't be too hard. Sure, I'll go on Friday. Hey, if she wants to pay me to tell little kids what they're doing wrong on the basketball court, I'll take the money and run. Daf probably told her I was a better player than he is, so she's recruiting me to clean up his mess."

Mary was dumbfounded. She didn't know how to respond to her son's arrogant response. She realized at that moment that Jason had become a bully. She also realized that Sr. Dorothy's intervention might have come too late. Praying that this wasn't the case, she said, "I get off early on Friday afternoon, so I'll pick you up at school and drive you there so you can get there on time." The truth was that in order to leave work early, she would really have to fabricate a story to her boss and say she had a doctor's appointment. So be it, she thought. I'm not letting him forfeit this chance.

Jason nodded curtly without a word of thanks. Picking up his backpack, he wandered off through the kitchen to the back door and out to the narrow back yard with its sparse grass and few flowers that had arrived like hobos, traveling to the dismal plot on the winds of discord.

Mary telephoned Miriam and told her Jason agreed to accept the job. She then made one request of the counselor. "I want you to make sure he doesn't bully the kids. I'm worried that the power he has will go to his head."

Miriam answered gently, "Don't worry. We have intensive meetings with the high school kids before they start working. Each one has to sign a contract saying they will enforce our no-bullying policy. Don't worry, I'll make it exceptionally clear to Jason that that includes bullying by coaches. He'll also have to commit to working 15 hours a week all summer, and he'll have to show up on time every day. Hopefully, by the end of August, you'll have a much more responsible son."

Mary thanked Miriam profusely before hanging up. She went to work that afternoon feeling better than she had in years.

Mary dropped Jason off at West End House on Friday afternoon at 4:15. She was lucky that her store manager was out ill that day, and his assistant took the doctor's appointment story at face value. After all, she was always taking Jude to the doctor, so her excuse was highly plausible.

Jason entered the building and spoke to the receptionist. Eyeing the tall young man, she thought how arrogant he was, and how it felt as if a toxic cloud had entered the building with his arrival. She ushered him into Miriam's office with no preamble and closed the door behind him. This one would require all of Miriam's skills, she thought to herself.

For her part, Miriam thought that Jason was just plain rude. She wouldn't tolerate rudeness from anyone, and he was no exception. When he sat down without so much as introducing himself or offering to shake her hand, she called him on it. "Mr. Kelly, it is customary when entering an office to introduce oneself politely. I expect my guests to do so. Please remember that in future."

Jason was taken aback. No one had ever spoken to him so directly unless they were angry at him. However, Mrs. Hernandez didn't seem angry. She just seemed righteously firm. Whoa, he thought, this one's going to be tough.

Miriam sized up his reaction and sensed the wheels turning in his head. He's read me correctly, she thought. Good. That will get us off on a firm footing.

***

When Dafidi went to West End House for his coaching assignment the following Tuesday afternoon, two of his players told him about Mr. Kelly, the new summer coach they met the previous day. The kids told Dafidi that the new coach didn't seem very nice, and that he just wanted to show off what a good player he was. Hearing this, there was no doubt in Dafidi's mind that they were talking about Jason. As soon as practice ended, he walked to Mrs. Hernandez's office to ask her about it.

Miriam was putting papers in her briefcase as Dafidi knocked on her door. Smiling at him, she said, "Come in. I'm just getting ready to go home, but I can talk for a few minutes."

Dafidi got right to the point. "Is the new summer coach Jason Kelly?"

Nodding, Miriam looked at Daf and asked, "Why do you ask?"

Dafidi found it hard to put into words what he wanted to say. What came out was, "I hate to say this. He's a great player, but he isn't very nice sometimes. My friends have had run-ins with him because he's a bully. I just worry that the kids will learn bad habits from him."

Miriam smiled at the earnest delivery with which Dafidi gave his short speech. She then said cryptically, "Don't let it worry you. I've got my eye on him. Maybe what he needs is to have some little kids to see right through him."

As she closed her briefcase she added, "You and Abdul are doing a great job with the kids. I'd like you both to stay on and work part-time this summer. I'm going to discuss it with Abdul on Thursday too. Talk it over with your mother and we'll discuss it next week. I've got to rush now because I am picking up my husband at work."

Dafidi smiled and said, "I'd love to work this summer as long as I can fit it in with my schedule at *Bettina's*. I'll talk to Mom tonight and call you tomorrow. Thanks, Mrs. Hernandez. You're the best!"

After discussing the coaching offer that night with his mother, Dafidi telephoned *Bettina's* the following morning to find out what his summer schedule would be. Bettina herself answered the phone, and in her straightforward way, she told Dafidi that she would like him to work as many hours as possible all summer. She then did something she rarely did – she gave him a compliment.

"Dafidi, you are an extremely hard worker and a very nice young man. You and Tom Gill are my two best waiters, and I rely on both of you a lot. The regular customers always tell me how nice you and Tom are, and this brings them back again and again. I need you to work a lot this summer. With the economy being so terrible, I need all the help I can get to keep my customers."

Hearing this, Dafidi felt guilty. He really wanted to decrease his hours at *Bettina's* somewhat in order to spend more time coaching at West End House. However, he also knew he couldn't let Bettina down. After all, she hired him when he had no experience, and she encouraged him to succeed. Although her manner was sometimes brusque, he knew Bettina had a kind heart and he just couldn't bear to hurt her. Therefore, despite knowing how difficult it would be to work two time-consuming jobs all summer, Dafidi answered, "No problem. I'll work whatever hours you need, except for the hours I already have scheduled at my coaching job."

They spoke for another few minutes, as Bettina outlined the schedule she wanted Dafidi to work. After hanging up the phone, Dafidi realized the extent of the commitment he had made. Shaking his head ruefully, he walked back into the kitchen to tell his mother the news.

"Mom, I'm going to be working like a fiend this summer! Bettina offered me three more shifts a week and told me that I can extend them whenever someone calls out sick. Looks like I'm going to be rich!"

Peggy laughed. "You'll be rich, but you'll be so sleepy that you won't be able to enjoy all that wealth."

Daf nodded, smiling as he responded, "And just think, Mom. You won't have to cook for me this summer. Just consider it as a mini-vacation from cooking!"

Peggy smiled at her son. "Sounds good, but try not to burn out with too much work. If it gets to be too much, you have to promise to tell me, OK?"

"Sure, Mom. No worries."

With that, Dafidi picked up his backpack and said, "I'm off. See you tonight."

Peggy waved good-bye to him and said "Have a good day, honey" as he closed the front door. Sitting at the kitchen table alone, coffee mug in hand, she reflected on how much her son had grown up during the short time since they moved to Brookline.

The following day after school, Abdul and Dafidi boarded the bus to Allston. Both boys had agreed to meet with Miriam Hernandez to go over their summer duties, and they felt more comfortable seeing her together. They were both worried that she might force them to work alongside Jason Kelly, and they sought support from one another.

When they arrived, Miriam was obviously happy to see them. She welcomed them warmly and told them that they would be working with the older kids during the summer, whereas Jason would be assigned to the younger players. Both Dafidi and Abdul wondered at the wisdom of this decision, feeling that Jason might really scare the younger kids with his bullying tactics. However, neither boy felt comfortable voicing this to Mrs. Hernandez. Sensing their unease and intuitively discerning its cause, she looked at both boys and said, "You are now both seasoned coaches. Jason, however, needs to start with the younger kids so he can gain experience."

Both Abdul and Dafidi were surprised at this remark but said nothing. Somewhere in the back of their consciousness lurked the idea that Mrs. Hernandez had more up her sleeve than she was willing to reveal.

After she went over their new responsibilities and the specific tasks they were to perform, she asked them an unexpected question.

"Do either of you know where Jason will be living when he goes to BC in the fall?"

Both boys shook their heads. Jason hadn't mentioned any dorm or apartment, and he hadn't said much of anything at all to them about BC. They were truly surprised by the question.

Miriam continued, "Well, I thought you might know, but if you don't, no problem. I just thought I would try to help find him a suitable roommate."

Dafidi frowned and thought, That's weird. Why would. Mrs. Hernandez want to find Jason a roommate?

On their way home from Allston the pair talked about the conversation with Mrs. Hernandez. Neither boy could figure out what she was up to, so they eventually gave up trying. They would just have to wait and see.

Miriam did have something up her sleeve. She had spoken at length to Sr. Dorothy Brennan that morning. During the conversation she learned the extent of the challenges facing Jason's mother. Miriam and Sr. Dorothy had wisely counseled that in order for Jason to succeed at BC, he would need to be in an atmosphere totally different from that of his home life. Therefore, they were searching for an inexpensive housing alternative that would provide the troubled boy with support and friendship, as well as structure and boundaries.

After telephoning numerous facilities, Miriam hung up the phone in frustration. Boston College required freshman to live in on-site dormitories. Although Jason had received a full scholarship, how would he ever be able to afford all of the "extras" inherent in dormitory living: pizza parties, movies and dating? Miriam felt that being financially frustrated would exacerbate Jason's anger.

What was really needed was a safe haven where Jason could retreat to study and think, without having to prove anything to anyone. She wracked her brains for an answer but couldn't arrive at one. Miraculously, her answer, and Jason's salvation, came an hour later in the form of a serendipitous telephone call from a friend who managed the Multicultural Leadership Experience Floors in Vouté Hall at BC, one of the dormitories available to freshman students.

Miriam's friend, Guillermo Manzano, asked her if she knew of any strong freshman student who would be willing to work with the maintenance staff in exchange for reduced room and board fees. Guillermo went on to explain that due to budget cuts, the size of the regular maintenance crew had been reduced by three people. Due to the 24/7 standby requirement, the current staff wasn't large enough to cover all the hours needed.

Miriam jumped at Guillermo's offer and told him she would call him back the following morning. Staring at the phone after hanging up, she pondered on how to best approach Jason with the offer, knowing that if it even hinted of charity, he would be offended and would become defensive and angry. Miriam sat there for some time thinking it through. When she finally arrived at a possible solution, she picked up the telephone and dialed Jason's counselor at Brookline High. After a protracted discussion, a feasible plan took shape. Miriam felt gratified after the call; the counselor had embraced the idea.

Thus it was that Friday morning, Jason Kelly was told by his teacher to report to his counselor at 10 am. Always prepared for the worst, Jason assumed he would be chastised by the counselor, and therefore, he assumed his most combative posture. However, when he arrived at Mr. Murray's office, Jason found himself faced instead with an offered chair and a welcoming smile. Taken off guard, he mutely sat down and waited.

Mr. Murray congratulated Jason on his acceptance at BC, and then told him that he wanted to discuss his college plans with him. Jason couldn't figure out why some geriatric high school counselor would have any interest in his plans. Cynically, the only thing Jason could come up with was that Mr. Murray might receive a bonus for every kid who went to college.

As Mr. Murray queried him on his plans, Jason became more and more confused. The counselor just asked questions; he wasn't at all trying to influence Jason in any way. After about ten minutes of general discussion, Mr. Murray said casually, "Oh, by the way, I might have a way for you to earn some extra money at BC. Have you chosen a dorm yet?"

Jason looked at Mr. Murray quizzically. This was the last thing he had expected the older man to ask. Finally, he shook his head and said, "No. Mom and I haven't had time to look over the paperwork yet. Also, since I'm on scholarship, I think that limits me anyway."

Mr. Murray nodded and smiled. He then picked up a business card from his desk and handed it to Jason, saying, "Well, you might want to call a friend of mine, Guillermo Manzano. He's desperate for some extra help in one of the dorms, so in addition to pay, he's offering reduced dorm fees. Another couple of students are also looking into it, so if you're interested, you'd best hurry and call him."

John Murray hoped his tone was light and casual. He was notoriously bad at lying, and had added the phrase about other students as an afterthought, hoping that Jason's competitive drive would ensure he'd call Guillermo immediately , if only to beat the other students to it.

Jason took the business card and read it perfunctorily. Then he rose and said "Thanks, Mr. Murray. I'll let you know. Can I go now?"

The counselor saw the impatience in Jason and recognized the young man's dismissive attitude for what it truly was – insecurity masking itself as arrogance. Jason's manner reeked of rudeness, but Mr. Murray ignored it, choosing to model polite behavior instead.

"Yes, you may go, Jason. Please come by tomorrow and tell me what Mr. Manzano says."

Jason left the office and looked at the business card one last time before putting it into the back pocket of his jeans. *Well*, he thought, *if this guy is so desperate for help, maybe I can talk him into giving me big money. Yeah, I'll call him.*

Saturday morning dawned bright and clear. As he struggled out of a deep sleep, Jason felt the warm rays of the sun strike his face through the tattered sash window above his bed. The light forced him awake. As he groggily rubbed his eyes, he remembered he had to call Mr. Manzano about the job. Another thought came into his mind – the other students Mr. Murray mentioned might have already telephoned and the jobs might already be taken. He decided to get up and call right away.

Jason turned over on his side and reached for the tiny red plastic alarm clock beside his bed. Looking at it, he discovered it was already 9:17. Raising himself up on his elbow, he put the clock back on the table and pushed back the covers, sliding his long legs out of the bed. After washing up and getting dressed, he wandered out to the kitchen in jeans and a grey T shirt, and looked to see if his mother left any coffee in the pot. Finding it was still hot, he poured some into a chipped yellow mug and sat down at the kitchen table. Sipping the hot liquid, he mulled over what he would say to Mr. Manzano.

A few minutes later, Guillermo Manzano's office phone rang. It was unusual for him to receive many telephone calls on weekends, so he answered it with some trepidation, thinking that it might be an emergency plumbing or electrical problem in one of the dormitories. He hated those kinds of calls on weekends, because it meant calling in staff and paying them overtime, thus further stretching his already limited maintenance budget.

However, he smiled when he found instead that it was Jason inquiring about the part-time job. As the young man explained his discussion with his school counselor, Guillermo realized that Miriam had spoken to the counselor in advance. Therefore, when Jason asked questions, Guillermo neither agreed with nor denied that other students had already applied for the position. Instead, he just said, "I am currently reviewing my staffing needs. Please come by today, if possible, and fill out the application.

After agreeing to meet with Mr. Manzano at 2 pm, Jason hung up the phone. He felt restless and confused, and everything felt as if it was moving too fast.

He reflected on how he suddenly might have two jobs – coaching during the summer and now, possibly the BC job. How would he ever study as much as he needed to? Jason was a compartmentalized thinker, a skill that had stood him in good stead when he had to block out the stresses of his home life to concentrate on schoolwork or basketball. However, he lacked flexibility and spontaneity, and couldn't get his mind around such life-altering events. Pacing around the kitchen, coffee cup in hand, he finally decided to head to the basketball court to practice - his favorite way of releasing stress and anxiety, although he had never admitted that to himself or anyone else.

Dafidi and Abdul had decided to practice that Saturday also. Just as they were walking onto one of the courts, they spotted Jason shooting jump shots by himself on another court. Both boys were reluctant to ask him to join them, yet both felt guilty for not doing so. After speaking briefly, they decided that if any of their friends happened to come along to play, they would ask Jason to make up a foursome. That seemed fair, and somewhat assuaged their guilt, but it didn't commit them to interacting with Jason immediately.

Soon the two were playing a brisk one-on-one game and totally forgot about Jason. Twenty minutes later, they heard Abdul's name being called, and stopped playing for a moment to see who was calling. Looking towards the parking lot, they saw Mike Ramsay getting out of his father's silver Honda Accord and waving. "Hey, guys. I was going to practice alone, but can I join you?"

Abdul yelled back, "Sure. Hey, say hi to your dad for us."

Holding the passenger door open, Mike leaned into the car and spoke to his father, who then responded to Abdul's greeting with a wave and a smile. Mike then closed the door and his father drove off.

Once Mike was close enough to the pair to speak at normal volume, he said, "I see Jason's over on the north court. I guess we should see if he wants to join us, even though truthfully, I'd rather not."

Dafidi responded, "Yeah, that's how we felt, but if we don't, he'll be even nastier to us during the game next Friday."

So it was that Mike walked over to Jason and asked if he'd join their group for an hour or so of practice.

Jason reluctantly joined the group. Unknown to the others, the only reason he did so was so he could ask if any of them had applied for the job at BC. After the group played for a while, they stopped for a water break, and it was then that Jason yelled. "Hey, Daf, you're going to BC. Have you gotten that maintenance job yet that you applied for?"

Dafidi looked at Jason with a quizzical expression on his face . "What maintenance job? I haven't applied for anything at BC. You must be confused."

Jason looked back and smiled, thinking, *one down, two more to go.*

Putting his water bottle back down on the bench, Abdul turned towards Jason and innocently asked, "What job are you talking about? No one has mentioned any maintenance work that I can remember."

Two down, Jason thought.

It was Mike's turn to comment, but he hadn't told Jason yet where he was going to college, so he wasn't certain he should say anything at all. Finally, he said, "I haven't heard anything about it. But then again, I might not go to BC. Actually, I'm not sure yet where I'll be going."

Three down registered Jason's mind. It was then that Dafidi noticed that Jason had a smug look on his face. Jason smiled and said unexpectedly, "Gotta go. Have an appointment. Bye."

With that, he hurried off the court, leaving the others totally dismayed at the sudden change in his demeanor. Looking at one another, they shrugged their shoulders and then returned to play for another half hour before breaking up so that Dafidi could go home to get ready for work.

After Jason left the basketball court he walked home to shower and change for the job interview. His mother was in the basement doing laundry when he arrived, but he ignored her and went straight to his room. Hearing the shower running a few minutes later, Mary went upstairs and approached the bathroom door, shouting, "Jason, do you want some lunch?"

Her son heard her but chose not to answer the question. Jason's mind was focused on the upcoming interview, and in his typical compartmentalized way, he just shut his mother's voice out of his mind. When Jason didn't answer, Mary simply walked away, knowing that he heard her. She was at a loss as to how to stir up her son's interest. After making herself a sandwich, she climbed downstairs to the basement and began folding laundry again. Unbidden tears began to flow down her cheeks as she stood there; she felt ignored and useless, a failure as a mother.

Forty minutes later Jason was climbing the steps to Vouté Hall. After searching for a few minutes, he found a building directory and made his way down a wide flight of stairs to the corner of the basement where Mr. Manzano's office was located. The air in the basement felt stuffy and stale, although the air conditioning was running full blast. Jason thought to himself, *This guy must not be too high up on the food chain to have an office down here.*

Walking along a short hallway painted in institutional beige, Jason came to a closed door with a small brass plaque on which *Guillermo Manzano, Maintenance Director* was written. Feeling suddenly anxious, Jason tapped hesitantly on the door. His knock was answered immediately by a gruff voice saying in a thick Boston accent, "Come in and close the door tightly. The air conditioning is too expensive to waste."

Jason opened the door and saw a short, stocky middle-aged man with ruddy, sun-lined skin and wavy grey hair sitting in a black leather office chair at a meticulously clean metal desk. An Excel spreadsheet was visible on his computer screen and he had obviously been working on the data. The man looked up at Jason and smiled, saying, "So you must be my 2 O'clock candidate. Make yourself comfortable, and I'll be with you in a moment." With that, Guillermo went back to his keyboard, typing numbers at a furious pace and staring at the screen intently. He finally stopped, shook his head, and said cryptically, "How the hell I'm supposed to make budget, I'll never know."

Guillermo stood up, walked over to a file cabinet and opening it, took a blue folder from the top drawer. Walking back to his desk, he turned to Jason and asked, "You must be Jason Kelly."

Jason nodded. "Yes. I came about the part-time job." For some reason, Jason felt intimidated, despite his usual bravado.

"OK. Then let's get down to business. Your school counselor sent me your profile, and I see that you're a bright guy and a star athlete. The only concern I have is whether you'd be responsible on the job. I need people I can count on. You look strong and the job requires a lot of heavy lifting of furniture and such. I can train you to do the maintenance work, but I can't force you to show up on time. Think you could be self-disciplined enough to do that on a regular basis?"

Jason had never been spoken to so directly by an authority figure. He felt cowed and awkward. After a few seconds, he answered in a muted voice, "I always get to school and practice on time, so it shouldn't be a problem."

Guillermo sensed the boy's unease and threw him a lifeline. "OK, then. Problem solved. Can you begin work the week before school starts? We'll be painting the dorm the week of August 30th. I'll expect you here at 9 am sharp on Monday the 31st. Make sure you bring your Social Security card and license for ID."

Jason hesitated in responding. No mention had been made of money, and he couldn't figure out how to ask about the pay. Finally, he repeated a phrase he'd always seen businessmen say in movies, "I'd like to think it over. I'll get back to you."

Guillermo couldn't believe the arrogance of Jason's statement. He was caught off guard and felt insulted by the boy's behavior. Here he was offering this troubled kid with no experience, a good job, and the boy was acting as if it was beneath him. Closing his eyes for a moment to regain his composure, he looked at Jason and said, "Thank you, that's all. I have a 3 O'clock candidate coming soon. You can let yourself out."

Jason couldn't believe it. Mr. Manzano didn't even shake his hand in farewell. He closed the door and stepped out into the stuffy hallway feeling like a total failure. He just couldn't figure out what he had done wrong.

Miriam Hernandez telephoned Mary Kelly that evening to find out how Jason's interview had gone. Mary was surprised by the call and explained to Miriam that she had no idea Jason had even had an interview. Miriam couldn't believe that the boy didn't tell his mother. She then told Mary about the job offer and the circumstances behind it, and requested that she keep the call confidential. Mary was grateful to Sr. Dorothy and Miriam for their help, but she was furious with Jason for not telling her anything about the interview. After thanking Miriam profusely, she hung up and sat down on the sofa with her head in her hands, crying.

Jason arrived home an hour later to find his mother had already left for her night shift at the supermarket. He made himself a ham sandwich and walked with it into the living room to watch TV. He heard childish music coming from the bedroom which he shared with Jude, but he had no intention of interacting with his brother. Jason turned the television to one of his favorite shows, *The Apprentice*.

He loved watching Donald Trump tear down the contestants, bruising their egos and humiliating them in front of their competitors. *Some day I'll have that kind of power and wealth*, he thought to himself.

When Mary arrived home early the following morning, she found Jason sleeping, slumped uncomfortably on the rumpled sofa cushions, snoring loudly. She felt both physically and emotionally depleted and didn't have the energy to deal with his moods right at that moment, so she left him where he slept. Jason could wait. Mary padded silently to her bedroom and closed the door. All she wanted was to escape to solitude and sleep.

The phone rang shrilly two hours later, rousing both mother and son from their slumber. Jason jumped up from the sofa, feeling disoriented and fuzzy-headed. He sat back down. Hearing the phone ring again, he got up and walked over and picked up the receiver, saying in a hoarse voice, "Hello."

On the other end of the line, Miriam Hernandez hesitated to answer. After Jason said "Hello" again in a questioning tone, she finally answered. "Hi, Jason. Is there any possibility you can come into work today? We're having a birthday party for one of the players you'll be coaching this summer, and I thought it might be a good way for you to meet the kids. The party starts at 1 pm. Can you come?"

Jason thought *What a waste of my time. All those snotty-nosed kids stuffing themselves with cake.* But he also realized that he had to stay on Miriam's good side in order to keep his summer job. Therefore, he answered, "Sure. I'll be there. Do I need to get dressed up?"

"No need. The kids will be in jeans. Just come and share some hamburgers and cake and ice cream and get to meet them. Come to the side entrance and knock and I'll let you in. See you then." Miriam hung up without saying anything else.

Oh well, at least I'll get something good to eat, Jason thought. He looked around him and suddenly realized he had slept all night on the sofa. Rising and walking to the kitchen, he turned on the tap and poured a glass of water, savoring it as it cleaned his palate of the stale salty taste left behind by the ham sandwich he ate the night before. Afterwards, he walked to the bathroom, showered and then walked into his bedroom with a towel wrapped around him. Jude was sitting cross-legged on the floor, enjoying his *Jungle Book* DVD. Holding his knees and weaving back and forth to the music, Jude was concentrating intently on the film and was totally oblivious of Jason's arrival. Relieved, Jason changed into clean clothes, sat down on the bed and put on his shoes. He managed to walk out of the room a few minutes later without having said a single word to his younger brother.

Mary was still sound asleep and didn't hear the front door close as her son left the house. Jason walked the short distance to the bus stop and waited only a few minutes before the Allston bus arrived. His feelings were all over the place; he kept thinking about the BC job offer, obsessing over what he had done to blow the interview. However, he didn't actually remember Mr. Manzano saying he did not have the job. Maybe he should telephone him and ask. Confusion reigned in Jason's mind as thoughts like these kept racing across his consciousness.

Jason felt relieved when he finally arrived at West End House. At least he wouldn't have to think about the BC job for a few hours. He slipped his mind into its West End House compartment, and walked up to the side entrance of the building and knocked. As promised, Miriam answered the door, a smile playing about her mouth. "Hi, Jason. Come on in. Welcome to Nicky Perkins' birthday party."

Entering the large room and looking around, Jason saw a long wooden trestle table covered in a colorful paper tablecloth and laden with food of all sorts. A banner stating "Happy 9th birthday, Nicky" was hung above it, cheering up the institutional room with its bright colors. A grey card table in one corner was piled high with gifts in festive looking wrappings. Jason thought suddenly, *I hope I wasn't supposed to have brought a gift. I don't even know this kid!*

Alongside the front wall, under high windows, another long table held paper plates and cups, plastic cutlery and a huge green cake in the shape of a dinosaur. Jason had never had a birthday party of his own, and he was astounded that adults had expended all of this effort on a little kid. Had he been honest with himself, he would have realized how envious of Nicky Perkins he felt at that moment. As it was, he just felt perplexed.

Miriam introduced him first to the other counselors and those parents who were able to attend. When Jason met Nicky's mother, Martha Perkins, he was taken by surprise. Martha was in a wheelchair and appeared to be in some pain. Despite this, a warm smile beamed on her face, and she extended her soft brown hand to Jason in a genuinely friendly handshake. Jason shook her hand and then quickly put his hands in his pockets. He wasn't used to tactile displays of friendship and he felt awkward.

Martha saw his nervousness, and thinking it was brought on by being faced with so many little children to coach, sought to put him at ease. "Honey, these kids won't eat you. They just want to learn how to play basketball the right way. Go introduce yourself to them and they'll be your friends forever." Laughing, she added, "And honey – just have fun!"

Despite himself, Jason smiled back at Martha. Her laughter was infectious, a robust tinkling sound. He wished his own mother could smile like that and be as relaxed as this disabled young black woman. He turned toward the group of children at the other end of the room, smiling and nodding to Martha as he did so.

Within a few minutes he was surrounded by an energetic group of 4th graders, each one vying for "Mr." Kelly's attention. They were talking raucously and every so often, one or two would laugh hysterically or punch one another in the arm. Jason had never been around so many happy youngsters and he couldn't remember ever being like this himself. He soon forgot his nervousness and was asking them what they wanted to improve on in their game. His questions brought a babble of answers as the children all tried to speak at once. Finally, Miriam came over and announced it was time for the cake and ice cream. The kids all turned and ran towards the table under the windows. Jason followed them slowly, feeling like a fish out of water. However, he also felt happy, a rare feeling for him

Miriam saw that he was more relaxed and surmised that an opportune moment had come for her to speak with him. As he munched happily on dinosaur cake, she walked over and said very casually, "Oh, by the way, your counselor, Mr. Murray telephoned me yesterday. He said you had a job interview at BC. How did it go?"

Jason almost choked on the cake. Coughing, he sputtered out, "I d-don't know. Other people were a-applying to Mr. Manzano too."

Miriam looked at him and said, "Well, you should still get back to him. It is the polite thing to do. Show some interest and maybe you'll get the job."

Jason looked dejected as he answered, "Actually, I think I blew the interview, but I don't know why. Maybe I should just forget about it."

Miriam shook her head. "No, you call him tomorrow morning and say you're interested. He'll let you know one way or the other, but at least this way, you'll have a chance. OK?"

Jason felt coerced, but he knew he couldn't refuse. Mrs. Hernandez would hound him until he did as she suggested. She held the reins to his summer job, and he couldn't afford to displease her.

"OK, Mrs. H. I will. I'll let you know how it goes when I come tomorrow afternoon to sign my paperwork for the summer job."

"Great, Jason. I'll look forward to hearing good news. Now, go eat some more cake and have some chocolate ice cream. Nicky is addicted to the stuff." Smiling, Miriam patted Jason on the shoulder and walked away.

Jason was soon joined by Nicky Perkins, who insisted the older boy join his group playing *Monopoly*. The skinny little boy with closely cropped black hair had his mother's engaging smile and a wicked twinkle in his big brown eyes. Jason liked him immediately and let himself be roped into playing *Monopoly* with a group of nine year-olds for a solid hour. Soon after that the party broke up. Jason left appearing happy and rewarded, feelings that were totally new for him.

The next morning at 10 am, between classes, Jason telephoned Guillermo Manzano and following Mrs. Hernandez's directions, politely told him that he was interested in the job and asked if it was still available. To Jason's surprise, Mr. Manzano said, "Great. Come by later this afternoon and bring your identification. We'll sort out the paperwork now, and then when September arrives, you'll be ready to hit the ground running."

Stuttering from shock, Jason could only respond, "Th-Th-Thank you. I-I'll be there. Bye."

Jason sat there with the phone in his hands staring into space. He hadn't failed after all. He had gotten the job!

Jason walked on air all day. After school, he headed to West End house and told Mrs. Hernandez the good news. Had he been more perceptive, he would have seen that she struggled to act surprised. However, her congratulations were truly heartfelt, and the sincerity in her voice made Jason like her even more than he already did.

Chapter 11
Last Game at Brookline

That week, Tuesday was Abdul's day to coach the 5th graders at West End House. The afternoon began very auspiciously. A parent had mailed Mrs. Hernandez a note complimenting Abdul on his handling of a dispute involving her son and another boy. Abdul stopped the increasing shouting and pushing before it escalated into an all-out fight. The parent also remarked how mature and polite Abdul was when she met him. Mrs. Hernandez congratulated Abdul on his success, and told him that the note would go into his file and would count towards his review at the end of summer.

An hour later, however, Abdul found himself struggling to run around the court after the kids. For some reason, his back pain was worse than usual, and it felt as if he had a permanent stitch in his left side. He finally sat down on one of the benches. He sat there for a few minutes, his head in his hands with his eyes closed. He then raised his head and began again to yell commands to the kids. This wasn't at all like him, and one perceptive little girl came up to him and asked, "Are you all right, Mr. Rashid? You look sick. Should I get Mrs. Hernandez?"

"No, it's all right, Emily. I'm just winded. Keep playing. You guys are doing a great job today and I'm really proud of you."

Emily left him and ran back to the game, and soon the children were playing at a fast pace again. Abdul forced himself to stand up and to walk over and stand by the south-facing basket to watch the game. His side felt better, but something was definitely still not right.

The next day at lunch, Dafidi and Abdul sat in the cafeteria eating and talking. Abdul mentioned the back pain incident to his friend, and Dafidi said, "You know, you've been having this problem periodically for about a year, I think. Why hasn't your doctor found what's wrong?"

"He always says it's a pulled muscle or something, which it probably is. Maybe I'm making too big a deal of it, but it really hurt this time. I mean it was a wicked pain, not just an ache."

"Tell your mom tonight, OK? You can't be sick for Friday's game. It's too important that we win this one."

"Enough, pushy friend! I'll mention it, but it is probably nothing."

Dafidi laughed and went back to eating his tuna sandwich.

Asiya Rashid picked up Maroun at work early the following evening, and they went shopping for a graduation gift for Abdul on the way home. After scouring a few car dealerships, they stopped at their local gas station to ask if the owner knew of any good used cars for sale in their neighborhood. As it turned out, he had been approached by a Harvard graduate student the day before who wanted to sell a used Toyota Yaris because he was graduating and was leaving to go home to Malaysia. The owner gave Maroun the boy's name and telephone number and wished them good luck, adding further that the car was in excellent condition and that he had been servicing it ever since the boy bought it.

Maroun telephoned the boy from his cell phone, and he and Asiya were soon driving to Forest Street near Porter Square in Cambridge to look at the car. As they drove around numerous blocks trying to find a free parking space in the heavily congested area, they became frustrated. Finally, they found a metered space on Mass Ave. near the corner of Forest Street. Praying that they could conduct their business quickly enough before the meter expired, to avoid getting a parking ticket, they walked the short distance to the three story brick apartment building where Steven Singh lived. They rang the buzzer, and a slender young man greeted them with a shy smile and led them down the street to a "Residents Only" parking space housing a tiny navy blue Toyota Yaris. The car was pristinely clean inside and out, and Maroun was pleased with its low mileage. He and Steven talked for a while, and it was agreed that Maroun would come the following evening to pay for and pick up the car. Both parties were immensely happy with the deal because Maroun felt sorry for the young student who reminded him of himself at that age. He agreed to pay a few hundred dollars higher than the gas station owner had said Steven originally proposed. Asiya was happy because the car looked solid, and although tiny, she knew the model had a good safety record.

When his parents arrived home later that evening, Abdul suspected they had been up to something. Both of them seemed very happy but hesitant to talk too much. They refused any dinner, saying they had gone out to eat in Cambridge on the way home. Abdul thought this was odd, as it was totally out of the way from the route his father normally took to get home from work. However, since he had no inkling of what was on their minds, he just assumed they had enjoyed a romantic dinner somewhere new and felt it was a private matter. He even thought to himself, *Maybe it's their anniversary and I forgot!*

Later that evening, Abdul approached his mother as she was unloading clean dishes from the dishwasher. "Mom, my back was acting up again today. When is my next appointment with Dr. Simmons?"

Asiya put down the cup in her hand and answered, "I telephoned this morning to make an appointment but they can't see you until late next month. You know how far in advance I have to make appointments. He is a very busy man."

Abdul nodded to his mother and said, "I know. No problem. I just thought maybe I should get it checked out again. I need to be in top form for the game on Friday night, that's all."

With a worried look on her face, Asiya asked her son, "What exactly does it feel like? Is it an ache or a pain or what?"

Abdul thought for a moment, trying to find the words to describe his mysterious ailment. Finally, he said, "Well, I guess it feels as if something sharp is digging into the left side of my back sometimes. It hurts more than a pulled muscle. Sometimes it goes away quickly, but sometimes it lasts longer. It was so bad yesterday that I took Ibuprofen and had to sit down for about fifteen minutes until it went away."

Asiya walked over to Abdul and put her hand on the left side of his lower back. "Is this where it hurts? Does it hurt when I touch it?"

"No, Mom. Not right now. It just feels a little achy where your fingers are - sort of like having someone touch a bruise."

Asiya nodded and said, "I'll telephone tomorrow and see if we can have the appointment moved earlier, but I can't guarantee he'll be able to see you before the game on Friday."

"Thanks, Mom. It's probably nothing anyway. Daf talked me into telling you, that's all."

Asiya laughed. "You and Dafidi are quite a pair. Neither of you listens to your parents, but you always listen to each other. If I didn't know better, I'd think you were twins separated at birth."

"No way, Mom. I'm a lot better looking!" Abdul giggled after saying this.

Asiya ruffled her son's think hair and said, "Go on now, finish your homework and let me empty the dishwasher. *Masterpiece Theatre* starts in a few minutes and I want to watch it tonight. I love Jane Austen stories."

"No probs, homework beckons." With that, Abdul grabbed a few cookies from a package on the kitchen table and walked out of the room. Watching him leave the room, Asiya thought to herself, *I am truly blessed with a wonderful child.*

When Abdul's mother telephoned Dr. Simmons' office the next morning, she was told that, unfortunately, there were no earlier appointments available. Asiya hung up the phone and gave herself a brief pep talk, trying to allay her fears about her son's health. *He just has a pulled muscle from playing too much basketball, that's all it is.*

With only two weeks until graduation, time seemed to accelerate for Abdul and Dafidi. Enmeshed in studying for final exams and practicing for the final basketball game of their high school careers, both boys were nervous and edgy, running on adrenaline. Daf was having trouble sleeping and Abdul had lost his appetite.

The game against Natick would be a difficult one; the opponents' team was composed of fierce competitors, one of whom would be their good friend, Yosha Stern. Both Abdul and Daf knew that the Natick team was well-trained and exceptionally skilled. They also knew that one of Natick's former players, Rinton Abiola, now going into his senior year at Boston College, was an advisor to the Natick team. Abiola excelled at all facets of the game and instilled terror into opponents' teams. Shouts of "Rin will win" echoed across the Boston College court at every game.

Rin Abiola's fame as the star of the BC team, and his legacy of outstanding games at Natick High would bring the media to the Natick-Brookline game. The Brookline players had already been told that television crews would be filming the game live for the weekly "High School High Five program" that ran on Friday nights during the season. This news only increased the pressure on the Brookline players, making them even more nervous. This was their time to shine or to be shamed and they knew it.

Abdul felt the pressure acutely. He was totally exhausted from staying up studying into the early morning hours, and he had been playing full throttle, though in intermittent back pain, for the past month. He just couldn't wait for it all to be over and for graduation day to finally arrive.

Dafidi was nervous but confident in his ability. He knew that he actually played best when the pressure was high; something in his makeup craved the extra challenge to force him to excel. It was the same with studying: procrastination and the subsequent cramming for exams brought out knowledge he hadn't even realized he had acquired. Therefore, he looked forward to the game almost as much as he did to graduation.

Their friend, Yosha, also knew the pressure was on. The Natick team counted on him as their best shooter, and if he did well in the televised game, it was probable that BC would offer him a slot on their team when he started school there in the autumn. This was one of his dreams...to follow in the footsteps of Rin Abiola.

The two boys could not have been less alike. Yosha was of average height, stocky and muscular, with thick, straight reddish hair and pale freckled skin. Rin Abiola was exceptionally tall and angular, with big brown eyes, glowing ebony skin, and tight black curls. Yet both had the same fire inside of them to excel at the game. The Natick coaches recognized this in both young men and helped to develop their intrinsic skill into full-blown talent.

As the game drew near, both teams practiced non-stop. Coach Rebor told Dafidi that he counted on him to guide the team to victory. For his part, the Natick coach imparted the same information to Yosha. Thus it was that the two good friends would be pitted against each other on the basketball court. Both boys were consummate professionals when it came to basketball and would not allow their personal feelings to affect their play. They saw the game for what it truly was – a competitive exercise and entertainment. Both would do their best to win for their teams.

Jason Kelly also anticipated the last game of the year. He saw it as his chance to finally get the recognition he thought he deserved. With a television crew there, all of Boston would finally know what a fantastic player he really was. Jason felt so confident that he blew off practice on Wednesday afternoon, preferring to study for his English final. Coach Rebor was livid at Jason's arrogant behavior, and unknown to the narcissistic young man, decided to substitute Dafidi in his place as team captain. Jason would receive a huge shock when he arrived for the game on Friday.

The week progressed smoothly despite the young men's concerns. Dafidi felt confident that he had done well on his finals, and Abdul accepted that he had done his best. Neither boy considered himself to be an exceptional student, but they both had worked diligently to succeed on their exams.

When Friday evening finally came and all of their exams were behind them, Daf and Abdul walked towards the gym together to suit up for the game. Daf was the first to speak.

"Well, here we go, my friend. Can you believe it? This is our last game at Brookline."

Abdul nodded, chuckled and responded, "Yeah, now we're really in trouble! BC is going to expect a lot more of us. I just hope we can live up to their expectations."

Daf laughed ruefully, "Just try to contain Yosha, and we'll do all right."

Abdul looked sideways at Daf, saying, "It's Yosha's strength I'm worried about tonight. He might bulldoze us."

Just as they reached the gym they saw Jason approaching. Walking with a slight swagger, showing how confident he felt, he edged up to Abdul and said, "Hope you've got what it takes. Rashid. No wimps allowed on the court tonight."

Abdul ignored the insult and kept walking, staring straight ahead so he wouldn't have to face his tormentor.

Dafidi knew better than to defend his friend, because this would only set off a flurry of derogatory comments from Jason. Instead, he followed Abdul's lead and strode deliberately forward until he reached the door to the dressing rooms. Opening it, he allowed Abdul to go ahead of him and then let the door close on its own just as Jason got to it. The thought *I must be exhibiting passive-aggressive behavior* briefly crossed Dafidi's mind as he heard the door slam shut in Jason's face.

Once inside the dressing room the two boys headed for their lockers, thankful that a half-wall separated them from Jason's. Taking their clean uniforms out of their backpacks, they hurriedly suited up. Abdul was so nervous he had to use the bathroom before going onto the court. Once he was done, he and Daf walked towards the gym together. At the large wooden entry door to the basketball court, both boys stood still for an instant and high-fived one another for good luck. Jason, who was walking a few feet behind them, shook his head and laughed maliciously at this gesture of their unity. He didn't even deign to comment on it, thinking it absurd.

Arriving at the benches and greeting the rest of the team, Daf and Abdul realized that Coach Rebor wasn't there yet. They looked around, but there was no sign of him. The team sat on the benches talking for a few minutes before they saw their coach open the door and approach them. He hesitated a few feet away and said, "Kelly, come with me for a moment, please."

Expecting to be complimented or to be given special instructions for the game, Jason swaggered over to Coach Rebor and smiled, saying, "Hi, Coach. So what do you have for me?"

The coach frowned as he realized how hard what he had to say was going to be for the young man to accept. He hesitated and, not wanting to humiliate Jason in front of the other players, said, "Kelly, come outside the door. I have something to discuss with you."

Once the door was closed behind them, Coach Rebor broke the news immediately that Dafidi would lead the team that night. Jason was so taken aback that he didn't know what to say. He froze, his face carrying an enigmatic look of confusion and sheer anger.

Coach Rebor recognized the look as a combination of fear and self-loathing. Jason knew deep down that he had done something wrong and was being punished, but his defensiveness wouldn't allow him to admit it or apologize to the coach.

With arrogant disdain, Jason shrugged and said, "Your call, Coach. Just remember it will also be your fault if we lose."

Coach Rebor couldn't believe the impudence of the boy. Looking into Jason's face, he responded, "If I could, I'd pull you from the game tonight. It's lucky for you this is the last game you'll ever play for me. Your rudeness has crossed the line once too often, Mr. Kelly."

"And know this, you will not receive any recommendation from me to the coach at BC. You're on your own now."

Hearing those words, Jason's face took on a totally different look; he looked stricken. His entire body slumped and he looked down at the floor. He couldn't meet the coach's eyes with his own. It was as if a plug had been pulled and all the energy in his body had been extinguished.

Coach Rebor saw this, and the kind man that he was, sought to defuse the moment. He said, "OK, Kelly. Time to play. Let's get back in there." With that, the coach opened the heavy wooden door and waited for Jason to walk through it. As Jason slowly did so, Coach Rebor knew he had finally given the boy something to think about. He just hoped that Jason wouldn't sabotage the game.

As it turned out, Brookline won by 4 points. Yosha played his heart out, but two of the other Natick players committed fouls that decided the game. As the Brookline cheerleaders and the crowd hailed the team's success, Daf and Abdul grabbed each other in a bear hug and jumped up and down a few times. "We did it…we did it!" Daf yelled.

Yosha and his team lined up across from the Brookline team and the players all walked down the line touching fists in a courtesy gesture that exhibited good sportsmanship. When Jason got to Yosha, he withdrew his fist in a stubborn display of dislike. Yosha, taking the high road, chose to ignore the slight and continued walking down the line.

When the Brookline team returned to the locker room, Jason was nowhere in sight. Dafidi and Abdul showered and changed and put their uniforms back in their backpacks. Joining two other players as they walked out of the gym, the group of four boys talked animatedly, reliving their victory play by play. Laughing and smiling, Dafidi and Abdul waved goodbye to the other players and began walking towards the front of the school, where Peggy had agreed to pick them up.

When Dafidi saw his mother drive up to the curb, he smiled broadly and waved.

As he and Abdul got into the Subaru, Dafidi asked his mother, "So, did you see it? Did you see how well we did, Mom?"

Peggy chuckled and responded, "I most certainly did see it. You guys are stars! I am so proud of you. And Abdul, I know your parents are waiting to tell you the same thing. In fact, we all have a surprise for you."

Neither Dafidi nor Abdul was expecting a surprise, so when Peggy got onto the Mass. Turnpike and began driving towards Boston, both boys were astounded. She turned off at the exit for Cambridge and drove down Mass. Ave., finally stopping in front of a small French restaurant located between Harvard and Porter Square and parking behind a navy blue Toyota Yaris,. The boys got out of the car, and Peggy ushered them into a tastefully decorated bistro, where they could see Asiya and Maroun seated at a large mahogany table covered with a crisp white damask tablecloth.

When Peggy and the boys reached the table, both Maroun and Asiya rose and kissed Abdul on both cheeks, causing him to blush with embarrassment. The party then sat down and chatted, smiling and laughing as the boys told them about the game. Finally, a waiter came over and took their orders, sending everyone into fits of laughter after he left, because he pronounced the items on the menu with a decidedly Bostonian pseudo-French accent.

Peggy turned to Asiya and Maroun and said, "Our waiter reminds me of the one on *Fawlty Towers*. Do you remember that show?"

Maroun chuckled, saying, "One of my absolute all-time favorites. I even have the DVD of all the episodes."

Abdul chimed in, "I love that show! It is so retro that even though none of what they say is politically correct, they got away with it."

Maroun, Asiya and Peggy laughed. Peggy then commented, "It's nice to know that my generation is now considered retro. I guess that means we're cool. Who knows – we might even be awesome!"

Daf and Abdul both rolled their eyes and smiled, showing how corny they thought Peggy's comment was. It was all good-natured, however, and the meal progressed in a genial atmosphere, with both parents and children enjoying themselves immensely.

When the comic waiter finally brought out their desserts and coffee, Maroun lifted his cup and said, "Here is a toast to my son and his good friend. May they always have a smooth ride through life."

Asiya nodded assent and then said, "And Abdul, your father and I have a surprise for you." Reaching into her purse, she pulled out a set of shiny keys and handed them to her son, smiled and said, "And may you also have a smooth ride down Mass Ave.!"

Abdul grinned from ear to ear. Looking from his mother to his father, he asked, "Are these for what I think they are – a car?"

Maroun laughed. "Well, it's about half the size of a real car, but yes, it is yours. Let's eat our dessert and then we can go outside and you can check it out. Just promise me you'll drive cautiously."

Abdul responded, "I'll drive so cautiously, you'll think I'm an old lady!" With that, he leaned over and kissed his mother on her cheek and then took his father's hand in his. "Thank you so much. You are the best parents ever."

Peggy nodded and added, "And they are also great at keeping a secret. Your car has been parked in a guest space in our building's underground lot for an entire week!"

Everyone laughed at this comment. Daf slapped Abdul on the back and said, "And now you can chauffeur me everywhere, old friend."

Upon leaving the restaurant, Abdul stated that he felt nervous about driving his new car for the first time on heavily congested Massachusetts Avenue. With numerous buses, bicycles, pedestrians, and the ubiquitous erratic Boston drivers, it was decided that Maroun would drive the car back to Brookline with Abdul as his passenger. That way, Abdul could enjoy his new car without panic. Daf asked to ride along in the tiny back seat and Maroun assented.

Peggy and Asiya stood on the sidewalk chatting for a few minutes more before driving off in their respective cars. Both women expressed their pride in their sons and agreed to sit together at the graduation ceremony the following Monday morning.

Chapter 12
Graduation Day

Dafidi awoke early on Graduation Day, eager to enjoy the festivities. At his English teacher's request, he had helped the valedictorian, Sara Mendelsohn, write her speech and he was anxious to see it delivered correctly. He knew that Sara was nervous about it. Although she was probably the brightest student in the class, she was sometimes reticent about speaking publicly because she thought she had to perform perfectly, or she would be a failure. Sara's perfectionism drove her to excel, but it also sometimes hampered her performance.

The day was perfect for the outdoor ceremony. With no discernible humidity, the warm spring breeze filtering through Dafidi's bedroom window felt fresh and clean. Looking out, he saw a clear blue sky dotted with fluffy white clouds.

Climbing out of bed and walking to the kitchen in his bare feet, he ruminated about how the day would be the beginning of his adult life. Lost in thought, he almost tripped over his mother's briefcase as it lay in the hallway. Catching himself and holding on to the door knob, he laughed out loud, thinking to himself *well, it looks as if I'll be as clumsy as an adult as I am as a teenager.*

Flipping the switch on the electric kettle and reaching for the French press pot, he prepared coffee for both himself and his mother. As the water came to a boil, he opened the refrigerator door, shook his head, and closed the door, changing his mind. He walked back over to the counter and poured steaming water from the kettle into the pot. Pouring coffee into two large mugs, he carried them into his mother's bedroom and set one down on her bedside table.

Peggy awoke as she heard Dafidi walk into the room. Rolling over and rubbing her still closed eyes, she looked up at him and whispered hoarsely, "Is that coffee I smell?"

Looking over at the bedside table and seeing the mug of coffee, she smiled. "Thanks, Daf. To what do I owe this considerate gesture?"

"I just thought that since today is my graduation, I'd like to take you out to breakfast. You deserve a break from cooking today. I thought we could just have coffee first and then, after we're all dressed up for the ceremony, we could swing by the Busy Bee on the way and have a full breakfast. I know you love their mushroom omelettes."

Peggy chuckled. "You are absolutely the best son ever. You're on, kiddo."

After his mother raised herself to a sitting position, Dafidi reached over and handed her the mug of coffee. He sat down on the foot of the bed and mother and son sipped the hot brew in silence. Peggy finally broke the silence by asking, "So, are you looking forward to the ceremony?"

Dafidi nodded. "Yeah, I can't wait. I just hope everyone likes Sara's speech. When I was helping her with it, we both decided it should be relevant to everything that is happening in the world right now. I'm a little worried it might not be totally politically correct. We all know how some of the parents in Brookline are so adamant about political issues. I just don't want to offend anyone."

Peggy looked at Dafidi and sighed, "You can't please everyone, honey. If you and Sara did your best, that's all you can ask for."

"Yeah, we did try our best. Let's just hope it's good enough."

After an hour spent relaxing over a huge breakfast at their favorite local coffee shop, Dafidi and Peggy drove towards Brookline High. As they approached, they saw a line of cars snaking into the stadium parking lot. Peggy joined the line, and they inched their way closer and closer until they were finally guided by a student attendant into a parking space far away from the stadium itself.

As they walked towards the stadium, Dafidi began to feel nervous. He kept this to himself, not wanting to ruin the day for his mother. She worked hard to give him this moment, and he wanted her to savor it. He held tightly to his robe and mortarboard and kept his own counsel.

Dafidi looked around the bleachers, searching for the Rashid family. He finally spotted Maroun and pointing, whispered to Peggy to go up the stairs towards where his friend's family was seated. She climbed higher and finally reached the row where she could see Asiya and her husband seated across the row from where she was standing. As others in the row stood to let her walk towards her seat, Peggy smiled and spoke to those parents she knew from the PTO. Once Dafidi saw his mother was seated, he walked down the steps towards where his class was seated on folding chairs on the football field.

Peggy and the Rashids chatted quietly until the Principal

announced the beginning of the ceremony. With the school band playing *Wind Beneath my Wings*, the principal thanked the parents and others assembled for their support of the students during their high school years. He went on to announce various awards the students had won and to congratulate those students who were graduating with honors. Both Dafidi and Abdul were among those named, and Asiya and Peggy clasped each other's hands as their sons' names were called. A proud father, Maroun was beaming with happiness from ear to ear, his black eyes twinkling with tears of joy.

It was finally time for the valedictorian to give the long-awaited speech. Just as students had done for generations, Sara Mendelsohn stepped nervously up to the podium. Her long, shiny dark brown hair hid part of her face, preventing the audience from seeing that her lips were trembling. Taking a deep breath, she hesitantly began her speech, thanking all assembled for their support. Stumbling over a word, she paused and recovered herself. She then continued, speaking with a firmer voice and a more relaxed demeanor.

The 2009 graduating class of Brookline High welcomes you to today's ceremony. Today, we go forth to begin our adult lives. As we do so, we enter a world in crisis, ravaged by economic, political and religious upheaval. The society that we join today as young adults is a confused world that seeks answers, an injured world that needs healing. As we take our place as participants in and contributors to this world, we need to ask ourselves three fundamental questions:

Are we striving to find answers to the world's many problems?

Are we helpers and healers rather than users and destroyers?

What can we contribute to make this world we share a better place?

In the sixties and seventies, our parents came of age in what was labeled "The Age of Aquarius" - an era in which young people sought to right the wrongs of the past and to transform society. As the Vietnam War raged and apartheid still reigned, they felt it was their duty to stand up against these evils through non-violence, as espoused and practiced by Mahatma Gandhi and the Reverend Martin Luther King Jr.. Following the lead of these two great men, they staged rallies and marches, hunger strikes and sit-ins. Their methods were thought to be revolutionary, but they were actually evolutionary. The world changed as a result of their efforts.

As they looked forward to transforming their world through the peace movement, those brave young people of the sixties and seventies challenged authority and took risks. Through their ongoing efforts, they helped end segregation in schools in the United States and apartheid in South Africa. They forced the government of the United States to hold President Nixon accountable for his duplicity during the Watergate scandal, and ushered in a new era of equality in the workplace for women.

However, as much as the world changed for the better during that era, it is today in trouble again. Wars are raging in Afghanistan and in Iraq. Internecine warfare is endemic in Sri Lanka and Pakistan. Women's rights are violated in the most brutal ways possible in Darfur and Somalia. Innocent children are starving, and an entire generation is being wiped out by the AIDS epidemic in Sub-Saharan Africa. Despite the signicant societal changes effected by our parents' generation, the world is still not the peaceful domain they envisioned.

Our parents came of age in The Age of Aquarius, whereas we are maturing into what many have dubbed The Age of Nefarious – a time of institutionalized deception practiced by corporations and Ponzi schemers; a time where many with extreme wealth use their power to grow their fortunes through exploitation of those who live in ever-increasing poverty.

The world we inherit is in turmoil; its inhabitants are agonized by their fears for the future. Their purses and souls are bankrupt. Need is all around us.

As we go forth into this maelstrom, how can we as young adults cope with it? What choices can we make to alleviate suffering and put the world back on the path of peace?

We have learned from the likes of Bill and Melinda Gates, and from Warren Buffet that what matters most in life is not how much wealth you accumulate, but how much you give to make life better for others. They have given hope to millions of people worldwide who would otherwise have no treatment for AIDs, malaria or other illnesses. They are the living embodiment of the biblical cliché "To whom much is given, much is expected."

It is my hope that we, the Class of 2009, will go forth as healers and helpers, teachers and mentors, innovators and contributors - harbingers of peace. May we strive to bring hope, prosperity and security to our troubled world. May we seek equality for all people, hope for the disenfranchised, and healing for the ill and injured. May we be not afraid of struggles and risks, always believing that our efforts will result in success. May we face our fears, recognize our weaknesses and will our spirits to overcome these internal demons. May we commit ourselves to help others to live better lives, for it is in doing so that we will heal our world.

I quote from a man of peace, Mahatma Gandhi. "One needs to be slow to form convictions, but once formed they must be defended against the heaviest odds. Strength does not come from physical capacity; it comes from an indomitable will. We must become the change we want to see."

In closing, I leave you with one final thought. Despite our future challenges, as we graduate today, we are happy and lighthearted. Therefore, I quote another pioneer of peace, Mr. Spock of Star Trek fame:

"Peace and Long Life. Live Long and Prosper"

As she said these last words, Sara smiled broadly and raised her right hand, forming the split-fingered salute made famous by the avuncular Vulcan on the TV show. When her class members saw her do this, they stood in one fluid movement, with their blue graduation robes fluttering in the breeze, and raised their hands solemnly in the same unique gesture. As the crowd in the bleachers looked over the sea of blue on the field, they saw over a hundred young people standing silent for a few moments, hands raised in a gesture of peace and blessing.

A comforting thought went through Asiya's mind as she witnessed this: maybe, just maybe, these kids will get it right and put our world back on the course to peace.

After graduation ceremony, the two families drove to the Rashid home for a small celebratory luncheon. Asiya had outdone herself; balloons decorated the living room, and beautiful flower arrangements graced the dining room table. She cooked all the day before and again the morning of the ceremony, and plates of luscious vegetables and meats were piled on the table. Peggy and Dafidi were struggling to eat, as they stuffed themselves during brunch that morning at the Busy

Bee Restaurant. Daf finally held up a hand and said, "Excuse me, Mrs. Rashid, but I can't eat another bite. I think I'm going to explode!"

Everyone at the table laughed. Peggy went on to explain that they had already eaten a hearty meal only three hours earlier. Maroun chuckled and said, "So here is what I propose: we all go outside and play a friendly game of basketball for an hour or so to wear off all of this food. Do I have any takers?"

Abdul smiled and asked, "You oldies against Daf and me?"

Maroun laughed and responded, "Why don't we politely reword that comment to Senior against junior players?"

Abdul grinned. "OK, Dad, but don't give it too much hope. After all, we're pros."

"We'll see about that," his father answered.

Five minutes later, the group walked through the kitchen and outside to the basketball court Maroun had created from a section of the back garden. Knowing his son's penchant for the game, he wanted to foster Abdul's interest. He himself played the game on his college team, and still liked to practice sometimes for relaxation and stress relief. Abdul had seen his father sometimes play by himself for hours, well after darkness fell, turning on the outside lights to illuminate the court. At those times, the son felt uncomfortable approaching his father about joining him. Abdul knew that Maroun needed the time alone to decompress from his frenetic work schedule.

Peggy and Asiya kicked off their high heeled sandals and walked in their bare feet to the court. The day was warm but not hot, and both women were wearing lightweight comfortable clothes, so they willingly joined in the game. Peggy stood there dribbling, looking to left and right, feeling indecisive as to which way to run. She then laughed as Abdul blocked her and stole the ball, dribbling it near to the basket and then throwing it in cleanly.

For his part, Maroun did quite well. He blocked his son efficiently and effected a jump shot from far back, bringing on cheers and laughter from the others. At one point, he stole the ball from Dafidi and took a long shot which, to the surprise of the others, bounced off the backboard and fell through the net. Another round of cheers went up. Abdul walked up and patted his father on the back in congratulations.

The game went on for almost an hour before everyone decided it was time to call it a day. They opted to sit at the patio table and enjoy cold drinks and dessert. While seated there, they heard a car drive up and park in the driveway. Maroun got up and opened the backyard gate to see who it was. He smiled and held the gate open for the visitors, allowing Mike Ramsay and Sara Mendelsohn to come in.

Sara grinned when she saw Dafidi and exclaimed, "The speech was a hit, Daf! A reporter from *The Boston Globe* was at graduation, and he's going to write an article about it in the local news section. He remembered the letter you and Abdul wrote to the editor and asked if I knew you. When I told him you helped to write the speech, he said he wanted to interview you for the article. Just think - our speech will be famous!"

Dafidi and the others laughed. Daf said, "You did most of the work. I was just an advisor. Why doesn't he interview you?"

"Oh, he will." Sara said. "But he really wants to talk to you. He said to me that you might have new ideas that will give new energy to the current peace movement."

Asiya politely interrupted Sara and asked her and Mike to stay for dessert. Both acquiesced and the group enjoyed another hour together, cheerfully recounting the graduation ceremony and talking about everyone's college plans. Mike finally stood up and said, "We've got to get going. We're going to grad night at Copley Place, and we both need to shower and change before the limo picks us up. Will we see you there?"

Abdul answered, "Yeah. But we're going with a big group. Unfortunately, neither of us has a date. One of the guys is picking us up here at six-thirty."

Mike smiled and nodded. "OK, guys, see you there. Bye, everybody!"

After Mike and Sara left and drove away, Peggy said that she and Daf had to leave also, so that she would have time to pick up Daf's tuxedo at the cleaners where she took it to be altered. She went on to explain to the group that the tuxedo had been her husband's, and since he was about three inches taller than Dafidi, the trousers had to be shortened. Dafidi frowned when she said this. He couldn't remember exactly how tall his father had been and it bothered him to admit this to himself.

Once he was seated next to Peggy in the car, he looked at her and asked, "Do you have any photos of my Dad? I can't remember exactly what he looked like. It's weird, because I kind of have a memory of him being tall, but I was so small when we were in Africa, that I might have just imagined him that way."

Peggy sighed. Keeping her eyes on the road, she answered, "I have a few photos but not many. I don't even know where I put them when we moved. I'll have to look for them."

Sensing that his mother was uncomfortable talking about his father, Dafidi responded, "No worries. Maybe some rainy Saturday we can look for them, when we both have the time."

Peggy knew her son was anxious to reconcile his feelings for his father, but she just couldn't bring herself to talk about it right then. She remained silent for a few minutes and then casually changed the subject, asking Dafidi about the group attending the graduation party at the Copley.

Mother and son talked spiritedly as they drove to the cleaners and then home, but no more mention of Jack Abraham was made.

The group of four boys drove through heavy traffic up to the Westin Copley Place, and circled around the area's one-way streets, trying to find a place to park, finally choosing the nearby underground Hynes Convention Center lot. The three other boys offered to help the driver pay for parking, since they knew it would be expensive. They parked and were walking towards the hotel when Daf saw Mike and Sara walking ahead of them. He shouted and they turned around and waved.

Dafidi's heart lurched when he saw Sara wave. He couldn't believe how beautiful she looked. Dressed in a long pale peach chiffon strapless gown and silver high heels, with her dark hair pulled back and clasped with a hibiscus behind one ear, she looked like a tropical flower herself. He spent hours going over the speech with her and had registered what a nice, friendly person she was, but he hadn't seen her looking so dazzling. Now he was envious of Mike, for it was obvious he was her date.

Dafidi looked down at the pavement and kept his head bent to avoid eye contact as the group of boys walked into the hotel. He was blushing furiously and he didn't want the others to see.

They saw an announcement board in the lobby stating that the party was being held in the *America Ballroom* on the fourth floor. They walked to the bank of elevators, remarking to each other about the luxurious interior of the hotel. They remained silent in the crowded elevator, but were soon chatting again as they made their way down a short hallway to the ballroom. Voices and music drifted from the room, and the boys were astounded to see how crowded it was inside.

As they recognized friends in the crowd, they dispersed.

Dafidi had trouble recognizing some of his classmates, especially the girls. They were like flocks of exotic birds, their plumage shining in vivid colors. He spoke to a few, laughing and chattering about the graduation ceremony. As he walked to the large buffet table laden with food, he spotted Sara off to one side, standing alone, scanning the room. She felt someone looking at her and glanced his way. When she saw him, she waved and gestured for him to join her.

Dafidi could barely move. He felt frozen in place with nervousness. Forcing himself to look normal, he picked up a plate and put some hors d'oeuvres on it. He then willed his feet to walk the short distance to where Sara was standing.

When he came close enough to hear her voice, Sara said, "Daf, you look nervous. Don't be – it's just a party after all. Come stand over here by me so that jerk, Jason, doesn't ask me to dance with him again. He's been bugging me for the last fifteen minutes since Mike went off with Alyssa Brunner to dance."

Dafidi couldn't visualize Jason asking anyone to dance, let alone Sara. The two were so different. Jason was a brilliant student but he was primarily known to be a 'jock' who thought of nothing but sports. On the other hand, Sara was an intellectual. She was the editor of the school paper, took AP classes in all subjects, and spent hours at the library studying. Dafidi realized that the attraction Jason felt for Sara was anything but intellectual, and this made him uncomfortable.

Daf knew he had to say something in response to Sara's request. He blurted out, "No worries. I'll stand here and keep you company. By the way, you did a remarkable job on the speech today. It was really good."

Sara tilted her head slightly towards him and brushed her hair back with one hand, a classic flirtatious gesture. Daf felt the butterflies in his stomach again as he looked at her and thought *She's really beautiful. Why didn't I see that before?*

Sara smiled and responded, "I couldn't have done it without your help. I was really nervous up there, but since we had practiced it so much together, I had it pretty much memorized. The hard part was trying not to just read it."

As she talked, Dafidi felt a presence come up behind him. Sara looked beyond Dafidi, frowned and stopped speaking, and looked down at the floor. Dafidi wheeled around and found Jason Kelly standing behind him, a wickedly malicious look on his face.

"So, Daf, I just overheard Sara say that you practiced a lot. Are you sure it was just on the speech?" Jason laughed at his own innuendo.

Dafidi couldn't stand the implication and felt he had to protect Sara's reputation. "Yeah, just on the speech. Some of us are gentlemen, unlike you."

"Hey, Abraham, don't get your tidy whities in a twist. I just thought you two looked like a couple. Guess not, now that you've told me that. Of course, you might not be telling the truth. Maybe you just want to protect 'Little Miss Perfect'."

Dafidi strove to restrain himself. He wanted to punch Jason on the nose. However, as he always did when provoked, he took in a deep breath and forced himself to remain calm. Before he could speak, Sara defused the situation.

Looking at Jason, she said, "Just leave me alone, please, Jason. Who I choose to date or not date is my business, not yours. Go bug someone else."

Jason looked stricken. He couldn't believe that Sara would embarrass him like that in front of Daf. He turned on his heel and was gone in a split second. Although they couldn't see it, he had tears welling up in his eyes.

After Jason left them, Sara sighed and said, "Sorry you had to incur the brunt of his anger, Daf. He's been bugging me for a month, trying to get me to go out with him, even though I keep refusing. He just doesn't know when to stop."

The two continued talking, and Dafidi finally got up the courage to ask Sara to dance. They walked to the dance floor and joined a huge group of kids gyrating, laughing and shouting to one another and singing along with the music. As he watched Sara dance gracefully, Dafidi felt as if he was in paradise. He remembered his own triumph as champion of the TV Dance Contest.

While they were dancing, Alyssa Brunner, Mike Ramsay and Abdul were seated at a table involved in an intense discussion about whether Mike should attend BC or Notre Dame. Mike had finally received his acceptance letter from Boston College, but his parents were pressuring him to choose Notre Dame. He himself was ambivalent; either school was fine with him, except that going to Notre Dame meant leaving his good friends behind. However, he and Dafidi had talked at length the previous week about how they could each visit if he went out of state, so he really wasn't afraid of losing contact.

Mike sat there listening as Alyssa and Abdul discussed his future. Hearing the emotion behind her words, he finally realized that Alyssa didn't want him to go to Notre Dame because she had a crush on him. Mike was flattered. Alyssa was pretty and smart. Tall and slim, with long silky golden blond hair, she had been captain of the Brookline girls' varsity basketball team, and in addition to being a great player, she could talk knowledgeably about sports. Mike really liked her, and he felt comfortable around her. She was going to attend Simmons College in the fall and would live in a dorm near the Fenway, not far from BC. Mike began to reconsider his choice of college, thinking that maybe BC would be a better option after all. As the evening progressed, he became more convinced this was the right choice. He now knew he wanted to remain in Boston so that he could get to know Alyssa better.

Jason left Copley Place Hotel immediately after the scene with Sara and Dafidi. He walked the short distance to the T and took the Green Line home. Dressed in a rented tuxedo, he felt out of place on the train. People gawked at the tall boy in the black formal suit, wondering why he wasn't with a date. When Jason finally stepped off the train, he felt relieved.

Loosening his shirt collar and taking off his tie and putting it in his pocket, Jason reflected on what a waste of hard-earned money the tuxedo rental had been. His mother talked him into going to the party, even though it was an expensive event. Mary wanted her son to have a normal high school graduation and to not feel deprived. She even gave

Jason a crisp $100 bill to pay for the tuxedo rental. Now her son just wished he had the hundred dollars back and that he had never gone to the party.

When he arrived home, he found Mary sitting on the living room sofa watching television, a bowl of popcorn in front of her on the coffee table and a knitted blue woolen afghan draped across her knees. She turned around, looking over her shoulder, and smiled at Jason as he closed the front door.

"Hi, honey. Was the party fun? I thought you'd be coming home a lot later."

Jason walked past her silently, without even glancing her way, and went straight to the bathroom, where he peeled off the tuxedo and turned the shower on full blast. He wanted to wash any memory of the night away. As he stepped under the hot spray, he vowed he would never have anything to do with Dafidi or Sara again. He was going to begin a new chapter of his life when he went to BC. Daf and Sara were relegated to an old compartment of his mind; BC to a new one.

Mary sat in front of the television, looking at it but not seeing it, wondering if she should try to speak to Jason. Something had obviously happened to upset him. She finally pushed the woolen afghan off of her legs, stood up and carried the half-eaten bowl of popcorn into the kitchen. She put it in the sink and sat down at the kitchen table, one foot tucked under her, thinking. Jason found her still sitting there that way when he entered the kitchen a few minutes later.

Mary looked up at her son, seeing a skinny young man in navy sweat pants and a gray T shirt, his wet hair dripping water onto his shoulders, turning the shirt's fabric a darker grey where it landed. She hesitated to speak. Jason broke the silence, saying in a sarcastic tone, "OK, so do you want to know what happened tonight? You want the gory details? I didn't fit in. I'll never fit in. That's the long and short of it, OK?"

Mary looked at her son, her haggard face registering profound sadness. She couldn't bring herself to ask the questions she most wanted to: *Did you even try to fit in? Did you at least try to be friendly?*

Jason opened the refrigerator, took out a milk carton and swigged directly from it. He then put it back and reached for a large yellow ceramic bowl of chili covered in plastic cling-film. As he went to lift the bowl from the shelf, he lost his grip, and the bowl crashed onto the kitchen floor, spilling its blood-red contents and splattering Mary on her bare legs.

Jason stood for a moment looking at the mess and then slid to the floor and covered his face with his hands. He began sobbing, first quietly and then with huge heart-wrenching sobs that seemed to emanate from his soul. He sat there for some minutes, oblivious of the detritus of the chili bowl surrounding him.

Mary knelt down and put her arm around his shoulders. At first he tried to brush her arm off, but when she remained holding him, he leaned into her and put his face on her shoulder. Words began spilling out of him, words that scared her even more than the tears.

"I can't take it anymore. Nothing goes right. I'm a total failure. Nobody likes me, not even you. I just want to die."

Mary heard these words and began crying herself. The pain and grief of the past few years began flowing out from both mother and son. As Jason shifted his body, Mary held her son in much the way that the Michelangelo's Pietà shows the Virgin Mary holding Jesus in her arms. The same emotions were playing out across Mary Kelly's face – profound love, extreme sadness and grief.

Mary finally spoke. Placing her hand on her son's forehead, she brushed back his hair in the same gentle manner she had done when he was very young and he was running a fever. As she did so, she whispered, "I'm so, so sorry your father died. He loved you very much. I love you so much. Please, please don't ever think he didn't love you or that I don't love you. You aren't a failure; you're just hurting and confused. I am too. We need help."

When he heard her last words, Jason looked up at his mother, his red-streaked eyes scanning her tear-stained face. He didn't say anything; he just looked at her and then turned away again. Taking her hand gently, he removed it from his shoulder and pushed himself up into a standing position. He walked silently towards the sink, plucked some paper towels off of their roller and began wiping up the mess on the floor. He still didn't speak.

Mary stood up awkwardly, her knees aching as she did so. She opened a cabinet under the sink and pulled some cleaning rags from a bucket and soaked them under the faucet. She knelt down again and began wiping the floor in a circular motion, cleansing the dregs of chili left behind after Jason's attempts to remove them.

She stood again and rung the rags under the tap, letting the chili beans seep into the garbage disposal below. Finally, she spoke. "Let me clean this up. Why don't you just go to bed. We'll talk in the morning."

Jason looked at his mother and nodded silently. He then did something so unexpected that Mary couldn't believe it. He bent over and kissed her on the cheek. Turning away quickly, he then walked into his bedroom and shut the door, thankful that his brother, Jude, was already sound asleep. For once, Jason felt grateful to hear the grating sound of his brother's snoring.

The graduation party wound down around 1 am, and Mike came over to where Dafidi and Sara were sitting and asked if she was ready to go home. Sara felt conflicted. She was exhausted and Mike was her ride home, but part of her just wanted to talk to Dafidi all night. Sensing her unease, Mike said, "I'll meet you down in the lobby in ten minutes, OK?"

Sara nodded. "Thanks, Mike. See you then."

Sara turned to Dafidi and struggled to put what she wanted to say into words. Looking at him she finally said, "Let's not lose touch in the fall, OK? After all, I'll be at BU, so our schools won't be that far away from each other."

Dafidi smiled. He had wanted to say much the same thing. He also wanted to kiss Sara. He looked back at her and said, "Don't worry, we won't lose touch. In fact, why don't we go to a movie as soon as I can get a night off from *Bettina*'s? I'll call you next week, OK?"

Sara grinned and suddenly felt lighter than air. She nodded and answered, "Great. Sounds good. I'd like that."

Dafidi stood up and said, "I'll walk you down to the lobby. I've got to get going anyway, but I'll have to go round up the other guys. I haven't seen any of them all night, and I just hope none of them left with the kids who were going out to drink. The last thing I want is to have to call my mom to come get me so that I don't have to be driven home by a drunk driver."

The two walked to the elevator and when it came, they and three other party-goers descended to the ornate lobby. Mike was sitting in a chair by the front entrance and he hailed them with a wave as they came out of the elevator. Dafidi leaned down near Sara's ear and said softly, "See you next week. Have fun until then. Make sure Mike drives safely, OK?"

Sara smiled and giggled, answering, "Maybe I'll make him let me drive home!"

Daf laughed and patted her on the shoulder. She walked across the lobby to where Mike was standing and then turned and waved to Dafidi before walking out. As he saw her pale peach dress glide through the wide entrance door, Dafidi thought he would burst with happiness.

Chapter 13
Healing Wounds

Mary Kelly telephoned Sr. Dorothy early the following morning, immediately after Jason left for his coaching job at West End House. She was awake all night thinking about what to say to the counselor.

Sr. Dorothy picked up the phone, saying "Hello, Dorothy Brennan here. May I help you?"

Mary always thought how odd it was that Sr. Dorothy didn't append "Sister" to her name when she answered the phone. Mary had gone to Catholic schools, but she wasn't well-versed in the newly relaxed etiquette of the 21st century church.

Mary took a deep breath and began telling Sr. Dorothy about the previous night. She broke into tears and gasped for air as she became more emotional. Sr. Dorothy pieced together the disjointed phrases and arrived at an accurate idea of what had transpired between the mother and her troubled son.

Sr. Dorothy asked Mary if it would be all right for her to come by the house that night. She knew from long experience that face-to-face contact was much more effective than trying to counsel someone over the telephone. Mary agreed, and Sr. Dorothy told her she would be there by six. Mary invited her to dinner and Sr. Dorothy graciously accepted.

As soon as she finished speaking with Mary, Sr. Dorothy telephoned Miriam Hernandez. The two women talked at length about Jason and his mother. Sr. Dorothy was especially relieved to hear from Miriam that Jason was succeeding with his coaching assignment. He hadn't bullied any small children, and in fact, the youngsters told Miriam that they really liked their new coach.

Miriam was happy that Sr. Dorothy was intervening to help the Kellys. Miriam knew of the nun's success with other families, and she firmly believed that Sr. Dorothy could turn the situation around, if anyone could.

So it was that at six that night, Sr. Dorothy arrived promptly at the Kelly home. Looking around her as she got out of her car, Dorothy Brennan could see the traces of poverty permeating the house. The heavy wooden door was scuffed, the stairs leading up to it were creaky and cracked, and the banister was full of splinters. The entire exterior of the house needed major repair and painting. Sr. Dorothy made a mental note to contact a priest she knew who regularly volunteered for Habitat for Humanity. Father Jim's ministry included performing free household repairs for the poor.

Mary came to the front door with a smile on her face that hid her pain. She greeted Sr. Dorothy warmly and offered her a glass of wine. Thanking Mary, Sr. Dorothy sat down on the faded sofa and covertly studied the room. There were numerous basketball trophies on one battered maple bookcase and a photograph of Mary and her two sons in an inexpensive Lucite frame. It was obvious from the photo that Jude had Down Syndrome.

Mary returned from the kitchen with two glasses of red wine and handed one to Sr. Dorothy. Sipping it slowly, the nun looked over the rim of the glass at Mary. Jason's mother looked physically depleted. Sr. Dorothy thought that if one word could describe Mary, it would be the color gray. She looked washed out, as if life had scoured all the energy out of her.

Mary lifted her eyes and saw Sr. Dorothy peering at her. She knew the nun was there to help her, so she wasn't uncomfortable being watched, just curious. She spoke to Sr. Dorothy, asking directly, "Why are you looking at me like that. Do I look OK?"

Sr. Dorothy smiled warmly and answered, "I was just thinking how tired you look. You work two jobs, and it must be exhausting. Is there any chance you could take a few days off?"

Mary smiled ruefully. "Not unless I want to go without food or electricity. Every penny goes into this house and the kids' stomachs. You can't imagine how much it takes just to feed two growing boys!"

"Oh, yes I can. I supported two younger brothers and a sister after my parents were killed in a car accident. I used to do a morning shift at one hospital and a part-time night shift at another. When it got to be too much, I took higher paying per-diem jobs and worked twelve days in a row and then collapsed for two days before doing it all over again. I know exactly how you feel. You can't think straight when you're so tired. It takes all of your physical and emotional reserves just to fix dinner or drive home without falling asleep at the wheel."

Mary began crying, her shoulder shaking with the sobs. "Oh, you do understand. I didn't think anybody could. I've been alone for so long."

Sr. Dorothy rose from the sofa and went over to Mary's chair. She leaned down and put a gentle comforting arm around Mary's shoulders. "Now, now, it'll be OK. Really, it will. I've got a plan to help you. Go rinse off your face, and then we'll have a nice glass of wine and dinner together and afterwards we'll discuss it."

Mary stood up and wiped her eyes with the back of her hand. She said, "I'll be back in a minute." Walking to the kitchen, she turned on the cold water and rinsed her face, throwing water against it with her cupped hands. Feeling marginally better, she dried her face with a paper towel and walked back into the living room.

Sr. Dorothy was sitting serenely, sipping her wine with her eyes closed. She sighed contentedly, opened her eyes and looked up at Mary as she heard her footsteps. Smiling, she said, "You look 50% better. Of course, I won't be satisfied until it's 100%!"

Mary laughed at the nun's comment, realizing suddenly that it was the first time she had laughed for ages. *Yes*, she thought to herself, *Sr. Dorothy really can help us.*

To make Mary feel at ease, Sr. Dorothy steered the conversation away from Jason and instead asked about her work. Mary's job at the supermarket wasn't rocket science, but she told Sr. Dorothy that she really liked her co-workers and that she felt at home there. It also offered the schedule flexibility she needed in order to take Jude to his multitude of appointments with health care providers. She could work "mother's hours" most weeks and then trade for other shifts as the need arose.

Mary went on to say that her job as a part-time CNA at St Elizabeth's Hospital was more difficult, both physically and emotionally. Hearing her talk, Sr. Dorothy realized that at least Mary's supermarket job was one positive aspect of her life.

The two women talked about a variety of issues until Jason arrived home. As he came through the front door and entered the living room, he saw a stranger sitting on the sofa. To him, she looked as if she might be someone's grandmother.

Mary spoke first. "Jason, I'd like to introduce you to Sister Dorothy Brennan. She works at St. Elizabeth's Hospital with me."

Sr. Dorothy stood up and extended her hand for Jason to shake. He walked forward hesitantly and did so. *Weird*, he thought. *She's not wearing nun clothes.*

Looking at Sr. Dorothy, he noticed the gold crucifix hanging on a long chain around her neck. He felt Sr. Dorothy looking at him as he stared at it, and he lowered his eyes, backed away from her and put his hands in his pockets.

Mary continued speaking. "Sr. Dorothy is having dinner with us tonight. Go get cleaned up and meet us in the dining room. And tell your brother that dinner is ready, and make sure he washes his hands, please."

Jason went off to the bedroom, closing the door behind him. He walked over and turned off the tiny television set his brother was watching. Jude was sitting on the floor with his back against the bed. Jason looked down at him and said, "Hey, go get ready for dinner. Mom's got a guest here."

Jude pushed himself up and lumbered out the door to the bathroom. Jason could hear water running and then the toilet flush. When Jude came back into the room, Jason said, "Go wash your hands again."

After Jude returned to the bedroom, Jason walked hurriedly to the bathroom and washed his face and brushed his teeth. He always felt grubby after he got home from coaching, and he had pizza breath from lunch. For some reason, he felt he needed to look presentable for the visiting nun. He walked back into his room and over to the closet and took out a clean sports shirt, hastily putting it on.

He then pushed Jude in front of him and said to his brother, "OK, Buddy. Let's go have dinner."

Sr. Dorothy watched the two boys enter the dining room. Jason was steering his brother in front of him, half pushing him as he did so. Jude didn't seem to mind, however. Jason pulled out a chair and Jude sat down in it, perching on the edge of the seat and looking right and left to see if the food was out yet. When he didn't see any, he yelled "Mom, where's dinner?"

Mary shouted back, "One minute, honey. I'm coming."

Her remark calmed Jude, and he sat back in his chair. He looked at Sr. Dorothy and said, "Who are you?"

She smiled warmly and answered, "I'm a friend, Jude. How old are you?"

He held up both hands and smiled.

Sr. Dorothy smiled back. "So you're ten years old. You must have fun at school. What sort of things do you do there?"

Jude had never had anyone ask him so many questions at once before. He thought for a moment and then answered, "We do art. I draw horses and dogs. I like dogs."

Sr. Dorothy responded, "Well, then, you'll have to come over to my house someday and meet my dog, Daisy. She's a black and white Border Collie and very, very smart."

Jude grinned at her and said, "I like dogs. I'm going to meet Daisy dog."

Just then, Mary came through the kitchen door bearing a beef roast on a small platter. She turned to Jason and asked him to bring in the bowls of vegetables. She went back to the kitchen and took a cookie sheet of dinner rolls out of the oven and placed them in a basket lined with a napkin. Following his mother back into the dining room, Jason came carrying two small bowls, one of peas and one of scalloped potatoes. Everything smelled delicious, and Sr. Dorothy said so, making Mary smile.

After Mary and Jason sat down, Sr. Dorothy spoke. "I would like to say grace before the meal, if you don't mind."

Mary nodded. She bent her head and closed her eyes, holding her hands together in her lap. Sr. Dorothy bent her head and began speaking. "God, please watch over this family and keep them safe. We are especially thankful for this beautifully prepared meal and for the work that Mary put into it. We are also thankful for dogs. Amen."

Mary chuckled to herself, knowing that Sr. Dorothy put the last sentence in for Jude's benefit. It was a sweet gesture and she appreciated it. Jason however, thought it was stupid. He didn't say so, but he grinned when she said it. Sr. Dorothy saw him frown, but she didn't care what Jason thought about it; she did it solely to make Jude happy.

Jude, who had never before even heard grace said at the dinner table, looked over at Sr. Dorothy and smiling, said, "You really like dogs. I do too."

The dinner progressed smoothly. Mary and Sr. Dorothy stuck to innocuous topics of conversation, and they all enjoyed the delicious food. Afterwards, as Mary and Sr. Dorothy sat at the table drinking coffee after Jason and Jude were excused from the table, Sr. Dorothy outlined her plan.

"Mary, you need a respite from caring for Jude. Two of my fellow sisters have offered to be Jude's chauffeurs to his doctors' appointments. You just have to telephone them a few days in advance so they can clear their schedules. Both are only working part-time now at the hospital because they're semi-retired. They enjoy an occasional change of scenery and both used to teach school. I think they'll get along with Jude and that he'll like them. This way, you won't have to change shifts at work so often and maybe you can just work days, even if you have to work long shifts sometimes for the extra money. I think a few weeks of going to bed at a normal hour would do you a world of good."

Mary nodded and half-smiled, biting her bottom lip in a nervous gesture. "Not having to drive into Allston twice a week would help a lot. It's not that far to St. E's, but the traffic and the parking are torture. But are you sure the other sisters are up to it?"

Sr. Dorothy laughed. "Most definitely. They are hearty Mid-westerners. Sr. Olivia helped her widowed mother raise her twelve siblings on an Iowa farm. She can cope with anything!"

Mary laughed at this too.

Sr. Dorothy continued. "My plans for Jason are a bit more complicated. He needs to learn that he doesn't have to be perfect to be loved. It seems strange to say this, but I think that is the reason he can't understand why you cherish Jude so much. He sees his younger brother as imperfect and can't understand why someone who isn't perfect could be loved. Do you understand?"

Mary looked up at Sr. Dorothy, pain visible in her countenance. She nodded and began speaking.

"Jason wasn't always a perfectionist. He used to be a normal sloppy little kid. But when his father died, he suddenly began organizing things. He had to have his closet just so, with his shirts all lined up – all the short sleeved ones together, and all the long-sleeved ones together. Then he began studying harder, long into the night. I would see piles of wasted notebook paper in the trash. Once I pulled it out and looked at it, and it was all the same assignment. If he made a mistake he re-wrote the entire thing until there weren't any cross-outs or erasures. He had to have everything perfect. He had to catalog everything."

Sr. Dorothy nodded. She had seen this same syndrome before in other children. She began speaking in a very gentle voice. "Mary, what you have here is a brilliant child who is trying to make sense out of something very painful. When his father died, he didn't understand why. Things felt chaotic and out of control. Jason's perfectionism is his way of bringing order out of the chaos of his life. He feels if he can sort out and organize the external components of his life, he'll feel orderly inside also. The only problem is that it doesn't work that way."

"Then how can he change? I don't want him to be unhappy all of his life."

Mary looked earnestly at Sr. Dorothy, awaiting an answer that would ease her mind.

"Well, first he has to learn to live with duality. He has to learn how to handle failure and he has to learn to succeed. Working through failure will make him more resilient, and earning success will give him more self-esteem. I am hoping that his two new jobs will help him do both."

"But what if he fails and cracks up? I worry he might commit suicide!"

Sr. Dorothy frowned and asked, "Has he ever suggested that he's thought of that? If so, then we have a totally different set of problems to solve."

Mary shook her head. "Thankfully, no, he's never mentioned it. It was just me projecting my own fears onto him, I guess. I've felt sometimes that suicide might be the only way out."

Sr. Dorothy concentrated on saying the right words. "Well, that's good news and bad news. I am very happy that Jason hasn't mentioned it, but I am extremely worried that you've thought of it. Mary, have you ever been evaluated for clinical depression?"

"Yes. After Jude was born I had a terrible time coping with his disability. I felt that I was somehow responsible– that I had done something wrong during the pregnancy. My doctor told me I had mild post-partum depression. He gave me pills and they helped. I was supposed to go for therapy too, but my insurance ran out and I couldn't afford it."

"I can refer you to a clinic where you can pay on a sliding-scale basis. You have insurance now through your job, so let's try to get you some help as soon as possible, OK? I think you need someone to talk to. You've been holding things in way too long."

Mary began to cry. "Th-thank you so, so much. You are a wonderful friend to do this for me. Nobody has tried to help me like this before."

"It's all right, Mary. You forget my vocation is to help. I need to do this to fulfill my destiny. It is part of who I am. I truly feel that God put me here to help others." After saying this, Sr. Dorothy said a silent prayer, asking God to ensure that what she was offering this troubled family would be sufficient to help them. She ended her prayer with a heartfelt *Amen.*

Jason's first day of coaching at West End House seemed as if it would never end. The day was overcast, hot and humid, and the air in the gym felt sticky. Sweat dripped down Jason's forehead as he ran around the court screaming commands at the children. He managed all morning to be focused and patient with the kids, but now he felt his patience ebbing away. Two of the children seemed inordinately clumsy, as if their arms and legs flailed in different directions at the same time. No matter how many times he tried to describe to the two boys how to position themselves to make jump shots, they just couldn't seem to accomplish it.

By noon, Jason felt he had reached his limit, but he still had three more hours of coaching to go. Thankfully, one of the program coordinators came into the gym and announced it was time for lunch. The children dropped what they were doing and ran towards the lunchroom, all the while chattering loudly. Jason felt he couldn't stand the noise any longer and headed in the opposite direction, towards the door to the street. Once outside, he took a breath of the muggy air and wiped his forehead with his hand.

After a few minutes of savoring the relative quiet outdoors, he re-entered the gym and walked towards the restroom. There he washed his face with cold water and dried it briskly with a paper towel. Feeling a little bit better, he decided he'd better eat something too. Mrs. Hernandez had told him that his lunch would be provided, so he walked into the lunchroom and was accosted by the twittering voices of small children as he did so. Taking a deep calming breath, he sighed and then got into line at the cafeteria-style buffet.

He chose an egg salad sandwich, chips and an apple juice, and took his lunch outside where he sat down on a low concrete wall. Although the sun shone ferociously, he felt more comfortable sitting there in the silence than he would have done inside at a table surrounded by noisy youngsters. Eating his sandwich, he thought about how his first day was going. *Well, the kids aren't great players, but at least they try to do what I tell them. And anyway, I get paid for this. Cool.*

After finishing his lunch, Jason meandered slowly back to the gym, arriving just as the afternoon group of eight year-olds were filing onto the court. Jason looked them over. Most were boys, and quite a few seemed overweight. Two girls were in the group also. One was slightly chubby, with flaming red hair, and the other was tall, thin, and with dark brown straight hair. They stood apart from the boys and giggled occasionally.

Jason shouted to the group to line up opposite one another in even pairs and to try to throw the ball across to the player opposite, zigzagging down the lines. The children attempted this, sometimes missing a catch and dropping the ball. As he watched them, Jason felt as if he could never make them into a real team. However, he noticed that the tall dark haired girl seemed more coordinated than most of the other kids.

After practicing throws, Jason had the kids sit down on the court and he briefly described the game to them. The boys whispered and giggled amongst themselves as he talked. Jason finally told them to keep quiet, and they immediately stopped talking. He couldn't believer it – they listened to him!

A few minutes later, Jason divided the group into two teams, assigning one of the two girls to each. The boys accepted the girls and play began. Jason noted that one boy, whom he only knew as Ernesto, stood out from the rest, effortlessly making baskets and working hard to block his opponents. The tall girl, named Silvana, also caught onto the game easily and was soon standing at the free throw line preparing to take a free throw. It went in cleanly and the children cheered. Silvana gave a high five to Ernesto and play began again. Jason had found his two team captains.

Independence Day

It was 5 pm on July 4th and Dafidi was struggling to keep awake at *Bettina's*. He regretted having agreed to join Yosha, Mike, LeShawn and Abdul on the roof garden of Mike's aunt's apartment in the North End to watch the fireworks. Betty Ramsay knew all the boys and invited them to join her in celebrating the holiday, knowing that her roof garden had one of the best free views of the festivities.

Daf had worked non-stop every night since the first of July, and he had also coached two days at West End House. As he carried plates back to the kitchen, he yawned and sighed. Placing the dirty plates down on the counter next to the dishwasher, he walked over to the coffeemaker and poured himself a cup of the strong brew. He gulped it appreciatively, relishing the hot liquid's comforting feel on his dry throat. Putting the cup down, he resumed his duties, attempting to put on his best face to the customers. When his shift finally ended at 8 pm, he grabbed his gear and headed a few blocks away to Betty Ramsay's apartment.

When she opened her front door, Betty saw an exhausted young man standing in front of her. Trying to suppress a yawn, he smiled at her shyly and said, "Sorry I'm late. We were really busy tonight at *Bettina's*. Hope I haven't missed the fireworks. Thanks for inviting me."

"Come on in, Daf. Everyone else is here and we were just about to carry the food up to the roof. Put down your stuff, grab something to drink and join us."

Dafidi set his backpack down by the front door and reached in it, and took out a small white cardboard box. He offered it to Betty, saying, "Here, I brought you some cannolis from *Bettina's*. She made them herself and they're really good."

"Thanks, Daf. It's a good thing I'm not dieting right now!" Betty laughed, as she was known to always be trying new diets to slim down her chubby figure.

Betty led Dafidi into the living room, where he was greeted by all the Ramsay clan, as well as his close friends. Just as he was about to sit down, the supersonic jets flew over the Esplanade. All eyes were glued to the television screen as Keith Lockhart, conductor of the Boston Pops led the Orchestra through "The Star-Spangled Banner."

The group then gathered up hors d'oevres, casseroles, serving utensils and plates, and carried them up the narrow staircase to the roof garden where they laid them on a large picnic table. Dafidi was astounded at how beautiful the roof looked. Topiary trees were placed in each corner and long white planters placed between them were filled with colorful flowers along the roof's edges. One could look out over the roofs of the North End and see as far as the airport to the northeast and as far as the Marriott Hotel in Cambridge to the northwest.

Everyone sang along as Neil Diamond belted out "Sweet Caroline."

Suddenly a loud 'boom' sounded, heralding the beginning of the fireworks. Barges on the Charles River sent forth huge multi-colored displays, each one more impressive than the last. Shapes of flowers and dragons lit up the night sky, mesmerizing the viewers. By the time the fireworks extravaganza ended, the happy group was replete with food, the adults were a bit groggy from too much to drink. Dafidi was sound asleep in a patio chair, his head resting on his chest.

Yosha came over and shook his friend's shoulder to wake him up. "Hey, Daf. Time to call it a night. I'm driving everybody home, so you'd better wake up. We're leaving in a few minutes."

Hearing Yosha's words, Dafidi struggled out of a sound sleep. He rubbed his eyes and said, "Sure, I'm coming. Thanks, Yosh."

Daf got to his feet and stretched. He suddenly felt wide awake. He smiled at Yosha and said, "Well, at least I saw most of the fireworks before I nodded off. I just hope I didn't snore."

"No one would have noticed, Daf; the fireworks were too loud. Let's go thank Mike's aunt and then hit the road. I've got to work early tomorrow at *Petals*."

The group of five boys piled into Yosha's car and headed through the congested city streets towards Brookline. People were milling about and roaming the city, celebrating far into the night. The traffic was as congested as rush hour, and it took the boys a solid hour to get home. Yosha waved good-bye and headed further west to Natick, happy that the crowds had thinned out once they got to Brookline. He had to be at the wholesale flower market at the Boston Flower Exchange at 5 am and would barely have time to sleep for a few hours, shower, change clothes and then drive back into the city. Yosha adored his new job.

There was something very rewarding in seeing recipients' happy faces when he delivered beautiful flowers to them. At those moments, he felt as if he were a cog in a wheel of kindness.

***

Guillermo Manzano sat at his large metal desk, waiting for Jason Kelly to show up to sign his new hire paperwork. Guillermo sipped at his mug of strong black coffee, enjoying its warmth on his tongue. He was tired from having attended to two emergency plumbing calls in the middle of the previous night. He couldn't wait to enlist more staff to help him keep up with the round-the-clock maintenance required of a large, multi-floor dormitory.

Hearing footsteps approach his office, he set the mug down on the desk and waited for the knock on his door. Hearing it, he shouted, "Come on in. The door's open."

Jason Kelly appeared in the doorway, he looked more subdued than he had on the first visit. Dressed in clean, ironed khakis and a white cotton button down shirt, he looked businesslike and competent. However, Guillermo was never fooled by appearances. He learned of Jason's history from Miriam Hernandez, and he knew the boy needed structured training if he was to succeed at work.

Jason sat back in the scuffed wooden-armed chair and put his hands down on his knees. Guillermo thought Jason seemed tense. He was correct in his assessment – Jason was a nervous wreck.

Jason hesitated to speak but fi nally got up the courage. "Do you have the p-paperwork I n-need to sign?"

Guillermo reached for the stack of papers, each headed with the Boston College logo. "Here, Jason. Why don't you move over to the small desk by the window to fill these out. Would you like a cup of coffee?"

Jason nodded and said, "OK. Thanks." He rose slowly from the chair and took the papers over to the small wooden desk which sat under a tiny transom window overhead. He riffled through the papers, looking at all of the questions he had to answer and examining the details he had to write down. He suddenly felt completely overwhelmed. When Guillermo handed him the steaming burgundy mug of coffee emblazoned with its gold BC logo, he almost dropped the cup. Recovering his composure, he sought a mental compartment in which to file the paperwork. Sipping the coffee to gain time, he finally put the mug down and began to fill out the top form.

Jason sat there for twenty-five minutes, concentrating intently on the multiple forms. He drained the mug of coffee and finally gathered up the forms and carried them over to Mr. Manzano. The man smiled and said, "OK, son. Give me a minute to finish writing this email, and then I'll give you a guided tour of the dorm where you'll be working."

Jason sat back down in the uncomfortable wooden chair and waited. He felt impatient but knew instinctively that he had to hide this from his new boss.

After what felt like an eternity, but was really only three minutes, Mr. Manzano logged off of his computer and rose from his chair. He gestured to Jason to follow him as he strode out of the office, leaving the door unlocked.

As the two walked along the basement hallway, Jason was ambivalent. In one way, he felt as if he was being trapped into doing something he didn't really want to do. However, in another way, he felt proud of having gotten the job. His feelings moved all over the spectrum as they walked without speaking.

After ascending to the second floor in the stuffy elevator, Mr. Manzano walked down a long corridor to a storeroom and taking a key ring out of his pocket, opened its door. Inside, Jason saw cleaning supplies, paper goods, mops, brooms and a vacuum cleaner. Mr. Manzano took out the vacuum and instructed Jason on how to use it and how to change the filter bag. He then told Jason never to mix chlorine bleach with ammonia, and to always make certain that any floor he washed was completely dry before he removed the "Wet Floor" signs around it.

As Mr. Manzano was speaking, a pretty young girl walked by and waved, smiling as she said, "Hi, Mr. M. Hope you have a great day!"

Mr. Manzano smiled back and answered, "Hi, Lisa. See you at Tai Chi later."

Jason looked quizzically at his boss, confused by Mr. Manzano's comment.

The older man saw this and said, "Oh, I teach Tai Chi two nights a week. Anybody in the dorm can come. It's free."

Jason was astounded. "How could this man work day and night and teach Tai Chi? When did he sleep?"

Mr. Manzano was unaware of Jason's thoughts and went on to describe Jason's new duties in detail. Per Miriam Hernandez's instructions, however, he left out two salient facts about the dormitory. One fact was that it was co-ed, and the other was that it was multi-cultural, encompassing students of many nationalities and diverse ethnic backgrounds. Miriam wanted Jason to experience the dorm and come to grips with his own prejudices. She didn't want to create a self-fulfilling prophecy where he would know in advance that people towards whom he felt prejudice lived there. Miriam's thought was that if he could meet numerous people and get to know them one-on-one, he would overcome his prejudices more quickly. It was a calculated risk but she felt confident it would work.

After walking Jason around the building, Mr. Manzano thanked him for coming and told him to report for work two days later at 9 am. He would work four hours a day, and Jason's first assignment would be to wash the insides of the windows in all of the dorm rooms. Mr. Manzano shook Jason's hand and wished him good luck in the new job and then walked off.

As Jason walked out of the building and down a wide stone ramp, he turned to look back at the building's façade. Although finished in 1988, Vouté Hall was reminiscent of older brick structures at the college, and the circular window above where he was standing added character to the building. It dawned on Jason as he stood there that he hadn't asked Mr. Manzano anything about the free accommodations into which he'd be moving once school started in September. Jason scanned the building trying to imagine where his room would be. Finally, he turned around and walked slowly away, trying to put his mind around all of the changes that had occurred so recently in his life.

Guillermo Manzano had evaluated the boy as he gave him the guided tour of the building. He could tell Jason had a sharp intellect and the capability to succeed. However, he also sensed insecurity and anger in the boy's attitude; even his stance was defensive, with arms crossed tightly across his chest as he spoke. Guillermo had a degree in psychology that he chose not to use, preferring instead to work with concrete entities rather than the more subtle and fluid movements of the human mind. He contented himself with teaching Tai Chi to allow expansion of the more esoteric features of his own nature. Guillermo was a pragmatist.

When he returned to his office, he telephoned Miriam Hernandez to give her an update on his meeting with Jason. Miriam expressed happiness that Jason even showed up, and she was delighted that he agreed to begin work on Wednesday morning. Miriam felt rewarded when she could help a young person turn their life around, and Jason offered a new challenge. She asked Guillermo to promise to telephone her on Wednesday after Jason finished his shift. Hanging up, Guillermo realized why he had always had a soft spot in his heart for Miriam – she was an angel – one who could always be counted on to help those in need or in emotional pain. He had known Miriam for 30 years, and knew her background. She was emotionally abused herself and she fought tooth and nail to stop her own victimization. If anyone could help troubled kids, it was her.

Later that afternoon, as Guillermo Manzano was tidying up his office and preparing to go home for the night, he had a flash of intuition regarding Jason. He laughed at the irony of the thought, considering his profession. Jason would be high maintenance.

Chapter 14
Summer 2009

Abdul picked up Dafidi in his new car on Tuesday, and they drove to West End House. Abdul had to coach that afternoon, and Dafidi had volunteered to help Miriam paint the lunchroom. Miriam offered Daf fifty dollars to do so, and he was appreciative, although he probably would have agreed to do it for free because he respected her so much.

When they arrived, Abdul was careful to park in a space next to a wall at the end of the small lot, so that only one side of his new car would be exposed to other cars parking. His father had drilled this idea into him for two weeks, saying it was a good way to avoid scratches and small door dings from careless drivers. Dafidi was amazed at Abdul's driving proficiency; he drove effortlessly and parked in one smooth maneuver.

Mrs. Hernandez came out to congratulate Abdul on his new automobile. She oohed and aahed, letting Abdul tell her about the car's every gadget. She saw the pride he had in the little car and knew he would be a careful driver. *If only all teenagers were this responsible*, she thought to herself.

Abdul walked over to the gym and gathered up his players. Soon they were engaged in a rowdy game, running and screaming, and thoroughly enjoying themselves. The happy sounds of their chattering and laughing could even be heard out in the courtyard and the parking lot

Mrs. Hernandez and Dafidi headed off towards the lunchroom. Once inside, Daf could see that Miriam had already been busy preparing the room for painting. Large blue plastic tarps were spread on the floors to act as drop cloths, and she had taped the edge over the wainscoting so that paint wouldn't spill over onto it.

Mrs. Hernandez directed Dafidi to a bucket of paint in the corner, and showed him how to pour it into the tray and use the roller so that it wouldn't be over-soaked with paint. The paint was a soft hue of light grass green. Dafidi thought it seemed cheerful and uplifting and that it offered a good contrast with the white beadboard below. He watched Mrs. Hernandez dip the roller in the tray and paint a small area, and then he replicated her movements and began to paint his assigned space. As he painted, he reflected on the school year ahead.

It felt relaxing to paint alongside Mrs. Hernandez, even though neither of them spoke a word. As they worked, they listened to classical music and their work soon took on a rhythm of its own, matching the cadence of the melodies. When Mrs. Hernandez finally told Dafidi it was time to stop, he was amazed to find that they had been painting for over three hours.

After cleaning their brushes, they both walked over to the gym to find Abdul. The basketball game had ended, and he was showing a small exhausted boy how to dribble correctly, fingers lightly on the ball. The little boy was clumsy, but he was trying his very best to copy Abdul's movements. Mrs. Hernandez and Dafidi stood there in silence as Abdul patiently encouraged the child.

When the little boy's mother arrived a few minutes later, Abdul waved goodbye to the child and came over to where Daf and Mrs. Hernandez were standing. He said, "Alberto really tries, but he just doesn't seem to have small muscle dexterity. He even has trouble holding the ball."

Mrs. Hernandez nodded and said, "That's because he was born with a mild case of cerebral palsy. He's getting better through practice however. The exercise helps his muscles."

Abdul and Dafidi talked with their mentor for a little while and then took their leave. Abdul buckled up, and he was as careful backing out of the parking space as he had been driving into it. Dafidi told him he was impressed, and Abdul smiled happily.

As they drove home, the two boys discussed what classes they were considering enrolling in at BC. Abdul cited Shakespeare, Anthropology and Comparative Religion. Dafidi looked over at his best friend, realizing in that instant that he didn't know him as well as he thought he did. Frowning, he asked Abdul, "So why are you choosing those subjects?"

Abdul concentrated on driving as he negotiated a busy intersection and then answered, "I've always wondered how other people think. I feel I need to learn how humans developed so I can figure out why they do what they do, so anthropology seemed like a logical class to take. I want to take Comparative Religion so I can analyze what I really think. Maybe if I learn about other religions, I'll understand my own better, or I might even question my own religion. As to Shakespeare, he just really seemed to understand human nature, even though he lived so long ago. Maybe I just need to explore my own feelings or something."

Dafidi nodded and said, "I know what you mean. Sometimes I wonder what it would be like if I had been born in India or China or something. Would I think about things in the same way I do now, or would I be totally different? But I'm glad that I was born in Africa."

Abdul responded, "I really think that down deep we are pretty much all the same. Maybe different religions exist just because God is so huge that one religion couldn't explain everything about him. Or maybe when the Bible says that we are made in God's image, maybe we live and die as cells in God's body the way that cells live, replicate and die in our bodies all the time. After all, we have helper cells and killer cells in our bodies. That would explain a lot, right?"

Dafidi said, "Wow, You've really thought about this. I just kind of take things at face value. Maybe you're right. Maybe I should take Comparative Religion too, if only so I can understand what you're talking about!"

Abdul laughed, saying "I might not be the deepest thinker, but I have my moments."

As the summer progressed, Dafidi got into a routine: he coached at West End House on Tuesday and Thursday afternoons and worked at *Bettina's* on Sunday, Monday and Wednesday during the day, and then again on Friday and Saturday nights. With no entire day off, he thought he'd be totally exhausted, but instead, he was energized. His bank balance had never been healthier, and he happily anticipated being able to buy a car by the end of August.

Peggy worried about her son working so much, but despite her fears, he seemed to be thriving with all of the activity. One Wednesday night over dinner in late July, she asked him to be truthful and to tell her if he was burning out. His response was honest and it allayed her fears. "Well, I'm pretty exhausted by Saturday night, but since I can go to bed earlier from Monday through Thursday, when I just work during the day, it isn't really a problem. What I am getting tired of is the long commute to *Bettina's* on the T. I can't wait until I can buy a car!"

Peggy responded, "Maybe we should start looking next week. I can take you around to some dealerships on Monday and Tuesday night. Or if you want, you could go to *Craigslist* and see if anyone has a good used car for sale privately. You might even get a better deal that way, right?"

"Yeah, I thought of that, Mom. The only thing is that dealerships offer warranties, and I won't have much money for repairs while I'm at BC. So I guess it's sort of a trade-off — either I pay less for the car up front and take a risk, or I pay more to a dealer and then have less of a headache if it needs repairs."

Peggy nodded in assent. "You're right. Well, let's just take it one car at a time and see what's out there, OK?"

"No worries. Will do."

***

Asiya opened her mail on a sweltering afternoon in late July, finding a letter from her aunt in Haifa among the envelopes. She opened it with some trepidation, fearing that possibly some catastrophe had happened. However, when she read her aunt's words, she smiled broadly.

The letter explained that her cousin, Alia, was finally walking again after suffering a devastating injury to her leg in a mortar attack in Gaza. She was now anxious to get back to her work as a nurse, and after hearing of a shortage of registered nurses in the United States, applied to numerous hospitals in Boston. Aunt Fatima wanted to know if Alia could stay with Asiya and Maroun while she interviewed for a nursing position.

Asiya was delighted. She was close to her cousin and would love to have her come to Boston. She felt, however, that it was only fair to propose the idea to Maroun first and to see if he was happy with the plan. With Abdul soon going off to college, the house would have plenty of room, and Asiya was often lonely for her family in Israel. It would be wonderful to have Alia here to share her thoughts. Her younger cousin was a bright and inquisitive woman with a big heart.

That night, while the family was eating dinner, Asiya read the letter to her husband and son and asked their opinions. Maroun and Abdul were both heartily in favor of the plan. Asiya felt immensely relieved. She would have felt guilty turning down the request from her beloved aunt.

Not content with writing, Asiya telephoned her aunt the next morning, allowing for the time difference between Boston and Haifa. As the phone rang, Asiya was again reminded of the long-lasting British influence in Israel as the "brr, brr" of the phone sounded its double ring tone just as it did in English homes. After a short pause, Aunt Fatima answered in her deep resonant voice.

Speaking in Arabic, Asiya quickly told her aunt that Alia was welcome to come to Boston, and the two women began planning the trip. Hence, twenty minutes later it was already decided that if her visa came through on time, Alia would fly to Boston through Rome on August 15th. Aunt Fatima promised to book the flights and pay the airfare. Before ringing off, she expressed her heartfelt gratitude to her niece and told her she would apprise Alia of the good news immediately.

Asiya felt gratified by the call. After all of the help her aunt had always given her, she was finally in a position to return the favor. She loved Alia like a sister and was thrilled that she would be able to see her again soon. She vowed to herself to help Alia find a permanent job in Boston.

The next morning, Asiya began scouring the classified ads, searching for any nursing positions. Each morning she would write the phone numbers and addresses in a small notebook and spend a few hours each day telephoning to inquire about how to apply for the listings. After a week, she had six applications ready for Alia to fill out. Some were permanent jobs and some were per diem assignments, but all were more lucrative than what Alia could earn in Israel. Also, Asiya's unspoken motivation was that working in Boston would be much safer for her cousin than working in Israel, and especially in Gaza. Even though she suffered a serious injury, Alia had a lucky break. She might not survive another mortar attack

***

Jack Abraham sat in the airport in Lagos, Nigeria awaiting the boarding call for British Airways flight 74, his overnight flight to London. As he waited, he scanned the *Animal Haven* website on his laptop. For two months he had been blogging about the welfare of mountain gorillas, corresponding with like-minded nature lovers on the website he had created. Jack was seeking to protect the animals he loved by using his IT skills to best advantage. As he waited in the noisy, crowded airport, he mulled over how he could continue his advocacy for the gorillas once he took up his new job in Rhode Island. In two days, he would be back on US soil, pursuing a new career.

A sonorous English-accented female voice announced over the loudspeaker that BA74 would now begin boarding. Jack closed his laptop, placed it back in its black leather case, and queued up with the other passengers. As he looked over the group of fellow travelers, he realized how much he would miss the variety of images in Nigeria. Women in colorful traditional garb jostled against sleek European businessmen in Armani suits; tiny children hugged their mothers' ankles, surveying the crowd around them with beautiful large dark brown eyes; a group of Canadian high-school students shouldered their *Roots* backpacks and laughed at one another's comments.

Once on board, Jack settled into his assigned aisle seat and strapped himself in. He watched the Canadian students as they stashed their gear into the overhead compartments and then settled as a noisy group into the middle of the economy section next to him. When a tall young black man asked Jack if the middle seat next to him was 42E, Jack nodded and assumed that he was also one of the Canadian students. Jack unbuckled and stood up, allowing the lanky young man to slide into the seat next to him. As he did, Jack noticed that the man was holding a Nigerian passport. He thought this odd, as the man's English pronunciation sounded North American.

Jack introduced himself and held out his hand for the man to shake. The young man smiled, shook his hand and introduced himself as Olufemi Abiola, qualifying it with the statement, "But everyone just calls me Femi."

Jack had never heard the name before and asked if it had any meaning. Smiling, Femi answered, "Yes, it means 'God loves me'."

Jack smiled and responded, "A good name. It looks as if we have passengers representing the entire United Nations on board."

Femi laughed. "It is always this way on the London-bound flight. I take it at least two times a year when I return from visiting my parents in Lagos. I am studying at Boston University and my brother is at Boston College, so we both travel back and forth frequently. Actually, I come more often, because he's their big basketball star there, so it isn't as easy for him to get away."

The two seatmates heard the tremendous roar of the powerful engines and sat in silence as the huge 747 surged forward on the runway and lifted effortlessly into the air, soon soaring high above Jack's beloved Africa.

The flight was smooth and uneventful, or as the petite blond flight attendant laughingly stated, "A real tranquil flight today, just as I like it. No spilled coffee on this flight."

As the plane began its descent to Heathrow, Jack and Femi leaned over and looked out the window. Although partially obscured by cloud cover, they could see the orderly green fields of Surrey and then London's ever-encroaching urban sprawl. Soon they saw what looked like airport hangars, the large grey buildings forming a demarcation line that defined the enormous airport. The landing gear engaged, and the plane floated down silently until, with their usual thud of safety, the wheels scraped the tarmac. Jack realized at that moment that this was the first time he'd been in London in fifteen years.

After deplaning, Jack and Femi walked together down the stark, brightly-lit and seemingly never-ending corridor to the arrival area. Jack had forgotten how busy and huge Heathrow really was. Even now, at 5:30 in the morning, the airport was alive with the frenetic activity of multiple overseas arrivals.

They walked together out to the main concourse and sought the check-in desk for their connecting flight to Boston. Both were on BA213, the 11:25 flight. They decided to have breakfast together. Jack was astounded by the food choices that now presented themselves at Heathrow, and he thought to himself that bagels and pizza were taking over the world.

The two settled into a booth at a cafeteria style eatery at the northern end of the concourse, savoring cups of hot coffee and tolerating the tepid bacon and eggs. Munching on buttered toast, Jack surveyed the airport through the large window.

"Wow, this place has grown like crazy since the last time I was here. It still feels the same – orderly but hectic, but it sure doesn't look the same."

Femi chuckled, "Yeah, Heathrow just gets bigger every year. Sometimes I think that soon the airport will be larger than the city!"

Jack and Femi chatted in a relaxed manner over several cups of coffee and tea respectively, with Jack relishing the invigorating power of the caffeine. As Femi spoke, Jack realized how much a citizen of the world the young man truly was. Femi described his studies at Boston University and told Jack about his dormitory and his roommate, Tom Gill. A born story-teller, he told Jack funny vignettes Tom had shared with him about his work as a waiter at a restaurant named *Bettina's* in Boston's North End. Femi also promised to treat Jack to lunch there in the near future.

As Jack listened to Femi, he wondered about his own son, Dafidi. Was he still in Kansas with Peggy? Would he possibly be able to see him soon? Jack's exhausted mind wandered as the young man spoke, and he completely missed Femi's brief mention of another waiter at *Bettina's* named 'Daf'', with whom Tom had shared some hilarious moments.

The pair finally left the cafeteria and wandered aimlessly down the concourse, stopping to buy newspapers and magazines for the flight to Boston. They still had three hours before the flight, so they decided to go outside and walk around to get some fresh air. As they stepped outside, they felt the warmth of the weak morning sun as it appeared briefly through fast moving clouds, and they were astounded to feel the humidity. It would be an incredibly hot day later that afternoon, but they would already be soaring high above the Atlantic by the time the sticky dampness of a typical English summer took hold.

Returning to Terminal 3, they were refreshed by the blast of air conditioning as the wide sliding glass entry doors parted. Each took turns watching the carry-on luggage as they went in turn to the men's room to freshen up and change clothes. Despite having just met, Jack instinctively trusted Femi, and the young man felt likewise. Femi also sensed something familiar in Jack but couldn't put his finger on what it was. It felt as if he had met him before or had met someone who looked like him.

The pair then went through security into the international passengers' concourse and spent some time perusing the duty-free shops. Femi bought a T-shirt for his brother and some Earl Grey tea. Jack enjoyed perusing the books at W.H. Smith and bought a mystery and two historical novels. As he was paying for these, he heard the boarding call for BA213 over the loudspeaker. He thanked the cashier and met up with Femi a few feet away, and they began walking down another long corridor to the boarding gate.

The 747 touched down smoothly at Logan Airport and rolled noisily along the runway until the reverse thrusters kicked in to bring it to a halt. Jack remained in his seat as other passengers immediately got up and opened the overhead bins, ignoring the flight attendants' safety warnings. His mind was tired and his thoughts were jumbled. He was having a hard time wrapping his mind around the immediacy of the change in his life this arrival would bring.

Femi sat calmly at his side, yawning and rubbing his eyes. He had fallen asleep after the meal service and had slept soundly for the last two hours of the flight. He finally turned to Jack and asked, "Do you have a pen so I can give you my phone number and address?"

Jack fished in his jacket pocket and brought out a small Filofax organizer and a pen. He handed these to Femi and asked him to write his contact information in the address section. Taking another pen out of his shirt pocket, Jack wrote down his new address in Providence, Rhode Island, and apologized for not yet knowing his new phone number. He did, however, give Femi his email address and told him to email him in the next few days so he could respond and send him the phone information.

Soon both were shaking hands outside the terminal, as Jack boarded the bus that would take him to Providence. Femi waited with him to make certain Jack caught the correct bus. As the bus drove off, Jack waved to the smiling young man and thought how nice it had been to spend time with someone of his own son's age.

***

Jack got home from a grueling day at his new office. He opened the refrigerator, took out a bottle of beer, and walked back out into the living room and over to his small glass-topped desk. Sitting down and taking a swig of Heineken, he turned on his laptop and went immediately to his email, hoping for a message from one particular person. *Sweetpea@zoonewengland.org* had been a regular contributor to the Animal Haven blog which Jack also frequented. She had been routinely corresponding with him for the past four weeks. He found the emails to be knowledgeable, informative and representing an animal rights activist with a world view acutely similar to his own. Because of the email address, he assumed the messages were from a young woman. However, the breadth of knowledge shown in her comments seemed to be that of an older person. Neither person had divulged any personal information, knowing too well how rampant deceit was on the Internet. Jack's email address, *gorrillaguru@hotmail.com*, could have been that of anyone of either gender.

Today's message from *Sweetpea* was about an upcoming lecture in Boston, to be held in late September. In it, she asked if *gorillaguru* was attending it or had heard the speaker before. Jack had never heard of the speaker, but thought the lecture topic, *Protecting the Protectors: Game Wardens who Monitor Mountain Gorillas at Risk in the Democratic Republic of Atanapa*, sounded interesting. He emailed back his thanks for apprising him of the lecture and said that he would definitely try to get a ticket. A few moments later he sent another email to *Sweetpea* saying that it would be nice to meet his email buddy in person at the lecture.

Peggy sat in her office at the zoo and read the two messages from *gorillaguru*. It was late in the afternoon, and she had been relaxing at her cluttered desk after work with a mug of tea, before forcing herself to brave the long commute home. She enjoyed their ongoing email discussions of a few weeks and was looking forward to more in the future. Now, however, she felt apprehensive. Who was *gorrilaguru*? She had no idea, even though in some ways she felt highly attuned to his or her way of thinking about the animals whose welfare she sought to protect. She had encountered *gorillaguru* the first time on the *Animal Haven* blog. Should she be courageous and offer to meet? After all, the lecture was to be held in a well-known theatre and would be completely safe. She sipped her tea and carefully considered how best to word her response.

Jack sat back in his chair and swallowed another mouthful of ale. He sighed and then shook his head and chuckled at his *hutzpah* in asking *Sweetpea* to meet him at the lecture. In his mind he saw *Sweetpea* as an attractive woman in her early thirties. Despite this vision, for all he knew, she could be a 90 year old man or a 10 year-old kid. What was he thinking?

Two minutes passed and then a message from Sweetpea appeared. "Would enjoy meeting in person. Why don't we meet at a nearby restaurant and have lunch before the lecture? I know a nice Italian place named Bettina's in the North End. We could easily walk to the theatre from there. How about meeting at noon since the lecture begins at 2:00 pm?"

Jack noticed that there was still no personal data in the email. He assumed that *Sweetpea* was savvy enough to know how to preserve one's safety on the Internet. He respected this.

He emailed back, "Sounds good. I'll see you at noon on Saturday, September 26th. Please email me directions."

Sweetpea read Jack's message and thought that it made it much easier that *gorillaguru* hadn't identified his or her identity by name or physical description. This way both of the parties would be assured anonymity if they sensed something uncomfortable about the meeting.

Peggy sent back a final note with directions to the restaurant from Interstate 93, saying simply "I hope these directions are clear. As I only know that you are located somewhere in New England, I figured that I-93 might be accessible from whatever route you'll be taking. When you get to Bettina's, just tell the waiter you're meeting 'the goofy zoo person.' That way, he'll be certain to seat you at to the right table.

Jack laughed. Now he was to speak in code! He emailed back, *Will do. See you then. Hope the food's good. Ciao!"*

Peggy read the last email and smiled. She put down her empty mug, logged off the computer and picked up her briefcase. Walking out of the office with a smile still on her face, she thought that, for once at least, she had something interesting to look forward to besides work.

Jack logged off his laptop and walked back to the kitchen. He put the beer bottle in the recycle bin, and opened the fridge, trying to find something appetizing for dinner. Giving up in despair, he decided to go out for Chinese food. Cooking had never been his strong suit.

As he drove to a small local Szechuan restaurant, he kept thinking that he had heard the name of the restaurant *Sweetpea* had suggested somewhere before. He just couldn't remember where. *Bettina's* rang a bell, but the bell was mute for the moment.

That same night, Tom Gill answered the telephone at *Bettina's* and was surprised to hear Dafidi's mother on the line. She told Tom about agreeing to attend the lecture with her email friend and explained about asking the person to use a code name instead of her real name when asking to be seated with her. Tom listened attentively and understood completely. If the person who asked him for the "*goofy zoo person*" was scary looking or odd, he or another waiter on duty could simply say that the "zoo person" hadn't shown up after all. That way, Peggy was totally safe.

When Tom returned to the dorm that night, he found Femi's huge green suitcase parked by his roommate's desk. Soon the door opened, and Femi stepped into the small room holding two large white paper bags from McDonald's. He grinned at Tom and held one out to him. Tom took it and opening it, sniffed pure cholesterol.

Femi laughed and said, "I've been craving burgers and fries for three days. Must have been the deprivation caused by airline food."

Tom reached into his bag and taking out some fries, munched happily. After swallowing, he asked, "So how were the senior Abiolas? Is everything good at the old country?"

Femi nodded. "Yeah, Mom and Dad are doing well and are as crazy as ever. Dad has put BC basketball posters all over his office, so that everywhere you look you see Rin's face staring back. It was kind of unnerving – like having clones of my brother everywhere."

Tom laughed. "Hey, he's on TV most nights here, so maybe he really has been cloned. The sportscasters can't get enough of him. It should be interesting once Dafidi and Yosha are on the team with him. Maybe they'll steal some of the limelight."

Femi responded, "I sure hope so. His head is getting bigger by the day."

The two young men sat up talking late into the night. Femi told Tom about his father's newest projects in Lagos and about the new AIDS clinic where his mother was doing volunteer work. He also told Tom about the nice businessman named Jack whom he met on the plane. According to Femi, this guy was a computer whiz and an animal lover. Femi told Tom that he suggested they meet some time for lunch at *Bettina's*, so maybe Tom would get to meet him. Femi, with his typical realism, also said that one never knew if one would ever actually see travel acquaintances again, despite agreeing to meet. He added that he hoped to meet Jack again, because he really liked him and thought he might be lonely after moving so far around the world.

Tom told Femi about the funny telephone call from Dafidi's mother and jokingly remarked that maybe she was actually dating again. Femi responded that if she was into dating, he would like to introduce her to Jack since, from what Tom had said, they sounded as if they were both about the same age and both were avid animal lovers. Yawning with fatigue and jet lag, Femi finally put a halt to the conversation and turned off the light in the common area and waved goodnight to Tom as he retreated to his own room. As he threw the greasy hamburger bags into the trash, Tom thought how nice it was to have Femi back. It had been lonely coming back to the dorm after work to the silent suite of rooms.

***

Alia cleared customs and walked out to the concourse at Logan Airport. She saw Asiya waving frantically to her and she waved back, grinning. The two cousins both walked swiftly towards one another and embraced. Tears rolled down Alia's cheeks as she said in Arabic, "I never thought that I would ever see you again. God is good to us, Asiya. We must never leave each other again, inshallah."

Asiya was crying too. "I am so happy you are here! We must hurry. Maroun and Abdul are in the car outside waiting for us. You won't believe how Abdul has grown since you last saw him." With that, Asiya pulled the trolley laden with Alia's baggage, and the two began walking to the sliding glass exit doors. As soon as they exited the terminal, Alia saw Maroun waving at her from the passenger window of a small Toyota.

Asiya guided Alia to the car, and they arrived just as Maroun was opening the trunk. He hugged his wife's cousin briefly and then quickly put her bags inside the crowded compartment and closed the lid. Opening the back door nearest the curb, he motioned for Alia to sit in the back seat and to put on the seat belt. Asiya went around the car and slid into the other back seat.

Alia looked at the car's driver with surprise and then burst out laughing. She asked, "Could our handsome young driver be the child I last saw in Haifa?"

Turning around and smiling at Alia, Abdul beamed with pride and said, "This is my car, aunt Alia, and although I don't think I'm handsome, yes, I am the same person you last saw in Haifa as a child."

Alia smiled the entire time they drove back to Brookline. She looked out of the window curiously, seeing architecture that was so unlike that to which she was accustomed. Everything about Boston seemed unique. Even the light seemed different. She had read about painters seeking northern light because it had a different quality, and now she realized it must be true.

Once they arrived at the house and Asiya had settled her cousin into the guest room, Alia began to truly relax. She said something to Asiya that made the older woman wince. "If you wake up at night and hear me thrashing around and speaking in Arabic, it is because of the nightmares. I still sometimes dream of the bombs falling everywhere. I just hope I don't wake you very often. It is so silent and peaceful here, maybe I won't have the nightmares anymore."

Asiya brought Alia out to the garden, and she sat outside with Maroun and Abdul and relaxed in the balmy night air while her hostess prepared dinner. Maroun told her not to even think of offering to assist with the meal, as he knew all too well how jet lag could catch up with anyone. He then went on to tell her about his job and about all the travel it entailed. Finally, Asiya brought out a hearty meal of roast lamb and fresh summer vegetables. By the time Alia finished her dinner, she was rubbing her eyes and yawning, barely able to stay awake. She told Maroun that he was right about jet lag, and she apologized for begging to be allowed to go to bed so early.

Asiya went with Alia and turned down the bedcovers while her cousin was in the bathroom showering. Practically stumbling from exhaustion, Alia stepped into the bedroom and collapsed on the bed. Stifling another yawn, she turned to Asiya and said, "I love you, my dearest cousin. You have saved my life." With that, she turned on her side and was soon fast asleep. Asiya walked over and drawing the blanket over Alia's shoulders, she leaned down, kissed the top of her head and murmured, "Sweet dreams, tonight, little cousin. You are safe."

Abdul went up to his bedroom and switched on the table lamp by his bed. He flopped onto the dark blue bedspread and putting his hands behind his head, leaned back on the pillows and closed his eyes. Today had been an awakening of sorts for the young man. He realized for the first time that he was no longer a child, but was now a young adult. He was no longer in high school but would soon be at Boston

College, studying for what would be his "real life."

Seeing Alia had awakened old childhood memories. He remembered her mother, whom he always called 'Auntie Fimi.' Now that he was an adult, he would be required by his culture to use her full name, Fatima. It was difficult to wrap his head around all the changes that had happened so suddenly: He would move out and live at BC; Alia would live with his parents while she looked for a nursing position; he and Dafidi would hopefully become basketball stars at BC. It was a lot to think about, and he suddenly felt overwhelmed and extremely tired. He slipped into a dreamless sleep while the bedside light still illuminated his room. His mother saw the light under his bedroom door and heard Abdul snoring. She opened the door silently and looked in. Her son was fast asleep, so she tiptoed in and turned off the light. As she exited the room, she felt the winds of change occurring too.

***

The next morning, Abdul left the house early to go to West End House. He was coaching older boys today for the first time, and he needed to warm up. When he arrived at the club, Miriam called him into her office for a few minutes.

"Abdul, I just want to let you know that the kids you'll be coaching today are a bit rough. If any of them gives you a bad time, let one of us know, okay?"

Abdul smiled and rolled his eyes expressively. He asked, "And how rough are they? It sounds as if I am being sent to a den to coach or something."

Miriam laughed. "Well, not quite that bad, but they can come across as threatening. Just banter back with them and don't take any verbal abuse. Remember that you are the one in charge, even if they might be a head taller than you are."

"Oh great – now I'm coaching giants!"

Miriam laughed again and said, "Well, not quite, but maybe in the future!"

Abdul left Miriam's office and walked slowly to the basketball courts. When he got there, a few tall young men were already playing one-on-one. They looked him over but didn't greet him. Abdul struggled to think of an effective opening statement so he could grab their attention.

Finally, he shouted, "Okay, do you want to be coached by the next star player at BC or not?"

One tall young man walked up to Abdul and lifted his hand in a high-five gesture. Abdul reached up and touched the boy's palm and knew in that instant that these kids would be fine. They might even challenge him to become a better player himself.

Arriving home that night, Abdul felt drained. He wandered into the kitchen and found his mother sitting at the breakfast bar, looking through a cookbook. She looked up as he came into the room and smiled at him. "So, how did it go today? You look exhausted!"

Abdul nodded and sat down wearily on the stool next to her. He briefly noted that the cookbook was open at a recipe for Pasta Primavera, so he asked his mother, "Are we having Italian tonight? I'm starving."

Asiya reached over and put her arm around his shoulders. "Honey, you look really beat. Dinner won't be for at least an hour, so why don't you go take a hot shower and lie down for a while. I'll call you when it's ready."

He nodded. "Sounds good. My back is aching, and I really need a shower. Just don't forget to wake me when dinner's ready, okay?"

Asiya laughed. "As if I have ever deprived you of food!"

Abdul grinned at his mother, turned and walked slowly out of the room, massaging his sore back with one hand as he did so, and thinking he would have to remember to take some aspirin before dinner.

At dinner that night, Alia told the family about her plans for the following day. She had an interview in the morning at Beth Israel Deaconess Medical Center for a position in the neo-natal unit. She was excited at the prospect, but also a bit fearful. "What if my qualifications aren't good enough? What if I become nervous and babble? What if…"

At that point, Asiya cut her off in mid-sentence. "Alia, you are highly qualified, and your skills have been tested under extremely stressful circumstances. Your references are impeccable, and I've never heard you babble in my life – except maybe tonight. You'll do fine."

Alia smiled at her cousin and said, "Thank you for your unflinching support. I'll try to remember your words tomorrow while I'm being interviewed."

As the family continued eating, Abdul told them about coaching the older boys that day. He expressed amazement at their skill and said he really had to play hard to keep up with them. He said the only two things they lacked were patience and a deeper knowledge of specific plays. He admitted that he was exactly the same way a few years before – impatient to score a basket and complacent about relying on plays he knew well and could execute effectively.

Maroun and Abdul talked sports for the remainder of the meal, while Alia and Asiya discussed the merits of the various job interviews that had been arranged. As Asiya brought in homemade tiramisu for dessert, Alia exclaimed that she had never been fed this much and would probably soon be too fat for her new interview suits. Asiya, obviously flattered, grinned from ear to ear.

The next morning, Asiya drove Alia to Beth Israel Deaconess Medical Center, negotiating the heavy traffic in the Longwood Medical area and struggling to find a place to park. She waited in the hospital café while Alia met with the director of the neo-natal unit. Asiya thought that the interview was taking a long time, as she sipped her coffee and treated herself to a forbidden secret pleasure – a glazed donut. Why, she wondered to herself, did hospital cafeterias serve such unhealthy food?

When Alia finally returned, it was obvious by her demeanor that the interview went well. As she sat down next to Asiya, the grin on her face and the twinkle in her eyes said it all. Excitedly, she told Asiya about how friendly and kind the director had been and how impressed he seemed with the fact that she worked for Médecins Sans Frontières in Gaza. He was astounded when she told him about the rocket attack that wounded her, and he commended her on her courage. After they talked for awhile, he took her on a tour of the neo-natal intensive care unit and introduced her to many of the nurses. At the end of the interview, he offered her the position for what seemed to her an astronomical sum of money. She wanted to accept the job immediately, but felt that she must ask Asiya for her opinion first. Therefore, she told the director she would telephone him the following morning with her decision.

Asiya was exhilarated to hear the good news. She also remembered something as Alia was speaking and asked her cousin, "Did you happen to meet a nurse named Tonya Johnson? One of Abdul's friend's mother works as a nurse in the neo-natal intensive care unit here."

Alia nodded. "Yes, she was absolutely lovely. She made me feel very welcome and she introduced me to two other nurses. Everyone was so nice."

Asiya's heart was happy for her cousin. "Alia, I think you should take this job. I just feel it is the right one and that you'll be happy here. That's my advice, for what it's worth."

Alia grinned. "I, too, knew in my heart it was the right place for me. I will be happy here. I can just feel it."

The cousins walked arm in arm to the multi-level car park and drove home in a happy daze. Alia was safe, and she would be happy after all. Asiya's silent prayers were answered, and she thanked God profusely as she negotiated the frenzied traffic.

Chapter 15
Boston College

August ended on an unhappy note. Abdul and Dafidi were saddened by the death of Senator Edward Kennedy two weeks after that of his sister Eunice Kennedy Shriver. Dafidi remarked, "He was the champion of the underprivileged, the poor, and the disadvantaged."

Abdul added, "And she was a visionary who made champions of people with disabilities or special needs. May they both rest in peace."

As September approached, the weather in Boston became glorious. The cloying humidity and clouds of late August gave way to bright sunny days with clear blue skies and dry, cool nights. Dafidi, Abdul and their regular group played basketball outside late into the night, reveling in the perfect weather. It was common for their games to break up near midnight.

Three days before their official move-in date to the dormitory, they all decided to celebrate. Asiya cooked a huge meal for Yosha, LeShawn, Mike, Abdul and Dafidi. The group sat outside in the garden and munched happily before beginning their nightly game. As they sat around eating and talking, Yosha told them he had heard through the grapevine that Jason Kelly would be working at one of the BC dorms. Evidently, he would be doing maintenance part-time in exchange for a room in Vouté Hall. The others couldn't believe their ears – Vouté was known as being the dorm where foreign language majors and students from overseas lived. How in heaven's name did Jason land there, when they all knew he was such a bigot? LeShawn commented, saying what they were all secretly thinking, "This should be interesting! Just wait until Jason shoots his mouth off."

The following day, Abdul and Dafidi drove to *Target* in Watertown, to buy last minute necessities for their dorm room. Abdul wanted a popcorn maker, and Dafidi insisted they needed an electric kettle and a French press coffee pot. He had become obsessed to strong coffee while working at *Bettina's* and wanted to make the same kind of brew he drank there. He explained to Abdul that this was his one luxury and that the caffeine burst each morning would help him focus better on his studies. Abdul just laughed and responded that Daf would become even more hyper than he already was. They headed back to Brookline with their "necessities" and separated for the afternoon as each began packing boxes for the move to BC.

Peggy came home from work that night to find six large, neatly labeled boxes stacked by the front door. She called to Daf to remind him that they needed to go to the appliance store to pick up the small refrigerator and microwave BC mandated each dorm room to have. Dafidi opened his bedroom door, showing the turmoil left behind by his packing. Peggy laughed and exclaimed, "It looks as if Hurricane Dafidi blew through your room. Come on, let's go pick up the fridge and then go out to dinner somewhere afterwards. I can't face cleaning up that mess tonight. I'm just too tired."

"It's okay, Mom. I'll clean it all up in the morning. When I move, the room will be immaculate. I promise."

Peggy smiled adoringly at her son and held her tongue. She knew only too well what 'immaculate' meant to an 18 year-old boy. Oh well, she would let him do his best, and then she'd clean the room more thoroughly once he was settled in at BC.

Motioning with her hand for Dafidi to follow her, Peggy began walking towards the front door and said, "Come on. I'm hungry and the appliance store closes at seven. Let's get going."

Over dinner at a new Thai restaurant that neither had tried before, Dafidi told his mother about the rumor that Jason was going to work in Vouté Hall. Peggy listened attentively and responded that maybe the job was exactly what Jason needed. She said that her reasoning was that he would be exposed to students from all over the world and would have to restrain himself from saying anything bigoted, if he were to keep his job. She thought it would force him to become more controlled and maybe, just maybe, he would begin to see that people everywhere were really the same deep down. She just hoped he didn't explode in one of his rages and lose the job, because she suspected he really needed it in order to live on campus.

Dafidi listened to his mother and understood her viewpoint. As much as he didn't care about Jason, he knew that the other boy's life was difficult and that it would be a financial strain for Jason to attend BC. Daf just hoped that Jason would grow out of his bursts of anger once he was in college. He didn't look forward to possibly bearing the brunt of Jason's rage during a televised BC basketball game.

After dinner, Daf and his mother drove home and sat up long into the night discussing the logistics of the move to the dorm. Luckily, it would take place on a Saturday, so Peggy wouldn't have to worry about fitting it in around her work schedule. However, what made it difficult was that they would have to make multiple trips because the Subaru just wasn't large enough to carry all of Dafidi's gear at once. They both knew that parking near the dormitory would be hard to find, so Daf was anticipating carrying the large boxes a fairly long distance. He hoped that the cooler, dry weather would hold. He dreaded moving on a hot, humid day.

As it turned out, the weather cooperated, and Saturday was breezy and beautiful, with fluffy white clouds and bright sunshine. Abdul drove to the Abrahams' apartment early in the morning and brought them coffee and donuts. Dafidi laughed when he opened the door and saw Abdul standing there in his sweats holding two enormous *Dunkin' Donuts* bags. Abdul thrust them into Dafidi's hands and said, "My friend, you and I are about to embark on one of life's greatest journeys. I just thought you could use a good send-off."

Dafidi gestured to Abdul to enter the apartment, and turning towards Peggy, who was standing in the kitchen doorway, he laughingly announced, "Hey, Mom. The King of Donuts has graciously blessed us with his company. Come and get some caffeine and cholesterol."

Peggy grinned back at the two boys, and soon the three were happily munching donuts and sipping coffee. Between bites, they talked about the impending move. Abdul was just as excited as Dafidi and both couldn't wait to get going. Peggy recognized their eagerness and putting down her cup, she said, "Okay, guys. Time to get moving. In a couple of hours you will be officially living on campus."

Abdul said he'd meet up with them in the parking lot at BC and he headed out to his car. Peggy and Daf each picked up a box and carried them to the elevator. Just as his mother was about to push the Parking Lot Level 2 button, Daf stopped her and ran back inside the apartment to grab the large plastic Target bag that held his precious coffeemaker and kettle. He got back in the elevator and smiled mischievously, saying, "Just in case our caffeine level drops once we get there." Peggy just laughed and rolled her eyes.

xxx

Jason moved two heavy boxes from his bedroom into the living room. Mr. Manzano scheduled him to begin work at 4 pm, so he'd have to move these into his dorm room and then go directly downstairs to get his instructions from his new boss. He just hoped nobody was there when he dropped off the boxes. He didn't want to have to explain about his job.

Jason was loading the boxes into the back seat of Mary's car just as his mother was closing the front door and locking it. Once she made certain the locks were secure, she walked out and climbed into the driver's seat and turned on the ignition. As she did so, she turned to Jason and said something that surprised him.

"I am very proud of you today. You are beginning a new chapter of your life, and I hope it brings you happiness. Remember that I love you dearly and just want the best for you."

Jason couldn't respond. He felt choked up with emotion. He looked out the passenger window and remained silent. He didn't see the hurt on his mother's face, but had he done so, he would probably have cried. She thought he was denigrating her words. What she didn't know was how much they had really meant to the troubled boy. Silence engulfed the car.

As they finally drove onto the BC campus, Jason struggled to say something to his mother. Once Mary turned off the ignition and was sitting there looking out at all the other parents and children unloading their cars, he turned to his left and looking at her, and whispered, "I love you too, Mom. Thank you for being proud of me."

Mary couldn't believe her ears. She began weeping and reached awkwardly in her handbag to pull out a tissue. Jason reached over and put his left hand on her right wrist and held it briefly. When he removed it, she looked up at him and saw that he too was crying. He wiped his eyes on the back of his shirt sleeve and then opened the passenger door and got out. As she saw him standing for a moment in the sunlight, Mary realized that her son was now a man, no longer a child. He would have to find his own way in the world now. She said a silent but fervent prayer that he would succeed.

***

The first few weeks at BC flew by for the group of five friends. Dafidi had solicited Tom Gill's help in enlisting his roommate's brother,

Rinton Abiola, to take them all on a tour of the campus and to introduce them to the basketball coach Bo Khao, and the team members. Rin was the team's star player and captain, so the new freshmen immediately garnered caché from being in his company. Dafidi and Abdul practically worshipped Rin, knowing it would be a long shot for them to achieve the success he had won on the court. For his part, Rin was remarkably down to earth and friendly. He remembered how scared his younger brother, Femi, felt during his first few weeks at Boston University, so he tried to make the young men feel comfortable and relaxed. He succeeded, and by their second week, the group felt totally at home at their new school.

The hardest part for Abdul was trying to figure out how to get from class to class on time. All six of his classes met on Mondays, Wednesdays and Thursdays, with three in a row each day. Dafidi had researched how to do it more efficiently, so he had two or three hours between classes, even though they were on the same days as Abdul's.

By the time the third week rolled around, Abdul was exhausted. He was staying up into the wee hours studying because his classes and basketball practice took up all the daylight hours. Dafidi, on the other hand, managed his time in such a way that he could study during the breaks between classes, and this gave him more time to practice or just goof off. Ironically, it turned out that it was Abdul who was drinking most of the strong coffee Daf brewed each morning. Daf sometimes thought his best friend lived on coffee and acetaminophen.

Yosha, Mike and LeShawn would stop by some nights and the friends would play card and eat greasy pizza. They all thought dorm life was great.

Jason's life was totally different. He was taking six classes that all met three days a week, and he was working an alternating schedule of three weeknights one week and two weekend days the following week. Like Abdul, he was exhausted. His exhaustion soon triggered his temper, and he was reprimanded by the dorm's Resident Assistant for yelling at a foreign student about the smell of fish sauce that emanated from his room's trash can – trash that Jason had to pick up twice a week. The RA patiently explained to Jason that in Vietnam the fish sauce was a common part of the diet, and that the student felt more comfortable eating the type of food he was used to at home. Jason kept his mouth shut, but he regarded both the student and the RA as idiots.

Guillermo Manzano watched Jason carefully and reported back to Miriam Hernandez on a regular basis. She would frequently call Jason into her office after his coaching sessions at the boys' and girls' club, and during these sessions, she would ask him in a casual manner to tell her about his week at BC. What Jason didn't realize was that these weren't just friendly chats, he was actually receiving therapy. Miriam would listen to his complaints, smelly fish sauce among them, and would suggest he reframe the various occurrences and look at them differently. Jason listened to Miriam because she was one of the few people he really respected. Soon Jason began learning from her, even though he didn't realize it. Jason was changing.

Yosha didn't expect to like BC as much as he did. He loved the peaceful beauty of the suburban campus and its proximity to the Chestnut Hill Reservoir, where he liked to go running in the morning. The length of the path around the reservoir provided a perfect workout for him. Yosha also liked the ambience of the school, with its stone buildings and quiet elegance. Living with his aunt and uncle was fine. They didn't intrude on his privacy, and Aunt Rachel's cooking was magnificent.

Mike finally decided to veto attending Notre Dame, and he and LeShawn shared a dorm room at BC. Cathy Ramsay would send bags of junk food and homemade cookies back with Mike after his weekend visits home, so his and LeShawn's room soon became a haven for their friends. Tonya and Lester bought LeShawn a wide-screen High Definition TV, so game day became an excuse for everyone to congregate there. Life was good.

Dafidi was seeing Sara Mendelsohn. As neither had any significant spending money, they met on Thursday nights at a Jewish community center in Cambridge for folk dancing. Sara and Dafidi both loved to dance. Sara loved the history associated with Eastern European and Israeli folk dances, feeling as if it were part of her family's past. Dafidi just liked to feel his body moving in rhythm to the music. He lost himself in the movement and moved as one with the sound. After all he was "Master of the Universe" when he won the TV Dance Contest many years ago. Folk dancing was entirely new to him, but after the first awkward session, he began to look forward to the dances. He also looked forward to seeing Sara, whom he found intelligent and funny. Dafidi soon learned that she was extremely serious about her studies and had a multi-dimensional personality. One moment she could be quiet and studious, and at the dances, she could be energetic and boisterous. He loved everything about her, from her unruly hair to her freckled nose.

As the weeks went on, Abdul noticed that Dafidi was texting and calling Sara more and more. One night, he mentioned this to Daf, who smiled and said succinctly, "Sara makes me happy." Abdul just smiled calculatingly and changed the subject.

Rin Abiola was a dynamo on the basketball court. He exploded with power and skill. No wonder he was the darling of the sports media.

Dafidi and Yosha sat on the bench and stared at him in awe. Practice was going great, but they both felt they could learn so much more from just watching Rin in action. Sometimes Rin's brother, Femi, would join them on the bench. He looked so much like his older brother, but the two had very different personalities. Rin was much more outgoing and confident, whereas Femi was more low-key and quiet. Both were polite and friendly, and both had a wickedly dry sense of humor.

Dafidi instantly took to Femi, and they soon became friends. Femi would sometimes accompany Sara on the T from BU when she came to folk dancing, and he would join them in the fun and dance vigorously. Sara and Femi had one class together, The Economics of Sustainability, and both were passionate about environmental causes. Sara was also trying to fix Femi up with her roommate, a Brazilian girl who was brilliant and beautiful but incredibly shy.

One night at folk dancing, Femi's arrival preceded that of Sara. When Dafidi asked him why they hadn't come together, Femi just shrugged and said that Sara had mentioned that she might bring someone with her and that they might be a bit late. When Sara finally appeared, she was speaking to a petite girl with incredibly shiny long black hair. Sara introduced her as Marta Barbosa. As Marta turned to say hello, Femi was so dumbstruck by Marta's beauty, he could barely stammer a greeting.

The first thought that went through Dafidi's mind was that Marta would be the perfect model for a painting of a saint. Marta had a luminous, other-worldly quality to her. She lit up a room when she entered, but she was totally unaware of her beauty. It was as if light followed her, much as it did in Renaissance era paintings of saints Dafidi saw in museums.

Once the dancing began, the four students relaxed and Femi began enjoying himself immensely. Soon he and Marta were routinely joining Daf and Sara at the dances. Daf thought it ironic that a Nigerian and a Brazilian would find a common interest in Eastern European and Israeli folk dancing. It just proved his point that everyone in the world was really alike.

Chapter 16
The Encounter

Peggy arrived at *Bettina's* just after 11 am on September 26th, seeking to speak to Tom Gill before *gorillaguru* showed up. She was glad that Dafidi was in school and no longer worked there, as she felt a bit embarrassed to have made a lunch date over the Internet. When she spoke to him on the phone, she swore Tom to secrecy, just in case. She kept reminding herself that at her age, there was virtually no opportunity to date, so she shouldn't get her hopes up. However, her hopes wouldn't be kept down, and she kept daydreaming about *gorillaguru* turning out to be a handsome and brave combination of Indiana Jones and George Clooney. Sighing, she shook her head at these thoughts and thought how insipid they seemed.

Tom saw Peggy sit down at a table by the front window and waved to her from the kitchen. She smiled and waved back and then hung her purse on the back of her chair and pulled the chair closer to the table. Afterwards, she sat looking out of the window, trying to evaluate people walking by to see if they might be her lunch partner.

As she was engrossed in watching a tour guide lead a group of Japanese tourists across the street outside, Tom came up to the table and placed a large basket of fresh bread down on it. Peggy turned around to speak to him and they talked for a few minutes before he went back to the kitchen and returned with a small glass of red wine.

Peggy smiled, saying, "I know I must seem to be a coward, Tom, but I've never arranged a meeting over the Internet before. I'm actually a bit scared. What if *gorillaguru* is a predator?"

Tom laughed. "Don't worry, Mrs. Abraham. *Bettina's* isn't known for being a gangster hangout or anything. If your correspondent turns out to look even remotely rough, I'll just say you never showed up. Not to worry."

Peggy responded, "You're the best, Tom. Now go back to the people at the other tables and ignore me. I'll sit here patiently until you let me know one way or the other."

Tom returned to his duties and Peggy sat there sipping wine and occasionally taking a small bite of the aromatic focaccia bread from the basket. At 12:05 she got up and went to the ladies' room. While she was there combing her hair and re-doing her lipstick, a tall, middle-aged man with grey hair opened the door to *Bettina's* and looked around him inquisitively.

Tom saw the newcomer and walked over to him. "How many will be in your party, Sir?"

Jack Abraham responded, "I'm meeting another person here. This might sound strange, but the person I'm meeting said to ask for 'the goofy zoo person'. Does that make any sense to you?"

Tom looked the stranger over carefully. The man was dressed conservatively and looked like what he was, a boring businessman. There was nothing at all threatening in his appearance or manner. Just then, Tom noticed that Peggy's table was empty, and he assumed correctly that she was in the ladies' room.

Taking a deep breath, Tom Gill made a snap decision based purely on gut instinct.

"Come this way, Sir. Your party is seated by the front window and will be returning to the table in a few minutes."

Peggy put her lipstick back in her purse and gave herself a mental pep talk. She took one last look in the mirror and turning, opened the ladies' room door and stepped back into the small corridor adjacent to the kitchen. She saw Tom approaching her with a smile. He stopped and said, "Show's on. The guy looks nice and normal. Have fun!"

Peggy was so nervous, she couldn't bring herself to look across the room at the table by the window. She walked across the small restaurant, all the while keeping her head down and looking at the floor in front of her. When she finally arrived at the table she looked up and gasped in shock when she recognized Jack. He was looking out the window as she approached, but then suddenly turned and looked directly at her. His eyes betrayed his surprise. Neither of them spoke.

Watching from the kitchen, Tom witnessed the meeting and immediately knew that something was wrong. He grabbed two menus and walked quickly to the front table, where Peggy was still standing frozen like a statue. Tom sought to bring normality to the situation, and pulling out her chair, said formally, "Please sit down and make yourself, comfortable, ma'am. Here are your menus."

Peggy sat down like an automaton. As soon as she was seated, Tom thrust a menu in each of their hands and retreated to the kitchen where he poured two glasses of water and returned with them to the table, from which an almost palpable sense of anxiety emanated. Tom had no idea what else to do.

It was Jack who finally defused the situation. He sighed and said to Tom, "Please bring us a bottle of Chianti. We'll order in a few minutes."

Peggy couldn't believe her ears. Jack was acting as if everything was totally normal. She was sitting there struggling not to hyperventilate from stress, and he was as relaxed as a sleeping cat.

When Tom appeared with the Chianti, Jack placed their order without even consulting with Peggy. After Tom left the table, Jack looked across at Peggy and said bluntly, "Well, we certainly had no idea we were going to meet up with each other. Let's be adults and have a decent lunch. I don't know about you, but I had to drive a long way to get here, and I'm starving. Also, if you don't mind me saying this, you look extremely well. Life must be agreeing with you."

Peggy lifted her head and looked in Jack's eyes. She noticed how tired he looked. She had to find something to say – something neutral. Finally, she said in a muted tone, "I like Boston. I have a good job and Dafidi is happy here."

Jack's face almost crumpled at the sound of his son's name. He struggled to get the next words out. "How is Dafidi? Is he still always dancing around? Does he still follow basketball on television? It has been a long time."

Peggy's heart went out to her estranged husband. Despite their many personal differences, she knew that Jack loved Dafidi dearly. When she and Daf lived in Kansas, Jack would send cards and gifts to Dafidi for every Christmas and birthday. However, when she decided to accept the job in Boston, she purposely decided to not divulge their new address to Jack. Now she felt guilty and deceptive.

Before Peggy could answer Jack's questions, Tom returned to the table and as he put her salad down on the table, he gave Peggy a look that silently asked '*is everything okay?*' Peggy nodded discreetly.

Although she felt as if she had a lump in her throat, Peggy began eating her salad. Jack couldn't stand the silence and sought to fill it with a description of his new company and its merits. When Peggy still didn't respond, he went on to tell her about the young man he met on the flight from Lagos to London. Peggy almost choked on her lettuce when Jack mentioned that the boy's name was Femi Abiola. Putting her fork down on the plate and coughing into her napkin, she finally spoke.

"Does he have a brother named Rinton?"

Jack was surprised at her words, and nodded in the affirmative.

Peggy put her left hand to her temple and resting it there, shook her head and said, "This is just far too much to absorb. Rinton Abiola is on the same basketball team as Dafidi. They both attend Boston College. On top of that, our waiter Tom Gill, is Femi's roommate at BU."

Jack was equally astounded. How could all of these bizarre coincidences have occurred? He sat there in shock, trying to wrap his head around the situation. What he finally voiced surprised Peggy.

"All I can think is that, for some reason, God wants me to see you and Dafidi again. This meeting was serendipitous. I had no idea who Femi Abiola was, and I could tell from your face when you first saw me today that you had no idea that I was to be your lunch date. This entire situation has occurred spontaneously and beyond our control. What we do about it now, however, is what is important in the long run."

Peggy sipped her wine and nodded, all the while looking down at the table and not at Jack. She looked distressed. A multitude of questions was racing through her mind: What should she do? How should she respond? She had dreamed many times of her beloved husband coming back to her, but not in this way. What about Dafidi? How would he feel? Should she even tell him that she saw his father? *God, help me*, she thought. *If ever I needed help, it's right now.*

Tom Gill was on the phone calling the Abrahams' apartment. The phone kept ringing and finally voicemail picked up. He hung up the phone without leaving a message. What could Daf do anyway? Tom had no idea who the man with Peggy was, but he knew there was some history there. Could he possibly be Dafidi's long-estranged father?

It was time for Tom to serve the lasagna. He carried the food-loaded plates over to Peggy and Jack's table and put them down. He then cleared away the salad course and took the dirty plates back to the kitchen, noting that the man was eating, but Peggy had barely touched her food.

As he was pouring coffee to take to another table, he looked up and saw Peggy standing by the kitchen door. She entreated him with her eyes and gestured discreetly with her head for him to come to the door. Tom put the two cups of coffee on a tray and walked the few paces over to where Peggy stood.

She spoke in a whisper. "Tom, could you please give me the bill? I need to leave now, and since this was all my fault, I want to pay for the lunch before I go. Please hurry. I'll explain everything to you later, but you must not tell Daf about this lunch, okay? I need time to think about everything before I decide if he is to know about today."

Tom fumbled in his black apron for the bill. He told Peggy the amount and quickly ran her credit card through the machine. She signed for it and then asked if *Bettina's* had a back entrance. Tom nodded and led her silently back through the kitchen. She smiled a sad smile and squeezed his hand briefly before stepping out into the back alley and disappearing.

When she didn't return from the ladies room after several minutes, Jack realized that Peggy had left. He raised his hand and hailed the young waiter. When Tom reached the table, Jack said, "Please give me the bill. My guest had an urgent appointment and had to leave."

Tom didn't know what else to say, so he told the truth. "Mrs. Abraham paid the check before she left."

"Did she say anything else?"

"No, sir, she didn't."

What Jack next asked took Tom by surprise. "Is your name Tom Gill?"

"Yes, sir. Excuse me, but did Mrs. Abraham tell you my name?"

Jack hesitated a moment before answering. He smiled and said, "No, I actually learned your name from a young man I sat next to on a long plane trip. His name is Femi Abiola, and I believe he's your roommate."

Tom looked visibly relaxed. "Oh, Femi; yeah, he is. Are you the computer whiz he talked to all the way from Lagos?

Jack responded, "Yep, that's me. I guess I talked his head off. He's a nice kid. Please say hi to him for me and tell him we're still on for lunch."

Tom pulled a pen and a notepad out of his apron and asked, "Give me your name and your telephone number, and I'll pass it along to him when I get off work. He'll be glad to hear from you."

Jack gave Tom the information, never realizing that Tom was secretly taking it down so that he could give it to Peggy if she ever wanted it. Tom knew that Femi already had Jack's contact information stored in his mobile phone. Tom had to put on his best poker face when Jack announced that his last name was Abraham. So he was right. This was Dafidi's long-lost father. Tom's face almost cracked with the strain of trying to keep a calm, appearance.

Arriving back at the dorm that evening, Tom found Femi stretched out on the sofa, relaxing in front of the TV. Tom sank into one of their two shabby arm chairs and poured out the story about Peggy and Jack's emotional encounter. Femi sat there mesmerized.

Finally, he spoke. "Tom, we have to let Daf know. He loves his father. He will be so happy!"

Tom shook his head. "No, neither of us can do that. I gave Mrs. Abraham my word that I wouldn't say anything to Daf. She has to be the one to break the news to him. All we can do is hope that she does. It is out of our control."

Femi bit his lower lip and nodded. "You're right. I just hope she has the courage to tell Daf the truth."

Peggy walked quickly down the back alley and out onto Hanover Street. She crossed the street and kept walking at a brisk pace until she came to the multi-level parking structure where her car was parked. Once she was in the car, she broke down sobbing. She sat there in the stifling heat, crying her eyes out. When she was finally composed, she turned on the ignition and backed out. Once she paid the attendant and exited, she headed north, going the opposite way from Brookline. Dafidi was coming to spend the weekend at home. She couldn't face him. Not yet.

Peggy had no real idea where she was going. She got onto I-93 north and just kept driving. When she reached the exit for Rte. 128 North, she took it. As she drove, a plan developed. She would drive to Rockport and stay overnight at a motel by the beach. She would walk by the sea and gather her thoughts. Maybe it would help, maybe not. Either way, it was all she could handle right now.

Peggy drove up Rte. 128 until it ended in Gloucester and then followed the heavily traveled two-lane road northeast into Rockport. She looked to her right and saw a long beach with dunes and then continued driving, arriving in the village, awash with weathered grey cottages and a quaint but touristy ambience. She followed the signs leading towards Halibut Point and just off Main Street, she found a small motel on the cliffs overlooking the harbor. After she checked in, she went to her room and freshened up before leaving to walk back down to Bearskin Neck, where she wandered aimlessly in and out of artists' studios and souvenir shops.

Peggy thought she could forget the debacle at lunch, but as she walked along, she had a sudden realization that she actually agreed with Jack's statement. Maybe they had been meant to meet again. What else could explain everything that had happened?

As afternoon turned to dusk, Peggy realized that she needed to contact Dafidi. He would worry if she didn't come home. He had no idea about her meeting with someone she met online, but it wasn't like her to just disappear, even for one night. She needed to give him a plausible reason for her absence.

As she passed a notice board, she noticed that there was to be a showing of a documentary about Jane Goodall at the local community center that night. Peggy was amazed at her good luck. This would be her excuse.

Taking her cell phone from her purse, Peggy dialed Dafidi's number and left a message. "Hi, honey. I've received a nice surprise. A friend from work invited me to go to a showing of a Jane Goodall documentary in Rockport, and she and I are going to spend the night there. I'll be home tomorrow morning. There's leftover spaghetti in the fridge you can nuke. There's plenty if Abdul wants to join you for dinner and stay over. I love you. Bye for now."

Peggy had never lied to Dafidi, and it felt strange to do so now, but she needed time to herself to think. One small white lie in the name of peace of mind couldn't hurt. She put her phone back in her purse and continued walking back to the motel. When she got there she lay down on the bed and closed her eyes, and within seconds was fast asleep. The strain had drained her.

She woke with a start in the early evening, not realizing at first where she was. When she remembered, she sighed and pushed herself into a sitting position. Her mind was balancing thoughts like a juggler: *What am I doing here? I need to think, that's what I'm doing here. Once and for all, I need to come to terms with my relationship to Jack. Seeing him today made me realize how much I've missed him. That's what really hurts, Peggy. Most importantly, now that he is in the US, you need to decide if you are going to tell Dafidi.*

Suddenly, her stomach growled, and she realized how hungry she felt. She stood up, went into the bathroom and washed her face. Soon she was driving to Gloucester where she knew a restaurant just off RT 128, that had excellent sea food. She stepped into Lobsta Land and was given a tiny table overlooking the Annisquam river. She quickly ordered a lobster roll, and then ate in a desultory manner. The beauty of the night was lost on her. She was miles away – swimming in an internal ocean of grief and regret.

Jack left *Bettina's* and drove back to Providence in an angry and petulant mood. He couldn't handle the fact that Dafidi was nearby but he had no idea where. How dare Peggy to withhold that information - Dafidi is his son too. Jack let himself into his small apartment and looked around, seeing it in a totally different way that he had previously. It was a cookie cutter building with no character. It had no warmth. Jack had an epiphany as he stood there. It wasn't the building that lacked warmth – it was his entire life. He needed to see his son and he still loved Peggy. What was he to do?

Chapter 17
Halloween

October brought beautiful Indian summer weather. Dafidi, Abdul and their friends stayed outside more than indoors and reveled in the beautiful sun-filled days. They practiced basketball and sat outside studying on the lawn in front of their dorm.

Mid-term exams were approaching, and Abdul was becoming nervous about his Comparative Religion class. He was always taught by his parents to respect other people's religion, but now his professor wanted him to write a long paper comparing and contrasting Christianity, Islam and Judaism, explaining their similarities and their differences. The professor also asked the students to pick one of the religions and describe it from the viewpoint of a follower of one of the other two religions. Abdul chose to describe Christianity from the point of a Jew, hoping that Dafidi could help him with the project. Now he was afraid that the professor, a Jesuit priest, would dislike his paper because of some of the things he wrote about church dogma. Indecisive, Abdul kept changing segments of the essay, not certain if he was wording things exactly as he should.

One Wednesday after class, as both boys were driving in Abdul's car, they discussed the religion project. Dafidi made a statement that Abdul found interesting. "Why would Father O'Connor be upset if you said that Judaism and Christianity both derived from the same root? They did! Just think, Jesus was a rabbi who studied the Old Testament, reading its psalms and prophecies just as priests and rabbis do today. I think you are worrying too much about offending your professor. After all, he has taught this class for years and the entire point of college is to hone our critical thinking skills. You worry too much, my friend."

Abdul knew that when Daf called him "my friend" he truly meant it. It was a term the two boys had used for years to denote how close they were. Therefore, he didn't take offense at anything Daf said, but instead, he reasoned that it was probably correct.

When he turned in his mid-term project, he received top marks. Father O'Connor remarked how thoughtfully crafted the paper was, and that it seemed to represent a lot of soul-searching on Abdul's part. Abdul secretly thought that it represented a lot of soul-searching on

Dafidi's part. After all, his best friend helped him formulate some of the ideas the paper expressed.

For his part, Dafidi was struggling with an English paper about John Donne. He read everything he could get his hands on, and all the research pointed to Donne's work having very sensual overtones. Dafidi felt he had to somehow convey this without offending the celibate priest who taught the class. However, as he attempted to do this, the paper began to sound bland and boring.

Dafidi finally came up with a solution. Instead of analyzing Donne's work, he would analyze the effect the author's life exerted on his work. That way, he could center his research on the author's experiences, rather than his writing. As it turned out, Dafidi received an A+, as the professor had never seen a student write such an original and well-researched paper about a well-known author. Dafidi's analysis and description of Donne's metaphysical ideas and of his obsession with death after his beloved wife died during the birth of their 12th child were extraordinary in scope, and the professor was astounded by the maturity of his student's conclusions.

To celebrate their success on their mid-terms, Daf, Sara, Mike, Yosha, LeShawn, Abdul, Femi and Marta, went to *Bettina's* for dinner on Halloween night. They sat family-style at a long table and enjoyed themselves immensely, laughing and joking while stuffing their faces with forkloads of pasta and baskets of bread. Afterwards, they all piled into Yosha's and Abdul's cars and drove up to the 'witch city' of Salem, to wander around and observe all the people who congregated there for Halloween. This had become an annual tradition, and each year they commented on how much stranger the Salem crowds had become.

Sara was dressed for the occasion, and she wore a gypsy fortune-teller's outfit, complete with gold coin earrings and a flouncy patchwork skirt. She looked very much like a gypsy, with her thick dark hair and big round eyes. Dafidi was proud of how beautiful she looked, and he was anxious to tell her. He had to wait until he and Sara were someplace alone though, as the group would tease him profusely if they heard his compliments.

They parked in the lot near the Peabody Essex Museum and walked as a group around the town, marveling at the eccentricities of their fellow Halloween revelers. When they were approaching the tiny historic Burying Point cemetery on Charter Street, they heard a familiar voice talking to someone walking behind them. Yosha turned around and was surprised to see Jason Kelly walking with a strangely dressed girl. Her skin was so pale that she looked as if her blood had been drained by a vampire. She had unnaturally black hair and was dressed in the Goth style popular with some college students. Jason himself was dressed oddly – he wore black from head to toe, and had heavy silver chains around his neck. Yosha couldn't believe his eyes.

Yosha stopped in his tracks and spoke to Jason, "Looks as if you're in the holiday spirit. Actually, it looks as if you are holiday spirits!"

Jason waved his hand as if to brush off Yosha's comment. He grabbed his companion by her elbow and turned her around so they could walk away from Yosha and his group.

Dafidi spoke first. "Yosh, just ignore him. He looks like an idiot tonight and he's acting like one. Let him have his fling with vampire girl and we'll go have our own fun. Who cares what he does?"

Yosha nodded ruefully. "Yeah, he's a real twit all right. Did you see those chains? He looked like something from a B rated horror film."

Sara laughed. "He's always acting like something from a horror film, even when he isn't dressed up like one of the characters. Come on, let's get our fortunes read by the woman in the booth over there by the cemetery fence. It looks like that'll provide some cheap thrills."

The group moved over to where a line of people were awaiting their turn to have their palms read by 'The Oracle' for $2.00 each. A tall middle-aged woman dressed in long white flowing robes with esoteric symbols embroidered in silver thread took each person's money, and then raised her hands over their head and closed her eyes. She then began to sway back and forth while she uttered the person's fate. Each of the friends went in turn, and their companions listened attentively, but with skepticism. The psychic announced that Dafidi would soon be reunited with a loved one, that Yosha would become immensely rich, and that LeShawn would go into politics. When Abdul's turn came, no one laughed, because for some reason, the self-proclaimed soothsayer told him that he would owe his life to his best friend. This sounded like a cloaked warning of some calamity about to befall Abdul. The group remained silent as they slowly drifted away from the cemetery and the ever-lengthening line of people waiting to see 'The Oracle.'

Sara finally broke the spell. "Let's go to Pickering Wharf and get some ice cream." The group nodded in unison and they crossed a busy street and walked towards a small ice cream shop named "Cone Coven." LeShawn laughed out loud when he saw the shop's name and exclaimed, "Why does everything in Salem have to be witch-related? That is the most stupid name I've ever seen! It doesn't even make sense. Covens are groups of witches, not groups of ice cream cones."

Dafidi laughed and said, "Maybe the ice cream is ghoulishly good!"

Abdul chuckled and rolled his eyes at his friend.

Laughing, Dafidi punched Abdul playfully on the arm, and the group sauntered into the ice cream shop to explore its magic. As it turned out, not one of them was bewitched that night.

For his part, Jason thought the Halloween revelers in Salem looked stupid. He felt that way himself. Céline talked him into donning a 'Goth' look for the night, just as she had done. Jason was astounded by this, because normally, she was extremely quiet, subdued and conservative – qualities he immediately liked when he met her three weeks before.

Céline Monette was French and like Jason, she was a freshman student at BC who lived in Vouté Hall. She came back from class early one day to find the door to her dorm room open and Jason replacing the lock. She was surprised to find him working there, because she noticed him a few days earlier in her Political Science class, when he asked their professor some extremely probing questions about President Obama's financial bail-out package. She introduced herself to Jason and struck up a conversation with him while he finished the repair to the door.

Jason found that he enjoyed talking to Céline. He found her soft speaking voice and melodious French accent very soothing. They spoke at length after class each day for a week until he finally got up the nerve to ask her out for a date. Jason told her he had heard about all the odd people that converged on Salem each Halloween, and he thought it would be fun to go there to see them. He also mentioned that it was something uniquely Bostonian that she wouldn't be able to experience in France. Céline agreed readily. She had been hoping that the tall young man would ask her out.

They took a commuter train to Salem and just walked around,

ogling the many bizarrely costumed revelers. Some of the historic buildings had free admission for the holiday, so they toured a few. They found that they both enjoyed just being together.

After they encountered Dafidi and his friends in Salem, Jason and Céline walked to a small restaurant and had dinner. Over pizza, they spoke about school and told each other about their families. Jason, however, left out any mention of his younger brother, Jude. Just as they were about to leave the restaurant, Céline said something that Jason would never forget. "Of course, I have not told you about my little sister, Claudine. It is most unfortunate, but she does not live with my family. Claudine has *arriération* - how do you say it in English — retardation. She is extremely sweet but does not understand too much. Do you know what I mean?"

Although Céline pronounced the word 'retardation' with French intonation so it sounded like 'raytahrdahseohn', Jason understood exactly what she was saying. He couldn't believe his ears. Why was Céline not embarrassed to tell someone about her sister? Jason couldn't fathom why she would openly divulge what he considered to be embarrassing information.

He didn't speak for a moment, but when Céline glanced at him with a puzzled look, thinking that she had somehow said something inappropriate, Jason made a snap decision.

Struggling to get out the words, he said, "I…I know exactly what you mean. My younger brother, Jude, has Down Syndrome. He lives at home with Mom and me, but he doesn't understand much either. It's really hard sometimes."

Observing how hard it was for Jason to convey this information, Céline nodded and placed her hand tentatively on his arm, as if to comfort him.

Jason was overcome. He had never spoken to anyone, except his mother and Miriam Hernandez, about Jude. He looked away briefly but didn't remove Céline's hand. Instead, he put his own over hers and said, "Let's go back out and check out the freaks." Céline smiled mischievously and said, "Maybe people will be checking us out and think we are the freaks!" Smiling and holding hands, they walked back out to the crowded street. Jason and Céline felt truly bewitched that night.

Chapter 18
Thanksgiving

November was unseasonably cold. Rain pelted Boston and ice formed on walkways. Jason was kept busy salting the sidewalks around Vouté Hall, and each icy morning he would be outside working by 6 am. He grew resentful of having to miss precious sleep, but he kept telling himself how lucky he was to live at Vouté, so that he could be close to Céline. He was extremely adept at compartmentalizing his time, but he had at least opened a gentler compartment where his time with Céline resided. She had softened some of Jason's rough edges.

Guillermo Manzano noticed the change. Jason didn't seem as impatient or angry. Even Dafidi noticed a slight difference. Jason no longer made sarcastic or disparaging comments to Abdul. The two couldn't be said to be friends, but at least they were no longer adversaries.

Thanksgiving break was approaching and Asiya Rashid was planning a huge holiday celebration. She telephoned Peggy to ask her for help in planning a Thanksgiving feast worthy of the Pilgrims themselves. Asiya explained to Peggy that she wanted Alia to know how thankful her family was that she was safe and was living with them in America.

Asiya intended to ask all of Abdul's friends and their parents to Thanksgiving dinner, and the two women went shopping for new tablecloths and serving dishes. Peggy insisted on paying for some of their purchases, saying that, because she worked so many long hours, she hadn't yet had all these people over. Asiya came up with a logical solution: the invitations would be sent out by both of them, even though the actual dinner would be held at the Rashids' house.

Dafidi and Abdul were looking forward to the party. They celebrated past Thanksgivings with Yosha's Aunt Rachel and Uncle Bernie and with the large extended Johnson family, but the Rashids had never hosted a large group for the holiday.

Asiya and Peggy sat for long hours pouring over recipe books, trying to find tasty and original dishes to make the meal special, but would be reasonable to prepare for such a large group. However, it was Alia who came up with an idea that not only seemed workable, but would also enhance the meal. She suggested that each family attending the dinner should bring a dish that they considered their Thanksgiving specialty.

Peggy looked at Asiya and smiled. "Trust Alia to come up with a solution that is not only do-able but which is inclusive and will make everyone feel truly part of the party. She is a gem!"

Asiya smiled at Alia and reaching over, tousled her dark hair, just as she did when they were children. "Yes, my little cousin is a gem - one more precious to me than any diamond."

Alia giggled and responded, "But unfortunately, a gem that eats you out of house and home!"

The next day, Peggy drove to the post office and mailed out invitations to the holiday feast. Asiya and Peggy decided that each guest would be asked to invite someone else as their own guest to the meal. Because of this, they rented a white marquee tent for the back garden to accommodate the large group they anticipated would come. Late on Wednesday afternoon, the truck from the party rental company drew up in front of the Rashid house, and workers began assembling the large tent and the heaters that would be necessary to warm it.

Dafidi invited Sara Mendelsohn as his guest. He also invited Tom Gill, and he asked Tom to invite his roommate, Femi, and Femi's brother Rinton, to come too. Daf knew that though Femi and Rin came from a wealthy family in Nigeria, they had no family in the States, and he didn't want them to miss out on a traditional Thanksgiving.

Sara called and said that both Femi and Rin would come with her. Dafidi had to drive to the Green Line to pick them up.

Before she left for class early Wednesday morning, Sara received a telephone call from Femi. He told her that the nice man whom he met on the plane had called him the night before to wish him a 'Happy Thanksgiving', and he asked Sara if she thought it would be okay to ask him to join them at the Rashids'. Femi said the man sounded a bit lonely, and he thought it would be good for him to be around people on the holiday. Sara responded that she would telephone Abdul and ask if it was all right for him to come.

When the phone rang late Wednesday morning, Alia answered it. She listened to Sara's request and then smiled and said, "Of course, it's okay. He's a friend of Femi's and believe me, there will be more than enough food. The more the merrier. Anyway, there will be plenty of people here for him to talk to. See you all later. Bye." Alia hung up and in the rush to get everything done, promptly forgot to tell Asiya that another person had been added to the guest list.

The day before Thanksgiving, Rachel Stern began baking three of her famous apple raisin pies. The scent of cloves and cinnamon permeated her kitchen. Rachel herself moved briskly and efficiently; having honed her baking skills from years of practice. Baking was not only Rachel's hobby, it was also an art form. When she pulled the steaming pies from the oven, each had a design inscribed on its golden top crust. One had an impression of a turkey, a second had a horn of plenty, and the third had the Hebrew letter *Beth* ב - to represent a house or sanctuary. Rachel thought this was appropriate because the Rashids had offered Alia a sanctuary from the horrors of war, and she hoped that Alia would understand the significance.

While Rachel was baking pies, Tonya Johnson was making her famous homemade spiced cranberry mousse. She took great pride in having created this unique recipe as a teenager when her parents vacationed at Oak Bluffs on Martha's Vineyard. On the way, her parents would always stop at farm stands and purchase fresh cranberries, and Tonya would experiment with new recipes gleaned from magazines. One day she added too much whipped cream to a new recipe, and when the result was a wonderfully light mousse, she knew she had invented a delicious dessert. Her family now looked forward to her concoction at every holiday feast.

Alia was cooking too. She was making sesame *halvah*. She knew the sweet concoction would be devoured by Abdul, and she hoped the other guests would also enjoy this traditional Israeli dessert.

Thanksgiving dawned sunny and a bit warmer. Asiya was thankful that there was no rain, and she walked out to the tent early in the morning to make certain that the small ceramic space heaters worked correctly. Assuring herself that all was well, she went back into the house and relaxed in the kitchen over a hot mug of coffee, happy that her holiday plans were going so well.

At noon, guests began showing up. Peggy and Dafidi came to the house an hour earlier, to help decorate the tent and to set up tables and chairs. Dafidi looked smart in a new navy blue sports coat, and Peggy looked almost angelic in a pale blue chiffon dress. Asiya and Maroun complimented her and she beamed.

Abdul wore a suit and tie, and when Alia kept teasing him that he looked like a groom, he blushed.

Dafidi walked upstairs to Abdul's room and went online on Abdul's laptop to check to see when the Green Line train would arrive closest to 2 pm, as this was the train agreed to with Sara. At 1:45, he left and drove the short distance to the train stop in his mother's Subaru. He waited only a few minutes before the train approached.

He saw Sara step out of the train with Rin Abiola behind her. Then he saw Femi and noticed he was walking alongside an older man with grey hair. The man looked familiar to Dafidi, even at a distance.

Daf started the car and drove closer to the intersection. He stopped by the curb where Sara was standing and opened the passenger door. She, in turn, opened the rear door and as she slid into the front seat, the remaining guests slid into the back seat. Dafidi was watching traffic out of his side window and didn't notice the older man sliding in between Rin and Femi. When he heard the rear door close, he said, "Seat belts on, please. Click it or ticket" and he pulled out into the heavy traffic.

As they drove, Sara and Femi discussed the relative merits of serving a Thanksgiving *tofurkey* to vegetarians, but no one else in the car spoke. Seven minutes later, Dafidi parked the car in front of the Rashid house, and his life would change forever.

Dafidi was the first to get out of the car, and as the others climbed out, he noticed the grey haired man. Seeing the man's back from the other side of the car, he didn't immediately recognize him. But when Jack turned around and smiled, Dafidi gasped. He felt as if he would faint.

Jack was as astounded as Dafidi. The young man who was staring at him looked just like an older version of his son. For long moments, the two looked at each other without blinking.

The others stood mesmerized watching the father and son. None of them could guess what was going on.

Finally, Femi broke the silence and politely said, "Dafidi, I'd like to introduce Jack Abraham, the friend I met on the plane coming back from Lagos."

Suddenly, recognition dawned in Sara and Abdul's heads. Sara spoke first. "Daf, you both have the same last name and you've both been in Africa. Are you distantly related?"

Jack smiled ruefully and looked Sara in the eye. "Not so distantly, Sara. I'm Dafidi's father."

Sara turned red with embarrassment and brought her hand to her mouth, saying, "Oh, My God, I had no idea. I didn't even know if you were alive."

Jack smiled and seeking to ease Sara's embarrassment, said cryptically, "Not to worry. Sometimes fate just steps in and takes over."

Dafidi didn't know what to do. He felt like running over to hug his father and he felt like crying. Finally, he did both.

Jack held his son in his arms and cried too. He whispered, "I thought I'd never see you again. Oh, how I've hoped for this moment."

The others stood silent, sharing the enormous emotion they were witnessing.

Finally, Rin took control of the situation. "Hey, this is a wonderful thing to happen on Thanksgiving. Come on, you two, let's go share the good news with the other guests."

Jack looked up at Rin and smiled, tears still streaming down his cheeks. He reached in his jacket and pulled out a handkerchief and wiped his eyes. He then handed it to Dafidi who did the same. Daf nodded toward Rin and said, "I think this is going to be the best Thanksgiving ever."

The group walked slowly to the back garden and entered the tent where about thirty people were milling about, eating hors d-oeuvres and talking. Both Asiya and Peggy were still in the kitchen preparing food, so they didn't see the newcomers arrive.

Ten minutes later, Peggy and Asiya walked into the marquee and each put a heavily laden platter down on the long buffet table. Asiya walked around the room making introductions, while Peggy busied herself arranging napkins and refilling the hors d'oeuvres trays. When he walked up behind her, she didn't hear Jack approach.

Jack stood for a brief second looking at his wife's back. He didn't want to make a scene, but he needed to let her know he was there before someone else came up to them. He reached out and gingerly tapped her shoulder to make her turn around. When Peggy did so, she gasped. Stammering her words, she looked at him with a frown and asked, "Wh..What are y..you doing here?"

Jack was direct. "Femi Abiola invited me to come. I had no idea you or Dafidi would be here."

Peggy was at a loss for words. She looked at Jack and thought how tired he looked. Seeing her face, Jack read the raw emotions there. "Peggy, we need to talk. With Dafidi so close by, it isn't right for me to not be able to see him. Maybe we have our differences, but we both love our son. Please, let's heal this once and for all."

Peggy nodded but remained silent. Still looking down at the floor, she finally responded, "Yes, you should see Daf. I am so sorry I didn't tell you when we moved away from Kansas. It wasn't right, and I apologize."

Jack reached over and took Peggy's hand. He whispered, "Apology accepted. We'll talk more later. Right now, you have guests to welcome and feed. Just make certain you give me your address and telephone number before I leave to go home."

Peggy bit her lip and nodded. Jack slowly let go of her hand and, seeking escape from the emotions which threatened to overwhelm her, Peggy walked quickly out of the tent and back to the kitchen. It would be a half hour before she reappeared at the party.

Jack walked over to where Dafidi was standing with Sara, and he began talking to both of them about how he and Femi had met. As he related the story, Sara realized that he was trying to put Dafidi at ease and was trying to defuse the emotionally charged atmosphere. After some minutes, she excused herself, allowing Jack and Dafidi some private time to catch up. Father and son walked over to a corner and sat there for over an hour, engrossed in each other. Sara smiled to herself as she walked past them, and she went over to tell Abdul how things were going. Sara thought to herself that she would remember this wonderful Thanksgiving forever. If ever there had been a reason to give thanks for a *b'rakhot*, a blessing, this was it.

Chapter 19
Basketball

The Group of Five decided to meet back at the Brookline High courts to play basketball each Sunday afternoon, as it was the only day of the week when none of them had classes or other commitment.

When the five friends arrived at the court, they each filled in the others on their past week, so it was as much a social as a sports gathering. However, with the basketball season about to begin, they all thought it prudent to challenge one another on the court as much as possible. They would perfect on their own what they learned from BC coach Bo Khao.

LeShawn told the others about something he recently read in a magazine. The article said that good basketball players were also good actors. It went on to point out that because basketball involved trying to wrest the ball from an opponent, it was necessary, as they all already knew, to fake out the opponent. Good fakes were distinct and varied and if done correctly, would freak out the opponent and make him so jittery that he would forget the moves he had planned.

The group listened intently and they decided that faking would be the skill they would practice that day. No one was to tell another what they planned. As the ball went into play, each player would try his best to feint a maneuver to put the other players off balance.

Dafidi had the first success. He raised his left hand up suddenly while LeShawn was trying to defend, and then shot a basket with his right hand. It landed cleanly and fell through the hoop and the other players cheered. As the afternoon went on, the players tried every maneuver they could think of, and tried to psyche out the other players' intended moves. As Abdul said afterwards, it felt like a mental workout as well as a physical one.

As dusk came early, the five friends left the court at about 4:30 pm. Abdul felt extraordinarily tired but tried not to let it show. Dafidi knew there was something wrong with his friend because Abdul wasn't talking much. He was walking with a stiffness that indicated that his back was hurting again. Dafidi questioned him about this once they were out of earshot of the other players. "So, my tired friend, does your back hurt or what? You're walking like an old man."

Abdul nodded. "Yeah, it's actually pretty bad. I didn't want to break up the game, but I was really struggling back there. It feels as if a hot poker is burning just above the back of my waist. In any case, I took some Ibuprofen and Naproxen, and it is getting better."

Daf frowned. "You know, you've been having problems off and on for a while now. I think you should call the doctor."

"I did – last week. But he was away, and I didn't know the doctor who was covering for him. It's embarrassing to see someone new. Next time maybe I'll see a chiropractor."

Daf laughed. "It would be more embarrassing to collapse during a BC game, right?"

***

Dafidi was playing basketball better than ever. Intense indoor practice during the bitter cold had honed both his defense and his shooting skills. Rin Abiola noticed the improvement and commented on it to Dafidi. "Hey Daf, pretty soon you'll be the number one player. I'd better watch my back around you." Rin chuckled and slapped Daf on the back in a friendly manner. Daf grinned. He was working hard and to have Rin Abiola compliment him was a huge honor.

Boston College won their first four games of the season. Dafidi's play was phenomenal in all the games. He averaged 20 points, 6 assists, and 6 rebounds a game. The upcoming nationally televised game with Duke would put him in the national spotlight.

Felix Bue inched his black SUV through the traffic on Beacon Street, narrowly avoiding a silver Lexus coupe that changed lanes at full speed in inimitable Boston fashion. The Fox 25 sports anchor was hurrying to the BC game, his mind racing with ideas for the upcoming interview with Dafidi Abraham. Turning right onto Chestnut Hill Avenue, he instantly felt more relaxed, knowing that he was approaching the stadium and would make it in time for the beginning of the game. As he proceeded down the beautiful tree-lined residential street with its stately mock-Tudor brick homes, he rehearsed in his mind what he would say to the young man. By the time he made the final left turn onto Commonwealth Ave., his mind was made up to address not only basketball in the interview, but also the charitable work on which the megastar was embarking.

Evidently, Dafidi and a friend, under the auspices of the college, were setting up an international summer camp for children displaced by the conflict in the Middle East. It was also to be attended by members of Boston College's *Baldwin's Bunch*, a group of local under-privileged children. After much publicity in the *Boston Globe*, Dafidi and his friend Abdul were invited to the United Nations to witness a meeting of the General Assembly and to speak about their Peace Camp proposal. Entering the campus through St. Ignatius Gate and sliding the SUV into a convenient parking spot, Bue turned off the key in the ignition as he thought to himself, "What in God's name could Daf Abraham know about politics?"

Entering Conte Forum, the sportscaster could feel the crowd's energy. This game was to be a big one – BC vs. Duke. The Duke roster was heavy with superb players and BC would have to struggle to win.

Meeting his cameraman by ESPN's *College Game Day* desk, Bue conferred with him briefly about the lighting. He then looked around to see if Arash Shah, the ESPN show's anchor, was anywhere nearby. The two sportscasters had been friends for years, and although they shared a friendly rivalry, they frequently discussed teams, sharing their information and experience with each other. Both men knew this enhanced their game coverage.

Felix heard his name called and turned around to find Arash walking up to him.

"Hey, Bue. What are you doing here tonight? I thought I had a monopoly on the Duke game!"

Grinning, Felix replied, "Very funny, Arash. You know I always beat you to the good ones."

"I'll bet you lunch tomorrow that Duke wins."

"You're on, Arash. How about Legal Seafoods at Chestnut Hill at noon? You'll be paying, and I'll be eating every oyster in sight."

"Felix, you old devil. You always pick the restaurants you like! OK, fish at noon it is."

The two men stood there chatting and sharing their ideas on how the game would pan out. Shah thought Duke would massacre the BC team, but Bue thought BC would annihilate Duke by using its star player, Dafidi Abraham, as point guard. As the announcer introduced the teams over the PA system, the two men moved to their assigned seats and waited to see which of them would win the bet.

The game began slowly, with each team seeking to gauge the rival's strategy. It was obvious to the Duke players that freshman Dafidi was a seasoned point guard. It also became evident that he felt he could beat the Duke players one-on-one, as he strove for wing isolation to allow himself the option of turning the corner to effect a successful drive to the basket. Moving with agility and speed, he put his opponents off balance and succeeded to land basket after basket. Even when he passed to another shooter, the ball found its mark. The Duke coach was becoming infuriated. His players couldn't stop Abraham.

For their part, the BC team was ecstatic. They learned their lessons well and were making their coach proud. Knowing they had such a strong point guard, they set him up for success by using a classic Celtics move from the their heyday in the 1960's – the Zipper Offense.

Dafidi initiated the offense by dribbling to the wing. He kept the Duke players confused. Coach Khao always taught him to minimize the margin of error by advancing the ball with as few passes as possible, and to always look at the ball handler. These were classic Celtics tactics. The BC team was looking to the past to succeed in the present.

The up-tempo game lasted just a little over two hours, with BC winning hands-down.

After the teams left the parquet, the crowd in the bleachers began filing out slowly. As Arash Shah and his fellow *ESPN* announcers dissected the winning plays, Felix Bue headed towards the locker room to interview Dafidi.

He found the young man surrounded by his teammates, high-fiving them and grinning from ear to ear. It was obvious he was the game's star player.

Stepping up to shake Dafidi's hand, the sportscaster smiled and introduced himself. Dafidi was taken aback – he had never met anyone famous before. He stuttered a bit from nervousness, saying the only thing that he could think of.

"Th-th -thank you for coming to the game, Mr. Bue. The team appreciates it."

Sensing the young man's nervousness, the seasoned announcer sought to reassure him.

"I should be thanking you, Dafidi. That game was magnificent! I haven't enjoyed my work so much in years."

Dafidi beamed with happiness.

Bue continued, "Anyway, I want to interview you and find out how the star player ticks. Can we move somewhere less congested? I'll get Buzz Ero, my cameraman, to find a spot with good lighting."

Dafidi nodded and smiled at the announcer, realizing for the first time how immensely important his playing had been to the team's success.

***

Seated in the coach's spacious office, Dafidi Abraham and Felix Bue discussed basketball in general before beginning the interview. Bue knew this would put the young man at ease. Finally, feeling that the moment was right, Bue began the formal interview by asking Dafidi about his motivation in wanting to set up the international summer camp.

Dafidi hesitated a moment, knowing that political correctness was an expectation on television. However, he also felt that he must state his case honestly and speak from his heart. Just as he did in basketball games, Dafidi knew when to back off and when to step forward.

Looking directly at the newscaster, he began speaking earnestly. "Mr. Bue, I am the child of Jewish parents, yet I am attending a Catholic university. My best friend is Christian, but of Arab descent, and has many relatives who are Muslim. In today's violent and prejudiced world, this may seem odd to many people. However, to me and my friend, we are just alike – two young men seeking to find our place in the world and trying to come to grips with it. We both feel strongly that our friendship has transcended our ethnic and religious differences and has enriched our lives for the better. We wish to share our experience with other young people and to enable them to know others of different cultures so that they, too, can become true friends. It all goes back to the saying, "friends are the family we choose for ourselves." Maybe the contribution Abdul and I make will allow children all over the world to think of their friends as 'family' and through this, religious prejudice and violence will end. That is our goal."

Bue was moved by the young man's words, and as he digested their meaning, it took him a moment to respond. Finally, he said, "Dafidi Abraham, not only are you a magnificent basketball player; you are also a magnificent human being. You have made your coach and team proud today, and you have just voiced the dream that so many people would like to attain. I wish you and Abdul much success. You are a star in life as well as in sports."

Dafidi couldn't respond. He was fighting back tears and feeling helplessly awkward. The seasoned cameraman sensed this and moved the camera onto the sportscaster. As the true professional that he was, Bue continued smoothly, listing the game's stats, and then concluded the interview by telling the audience that they had just begun to see this young man 's rise to stardom and that he would be a meteor in the sports firmament before long.

Buzz Ero packed up his video gear and Dafidi and Bue walked towards the door. Buzz opened it and before going through extended his hand to Dafidi. "Young man, I am astounded by your spirit. Go get 'em!"

After the two men left, Dafidi sat back in Coach Khao's leather chair and closed his eyes. He felt tears form and slide down his cheeks. He was so happy and yet so scared. Thoughts came at him from all sides. Could he and Abdul really help those kids? Could he continue to win games so easily? Would his mom have enough money to support him? Game day was over but the game of life was just beginning for Dafidi.

Chapter 20
December and Gifts

Jack telephoned Peggy and they agreed to meet for coffee the following week. It was a tense meeting, held at an unlikely place. Peggy drove to Providence and met with Jack at the café in the large Nordstrom store at Providence Place. She suggested the venue because it would be crowded and informal, and they wouldn't be likely to linger there. As she filed through the cafeteria style line while she waited for Jack to show up, she rehearsed what she would say. When the time came to say the words, however, she couldn't. As much as she knew that she wanted to tell Jack not to try to become a part of her and Dafidi's life again, she just couldn't say the words. Down deep, she wanted Jack back in her life. The problem was that she wanted the Jack whom she knew many years ago in Africa— the gentle, loving, supportive husband and doting father to Dafidi. The new Jack was a person she didn't know. It had been so many years, that in some ways, she felt that he was a stranger.

Jack arrived ten minutes later, looking flustered. He had never been to that mall before, and he struggled to find a parking spot with all the holiday shoppers.

When he saw Peggy sitting across the room in a booth below a wide window, he smiled and waved. He paid for his coffee and a piece of carrot cake, and brought his tray over to Peggy's table. Sitting down and taking off his sport coat, he tried to make small talk about the weather and the traffic. Peggy was grateful that he was keeping the conversation on neutral topics.

Finally, he took a long sip of hot coffee and looked her straight in the eye. He didn't look away when she looked down at the table, and when she looked up again, he was still staring at her with a serious look on his face.

"Peggy, I may be too old to have an emotional relationship again. I'm cynical, and I'm confused. But all of these issues don't make me a bad person. I love Dafidi and I've missed him horribly. I've missed you too."

"So, here's the deal. Why don't we just schedule time for the three of us to do things together on a regular basis? We don't have to do anything spectacular – just normal things like going out to dinner or a sports event. I'd love it if Daf and I can go together by ourselves sometimes too. Let's be frank – if you have a new relationship, I won't interfere."

Peggy looked at Jack and shook her head. She answered, "Since we're being frank, here's the scoop. I don't have any relationships and like you, I feel too burnt out to even contemplate one. My work takes up about 90% of my time, and I try to devote the remainder to our son. But now he's in college, and he has less time to spend with dear old Mom. If we can find any time to all go out, that's fine with me. With our schedules, it won't happen very often anyway."

Jack reached for his coffee. Taking a swig, he looked down into the cup and thought about how to word what he really wanted to say. He finally looked up and said, "Will there ever be any time when maybe just you and I can go out for dinner?"

Peggy's eyes grew big. She answered in a tiny voice, "I don't know what the future holds, Jack. Let's just go with the other plan for now, OK?"

Nodding and knowing he had to compromise, he responded, "Probably for the best. All right – I agree."

***

Dafidi and Abdul were waiting with bated breath for their grades to appear online. Finally, on December 21st, they went into the website and saw the posted grades. They whooped with joy as they read. Both had aced their examinations. Dafidi stood up and did a dance of happiness. Abdul just sat there grinning from ear to ear.

When Peggy arrived home that night, Dafidi had dinner waiting and a glass of wine poured for her. As she walked into the dining room, he told her to please sit down, as he had some important news. Peggy knew from his mischievous demeanor that the news could only be good. When he told her that he got top marks on all of his final exams she beamed and held up the wine glass, saying, "A toast to my host! You are absolutely the best. Now, even BC knows that!"

Dafidi laughed. He then sat down a the table and asked, "Can we call Dad and tell him?"

Peggy nodded, but her words put a slight damper on the moment. "*You* can call him and tell him. I'm going to go have a shower before my lavish dinner."

Dafidi would have preferred his mother to telephone his father, but he was so happy, he didn't feel like pressing the point. As soon as Peggy left the room, Daf telephoned his father and told him the good news. He also told him about the celebratory dinner he planned for Peggy that night.

Jack's response was ecstatic. "Well done, Daf. You are absolutely incredible. If you can make these kinds of grades while playing basketball for BC, just think how well you'll do when you get to graduate school and can live off of a scholarship and not have to play on the basketball team!"

Daf chuckled. "Dad, it sounds as if you've got my entire future planned. Remember, I'm only a freshman. Who knows what will happen in the next three years?"

Jack said, "You'll do fine all the way through college. You have drive, determination and persistence. I have absolutely no worries."

There was a brief pause and then Jack asked, "So, when can we go out and celebrate? I know you're busy, but can you make time for your old man?"

Dafidi answered, "Of course. How about this Sunday night?"

"Great, son. Why don't I drive up and we can go into Boston to someplace more upscale than usual. Ask your mom if she wants to come too."

"Okay, Dad. I can't promise about Mom, but I'm onboard. Would 6 be okay?"

"Yes. I'll pick you up then. Now go get your mother's fancy dinner ready. Bye for now."

Dafidi hung up the phone feeling completely exhilarated. His father was back in his life. He couldn't put words to his feelings. He just knew he was happier than he'd been in a long time.

***

Jason decided to buy his mother a real Christmas tree. Céline went with him to the lot, and they had picked out a tall Frasier fir. They stopped and bought a tree stand for it and drove it back to the Kelly house in Céline's battered old car. When they finally managed to get it standing straight, it looked magnificent. The fresh scent of pine permeated the tiny living room.

Céline reached in to her copious handbag and drew out a small plastic bag, saying, "This is for you. *Joyeux Noël.*" She stood on tiptoes and kissed Jason on his cheek.

Jason opened the plastic bag and found a box wrapped in gold paper containing a beautiful handmade star-shaped tree topper made of crystal. A label affixed to the star said *Lalique.* He had never heard the name before, but it sounded foreign, so he asked Céline, "Is this from France?"

Céline smiled. "Of course, silly. Lalique is the most famous crystal in France. Please, also read the card."

Jason opened the tiny gold-embossed white envelope and pulled out what was obviously a French Christmas card. Under *Joyeux Noël et Bonne Année Nouvelle,* Céline wrote, "You are a star, so I wanted you to have a star. May you shine bright and clear in the New Year. *Bisous,* Céline"

Jason blushed furiously. He had never been given a gift by a girl. He was also terribly embarrassed that he had no gift for Céline. He had no idea what to say or do.

He was saved from having to say anything because at that moment his mother came through the front door, her arms laden with groceries. Jason put the star down on a table and went forward to take one of the grocery bags from her. She stared in amazement at this behavior, He had never offered this kind of help before. Then Mary saw the young woman standing by the Christmas tree. Mary looked from one to the other with a puzzled look.

"Jason, please introduce me to your friend. Also, where did the tree come from?"

Jason looked at this mother and then at his girlfriend and answered both of his mother's questions. "Mom, this is Céline Monette. She lives in my dorm. And the tree is from me, I mean…us. We wanted you and Jude to have a real tree this year."

Mary couldn't believe her ears. Was this really her petulant, bullying son speaking? Could this petite young French girl have influenced him? Whatever had happened, Mary approved.

She responded. "Thank you both so much. That is the most beautiful Christmas tree I've ever seen. I'll have to go down to the basement and find the decorations we used to use – be...before - well, when your father was still with us."

Céline realized in that instant that the Kellys hadn't really celebrated Christmas since Jason's father died. She wanted to hug Jason and his mother and tell them it was okay to celebrate. Tears were welling up in her eyes.

Jason defused the moment by holding up the crystal star and saying, "Mom, look what Céline gave me for the tree. Isn't it beautiful?"

Mary looked at the star and nodded. "Celine, that was a most thoughtful gift. I think the least we can do is to ask you to stay for dinner tonight. It won't be fancy, but at least it won't be dorm food."

"I'd love to, Mrs. Kelly. If you like, I'll help you prepare it. I love to cook."

"Yes, I'd enjoy your company in the kitchen. While we're cooking, Jason can string lights on the tree."

Turning to Jason, Mary said, "Honey, I think the lights and decorations are in the cupboard under the stairs. I just hope the bulbs are still good."

With that, Mary picked up one of the grocery bags, and she and Céline walked into the kitchen. Jason followed them with the other bag and then disappeared down the back stairs to the basement. He soon found the lights and decorations and came back upstairs and through the kitchen to the living room.

When dinner was finally ready and on the table, Jason called to his mother and Céline and asked them to step into the living room for a moment. When they did, he turned on the lights on the tree. The tiny, twinkle multi-colored lights reflected off the crystal star on the top of the tree, sending dancing lights around the room. It looked as if the Aurora Borealis had come down to earth. That moment was a gift to Mary Kelly that she would never forget. Light had returned to their lives.

**

Asiya and Alia walked around The Mall at Chestnut Hill ogling the beautiful Christmas decorations and the expensive gifts. Asiya came seeking gifts for Maroun and Abdul, and Alia wanted to buy something special for each of the Rashids. When they came upon an upscale kitchen goods store, Alia suddenly asked Asiya if she could possibly go get them some coffee. Alia pleaded caffeine depletion and said she needed a rest and would just sit outside the store until Asiya returned. However, as her cousin rounded a corner and was out of view, Alia popped into the kitchen store. She had a mission to complete, and she didn't have much time.

By the time Asiya returned, Alia was seated once again on a bench outside the store. The two cousins sipped their coffee and then Asiya asked if she could browse for a bit in the kitchen store. Alia didn't want to go in with her, in case the salesclerk said anything to give away the surprise she planned, so she said she would go into the department store to use the ladies' room while Asiya browsed.

Asiya wandered around the well-stocked shop, looking at all of the beautiful cookware and appliances, knowing she couldn't afford to buy them, but wishing she could. Asiya loved to cook, especially for large groups of people. Cooking was a gift she gave others – a way to express her love for them.

When Alia returned to the bench, she found Asiya sitting there with a tiny paper bag in her hand. She opened it and showed Alia what she bought. It was a tiny whisk. Asiya explained her purchase to her cousin, "It is for when I whip meringues. Honestly, I just needed to buy myself a small treat, and it was all I could really afford."

Alia nodded and said she understood. She suggested that they treat themselves to lunch. "After all – you still need to eat, even if you can't afford to cook!"

Asiya laughed, and the two went in search of a restaurant neither could really afford.

***

Sr. Dorothy Brennan drove to West End House. She went inside and knocked on Miriam Hernandez' door. Miriam said "Come in" and smiled broadly when she saw who was visiting.

"Sister Dorothy, How are you? I haven't seen you in so long."

"Nor I you, Miriam. But I wanted to bring you a special Christmas gift. When you open this envelope, I think you'll smile."

Miriam took the festive red and white candy-striped envelope and quickly opened it. When she pulled out the card inside, something dropped soundlessly to the ground. She reached down to pick up the piece of paper and gasped when she turned it over. It was a check for $100,000.

All she could say was "But how…who?"

Sr. Dorothy smiled. "Just read the card, Miriam. It explains everything."

"This check is given to West End House Boys and Girls Club in appreciation of giving me a wonderful life. Without the kind people who work there, I would never have had a chance in life.

As it is, my life is bountiful and beautiful beyond what I could ever have dreamed. I have a lovely family, a good job and a nice home. The one thing I don't have is children. Rather than adopt one or two children, I have decided to help many children. Therefore, for the next ten years, I will donate $100,000 a year to your worthy establishment. Please be assured that this check is valid and you may cash it immediately.

Blessings from a former child you loved (who would like to remain anonymous.)"

The check was a bank check drawn on a large Boston bank. Miriam sat down heavily and began to cry. She looked up at Sr. Dorothy and said, "Do you realize how much this can help –especially in this economy?"

Sr. Dorothy said, "Yes. I do. I am so happy this happened. It is truly like a Christmas miracle."

Miriam nodded. "Oh, how I wish I could thank the donor in person. Who do you think it is?"

Sr. Dorothy blushed the tiniest bit and said "I have no idea. It could be anyone. It doesn't matter, does it? What matters is the good the check will enable you to do."

"You're right, of course. Oh, Sister Dorothy, what a lovely gift. Merry Christmas!"

When Sr. Dorothy Brennan was back in her car, she leaned back, closed her eyes, made the sign of the cross, and said a small prayer, asking forgiveness for a white lie she had told. "God, please forgive me for saying I had a family and a house. I just said that to put Miriam off the scent. Amen."

She reached into the glove compartment and pulled out a check stub. She would have to file it somewhere safely in her office, far away from prying eyes. She didn't want anyone to know about the large inheritance she received from a recently deceased woman whose family was grateful for the care Sr. Dorothy gave their relative during her last years. Maybe she would file away the stub with her childhood photos – the ones showing her as a skinny child with scuffed shoes and hand-me-down dresses, posing in front of West End House.

***

Jack scoured shops in the mall trying to find the perfect Hanukkah gift for Dafidi. After so many years away, he had no idea what his son would like. As he was walking, he passed a travel agent's shop and saw an Israel Tour poster in the window. Suddenly, he had an idea. He entered the shop, briefly spoke to a woman inside, and then stepped back out and headed to his car. He needed to get home quickly and go online.

Once he was back at his apartment, he went directly to his laptop and logged on. He brought up numerous discount travel sites and began writing down prices on a piece of paper. He sat and mulled over each offer and then went back online and compared it to others. He sat at his computer until it became dark outside, and he finally realized he had forgotten to turn on any lights.

After taking a beer from the fridge and making himself a sandwich, he headed back to his desk and began working again on his project. By 10 pm, he had finished. The task was done and Jack was a happy man. Dafidi would get the best gift ever this year.

***

Peggy dithered over whether she and Dafidi should give Jack a Hanukkah gift. She finally decided that the gift should come from Dafidi and that it should be something small. When she told her son this, he protested. "No, Mom. It should come from both of us. We're both his family."

"No, Daf. It would be inappropriate for me to give your father a gift. Please, just do as I say. I'll give you some money and you can choose his gift. Just put only your name on the card, please."

Dafidi knew when he was beat. He acquiesced to his mother's request and went in search of a gift for his father. Abdul was roped into going with him, and Abdul was the one who made an excellent suggestion as to where to buy the gift.

"I think your dad would like an antique. Maybe something African. Or maybe a book."

Dafidi nodded and said, "Sometimes, you amaze me, my friend.

- 216 -

Antique is your suggestion, and antique it will be."

The two scoured antique shops all over Boston. They finally found one on Charles Street that specialized in Scandinavian antiques. Although it seemed a stretch to find something African in such a store, Dafidi told the owner about their quest. He thought for a moment and then said, "I may have just the thing. Come with me."

He led them up a flight of stairs to the second floor. The downstairs had been light and clean and full of heavy pine furniture. Upstairs was totally different. Here there were bookcases filled with duty tomes, oriental rugs hung over the backs of heavily padded Victorian chairs, and a glaze of dust everywhere. The antique dealer reached towards a bookcase and pulled out a hardbound book, its cover in perfect condition, but the edge of the pages showing a pale buttery color. He leafed through it quickly and then presented it to Dafidi.

The beautifully embossed burgundy leather cover bore the name "Out of Africa" with the name Isak Dinesen written below. Dafidi recognized the name. He opened the book and looked at the date it was printed, 1937.

The owner saw him looking at the pages and said, "It is not a First Edition, but it is one that was printed the same year. There are very few left from this printing. A First Edition would be exorbitantly expensive, whereas I can sell you this copy for $110.00."

Dafidi and Abdul looked at each other and Abdul shrugged. He had no idea how much the book should be worth.

Dafidi liked the idea of the book. He remembered his father loving old books and reading to him from them when he was little. He made a decision.

"Yes. This book would be perfect, thank you. I'll pay you in cash."

After the owner wrapped the book in new tissue and placed it in into a bag bearing the store's logo and address, Dafidi and Abdul walked down Charles Street to a small pizza parlor. They sat there eating and talking and the more they talked, the more Dafidi decided he liked his choice of gift. His father would be happy.

***

Peggy was thoughtful as she chose gifts for Dafidi. He desperately needed a new back pack, so she bought that first. For some reason, as she chose an upgraded style with more features than his tattered old pack, she was drawn to a display of luggage. She and Dafidi hadn't traveled since arriving in Boston, but maybe he would need luggage for a trip in the future. After all, most of his classmates went to Europe or Australia for months at a time over the summer break, so he might do the same. He had saved money while he worked, so he could afford to travel.

Peggy left the store with a large duffel bag on wheels, made of the same fabric as the backpack. She could visualize Dafidi walking through a foreign airport, laden with a heavy suitcase and a bulging backpack. That's what college students should do, she thought. That's what Jack and I did, too. Her mind began to wander back to the days when she and Jack first dated. They traveled all over Europe and then to Morocco, where they were entranced by the exotic environment. She hoped Dafidi could do the same.

As she was walking past a sporting goods store, she saw the cross country skis that Dafidi had asked her to consider for this year's gift. Feeling generous, she went in and bought them. She hoped Dafidi would be happy with this year's Hanukkah gifts.

The eight nights of Hanukkah had come and gone. Peggy and Dafidi exchanged gifts and both enjoyed lighting their small sterling silver menorah and saying the traditional blessing each night.

Dafidi found a beautiful black leather briefcase for his mother – something she needed badly since her old one was falling apart. He also bought her three books that she was meaning to read. His other four gifts were tiny but heart-felt: a framed poem he had written to her in third grade, a tin of chocolate brownies he baked himself, a DVD of her favorite old film *Casablanca*, and a calendar from the World Wildlife Fund. Peggy was touched by the gifts because they showed so much thought and were so sentimental. She cried when she read the short poem again, remembering the first time he gave it to her on her 36th birthday.

Peggy gave Dafidi two tickets to a Celtics game, a pair of snowshoes, a much needed new backpack, and a burgundy colored hooded sweatshirt with the gold BC logo on it. Her four small gifts were a huge bag of gummy bear candy, a whimsical mouse pad in the shape of a mouse, a CD of his favorite music, and a bag of dark chocolate Hanukkah *gelt* - the traditional gold wrapped chocolate coins given to small children for the holiday.

***

Christmas season at the Rashid house was fairytale-like for Alia. It reminded her of Christmas films from the 1940's. In Haifa, Christmas Day was usually cool and sunny, and the holiday was celebrated more for its religious meaning.

In Boston, it was totally different. On December 23rd it was snowing - a light, fluffy snow that coated everything in a pristine layer of white. As she walked up the path to the house, she saw the Christmas tree lights flickering in the front window, evoking a feeling of magic and warmth. She had never felt more festive, and she had never felt more safe.

As she opened the front door, she saw a large box with a UPS label on it sitting on the floor to the left. She looked at the label and was surprised to find that it was the gift she had ordered for Asiya. Seeing Abdul sitting in the living room watching television, she walked in and asked him casually, "Is your mother home yet?"

"No. She's been gone all day. I haven't seen her since really early this morning. Oh, a package came this afternoon for you. It's in the front hall. If you want me to take it upstairs for you, I will."

"Thanks. Could you please? It's a surprise for your mother for Christmas. I don't want her to see it until then."

Abdul followed Alia up the stairs, carrying the heavy box. He set it down carefully inside her bedroom. As he stood up, he was gripped by a sharp pain in his back. Alia saw him wince and anxiously asked, "Did you hurt yourself? Was the box too heavy? Here, let me see where it hurts."

Abdul backed away and shook his head, saying, "No. It's nothing. I just carried it wrong. I forgot to bend my knees when I picked it up off the floor, that's all."

He turned and fled from the room. When he got to this own bedroom he flopped face down on the bed and decided that he would rest his back.

That night, he took four naproxen pills over a three hour period and fell into a deep sleep. When he got up in the morning the pain was dulled, but it still hadn't gone away. He took some ibuprofen from the medicine cabinet before he gathered the strength to brush his teeth.

Since it was Christmas vacation, he was able to stay in bed and vegetate, so he picked up the mystery novel which he bought for his father for Christmas, and began reading it. Soon he was fast asleep again, the book open on his chest. He didn't awake again until almost noon, and by then he felt better.

While Abdul was sleeping, Maroun was wrapping gifts for his family. He bought Alia a beautiful grey cashmere sweater. She had so few winter clothes, and because she wore a uniform to work, she rarely bought herself anything. Maroun wanted her to have something luxurious and special.

He wrapped the large box containing the snowshoes he bought for Abdul. He also bought his son cross-country skis, but these were too large to wrap. He would hide them behind the tree late at night on Christmas Eve to surprise Abdul in the morning.

For Asiya, he chose a pair of garnet earrings set in gold because he thought they would look beautiful on her.

Maroun also wrapped the gift that the Rashids bought for Peggy and Dafidi. It was a new state-of-the-art microwave to replace the antique one which they brought with them from Kansas. Asiya knew that Peggy's work schedule sometimes didn't allow her time to cook properly, but at least now they could microwave efficiently. Asiya laughed when she told Maroun about the gift., saying, "Food; it's always about food." They both laughed.

Christmas Day

Christmas Day was beautiful. A milky sun shown down on the pristine snow left overnight by a fast moving storm. Although cold, it wasn't bitterly so, and children played outside, making snowmen.

The Rashid house was buzzing with activity beginning very early in the morning. Asiya got up and made a pot of coffee, and put the homemade cinnamon rolls she left to rise on the counter the night before, into the oven. The other family members awoke to the comforting smells of hot coffee and cinnamon wafting through the house.

Abdul staggered downstairs in his sweats and practically pounced on the coffee pot. He sighed with satisfaction as he took the first sip from his mug. Asiya went over and wrapped her arms around her son's shoulders and said, "Merry Christmas, my dear son. Would you like eggs or just a cinnamon roll?"

Abdul grinned and answered, "How about eggs and two cinnamon rolls?"

"No problem, little prince. Your wish is my command."

Asiya served him and waited for the others to come downstairs. Fifteen minutes later, the entire family congregated around the kitchen table, happily devouring a huge holiday breakfast.

Maroun finally announced that it was time to open their gifts. Picking up his coffee mug, he walked slowly into the living room and bent down to turn on the tree lights. Clutching her dressing gown and carrying her coffee, Asiya followed him and was rewarded by the festive sight of the beautiful illuminated tree with a backdrop of snow seen through the window behind it.

Alia was prepared. She came into the room with a camera in hand and began snapping candid photos. Asiya put her hands up to cover her face, laughing and saying, "Without makeup, I'll look like a monster."

Abdul walked into the room while Alia was tormenting his parents with the camera, and he laughed at their antics. Then he noticed something sticking out behind the Christmas tree. He walked over and read the tag attached to the gift.

"Whoopee! I can't wait to ski. Dad, you're the best. Dafidi and I have been wanting to learn to cross-country ski for months. Thank you, thank you, thank you!"

Maroun grinned from ear to ear. He had managed to keep the skis a secret, even from Asiya.

Peggy woke up early on Christmas Day. She showered and dressed and made a pot of coffee. She then went into the living room and opened up a roll of silver gift wrap and began wrapping the gift she bought for Asiya and Maroun. It was a beautiful contemporary looking silver serving dish made in Israel. Although it cost a fortune, Peggy bought it anyway because she thought it was the perfect gift for her friends.

Rummaging through the back of her closet where she had hidden them, Peggy brought out the new suitcase and skis which she bought for Dafidi for Hanukkah. She wrapped these in large blue gift bags and then wrapped the large box containing the backpack. Hanukkah had arrived, beginning on December 11th and Peggy had given Daf eight small gifts of books, clothing and CDs. Knowing that she and Daf would spend Christmas Day at the Rashid home, she held back on giving him these large gifts until then, thinking it would be fun to surprise Dafidi with the unexpected presents.

Peggy packed the skis into the car while Dafidi was still sleeping. She drove the short distance to the Rashid home and dropped them off. Maroun answered the door and laughed as she told him why she came. He chuckled as he said, "I, too, bought Abdul cross-country skis. He was over the moon when he saw them, so I suspect that Dafidi will be also. Here, let me take them inside and you can scoot back home so that Daf doesn't become suspicious. We'll see you back here at noon." With that, he waved to her and carried the skis inside the house.

Once she was back home, Peggy poured a cup of coffee and sat for a few minutes reading the paper. As she was doing so, Dafidi came into the kitchen and asked her, "What time do we have to be at Abdul's house?"

Peggy answered, "Noon. We've got plenty of time. I'll make us some breakfast."

Daf watched his mother as she scrambled eggs and made toast. He thought to himself how wonderful it would be if his father could be there too. Knowing that she was sensitive about the subject, he kept his thoughts to himself.

Arriving at the Rashids' home at five minutes to twelve, Daf got out of the car and opened the back door to take out the wrapped gifts his mother had brought for his friend's family. He thought to himself how generous she had been, as he lifted out four large boxes. As he struggled to balance them while walking up to the front door, Peggy rushed up and grabbed the box that was teetering on the top of the pile, saying, "Here, let me get that one. I'll ring the doorbell."

Asiya answered the door and grinned at her guests as she motioned them inside. "Come in. Happy holidays. Here, put those down by the stairs and I'll have Maroun take them in and put them under the tree."

As Dafidi did so, Abdul came rushing into the hallway. "Daf, you won't believe it! Dad bought me the skis I wanted. "

Dafidi smiled at his ebullient friend. "Great. Now if I can afford to buy some soon, we can go to Lincoln and tackle that cross-country trail we saw last summer."

Asiya spoke up, "Enough about skiing. Let's go in and have some lunch. Afterwards, we can all exchange gifts."

The two families enjoyed the sumptuous meal that Asiya and Alia had prepared. The group lingered at the table, taking second helpings of the delicious prime rib and the sublime vegetable casserole. When they were full to bursting, Asiya brought in coffee and they sat there talking animatedly and enjoying one another's company. Alia suddenly got up from the table, and with a twinkle in her eye exclaimed, "I have a surprise for my favorite cousin. It seems like the perfect moment to give it to her after this wonderful feast. I'll be right back. Abdul, come with me. Don't anyone move!"

With that, Alia and Abdul went upstairs and retrieved the enormous box that was delivered to the house a few days before. Abdul noticed that Alia wrapped it in Christmas paper and that there was a huge red bow on it now. He carried the box downstairs and into the dining room. When the group saw it, they all stared at it with curiosity, but Alia was the only one to speak.

"Merry Christmas, my beloved cousin. You deserve to have the best. I hope you like this."

Asiya got up and walked over to the other end of the dining room. She bent down and read the card that was attached under the large red bow. When she lifted her head and looked up at Alia, the group could see that there were tears in her eyes.

"I hate to disturb this beautiful wrapping, but here goes."

Asiya tore the paper and as she did so, the name of a top-line cookware manufacturer was revealed on the box below. As she tore off more paper, the group could see the surprise more clearly. The box contained a sixteen piece set of stainless steel pots and pans designed for professional chefs.

As the contents of her gift were revealed, Asiya gasped. "Oh, I d… don't believe it! These are the pans I've been dreaming about for years, but I never thought I'd ever get them. Alia, this is wonderful. Oh, how did you know?"

Maroun smiled and answered, "Sometimes your husband actually listens to you, you know. And he sometimes speaks with your cousin… at least when he can get a word in during the rare moment when you two aren't talking!"

Asiya giggled at her husband's comments. She walked over to him and kissed his forehead and then walked to Alia and hugging her, said over her shoulder, "Oh, you are the best cousin ever! Thank you so much." Laughing, she added, "As I've always said, it's all about food in this house!!!"

The group laughed at her comment and then Maroun remarked, "Let's go into the living room and enjoy the other surprises under the tree."

The group got up from their chairs and walked into the other room, remarking on how festive it looked with the beautifully decorated Christmas tree and flames flickering in the cozy fireplace. As Alia snapped photos of everyone, Abdul walked up to the tree and began handing out gifts to their recipients. When Asiya opened Peggy's gift, she exclaimed, "Oh, the silver serving dish is so beautiful. I've seen some similar to this in Haifa but never here. Where did you find it?"

Peggy answered, "I saw it in the window of a Judaica store in Newton Centre and knew it was perfect for you. I'm so happy you like it."

The others began opening their gifts, smiling and laughing and thoroughly enjoying themselves. Once all the boxes had been opened, Maroun got up and walked to a closet in the hallway. As he left the living room, he turned and said, "Oh, just one more surprise. I'll be right back."

Dafidi was reading the cover notes of Maroun's new mystery novel as Abdul's father came back into the room, so at first he didn't see what he was carrying. When he finally looked up from the book, it was to find everyone grinning at him.

Peggy looked at her son and said, "I sure hope you like these, Daf. You can't imagine how hard they were to hide from you!"

Looking at the skis, Dafidi smiled broadly and got up and walked over to his mother. Hugging her, he said, "Mom, thank you so much. I can't believe this!"

The group enjoyed the afternoon, sitting around talking, drinking coffee and apple cider, and nibbling on homemade Christmas cookies.

As she munched happily, Alia looked at her friends and family and thought how perfect this Christmas had been and said a silent prayer of gratitude for her good fortune.

***

As previously agreed, Jack arrived at the apartment at 6 pm on December 27th to pick up Dafidi to take him out for holiday dinner. Peggy answered the door bell and looked at her estranged husband. Trying not to let her emotions show in her face, she ushered him politely into the hallway and called for Dafidi to come out to greet his father. Dafidi walked out of the living room with a big grin on his face. "Hi, Dad. I'm ready. Am I dressed okay for a fancy place?"

Jack laughed as he looked at his son's outfit of sport coat, tie and freshly ironed chinos. "You look every inch the gentleman. Come on. Let's get moving. The reservation is for 6:30."

Even though Peggy knew that the dinner was for only father and son, she was hurt that she had not been included. She put on her best poker face and kissed Daf on the cheek. She said, "Have fun. Hope the food's good." That was all she could get out before closing the door behind them. She walked slowly into the living room and collapsed on the sofa crying. All the suppressed pain of the past few years came out over the next hour. She finally lifted her head off the damp sofa pillow, rubbed her eyes and sighed. Getting up slowly, she walked to the bathroom and washed her face. Looking at herself in the mirror, she thought she looked old and drained. With a resigned air, she sighed and walked into the kitchen and poured a small glass of red wine. Sipping it, she returned to the living room and turned on the television. The well-crafted British historical drama about Margaret of York in the 1400's was completely lost on Peggy. She sat there like a zombie, eyes open but unseeing as characters in medieval garb appeared on the television screen. She was in another world – one more current and more painful.

Jack and Dafidi sat in a large booth at Legal Seafoods, nibbling on appetizers while they waited for their meal. Jack was waiting until they finished eating to present Dafidi with his gift. Dafidi's wrapped present for his father was placed next to him on the leather seat of the booth.

After finishing their broiled lobster, father and son talked for a while about Dafidi's political science class while they ate an elaborate dessert. Then they talked about basketball. Finally, they finished and their plates were removed. Jack ordered more coffee and reached into his jacket pocket for a large envelope. Before he could take it out, Dafidi said, "Dad, here is your Hanukkah gift. I hope you like it." Jack took the wrapped parcel and began tearing off the gift wrap. When he saw the book, he smiled broadly.

"Daf, where did you find this? I've wanted a copy for years. Did you know that?"

Dafidi smiled broadly, happy that he bought the right gift for his father. "No, Dad. I had no idea. It just seemed like something you'd like to read, and I know you like old books."

Jack responded, "Right on both counts. Thank you very much, son. Now, here's your gift, and I hope you like it too."

Dafidi took the large white envelope from his father. He could feel something inside but couldn't figure out what it was. He tore the envelope and pulled out an airline ticket and a printed itinerary. He gasped when he saw the destination.

"Da..Dad…Is this…is this really for me?"

Jack smiled and answered, "Yes, Daf. This is for July, when you are out of school. We are going to visit Israel."

Dafidi couldn't believe it. This was something he had wanted to do since he was a child. His grandfather had told him stories about Israel. Now he would walk the streets of Jerusalem, swim in the Dead Sea, re-live the bravery of Masada, get to say a prayer at the Western Wall. He would also like to visit Nazareth, and to meet Abdul's relatives. Dr. Joe had showed him hundreds of pictures from his visits to Israel, and Dafidi was looking forward to hopping on the plane bound for Tel Aviv. He would be going with his father – just the two of them. This was a miracle.

Dafidi could feel tears welling up in his eyes. He struggled to say what he felt. "Dad, I don't have words to say what this means to me. Thank you so much!"

Jack sat there and sipped his coffee without speaking. He finally raised his head and looked at Dafidi.

"Son, I just want you to know that I never wanted you to go out of my life. Having you back is the best thing that has ever happened to me. This gift is just my way of saying that I love you."

Dafidi felt a tear slide down his cheek. He wiped it against the back of his shirt sleeve. He looked at his father and nodded.

"I understand, Dad. I know that neither you nor Mom wanted to hurt me. It's just that I wish things could be different."

Jack hurt for his son, but he didn't feel it was fair to get his hopes up. He thought for a moment before responding, "I wish things could be different too, Daf. But relationships are hard and both parties have to come to terms with compromises. We can't always have things turn out the way we would like."

Dafidi nodded and bit his lip. Despite his father's wonderful Hanukkah gift, he still felt a lingering emptiness. For some reason, the famous Seder announcement, "Next year in Jerusalem!" floated unbidden into his mind. Maybe next year would be different.

Chapter 21
Health Problems

December 28th arrived with heavy snowfall and extreme cold. Abdul and Dafidi were anxious to try out their new cross-country skis, but the temperature plummeted, and it was just too cold to safely enjoy outdoor activities. The two boys both experienced severe 'cabin fever' as they relaxed at home.

The cold hung on until New Year's Day, when a brief warm-up ushered slightly higher temperatures and sunshine. Abdul called Dafidi early in the morning, and they decided to take advantage of the milder weather to head to the trails in Lincoln, Massachusetts to break in their new skis. Abdul affixed the two sets of cross-country skis to the roof rack on his car, and the two friends set off to spend the day enjoying the pastoral woods in a nearby rural suburb.

Once in Lincoln, Abdul parked the car at a well-known trailhead on Route 117. After putting on their skis, the two headed east past a frozen pond and worked their way through the woods, enjoying the quiet and serenity. Neither boy spoke. Each was wrapped up in trying to maneuver the new skis while taking in the beautiful scenery.

An hour later, as Dafidi was concentrating on negotiating a curving path through deeper snow and dense forest, he heard a thud behind him and then a moan. Stopping in his tracks, he turned awkwardly and saw that Abdul had fallen and appeared to be in pain.

"Daf, I felt a spasm in my back and I lost my balance. My back still hurts…"

Dafidi leaned down and tried to help Abdul stand up. As he put his hands under his friend's arms, he heard Abdul wince in pain. He looked at Abdul and said, "Come on, my friend. We need to get you home. Here, lean on me."

The two slid slowly down the trail, with Abdul holding onto Dafidi's right shoulder with both hands as Daf used his poles to propel them both forward. It was slow going, but finally they reached the car. When they did so, Dafidi opened the passenger door and helped Abdul collapse onto the seat. Taking off his friend's skis, Dafidi hurried to ease Abdul legs into the car and close the passenger door. He then secured the skis on the roof rack and went around to the driver's side and climbed in. Taking Abdul's car keys he put on his seat belt, turned on the ignition and drove out onto Route 117, heading east.

He saw a blue sign up the road at an intersection that said 'Hospital' with an arrow pointing to the right. As he came up to the intersection, he made a snap decision and turned the car around, following the arrow.

Arriving at Emerson Hospital a few minutes later, Dafidi followed the signs up a small hill towards the emergency room. He parked as near to the door as he could and ran in, leaving Abdul in the car. He remerged a few moments later with a wheelchair. He opened the passenger door and deftly bundled Abdul into the chair and pushed him through the automatic doors into a crowded waiting room. A kind and gentle looking golden honey-haired nurse came and introduced herself as Janet. She took the chair from him and pushed it into the more private triage area. Dafidi followed her. She helped Abdul climb onto a gurney.

Janet took down Dafidi's account of what had happened and then made additional notes based on what Abdul told her. Hearing Abdul relate the story of his previous sports injury, she assumed the current back pain might be a flare-up from it. Leaving the triage area, she walked into another room to consult with the attending ER doctor.

The doctor came into the room and introduced himself. "Hi, Abdul. I'm Dr. Gupta. How long you have been experiencing back pain? Is this the first time?"

Abdul shook his head and answered, "No. It's happened a few times before since I injured my back a few years ago playing basketball, but I usually just take over the counter pain killers and it gets better."

Dr. Gupta nodded, took some notes, and set down his clipboard. He did a neurological evaluation, and examined his neck and entire spine, and the chest and abdomen. Abdul was tender in the lower back, and Abdul gasped as the doctor palpated the area. Dr. Gupta removed his hands and reached for his clipboard. He jotted something down and then turned back to the young man lying on the gurney.

"I'll be back in a few minutes and we'll take some X-rays to make certain nothing is broken. Unfortunately, until we know what's going on, I can't give you any pain medication. Just lie still, and we'll try to get you down there as soon as possible."

Abdul nodded. He had no strength to do anything else.

Coming back to the room, nurse Janet said, "Okay, young man, I think we need to run some tests. While I take you up to radiology, your friend can wait in the waiting room."

Abdul and Dafidi nodded in unison. Daf looked at his ailing friend and said, "I'll call your mom. Don't worry. Everything's going to be all right."

Janet wheeled Abdul to a small room in the Radiology Department and. Abdul felt afraid and despondent. He had never been seriously ill before, and he had never had to call his mother or father to come to a hospital. He felt guilty for bothering them and he felt terribly alone. Janet sensed his anxiety, and tried to calm him down by talking about her cats.

Asiya arrived at the hospital 45 minutes later and found Dafidi sitting in the waiting room staring. When he looked up at her, he could see the worry in her face. She walked over and sat down beside him and he said, "They've taken him to radiology. The doctor said for me to tell the nurse when you arrived." With that, Dafidi got up and walked to the nurses' station and spoke to the nurse. Janet came over to Asiya and spoke gently to her. "Mrs. Rashid, your son is undergoing tests. We'll let you see Abdul as soon as he comes back from radiology. By then we should also know a bit more about his condition."

An hour later, nurse Janet came back and told Asiya that she and Dafidi could go in and speak to Abdul. She ushered them through the swinging doors into the emergency area and took them to the small room where Abdul was lying on a gurney. When Asiya saw her son, she leaned down and kissed him on the cheek and smoothed his hair back from his clammy forehead. She yearned to hold him to her but knew that would embarrass him.

Asiya and Dafidi sat on the two chairs by Abdul's bedside. Neither spoke. Abdul had his eyes closed, and they both assumed he had nodded off. Finally, Dr. Gupta came into the room and pulled the curtain closed around them.

"Mrs. Rashid, we did X-rays of his entire spine, and of the chest and abdomen and didn't find anything unusual, and there are no broken bones. Abdul seems to think that he has pulled a muscle that he previously injured playing sports. This is probably the cause of his back pain. However, I suggest that Abdul see his regular physician if his back is still hurting. I shall give him a prescription for Ibuprofen, and another for a muscle relaxant. Abdul can go home now."

Looking immensely relieved, Asiya nodded. "Thank you, doctor. I'll telephone Dr. Simmons and set up an appointment."

Later that afternoon, after Dafidi helped Abdul up the stairs to his bedroom. Asiya telephoned Dr. Simmons and left a message with his answering service. The doctor's office phoned her back a few hours later, saying that Dr. Simmons had hurt his ankle in a skiing accident the previous weekend and wouldn't be back at work for at least three days. She went on to suggest that Asiya telephone the doctor who was covering the practice for that time. The receptionist also surprised Asiya when she told her that Abdul had already made an appointment for later that month.

When she heard that Abdul had made an appointment without informing her, Asiya's 'mother's radar' went into full operation. Hanging up the phone, she sat there quietly thinking for a few minutes before telephoning Maroun at work. When she told her husband about their son's condition, he suggested that they take Abdul to the Pain and Wellness Center in Peabody, where his own back had been successfully treated a few years before, with a series of injections in the spine, and physical therapy.

Abdul's pain worsened overnight and, despite not wanting to worry his parents, he told his father the following morning. Maroun immediately telephoned the Pain and Wellness Center. The secretary, Lina told him that she could squeeze Abdul in that day if they could come at 3 pm. Maroun decided to call out of work that day so he could accompany his son and Asiya to the appointment.

As they were driving north on Rte. 128, Asiya's cell phone rang. It was Dr. Simmons calling to apologize for not being able to see Abdul. Asiya apprised Dr. Simmons of their choice to visit Maroun's former physician. When she did so, Dr. Simmons said, "I know Dr. Vered very well, and I've referred many patients to his clinic. I've actually visited the clinic and was quite impressed with the set-up. They have a multi-disciplinary group of practitioners, including physicians, nurse practitioners, chiropractor, physical therapists, acupuncturist, massage therapist, and psychologist, all under the same roof."

When the family was ushered into his office, Dr. Vered recognized Mr. Rashid right away. "I haven't seen you in ages. I hope that you are no longer having back problems?"

Maroun smiled, "You cured me, but I think my son Abdul may have inherited back problems from me. He's really suffering, and we need your help again."

Dr. V, as he is fondly called by most of the staff, took a detailed history from Abdul and typed the information into the electronic medical record system on his desktop computer. He then told his parents to wait in his office while he took him to an examination room. After carrying out a thorough physical and neurological examination, he told Abdul that he could dress and go back to the office to rejoin his parents.

When he returned to his office, Dr. V told the Rashids that he did not think the present pain was coming from the spine. He was concerned that Abdul could be suffering from *visceral pain* arising from a disorder of an abdominal organ. He did not appear to have *sciatica*. In order to be quite certain, however, he would obtain an MRI of both the spine and the abdomen. Since intravenous contrast would be injected to enhance the detail of the images, a blood test would be initially obtained to be sure that his kidneys could tolerate the contrast material called Gadolinium. Dr. V was worried about the amount of ibuprofen, naproxen, other NSAIDs, and acetaminophen that Abdul told him that he consumed. He counseled him about the risk of damage to his liver and kidneys, and instructed him to cut down on their use.

"Please call my office for a follow-up appointment after you have the MRI scan." With that, he printed and handed them two notes, one authorizing a blood test for *creatinine* and *BUN*, and the other for the MRI scan. Lina set up the tests before Abdul and his parents left the clinic.

The blood test was abnormal, so MRI was done without contrast injection.

Thursday dawned bright and clear and exceptionally cold – too cold to snow. Asiya and Abdul arrived at Dr. V's office. Both mother and son gratefully sank down into the waiting room's chairs, happy to be indoors and warm after enduring the brutal cold while walking the short distance from the parking lot.

Five minutes elapsed and Dr. V himself came out to lead them into his office. Abdul said that his back pain was much better, and that he was no longer taking Ibuprofen.

The doctor was brief and to the point. He informed Abdul that the MRI of the spine was normal. But it was done without intravenous contrast injection because the blood test was abnormal.

"I am worried that you might be suffering from a condition known as analgesic nephropathy. This is kidney damage which is often associated with long-term use of analgesic medications such as acetaminophen, and NSAIDs. It is mostly seen with self-medication with a combination of these over the counter pain killers. I am going to send a report to Dr. Simmons, and I would like you to call him to make an appointment to see him for further tests."

Asiya said a silent prayer, requesting health and safety for her beloved son. She thanked Dr. V, as she and Abdul left the office.

The following week, winter settled in and bitter cold enveloped Boston. Abdul, Dafidi and their friends spent weekdays attending classes and weeknights studying. The cold gripping the campus prevented all but the most hardy of students from venturing out to attend movies or go ice-skating at the Frog Pond. Dafidi and Abdul longed to go cross-country skiing again, but sheets of ice had supplanted snow, making the sport unfeasible and potentially dangerous.

As far as Dafidi could tell, Abdul seemed to feel better. Abdul himself was trying to put the emergency room incident behind him, although he still didn't feel quite right. Every now and then a nagging ache would return, and he was constantly thirsty. He also felt drained, as if most of his energy were sapped. He began going to bed earlier than usual, and he found getting up in the morning difficult. He pushed himself, knowing that his team mates counted on him to come off the bench and propel the team at critical moments . He didn't want to let the team down.

As January reached its mid-point, the extreme cold eased up and so did the players' spirits. They were unbeaten, and they were relaxed and playful.

In truth, each of the 'Group of Five' had their individual strengths on the court. Dafidi could penetrate with ease and had the ability to score effective mid-range jump shots. Yosha was talented at scoring from underneath the basket. Abdul was skilled at setting up a good screen. LeShawn was a great perimeter shooter, and Mike was an explosive player. Of course they all looked up to the captain, Rinton Abiola who was the consummate player, and a master in all aspects of the game. As a cohesive team, they came together as an extremely powerful unit.

Dafidi's classes were going well. He especially enjoyed *Contemporary American Politics,* a class he shared with Abdul and LeShawn. The three young men studied together for long hours, discussing President Obama's financial stimulus package and his handling of the war in Afghanistan. They were astonished by the rapid shift of the focus of the national discourse from the economy to health care reform. Dafidi was astounded at LeShawn's grasp of political maneuvering. He thought back to Halloween when the supposed 'Oracle' predicted that LeShawn might someday go into politics. Dafidi wondered if, despite her dubious psychic credentials, she might have been right after all. Time would tell.

An idea had evolved out of one of the class mandated projects. Dafidi and Abdul were volunteering with *Baldwin's Bunch* and really enjoyed mentoring the little kids in the group. A remark by Alia one night over dinner at the Rashid house gave the two boys an idea. Alia had said, "Wow, I wish there was a group like *Baldwin's Bunch* for the kids I met in Gaza. So many of them seemed to have no direction, and I really think that a group of mentors could give them some hope for the future and keep them focused."

Dafidi and Abdul's idea was to open a summer camp to be attended by children from both sides of the middle-east conflict. Airfare for the children would be paid by donations solicited at BC sports events, and the BC basketball team would film television advertisements. Two professional basketball players from the NBA who were BC alumni had offered to set up a non-profit organization to help fund the camp. It would also be a tax shelter for them.

By the second week of February, the camp idea had taken hold and was being officially formulated and sanctioned by the college. Boston newscasters interviewed Dafidi and Abdul and details of the camp to be held the following summer were broadcast on television and radio.

Rin Abiola also offered his support in setting up the camp, and soon Dafidi's name became inextricably linked with Rin's in the sports headlines. The two basketball players were regarded as stars both on and off of the court.

On Sunday, Dafidi and Abdul decided to go cross-country skiing again, despite Asiya's request that they put it off until after Abdul's appointment with Dr. Simmons the following Monday. Abdul listened to his mother's worried protest and then assured her there was nothing to fear, as he felt totally fit. Asiya, however, wasn't to be swayed.

"Daf, you must get him to come home right away if he exhibits any symptoms,. He has a doctor's appointment tomorrow, and if Dr. Simmons finds him to be well, then you have all the rest of the winter to go skiing. Please watch him closely."

Daf agreed to do as Mrs. Rashid asked, waved goodbye to her and walked out to the car. As Abdul was backing out of the driveway, Dafidi asked his friend, "If you feel any pain while we're skiing, you'll tell me, right? I don't want a repeat performance of what happened last time."

Smiling, Abdul nodded. "No worries, my friend. I don't want to land in the emergency room again."

The two friends decided to try an easier trail in Carlisle. When they arrived, the sun was shining and the weather was perfect – briskly cold but with no wind. They spent two hours slowly traversing a flat trail that wound through farmland. Both felt exhilarated afterwards.

When they arrived back home, Asiya was relieved to hear that the trip had been uneventful. She invited Dafidi to stay for dinner, and he and Abdul enjoyed telling everyone about their skiing adventure.

That night, Abdul woke up around 2 am with a searing pain in his left side. He pulled himself up in bed, but then dropped his head back on the pillow, feeling dizzy. When he tried again to get up, he felt nausea overtake him. He lay there feeling wretched and frightened, afraid to call for his parents, but afraid not to do so. He suspected that something was terribly wrong.

Abdul finally fell back asleep. When his alarm went off and he didn't get up, his mother opened his bedroom door and called to him. When he didn't respond, she went over to the bed and gently shook his shoulder, saying, "Honey, you're going to be late for class. Remember, you have to drive – you're not waking up in the dorm this morning."

When her son responded with a muffled moan, Asiya felt his forehead. He was burning up. Suddenly, his body was wracked by spasmodic chills. Asiya rushed from the room and called to Maroun from the landing above the stairway. When he ran up the stairs and into the room, he found Abdul in his mother's arms, shaking uncontrollably. Asiya saying soothing words and smoothing his hair back from his clammy forehead. Her face showed her concern.

"Maroun, telephone Dr. Simmons. I think we need to take Abdul to the emergency room."

Maroun nodded and ran to the telephone. He returned a few minutes later and said, "Dr. Simmons said to call 911. I've already done so. An ambulance should be here soon. Oh God, what's wrong with him?"

Asiya shook her head despondently and said, "I don't know. I just don't know."

Three minutes later the ambulance arrived and whisked Abdul off to Brigham and Women's Hospital emergency room, with Maroun and Asiya trailing behind the ambulance in their car. Asiya sobbed as they drove, while Maroun concentrated intently on driving, trying to stay calm and focused. Neither parent spoke.

At 1 pm that afternoon, Peggy's office phone rang. She picked up the receiver and was shocked to hear Asiya on the other end of the phone, telling her that Abdul was critically ill and in the emergency room. Peggy listened to her friend's words as Asiya struggled between sobs to tell her everything. Peggy finally spoke.

"I'll be there as fast as I can. I'll telephone Daf, but he might be in class. Try to relax. Abdul's in a topnotch hospital."

Asiya thanked Peggy and hung up. Peggy quickly apprised her receptionist of the situation, left the office and ran towards her car. She drove as fast as possible to Brigham and Women's Hospital and cursed because of how long it took to find a parking space in the crowded garage on Francis Street.

When she finally arrived in the ER's jam-packed waiting room, she found Asiya and Maroun seated in a distant corner, with Asiya slumped against her husband's shoulder. Maroun explained to Peggy that Dr. Simmons had just arrived and was in conference with the attending doctors, and he said that he would be out as soon as possible to let them know what was going on.

Forty-five minutes later, Dr. Simmons came out to speak with the Rashids. His face was glum and his demeanor subdued. Looking at him, Peggy knew instantly that something was terribly wrong with her son's best friend. Dr. Simmons stood in front of the Rashids and spoke softly.

"We believe that Abdul has chronic kidney disease. He will be undergoing tests for some hours, and once we have the results, we can discuss possible treatments. I've ordered several tests of kidney function. I'm so sorry."

Asiya looked up at the doctor and nodded. Speaking softly, she said, "Thank you, Dr. Simmons. We'll stay here until we find out what's wrong. Can we see him soon?"

Dr. Simmons shook his head. "Unfortunately, no. Right now he is having blood drawn. Once the tests are over, you'll be able to go in to see him. You must be patient and keep positive. Kidney disease is treatable, and your son is an athlete and quite fit. I'll come back later to review the tests, and I'll speak with you at length then."

Maroun thanked Dr. Simmons and shook his hand. After the doctor left, Asiya began sobbing, and Maroun felt at a loss as to how to comfort her. Trying to defuse the situation, Peggy asked him to go get them all coffee and said she would sit with Asiya. Reaching over, she put a gentle arm around her friend's shoulders. "Oh, Asiya. My heart goes out to you. But it will be okay. I just know it will. Please don't cry."

Asiya's tear-stained face looked up into Peggy's and she muttered, "He is my only child – the love of my life."

Peggy patted her friend's back. Maroun found them seated that way when he returned with a tray of coffee and pastries. He thanked God that he and Asiya had such a good friend in Peggy.

Answering the phone Dafidi knew from his mother's voice that something was terribly wrong. When she explained about Abdul's condition, he knew he needed to get to the hospital a soon as possible. Thus it was that, an hour later, he was present when Dr. Simmons came to report the test results.

Dr. Simmons took Asiya's hands in his and held them. Looking directly at her, he said gently, "You must be strong, Mrs. Rashid. Your son is going to need your help. He is very sick. Abdul has advanced chronic kidney disease and his left kidney has ceased functioning. Dialysis is urgently needed to rid the blood of impurities. We are preparing him for dialysis right now."

"I will be totally truthful with you. Sometimes dialysis can control the problem indefinitely, but sometimes it cannot. If it fails to do so, Abdul will need a kidney transplant. I suggest that we try to find a match for him just in case. That would prevent a dangerous delay, should the treatment not work. I will also need your signature on the consent form for dialysis."

Dr. Simmons handed Maroun the consent form, and both Maroun and Asiya signed it with shaking hands. Maroun handed it back to the doctor.

"Thank you, Mr. Rashid. We will try our best to help Abdul. You can go in and see him now. Come with me and I'll take you to his room. You must make your visit brief, however, as he'll be transferred to the dialysis unit in a short time."

Dr. Simmons left carrying the consent form, with Maroun and Asiya trailing behind him.

Peggy reached over and took Dafidi's hand. "Honey, let's go downstairs to the cafeteria and get more coffee for everyone. I think this is going to be a long night."

Peggy and Dafidi left late at night, after being assured by Dr. Simmons that there was no imminent danger. Maroun and Asiya finally went home early the next morning. Abdul was resting comfortably, and there was nothing further they could do for him.

The following evening, Abdul was allowed to go home with his parents. After his father helped him up the stairs to his bedroom, Abdul climbed gratefully into his bed, stretched out and closed his eyes. Within minutes he was asleep.

Maroun drew the blanket over his son and leant down and kissed his forehead. He made the sign of the cross and said a silent prayer that his son would soon be well.

As January continued, so did Abdul's dialysis treatments. His back ached less, but he still felt exhausted. Although he returned to the BC dormitory with Dafidi, he was under doctor's orders to forego basketball.. This frustrated Abdul immensely. He had trained so rigorously to improve his skills but now he had to sit on the bench while the rest of the team played. Knowing his friend so well, Dafidi could sense Abdul becoming angry and withdrawn.

One evening, as they were studying back in the dorm, Dafidi decided to broach the subject of Abdul's withdrawn attitude. Neither boy usually spoke a lot about their innermost feelings, so it felt awkward for Dafidi, but he knew he needed to do it.

"Hey, my friend, let's take a break." Standing up and stretching, Dafidi walked over to the tiny refrigerator. Reaching inside it, he brought out a gallon of chocolate ice cream and some hot fudge sauce. He prepared two bowls and handed one to Abdul, who took it with a nod and a smile.

After taking a spoonful of ice cream, Dafidi bravely initiated the difficult conversation. "So, why the long face lately? I know it must be hard not playing because you're sick, but at least you're getting better. What's going on?"

Abdul looked up at Dafidi and shook his head. He set the bowl of ice cream down on his desk and sat silently for a few seconds before replying.

"You can't imagine how frustrating it is. I feel like an old man! Everyone else is all excited about our team, and I'm supposed to sit there and act happy for them. All those years I practiced and for what?"

Daf saw the pain in Abdul's face and heard it in his voice. He thought for a moment before responding.

"But you'll play again soon. The dialysis will fix everything, and you'll probably be up and playing by March. You're letting your imagination run away with you!"

Abdul grimaced and shook his head. "No, my friend. Unfortunately, you are wrong. I am not getting much better. I'm tired all the time and my blood tests haven't been good. I might have to be hooked up to that damned machine for the rest of my life."

Dafidi heard the sadness in Abdul's voice. He realized that he too would feel the same way if he were in the same position. He struggled to say something that would let Abdul know that he understood.

"I know it must be the pits, and I'd feel the same way. But you've got to somehow get to a more positive outlook. It can't be good for you to be so depressed!"

Abdul nodded. "I know, Daf. But I just can't force myself to feel happy. Truthfully, I'm bone-tired and I'm scared. My parents are trying so hard to be upbeat, and I can't let them know how I feel. Truthfully, I'm afraid I'm going to die soon."

Dafidi didn't know what to say. He just sat there frowning. Finally, he muttered, "So we have to find a way for that not to happen. I am going to give my friend Dr. Joe a call. I know that he will give us good advice."

Abdul nodded and said, "Easy for you to say."

Right there and then, Dafidi reached in his pocket and took out his Iphone and telephoned Dr. Joe. He explained Abdul's predicament. Dr. Joe asked to speak with Abdul. After 10 minutes on the phone, Abdul had a smile on his face. Dr. Joe assured him that he was in good hands at the Brigham and Women's Hospital. He gave Abdul his phone number and said that he should feel free to call if he had any questions or concern. He also offered to speak with Dr. Simmons and the kidney specialists.

As February began, snowstorms buffeted Boston. Trudging through ankle deep snow and along icy walkways to reach their classes, Dafidi and Abdul longed for spring to arrive. As they walked, Dafidi noticed that Abdul seemed to struggle for breath at times and just wasn't his usual fit self. Although Abdul never complained, Dafidi could tell that something was definitely wrong.

Dafidi went home for dinner on Tuesday night during the first week of February. As he ate dinner with his mother, he shared his concerns about Abdul with her.

"He's just not right, Mom. Something is really wrong. He falls asleep at 8 O'clock at night, and he gets up a few times in the middle of the night. I feel as if I should tell his parents, but he'd hate me if I did."

Peggy nodded and said, "If it were a less dangerous situation, I would advise you not to betray his trust. But Daf, he could die. I think his parents need to know. Why don't I mention to Asiya that you told me your concerns. That way, if Abdul becomes angry it will be towards me, not you."

Dafidi looked at his mother with gratitude. "Thanks, Mom. I knew you'd figure out how to help somehow."

The following morning, Maroun and Asiya drove Abdul back to BWH for more tests. After he was whisked off by a nurse, they sat patiently in the waiting area, assuming he would be brought back in a short while. When minutes turned to hours, they became worried.

Asiya sipped at a cup of tea while Maroun tried to read *Sports Illustrated*. Neither could concentrate. Asiya jumped in her seat when she saw Dr. Simmons approaching them down the hallway. As she put down her cup with shaking hands, tea sloshed onto her white blouse, but she was oblivious to the stain. Dr. Simmons pulled up a chair and sat facing Abdul's parents. Looking at them, he said, "I am truly sorry to bring you this news, but Abdul took a turn for the worse this morning. Dialysis is not effectively controlling his electrolytes. He will probably need a kidney transplant in the very near future. I have put in a call to Dr. Joseph Smith who is our top transplant surgeon."

Asiya gasped. Maroun took her hand in his and held it tightly. He turned to Dr. Simmons and said, "But I've heard it is very difficult to find a donor. How do we do this?"

Dr. Simmons answered, "Yes. It is extremely difficult to find a perfect match. We can, of course, use a kidney from a deceased donor. However, a kidney from a living donor is optimal. There are approximately 50,000 patients waiting at any one time for a donor kidney, so the wait could be long. Unfortunately, I don't think that Abdul can wait too long."

Maroun spoke. "So you are telling me that the best solution would be a living donor. Would I be a match? I would assume a family member would match most closely. Is that correct?"

Dr. Simmons nodded. "Sometimes that is the case. However, occasionally it is not. Potential donors would have to undergo tests to determine compatibility. Tissue matching involves genetic matching between the recipient and potential donor. Typically, six antigens are tested. A six-antigen match is rare and only occurs in 25 percent of siblings and less in the general population. A six-point match would be the very best. However, with new immunosuppressive medications, a less exact match is also feasible."

Maroun asked, "Can I go through a test today?"

Asiya spoke before Dr. Simmons could answer. "I would also like to be tested. Please, can we both do this as soon as possible?"

Dr. Simmons nodded. Come with me and I will introduce you to the transplant nurse, Aimee Barber who will give you more information.

The test results came back later, and Asiya was only a two point match but Maroun was a three-point match. Both were possible donors but the match could be better for optimal success.

When Peggy telephoned Asiya at dinner time that night, her friend told her the disturbing news. When Peggy asked if a non-relative could be a possible donor, Asiya answered that it was possible. Peggy hung up the phone and immediately began making telephone calls. She first phoned Tonya Johnson to find out if she knew what the donor tests entailed. Tonya explained the procedure and then volunteered herself, Lester, LeShawn and his twin sisters for testing. She said that she would have LeShawn telephone Abdul's friends to suggest that they be tested. By the next morning, Peggy had compiled a list of 32 potential donors, including herself and Dafidi.

Aimee Barber was astonished when all 32 people showed up for testing. Not only were Abdul's best friends there; the group also included Brookline High School coach Tom Rebor, Rachel and Bernie Stern, Sara Mendelsohn, Femi Abiola and Miriam Hernandez. Ten minutes before the last person was to be tested, a tall, arrogant looking young man strode into the waiting room accompanied by an older gentleman. Dafidi was amazed when he recognized Jason Kelly and Guillermo Manzano. Miriam had telephoned her friend that morning and told him about Abdul's plight. Knowing Jason was Abdul's teammate, Guillermo persuaded the young man into offering to be tested.

When the test results came back, it turned out that Peggy was not a good match. Neither were 29 of the others. Alia was a three point match. Incredibly, Dafidi was a six-point match – the 'golden bullet' for a kidney transplant. Also, both he and Abdul had type O blood.

A decision had to be made soon. Abdul's body was not properly excreting waste products, and the dialysis was only partially working.

Dafidi was ushered into Dr. Smith's office. He sat down and looked across the desk at his friend's doctor. The surgeon looked stressed and tired. When he spoke, the exhaustion could be heard in his voice.

"Dr. Joe spoke to me about you. And of course I have read about your remarkable success in basketball. I know that you sincerely want to help Abdul, Dafidi. However, I must advise you that donating a kidney is a major decision. Your kidney can be taken by a minimally invasive laparoscopic technique, but it still involves risks. Bleeding, pain, breathing problems, and infection, are perhaps the commonest risks. We have a good track record. And by the way, the first successful kidney transplant in history was performed at this hospital. Dr. Joe and I worked with Dr. Murray, a plastic surgeon, who pioneered the work. Before you agree to be Abdul's donor, I want you to go home tonight and think about the risks. I'll telephone you tomorrow morning to ask you for your decision."

Dafidi nodded. He thanked Dr. Smith and left hurriedly. He needed to get his mind around the implications of what the doctor had said. As he walked to the T to take the train home, he realized that he could even die from the surgery. However, he also knew that Abdul would definitely die without the transplant.

In that moment Dafidi made up his mind. He would donate a kidney after the basketball season.

Over dinner that night, Peggy tried to explain to Dafidi her fears about the surgery. What if it didn't help Abdul after all and Daf was left with only one kidney? What if Dafidi became ill himself with kidney disease and needed a transplant? What if…what if…

Dafidi's mind was made up. Nothing his mother could say would deter him. That night something popped into his brain just as he was falling asleep. On Halloween, the odd looking woman in Salem who purported to be a psychic had said that Abdul would owe his life to his best friend. It was a sign. He would be the donor.

Trauma and Triumph

BC was the cinderella team as the NCAA Men's Division I basketball championship began.

In the First Round of the East Regionals held at the Dunkin Donuts Center in Providence, Rhode Island, #1 seed BC thumped #16 seed Boise State, winning 110 to 62. Dafidi played at top form and scored a record 46 points. When BC won the game, the crowd went wild. After the game, Rin Abiola congratulated Daf on his playing, slapping him on the back and saying, "You never cease to amaze me!" Standing next to Dafidi as Rin said this, Sara Mendelsohn nodded and laughed, saying "I'll second that!" Daf's face turned beet red as she reached over and kissed him on the cheek in front of the entire team.

The days seemed to fly by for Daf as he struggled to further improve his offensive skills during daily practice. Each night after practice, he would telephone Abdul and solicit his advice on certain plays, hoping that in doing so he was including Abdul in the games vicariously. Abdul appreciated the daily calls but saw right through them, surmising Daf's kindly motives. He appreciated his friend's good intentions, but felt awkward giving advice when he was too ill to play himself.

Abdul put up a good front, but he was depressed and extremely frightened. He knew that if the dialysis didn't improve his situation soon he would need a kidney transplant. Although he was grateful to Dafidi for offering to be his donor, he felt horribly guilty that his best friend might have to undergo surgery and with it, pain. Abdul couldn't bring himself to verbalize these feelings to Dafidi, but he felt them nonetheless.

In the Second Round, BC throttled #6 seed Oklahoma Sooners by a score of 73 to 56 to reach the Regional Semifinals. Dafidi was struggling with so many conflicting feelings, he had a difficult time concentrating on the game. Despite his struggle, he led the BC team to victory, making all of the 12 free throws and scored a total of 36 points to lead all scorers. In the eyes of his coach, his team, and basketball fans, Daf was a rising star.

Dafidi hid his feelings from his teammates. He felt guilty for playing so well when Abdul was so ill and couldn't play at all. Only Peggy sensed that Daf was struggling emotionally to come to grips with his friend's illness. She tried to draw Dafidi out, asking him questions designed to elicit responses about this feelings, but he hung back, not responding as she would wish. She finally gave up and just let him be, trusting him to be mature enough to sort out his own emotions.

By the time the Regional Semifinals came to pass, Abdul's condition had worsened considerably.

Peggy answered the persistent ring of the phone early in the morning. Coffee cup in hand, she picked up the receiver assuming the call was from a co-worker whose car was being repaired needing a ride to work. She almost dropped her cup when instead she heard Asiya's tearful voice telling her that Abdul had been rushed to Brigham and Women's Hospital. Abdul needed a kidney transplant and the surgeon said that it should be within the next few days.

Peggy tried to calm her friend and told her that she would get in touch with Dafidi immediately. Now Dafidi was going to be risking his life to save his best friend. The emotions Peggy experienced at that moment overwhelmed her, and tears began streaming down her face.

Dafidi received the news from his mother just hours before the game against Georgetown. He told coach Khao that he would leave the team after the game and proceed to Boston to give Abdul a kidney, noting "There are things in life that are more important than basketball."

The news spread like wild fire. All the major news services interrupted their programs to report that Dafidi was abandoning the quest for basketball glory so that he could save his friend's life.

Dafidi and the BC team were pitched against arch rivals and 4th seed Georgetown Hoyas in the round of Sweet 16 . Georgetown had a great season, and were poised to reach the Final Four for the sixth time. Though seeded #4, many basketball pundits predicted that they would upset BC.

This was going to be Dafidi's last game of the season. Would he be distracted by the impending surgery? Or could he rise to the occasion and give another spectacular performance that he had become famous for? Would he give a performance that would be remembered by generations to come? Or would he be just a mere mortal tonight?

Georgetown coach raised eyebrows when he announced at a press conference that "I guarantee that the Hoyas will win hands down. The Boston College Eagles are too inexperienced to withstand our strength and depth. Dafidi will be easily contained."

Such trash talk usually came from a player. It was puzzling that it came from a coach. Was it meant to frustrate Dafidi?

Many signs held by fans wished *"DAFIDI AND ABDUL GOOD LUCK!"*

A couple of signs read *"DAFIDI 2011,"* hoping to see BC back next year.

Georgetown started off the blocks with blazing speed and scored the first 8 points of the game. Boston College was slow and appeared to be nervous. Dafidi missed his first 2 shots. All eyes were on him, on this his last game of the season. The TV announcer wondered if he was preoccupied by his impending kidney donation surgery tomorrow. Coach Bo called an early time out to regroup.

BC scored 2 quick baskets. Georgetown missed at the other end, Dafidi got the rebound, took the ball from coast to coast, and scored on a slam dunk. Just like that BC was back in the game.

It was a cat-and-mouse game throughout the first half, and the game was knotted at 30.

The Georgetown players were strong and fast and provided tough competition. Rin Abiola and Mike Ramsay fought tooth and nail to keep BC ahead in the game, but it was ultimately Dafidi who saved the day. BC won when superstar Dafidi Abraham handily evaded a giant defensive player and slam-dunked an alley-oop pass from Yosha Stern with just seconds to go in the game. The BC crowd went ballistic.

Dafidi received a standing ovation. It was an emotional finish to his season as his team mates stood in line to give him a hug and a high five. Every member of the Georgetown team also gave him a hug. The coach of the Hoyas whispered something into his ear.

***

Abdul and Dafidi were wheeled into adjacent operating rooms. Dafidi was to undergo a laparoscopic donor nephrectomy, a newer procedure that required a smaller and less-invasive incision and shorter recovery time. He would have to stay in the hospital for one to two days afterwards and then be monitored at home for about a week.

Abdul's surgery would take from two to four hours. Even if the surgery proved successful, he might have to undergo dialysis once or twice afterwards to jump start his 'sleepy' new kidney. He would stay in the hospital longer than Dafidi, but could be back at home in about a week if all went well.

Both surgeries went flawlessly. Dr. Joe visited Dafidi in the Recovery Room, and assured him that the transplant was going on very well and that Abdul's condition was stable. Hours later, both boys were resting comfortably. Now they were truly brothers. Each made an uncomplicated recovery. Abdul's new kidney began to work right away.

When Dafidi went home from the hospital two days after surgery, he felt tired and his back ached, but the doctors gave him a clean bill of health. He looked forward to joining his teammates again for March Madness.

Abdul was discharged home a few days later. He received a constant stream of visitors, many of whom had volunteered to be his living donor.

Yosha put his burly arms around Abdul and gathered him in a big bear hug. "Shalom, my friend. It is a blessing to see you fit again."

Abdul laughed. "You sound just like your Uncle Bernie, Yosh. You'll become a rabbi yet!!!"

Cathy Ramsay walked up to Abdul and grinning, placed a huge tray of homemade cookies in his lap, "You need to build your strength. I think that chocolate chip cookies always help with that, don't you?"

Abdul laughed and thanked her. It was good to be home.

He thanked them all from the bottom of his heart.

***

Meanwhile, #2 seed North Carolina Tar Heels met #3 seed Xavier Musketeers in the other East Regional semifinal. North Carolina won by a score of 80 to 76 to set up a show down with Boston College in the Regional Finals.

BC defeated North Carolina by a score of 72 to 70. Jason Kelly was the star of the game. He dedicated the victory to Dafidi who did not play.

In their first ever appearance at the Final Four, BC ran by UNLV by a score of 88 to 82. Dafidi watched the game from home and he itched to be back playing basketball with his team. Louisville narrowly beat Kansas 73-71 to set the stage for the national championship against BC at the TD Garden.

Chapter 22

Championship Game

The anticipated night finally arrived. Never in the history of college basketball had the nation seen such frenzy. The excitement generated was greater than anything ever seen in college sports. Companies shelled out millions of dollars for 15 second advertisements, knowing full well that millions would be watching the game.

Unfortunately, the *phenom* at the center of this frenzy would be merely a bench warmer tonight, not the champion that thousands came to see and millions tuned their television sets to watch. The fabulous freshman, Dafidi Abraham, would be cheering, not playing. Tonight would belong to someone else. But who would that person be? Could any other college player generate the excitement that the whole world had come to expect from Dafidi? In his freshman year, he had been a megastar point guard, leading the team in every aspect of the game. Averaging 26 points and 9 rebounds per game, with his 3-point percentage at 0.600, and free throw at 0.8200, he was the only player on the team with an All-Star pedigree, a thoroughbred. Tonight, however, he would remain a spectator, albeit a knowledgeable and excited one.

The *New York Times* wrote, "This year's edition of March Madness is more Madder than Madness. It is nothing less than insanity! It is national hysteria. It is a total national mental meltdown."

The *Boston Globe* headline was "Can the Eagles Clip the Cardinals without Dafidi?"

The temperature of anticipation was rising by the minute. Tailgate parties began over 12 hours before game time. Sausages were sizzling and beer was flowing. Game tickets were snatched off *eBay* in minutes. Scalpers were selling premium seats for thousands of dollars, with buyers eagerly handing them their hard-earned cash.

Coach Bo Khao gave an emotional speech to his team in the dressing room before they ran out to the parquet court, his anxiety evident in his voice.

"I can't stress enough how important this game is, both for you and for me. For many of you it will be the greatest game of your life. We want to win it hands down, but we have a big problem: Daf will not be playing in this game, and for good reason. He just donated a kidney to save the life of his best friend.

No matter who is out of the game, the train must roll on. We are a strong team. We have depth. In the midst of our dilemma is an opportunity for one of you to rise up and shine. I know that when your number is called, you will step up to the plate and give me your best. That is all I ask of you. Even without Daf, we are a better team than Louisville. If we play our best game, we will be victorious. We have one mission: victory, nothing more, nothing less.

Though he will not play, Daf will be in uniform and will be right there with the team. His cheering will be like rocket fuel. It will power our team to accelerate."

As their coach finished his speech, a sigh rose in unison from the team. Conflicting feelings showed on their faces: fear of losing the game, attempts to maintain tight emotional control, and a sense that they would tough it out and do their best to win, no matter what.

As the players filed out onto the court, the crowd cheered, but the loudest ovation came when they sighted Dafidi. The excited crowd gave him a standing ovation. Each member of the team gave him a high five before sitting on the team bench. Dafidi smiled and waved to the crowd, adjusting the abdominal binder he was wearing to reduce the pain from his recent surgery. A small grimace passed across his features as he felt the incision pull.

The television announcer remarked, "As I look around the full house, it is clear that this is the hottest ticket in town. The Vice President is here, as are the Secretary of State and the Governor of Massachusetts. I see that the Archbishop of Boston, the President of the Arab-American Association, and the leader of the Anti-Defamation League are all seated next to one another. What a night of fellowship! Michelle, you think you can get an interview?"

Louisville won the tip-off and took an early lead of 8-2. The Boston College Eagles started the game slowly and showed signs of nervousness. After all, this was the team's first appearance in a championship game. The Louisville Cardinals were making their 35th appearance at the *Big Dance*, and this was their 9th Final Four. Both teams struggled to make shots in the first half, and collectively made only 36%. BC saw solid performance from Rin Abiola, who scored

12 points, bringing the team close to Louisville with a 36-30 score at intermission.

Michelle got a quick interview with Coach Khao before he found his way to the locker room.

"How is your team doing, Coach?" Half-turning to the newscaster, Khao remarked, "Good."

Michelle persisted. "If you were to fall behind by 10 points, would you play Dafidi?"

Coach Khao looked askance at the young woman, replying tersely, "How many times do you want me to tell you that Daf is in no playing condition?" Taking a step forward and turning away from her, he muttered, "Gotta go now."

Abdul was watching the game on television. His attention was focused on his friend, Dafidi, wishing fervently that he could be at the Garden to cheer on the team with him.

His father sensed the sadness in Abdul's eyes. "What's the matter," he asked.

Abdul responded, "I really wish that I could be at the game. After all, Daf gave me tickets."

Without a second thought, his father telephoned the BC Eagles Entertainment Secretary. In no time, a limousine arrived to take Abdul and his dad to TD Garden, where they watched the remainder of the game on a wide screen television set in the office of its president.

With some help from her producer, Michelle was able to secure an interview with the Roman Catholic Archbishop of Boston. "Your Eminence, when did you become a basketball fan?"

Welcoming the question, he took the opportunity to name some of the great Celtics of the past. "Many of us at Catholic University were fans of the Boston Celtics. We were familiar with the likes of Red Auerbach, Bill Russell, Bob Cousy. How about Larry Bird, the chief, and Kevin McHale! But today, I am really here to honor two fine young men: Dafidi and Abdul. They are living examples of what we teach and preach every day."

The President of the Arab-American Association stepped into the picture and agreed, adding, "There will be peace in this world if we can all live and share by the example of these extraordinary boys. There will be nothing about which to fight."

BC scored the first 2 baskets of the second half to cut down on the deficit. The crowd began to witness the BC team's exceptional strength. Louisville had no answer for the press defense of BC. Several turnovers by Louisville allowed BC to control the tempo of the game. Mike Ramsay excelled at blocking shots. Jason Kelly was unselfish, and his screen plays allowed Rin Abiola to score at will.

The BC crowd roared as the game seemed to go their way. When Rin landed a 14 foot jump shot, they went wild and chanted, "Rin will win, Rin will win!"

With the score tied at 72 in the game's waning moments, Louisville had a golden opportunity to take the lead. Sampson got a defensive rebound and raced to the other end of the court, where his shot was cleanly rejected by Rin Abiola. The Cardinals' coach was irate, thinking that a shooting foul should have been called. Running out of the coaching box, he yelled obscenities at the officials while gesticulating angrily at them. A technical foul was called. The game clock showed only 2 seconds remaining.

Coach Khao didn't hesitate to call upon the captain of the team, Rin Abiola, to take the shots. A senior, Abiola was playing his last and greatest college basketball game. His parents came from Nigeria to watch their son in the height of his glory. Never had the talented player worked so hard to win. Perspiration dripped from his forehead and his right eye was swollen. Taking a deep breath, he reluctantly stepped up to the line. All of a sudden, he called a time out, stunning the coach, who just couldn't figure out what was wrong.

The team huddled quickly and Abiola suggested that the shots be taken by Dafidi, who was still seated on the bench. Coach Khao approved. Walking over to Daf, Rin told him what he wanted. Dafidi protested, citing the pain of his surgical incision. Waving his hands toward the team, Rin urged Daf to think of the big picture and implored his teammate to reconsider. Finally, Rin prevailed and Dafidi stood up as he handed him the ball.

The crowd sensed what was happening and cheers of "Dafidi, Dafidi, Dafidi" rang out. Even the television announcer joined the chorus.

Dafidi Abraham reached deep into his emotional and physical reserves and stepped up to the line. After adjusting the abdominal binder, he took a deep breath, looked up at the rim, and leaning backward, took the first shot. The ball landed off target, and he retrieved it. Concentrating intently, he took the second shot. The ball rolled around the rim for a moment and then dropped into the basket.

The joyous arena went wild. Rin Abiola ran up to Dafidi and hugged him tightly while ruffling his hair and grinning from ear to ear. Enduring the pain caused by the rough hug, and knowing it was a joyous moment for his team, Daf grinned also. Suddenly, Coach Khao and the rest of the team were circling him, patting him on the back and shouting happily. His joy dulled his pain somewhat, but one thing was still troubling him – he couldn't find his parents anywhere in the mêlée.

The crowd went berserk as Dafidi was announced as MVP of the tournament. A half hour later, not one single soul had left the Garden, choosing instead to enjoy the joyous tumult as long as possible.

Just then, Dafidi saw his parents. Turning towards them, he let himself be encircled by their arms. As onlookers saw Peggy smoothing Daf's hair and kissing his forehead gently, there wasn't a dry eye in the arena.

As Dafidi's parents were releasing him from their affectionate embrace, he noticed a large group of school children walking towards him. Dressed in the maroon and gold T-shirts of Baldwin's Bunch, they represented the future. Daf could only pray that the example he and Abdul have set would enable that future to be peaceful.

Amid the unending deafening cheers, a special telephone call came in. As President Obama's congratulations were broadcast over the speakers, the cheering subsided and onlookers listened intently. Suddenly, a young man in a wheelchair was seen being rolled onto the parquet. Giving the telephone to Coach Khao, Dafidi walked briskly towards the wheelchair and stood in front of it smiling. Taking Abdul's hands, he helped his friend to his feet and gave him a brotherly hug. The crowd went wild, erupting into further cheering.

The next morning, the front page of the *Boston Globe* ran a huge photo of the crowds cheering Dafidi and Abdul, accompanied by a long article about his unselfishness in agreeing to forgo the basketball tournament so that he could donate a kidney to his best friend. At the end of the article were the address of the National Kidney Foundation and directions about how to be a living donor. Within three days, the foundation's East Coast office was swamped by calls from the Boston area.

Television stations told the story of Dafidi and Abdul over and over. Oprah's producer telephoned the Abrahams and the Rashids, asking if they would consider going on the show to tell their story. Dafidi and Abdul were hailed by the media as "brothers beyond borders" – alluding to their different religions and heritage. The now famous letter which they wrote to the *Boston Globe* while they were in high school was reprinted in newspapers and broadcast worldwide. Their story touched the hearts of millions of people all over the world.